"You will be my wife and, therefore, subject to my will under the law. Does that really concern you?"

She huffed out a puff of air. "Does it concern me? No, Mr. Marlington, it terrifies me."

Gabriel frowned, his amusement draining away. "Whatever for? Do you really think I am such an ogre?"

Drusilla wanted to bang her head on the arm of the settee. Why had she even raised this topic?

She looked into his captivating, no-longer-laughing eyes. "Whether or not you are an ogre is utterly beside the point. Why should I have to give control over my person to any man—ogre or saint? Why should it not be you who is subject to my control and will?"

The way his mouth fell open was comical. "What?"

"I said—"

He held up a hand. "No, I heard you. I merely do not take your point."

"Of course you don't."

"You wish to be my master in this marriage." The flat way he spoke the words told her all she needed to know what he thought about that.

Also by Minerva Spencer

Dangerous

Barbarous

Scandalous

Minerva Spencer

Notorious

KENSINGTON BOOKS
www.kensingtonbooks.com

This book is a work of fiction. Names, characters, and incidents either are products of the author's imagination or are used fictitiously. Any resemblance to actual persons living or dead, or events, is entirely coincidental.

KENSINGTON BOOKS are published by

Kensington Publishing Corp.
119 West 40th Street
New York, NY 10018

All Kensington titles, imprints, and distributed lines are available at special quantity discounts for bulk purchases for sales promotion, premiums, fund-raising, educational, or institutional use.

Special book excerpts or customized printings can also be created to fit specific needs. For details, write or phone the office of the Kensington Sales Manager: Kensington Publishing Corp., 119 West 40th Street, New York, NY 10018. Attn. Sales Department. Phone: 1-800-221-2647.

ISBN-13: 978-1-4967-3284-2 (ebook)
ISBN-10: 1-4967-3284-7 (ebook)

ISBN-13: 978-1-4967-3283-5
ISBN-10: 1-4967-3283-9
First Kensington Trade Paperback Printing: December 2020

10 9 8 7 6 5 4 3 2

Printed in the United States of America

For Marla

Chapter 1

London
1817

Drusilla Clare plied her fan, using it for its intended purpose—cooling—rather than its expected purpose—flirting. After all, who would flirt with her?

"Dru, you're doing it again."

At the sound of her name, she looked at her companion. Lady Eva de Courtney should not, by all rights, have been sitting beside Drusilla in the wallflower section of the Duchess of Montfort's ballroom. Eva was not only the most beautiful debutante in London this Season, she was also richly dowered.

But she was also proof that pots of money and a gorgeous person were not, alas, enough to overcome a fractious personality or notorious heritage. Or at least her mother's notorious heritage. Because it was a well-known fact that the Marquess of Exley's first wife and Eva's mother—Lady Veronica Exley—had not only been a ravishing, mesmerizing temptress who'd driven men of all ages insane with desire and yearning, she'd also been barking mad.

Eva, reputed to be every bit as lovely as her dead mother, had neither the desire nor the charisma to drive anyone mad. Except perhaps her stern, perfectionist father.

"What, exactly, am I doing?" Drusilla asked Eva, who'd

pulled a lock of glossy dark hair from her once-perfect coiffure and was twisting it into a frazzled mess.

"You're frowning and getting that look." Eva thrust out her lower jaw, flattened her lips, and glared through squinty eyes.

Drusilla laughed at her friend's impersonation.

Eva's expression shifted back to its natural, perfect state. "There, that's much better. You're very pretty when you laugh or smile."

Drusilla rolled her eyes.

"And even when you roll your eyes." Eva's smile turned into a grin. "Come, tell me what you were thinking when you were looking so thunderous."

Drusilla could hardly tell her friend she'd been wondering when Eva's gorgeous but irritating stepbrother—Gabriel Marlington—would make an appearance, so she lied. "I was wondering if Lady Sissingdon was going to fall out of her dress."

They both turned to stare at the well-endowed widow in question.

Eva snorted and then covered her mouth with her hand. Drusilla couldn't help noticing her friend's previously white kid glove now had something that looked like cucumber soup—one of the dishes at dinner—on her knuckle and a stain that must be red wine on her index finger. Drusilla could not imagine how Eva had managed the stains as she had not been wearing her gloves to eat.

Eva's violet-blue eyes flickered from Lady Sissingdon's scandalous bodice back to Drusilla, and she opened her mouth to speak but then saw something over Drusilla's shoulder.

"Gabe!" She shot to her feet and waved her arm in broad, unladylike motions.

Drusilla slowly swiveled in her chair while Eva attracted not only the attention of her stepbrother, but everyone in their half of the ballroom. She knew she should remind her friend to employ a little decorum—it seemed to be her duty in life to keep Eva out of scrapes—but her heart was pounding, her palms damp, and her stomach was doing that odd, quivery thing it seemed destined to do when Gabriel Marlington entered her orbit. Something he'd been doing on an almost daily basis since the beginning of the Season, when he'd begun escorting his sister—and, by extension, Drusilla—to every function under the sun.

He stood near the entrance to the ballroom as the majordomo announced him. His name—as always—sent a frisson of excitement through the crowd. The women in the room—young, old, married, widowed, or single—raised their fans or quizzing glasses, the better to watch him.

The men, also, took notice of his arrival. Especially the clutch of men who slouched near the entrance—young bucks who looked as if they were undecided about whether they should remain at the ball or leave to engage in some vile, masculine pursuit. The men closed ranks as Gabriel walked past them, like a pack of wild dogs scenting a larger, more dangerous predator.

One of the group, Earl Visel, a man with perhaps the worst reputation in London—if not all of England—said something to Gabriel that made him stop.

The two faced each other, Visel's cronies hanging back as their leader stepped closer to Gabriel. They were, Drusilla realized, both tall, broad-shouldered, narrow-hipped men, although Visel was pale, blue-eyed, and blond while Gabriel was golden and heavy lidded, with hair that put her in mind of a glowing coal.

Whatever Gabriel said to Visel caused the men behind the earl to erupt into a flutter, the gabble of voices audible even over the noise of the ballroom. Visel was the only one who seemed unoffended. In fact, he threw back his head and laughed.

Gabriel appeared not to notice the reaction his response

created among the ball's denizens and scanned the crowd just like the Barbary falcon he resembled, his full lips curving into an easy smile when his eyes landed on his sister. His gaze kept moving and Drusilla couldn't help noticing how his expression turned to one of mocking amusement when he saw her. She told herself his reaction was entirely natural, especially since she'd done everything in her power to provoke and annoy him for the last five years.

She also told herself that she disliked him because he was everything she despised in the masculine species: arrogant, too attractive for either his own or anyone else's good, assured of his superiority, and so accustomed to female adulation he would never have noticed Drusilla's existence if she hadn't forced him to.

But she knew she was just lying to herself.

The real reason she disliked him—if that was indeed the emotion she bore him—was because Gabriel Marlington made her dislike herself, an emotion she'd believed she'd rooted out years ago. Every time he came near her, she was forced to recall her own less-than-prepossessing appearance. Drusilla knew she was not ugly, but she certainly could never be called pretty. No, handsome was the best she could ever hope for. Not that she cared about such superficial and vain matters. Yet another thing she told herself.

"Gabe!" Eva was bouncing up and down when her slipper caught on the grubby hem of her white gown. An audible *riiiiiiiiiiiiip!* drew the attention of everyone in the vicinity.

Her face, so happy only a second earlier, collapsed into a frown. "Oh bother."

It was a big rip, but nothing Eva hadn't done before.

Drusilla laid a hand on her friend's forearm. "Don't worry, Eva, I have plenty of pins and we'll fix it in a trice," she said as Gabriel stopped in front of them.

"Good evening, ladies." He greeted his stepsister by kissing her on both cheeks in a foreign fashion Drusilla secretly found charming. He never greeted Drusilla that way. But at least today he smiled at Drusilla after hearing her volunteer to fix Eva's gown.

"You have an excellent friend in Miss Clare, Eva. Not to mention a forward-thinking one to come armed with so many pins."

Drusilla tried not to bask in the grateful—almost warm—glance he shot her. Instead, she narrowed her eyes and dropped a slight curtsey. "Mr. Marlington."

He appeared not to notice her cool greeting. "You two ladies are looking in fine fettle this evening. Is that a new gown, Eva?"

Eva snorted at his poor attempt at fraternal flattery. "You are such a dunce, Gabe. How can a person tell one bland white gown from another?"

He laughed at her rough words. "It is not very ladylike to call one's brother a dunce, Evil."

Eva smacked him with her fan, but Drusilla knew her friend reveled in both the pet name and the brotherly affection; who wouldn't? Drusilla had no siblings—half or otherwise—and could only imagine what it would be like to have such a playful, teasing relationship. She was fond of her Aunt Violet, of course, but their relationship was neither close nor particularly deep. And she'd loved her kind but distant father, but he'd rarely had the time to spare for her when she'd been a girl, and he'd died when she was only fourteen, and still away at school. And that was the sum of her family, at least any she knew.

Drusilla did not understand how Eva managed to view the delicious man as nothing more than a brother. After all, not only did the two share no blood, but they'd just become acquainted with each other a little more than five years ago.

It was beyond maddening; just *thinking* about Gabriel Marlington made Drusilla swoon, but Eva seemed perfectly comfortable abusing him, physically mauling him, or ordering him around.

Eva grabbed his arm, bouncing up and down on the balls of her feet, her expression chiding but affectionate. "You're so late—it's almost the supper dance. I thought you might not come tonight."

"It was wretched weather just this side of Epping, so that slowed me down. But I gave you my word I'd be back tonight. You should know I always keep my word."

Gabriel looked from Eva to Drusilla, his warm smile still in place, but his eyelids lowering over his vivid green eyes.

"And how have you been, Miss Clare? Organized any prison rebellions while I was away?"

She sighed and unfurled her fan, adopting her most bored expression. "That never grows old, does it, Mr. Marlington?"

He chuckled. "I'm a man of simple pleasures."

Drusilla snorted. His *pleasures* provided more fodder for *ton* gossip mills than a dozen young bucks bundled together. If only ten percent of the rumors were true, then his pleasures were anything but simple.

"And I did *not* organize a prison rebellion."

"Ah, that's correct—you merely provided the funding."

Drusilla sighed. The incident he was referring to had taken place last year, when a group of militant prison reformers used the money she'd given them to provide necessary items for prisoners to stage a gaol protest that led to hundreds of pounds of damage and the escape of four hardened criminals who'd been slated for transportation. It had not been the best of months for her and she'd resolved to donate only to causes she was personally affiliated with, or those advocated by the members of her small, intimate reform group.

She gave him a contemptuous smile. "Surely you can come

up with something more recent to irk me about after so many months?"

"Oh, I don't know, it seems like a rebellion *and* an escape should be good for more than a few months of irksomeness." He turned to Eva. "Or is that irkishness?"

Eva chortled. "You're such a ninny, Gabe."

"*Ninny* would not be my first choice of word," Drusilla muttered.

His eyebrows arched high in mock confusion. "Whatever do you mean, Miss Clare?" He turned to his sister. "Do *you* know what word she means, Eva?"

"I don't think *you* want to know what word she means, Gabe."

He turned his distracting emerald gaze back to Drusilla, his lips curving in a way that made her breathing hitch. "Oh, but I do. Tell me, what word *would* you choose for me? *Witty? Handsome? Clever?*"

"The word I had in mind is hardly the type I wish to use in public, Mr. Marlington."

His eyes lit up. "Do tell, Miss Clare—where *do* you prefer to use such low words?" She ignored the question, but he was undeterred. "I must know how a proper young lady like yourself even knows of such words? Please—I am in danger of perishing with curiosity."

"I'm afraid you must perish."

He clutched his heart and grinned. "Cruel beauty."

Any heart palpitations she'd been experiencing from prolonged proximity to him dissipated at his words, which could only have been mockingly meant: Nobody could call her a beauty. Unless they were ridiculing her. Luckily such taunting only served to strengthen her resolve.

"As diverting as it is to contemplate your premature departure"—he laughed but Drusilla continued undaunted—"I'd much rather discuss your week in Newmarket, which—"

"Why, Miss Clare! I'm flattered you noticed how long I was gone and whither I went. It makes me believe you must have missed me."

"Believe whatever you wish, sir. But also keep in mind that I notice pestilence, famine, and war—but that hardly makes me miss them."

He threw his head back and laughed, and Drusilla tried not to feel proud but failed.

When he looked at her next, it was with eyes shining with humor and . . . admiration?

"What is the saying of the great English playwright, Miss Clare? "Methinks thou dost protest too much?""

Drusilla goggled in mock amazement. "My goodness, Mr. Marlington—quoting Shakespeare? It appears you *did* learn something at Oxford besides gambling, pugilism, and cocking."

"Not true, Miss Clare. I'm afraid any Shakespeare I know I learned from my position in the pit at Drury Lane."

Drusilla's face flamed like a torch. *Surely* he could not be alluding to his *notorious* exploits with the actresses Giselle Fontenot and Maria Beauchamp?

He winked at her.

Drusilla's eyes widened; that was *exactly* what he was alluding to.

His lips curved as he watched her face color and comprehension dawn. His green eyes pierced her protective façade and went straight to her overactive brain, as if he could see the images her imagination provided—images of this gorgeous man cavorting with his two ravishing lovers—and as if he could *hear* the bubbling caldron of jealousy within her.

Drusilla swallowed and unclenched her teeth, pulling her eyes away from his knowing gaze, ignoring the distracting sensation that pulsed in her belly and lower: a sensation she'd become accustomed to, courtesy of Mr. Marlington.

She looked across the room, searching frantically for something that would free her from his attention and the mortifying reactions it created in her body. Her gaze landed on a vision of blond perfection, and inspiration struck.

"You will be pleased to know Miss Kittridge has been inconsolable in your absence."

His dark auburn brows arched in surprise, but his gaze was already turning toward the east side of the ballroom, to where the luscious Miss Kittridge stood.

Drusilla gritted her teeth against the crushing knowledge that he'd known *exactly* where the other woman was without searching, as if beautiful people possessed some type of homing ability that allowed them to locate others of their kind.

And Lucinda Kittridge was, without a doubt, beautiful. She was also extremely wealthy—even more generously endowed in that area than Drusilla. And if that wasn't enough, she was four years younger and *far* more favorably blessed with charm. She was a blonde, blue-eyed angel with the body of a succubus and a mind like a military strategist, at least when it came to marriageable men. But as lovely a package as she was, her family business—England's largest abattoir—mitigated against her ever catching a peer. So she'd set her sights on the next best thing: a man related to many powerful peers by blood. Gabriel Marlington suited her needs to perfection. He might be steeped in notoriety and of dubious parentage, but his family connections were second to none. Drusilla knew full well Miss Kittridge and her mother had been angling for him since the first evening he'd appeared in London society.

Miss Kittridge looked up from her throng of admirers toward Gabriel, as if they were joined by some invisible bond, and Drusilla hated herself for drawing the perfect, wealthy heiress into her conversation with the gorgeous, irritating fortune hunter.

She bit her lip at that unkind thought; calling Gabriel Marlington a fortune hunter was nothing more than spite on her part. Not only did he have a respectable independence, but he'd never pursued Miss Kittridge. Quite the reverse.

The delectable debutante—known among the *ton* as "the Kitten"—had made her preference for Mr. Marlington clear whenever the opportunity arose. Both she and her social-climbing parents would overlook Gabriel's notorious past and scandalous liaisons thanks to his connections to the Marquess of Exley and the Duke of Carlisle, two of the wealthiest and most influential peers in the land.

While the *ton* might consider Gabriel Marlington, the exiled son of the former Sultan of Oran, a baseborn outsider, there were few people either brave enough—or stupid enough—to voice such thoughts. To be blunt, his aristocratic connections were far too impressive for anyone to ignore him, no matter how much some people might like to.

"I don't care for the Kitten."

Drusilla and Gabriel turned away from Miss Kittridge at the sound of Eva's voice.

The delicate but disheveled beauty was chewing on yet another raven-colored curl she'd pulled from her disastrous coiffeur and staring speculatively at the woman in question.

Gabriel gently detached the curl from his stepsister's hand and tucked it behind her ear. "Why is that, Evil? Because she is almost as pretty as you?"

Eva elbowed him in the ribs—hard.

Gabriel clutched his side. "Lord, you're such a barbarian."

Rather than appear chastised, Eva grinned, pleased with the accusation.

"Tell me, why don't you like the Kitten?" Gabriel persisted.

"She only looks all soft and cuddly like a kitten. I think she is rapacious and sharp clawed beneath all her pretty fur."

Drusilla agreed with her friend's astute observation. How

was it that men did not notice there was something hard about the exquisite and seemingly sweet heiress?

Gabriel cut Drusilla a sly glance. "And what about you, Miss Clare? Do you also dislike Miss Kittridge?"

"I have not wasted a second's thought on her," she lied.

His lips twitched, as if he knew how Miss Kittridge's open attraction to him—and his reciprocation of it—ate at Drusilla like an acid when she was alone at night. Or during the day. Or anytime the horrid thought gained purchase in her mind.

She scowled at him.

"You're not really going to offer for her, are you, Gabe?" Eva's brow was furrowed with concern and Drusilla's body clenched as she waited for his answer, the suspense painful.

But the annoying man merely smiled, as if he could sense her agony and enjoyed prolonging it.

Drusilla assured herself that was impossible: Gabriel Marlington could not know how she felt for him, not after she'd employed her considerable intellect to conceal her humiliating infatuation.

"Are you, Gabe?" Eva repeated, asking what Drusilla could not.

He shrugged. "You know how Mama has been these past few months, Eva. One of us must become leg-shackled before the Season is out if we're ever to have any peace in our lives. And since *you* are showing no signs of doing so, it seems that I must fall on my sword."

"I couldn't agree more. You *should* fall on your sword for the good of the rest of us; just make sure that sword isn't the Kitten."

He smiled down at his half sister, who was staring pensively at the sword in question.

Agony and futility as sharp as needles stabbed at Drusilla's heart. Was he so blind that he thought the Kitten might actually like—or love—him for who he was? Or maybe he didn't care about such things? Perhaps his only requirement when it came to a mate was a pretty face?

He eyed Drusilla with amused speculation, as if she'd just spoken out loud. "And what is your opinion, Miss Clare—because I know you will have one."

"Please, fall on whatever sword you wish."

He laughed with obvious delight.

But the thought of Gabriel Marlington married to the Kitten made Drusilla want to fall on a *real* sword. It also made her want to slap the smug look off his perfect features.

Instead of doing either, she used the only weapon left to her: her wit.

"You seem terribly confident that your unsavory antics won't sour Miss Kittridge's parents' eagerness for you and your suit, Mr. Marlington."

He turned to Drusilla, arrested. "How flattered I am that you take such an interest in my, er, suit, Miss Clare. And my antics."

She flicked a nonexistent piece of lint from the puffed sleeve of her pale blue gown. "Not interest, sir, merely an objective observation."

"Ah, I see. But tell me, Miss Clare, just what *unsavory* antics have you heard about?"

A wave of heat began to make its journey up her neck. She compressed her lips, as if that could somehow stop the tide. "I can only imagine."

"Can you? I'm all agog to hear the fascinating fruits of your active imagination."

Drusilla narrowed her eyes in what she hoped was a condescending and repressive fashion and gave him a deceptively sweet smile. "I hardly need to cudgel my brain to invent antics for you, do I, Mr. Marlington? Not when you are so good at providing all of us with real examples. Your notoriety is legend and tales of your behavior—or should I say *mis*behavior—abound, many of them as entertaining as an evening at the . . . theater." There, let him chew on *that*.

But if she had hoped to discompose or embarrass him with a veiled reference to his notorious liaisons, he disappointed her. Instead he gave her a smile of genuine delight

"Ah, Miss Clare, I never imagined you to be the type of woman to pay any mind to scurrilous gossip."

Drusilla widened her eyes in mock wonder. "Oh? Please, *do tell*, Mr. Marlington," she said, echoing his earlier words. "I'm *all agog* to hear the type of woman you imagine me to be."

He leaned toward her and said in a voice so low that only she could hear, "My imaginings are not the type of thing I can discuss in public."

Drusilla took a hasty step back and bumped into a passing dandy, the impact enough to send her sprawling.

Gabriel's response was quick and unobtrusive as he set a light hand beneath her elbow to steady her, giving the other man a dismissive nod before releasing her arm.

"The heat in here is quite oppressive, is it not?" He was looking at her with something suspiciously like concern.

She ignored her palpitating heart and his question, eager to move the subject away from herself and back to him.

"We were speaking of your recent trip to Newmarket, I believe," she said. "It has been disappointingly quiet thus far, but it is still early days, Mr. Marlington. Tell me, what stories can we expect? Reckless wagers? Impromptu mills? Duels? Orgies?"

He grinned in a way that made her wish she could take back her words. Or at least that last one.

"Orgies?" he repeated.

Her face became impossibly hotter.

"You *do* have an active imagination, Miss Clare. I should

dearly love to hear your thoughts on orgies. Not to mention how I fit in with such speculations about orgies."

"Quit saying *orgy*," she hissed.

"You started it."

"You sound like a twelve-year-old, Mr. Marlington."

His lids lowered and heat burned through her body, the conflagration hottest between her tightly clenched thighs. *"Orgy,"* he whispered.

Eva's laughter broke the terrifying trance. "You two! Always funning one another."

Drusilla and Gabriel turned to stare at Eva in amazement. How was it that she failed to recognize the hostility that characterized the relationship between her best friend and brother?

But Eva was gazing across at the beguiling debutante, oblivious to their astonished expressions. "It looks like you aren't the only one chasing the Kitten, Gabe."

Lord Visel had approached Miss Kittridge while Drusilla and Gabriel had been sparring. The girl—and her mother—were preening at the unprecedented experience of having attracted the interest of a duke's heir, no matter how scandalous the man's reputation for outrageous and reckless behavior.

If seeing his nemesis paying court to Miss Kittridge caused Mr. Marlington any heartache, he certainly did not show it.

Instead he turned to his sister. "I heard the marquess picked up Gerald Hine's chestnuts at Tatt's?"

The stepsiblings began talking horseflesh, a subject that seemed to occupy at least three-quarters of Eva's mind.

As much as Drusilla yearned for Gabriel Marlington's attention, she was weak with relief when she no longer had it. Sparring with him always made her feel as if she'd barely survived a treacherous journey. She relaxed and permitted herself furtive glances at his irresistible person, behaving just like a glutton at a banquet in Dante's Third Circle of Hell.

Dru had no idea what Gabriel's father had looked like, but

the former sultan and the Duke of Carlisle's daughter, Lady Euphemia, had certainly produced a heavenly son. Not only was he one of the most stunning men in the room, he was also one of the most distinctive. His speech was still quite heavily—and charmingly—accented. His appearance, as well, was rather exotic, his bronze complexion standing out among the pale, pasty-faced crowd of young bucks. And his hair? Well, that was truly his crowning glory. It was a dark, burnished auburn of a sort she'd not seen on any other person. It was true that all of the Marlingtons had red or reddish hair, and his mother—the marchioness—had particularly lovely copper curls. But Gabriel's hair was almost black with a sullen crimson undertone.

His nose was a great hawk's beak that should have made him ugly but instead served to keep him from being too perfect. It also heightened his resemblance to his illustrious maternal grandfather, the Duke of Carlisle.

Last, but certainly not least, were his eyes.

Drusilla heaved a half-worshipful, half-disgusted sigh, which earned her a quick questioning glance from the sooty-lashed, almond-shaped green orbs in question. She returned his mild querying expression with a haughty, superior stare she'd perfected years ago. He recoiled as if she'd reached out and poked him. Or kissed him.

The thought sent heat flaring through her body. Her *entire* body. She looked away. God save her if he ever had any idea of just how fascinating she found him. Or at least his person. No, that was not true. She found *all* of him too interesting. Which was unfortunate. If it had been only his appearance, she would have gotten past her obsession quickly. But he was also clever and funny and brave and mysterious and something else for which she had no word—but which made her tingle all over when she was around him. What woman could resist such a combination?

What she felt for him was something she kept deeply buried: a secret so mortifying she'd never even exhumed it and taken a look at it herself.

Couples began assembling for the next set, and Gabriel glanced around.

"Where has Mrs. Peel gone?" he asked, surveying the room for Drusilla's aunt, who was acting as their chaperone tonight.

"She didn't feel well and has gone to the retiring room to rest," Drusilla said.

His full lips thinned. "You two should not be here alone, unsupervised."

Drusilla bristled at his chiding, but Eva smacked him on the arm with her fan. "We're not toddlers, Gabe. Besides, we aren't alone: we're with *you*."

Gabriel shook his head at his sister but let the subject drop. Instead he asked, "And what are you both doing over here in the corner?"

Drusilla called him Gabriel in the privacy of her own mind. And why not? After the way she'd treated him these past five years, it was unlikely he would ever invite her to use his Christian name in real life.

"We like it here," Eva said.

He frowned down at his tiny stepsister. "You shan't meet any nice young men if you hide in the back."

"Lord, Gabe, you sound just like Mama: *nice young men* indeed. You should know better. You're the only *nice young man* within spitting distance."

His gaze flickered ceilingward, as if rendered speechless by his sister's vulgarism.

"Besides," Eva continued, either undeterred or unaware of her stepbrother's reaction. "Dru and I have already met every young man in London—nice or otherwise." She gestured to the aisle of empty space around them with her fan, which Drusilla noticed no longer closed properly. "And they can *see* where we are perfectly well if they are interested in dancing."

All three of them looked across the room toward the clutch of men Gabriel had passed—several of whom were looking in their direction, but not—Drusilla was sure—with any interest in dancing.

Eva was right. The young men of the *ton* had no interest in either of them. They shunned Eva because of her long-dead mother. And they ostracized Drusilla for philosophical reasons: *her* philosophies, to be precise.

While Dru didn't have a shocking family secret or keep two mistresses in the same house, she was just as notorious in her own way. It wasn't just the prison break she'd inadvertently funded, but her views on marriage and the rights of women that had relegated her to the fringes of society. Not even her considerable wealth could lure suitors.

The young men weren't staring at Drusilla and Eva, but Gabriel.

Lord Visel, in particular, seemed to be watching him. Women might swoon over Gabriel Marlington, but a good number of men seemed to dislike him. Drusilla could only imagine it was jealousy or envy that elicited such animus.

Eva elbowed him in the side again. "Now that you're here, Gabe, you can dance with Dru."

If Drusilla hadn't been staring at Gabriel like a condemned woman eyeing her last meal, she might have missed the lightning-fast expression of irritation that crossed his handsome features. But she *was* watching and she *did* see it. And when he cut her a quick glance, she could see that *he* knew *she* had seen it. And she wanted to kill her well-intentioned friend.

"Er, but what about your gown?" Gabriel said lamely. "Doesn't it need mending?"

Drusilla snatched her friend's arm before Eva did something even more humiliating, like beg Gabriel to dance with her.

"Yes, Eva, your gown. We must go and fix it."

Eva's sudden flush said she realized she'd been too impulsive. She glanced from Drusilla's mortified expression to her brother's wooden one. "You'll be here when we return, Gabe?"

"I'll be here. With Mrs. Peel temporarily out of commission, it appears I am your chaperone as well as your companion." The smile he gave his stepsister was warm and protective. And then his green eyes flickered past Drusilla as if she wasn't even there and settled on the lovely Lucinda Kittridge.

Chapter 2

Gabriel watched the two girls head toward the door leading from the ballroom to the ladies retiring room. Should he follow them to ensure they weren't meddled with? He shrugged the foolish thought away. Who the devil would meddle with them inside a room bursting with women? The retiring room was probably the safest place in the house for two young girls—safe, at least, when it came to their virtue. Not that a roomful of women was necessarily safe. Gabriel had grown up around mostly women and knew they could be just as dangerous—*more* dangerous, really—than most men.

He considered the matter of their absent chaperone, Mrs. Peel, his eyes sweeping over the clutch of nearby matrons He did not recognize any of his mother's acquaintances or he would have approached them and asked for help. Although the marchioness had told him his chaperoning duties were ornamental, Gabriel couldn't help his concern. In Oran his half sisters had never been allowed outside the palace without proper covering. But here?

Gabriel glanced around the room at the various necklines. He was still shocked at the dresses women would permit their eighteen-year-old daughters to wear. The English aristocracy seemed to have no trouble sending their daughters out into public half-dressed despite their puritanical attitudes toward sex and sexuality.

Well, there was little he could do about the situation tonight. He would seek out his mother tomorrow and raise the subject of Mrs. Peel, who was quite an elderly woman and had appeared to feel out of sorts often this past month. He believed the two girls required a more robust chaperone, but he could hardly suggest that to Miss Clare as Mrs. Peel was her aunt.

Miss Clare.

He snorted. The name brought to mind the face of one who perplexed and annoyed him more than any other woman he had ever met. More than any person, really. Even his half brother Assad—who'd tried to kill him more than once—had not been so tiresome.

Gabriel knew he wasn't alone when it came to his feelings about Eva's bosom friend. He'd heard other men talking about the sharp-faced, sour-tongued—but exceedingly wealthy—daughter of the late merchant king Edgar Clare. She was critical, brutally direct, and sanctimoniously opinionated with everyone, but she seemed to save a little extra judgement for Gabriel. Or at least it seemed that way over the past few months he'd been accompanying Eva and her friend to every wretched event.

When Eva had first written to him about the wonderful friend she'd made at her finishing school—his mercurial and awkward sister's *only* friend outside her family—Gabriel had been overjoyed.

But then he'd met Miss Clare.

Gabriel pursed his lips and shook his head. Just look at her tonight: she was a girl of one and twenty who devoted all her time, money, and efforts to charitable works and dressed like an aged spinster.

Not that he disapproved of her more modest necklines and

voluminous petticoats; no, he thought her gowns were appropriate for a girl her age, if not always a flattering color or cut. Nor did he mind her devotion to worthy causes. However, he did find her superior attitude toward him grating. She behaved as though he were a savage libertine with no self-restraint. Restraint was probably her middle name—or perhaps it was Censorious.

Miss Clare comported herself like a woman of forty. Older, really. Gabriel's mother, the Marchioness of Exley, behaved with more girlish spontaneity than Drusilla Clare.

Gabriel would like to have wiped her superior smirk off her face and told her the truth about where he'd spent the past week—*not* raking at Newmarket but down in Brighton on *serious* business—but that would have been foolish, considering how sensitive this particular business was. Besides, it wasn't as if Drusilla Clare's opinion of him mattered a jot. In fact, he *hoped* she imagined him off gambling, cocking, and whoring.

Ha! Drusilla: even her name was enough to dampen a person's spirits.

Gabriel snorted at his own stupidity. The first notes of a reel filled the cavernous ballroom and he saw the set had formed while he'd been woolgathering. The luscious Miss Kittridge glared at him from over the head of her short, squat partner.

Gabriel smiled and gave a slight shrug, earning a decidedly *un*kittenish glare and angry toss of blonde curls.

Perhaps he'd ask her for the next set—which was the supper dance, a waltz.

He waited until the steps brought her around again and she could see him, and then he mouthed the word *supper*. Her eyelids lowered and her frown melted away. She hesitated a long moment before giving him the slightest of nods.

Gabriel experienced a slight pang of something at her acceptance—disappointment? He shook the thought away. So what if they had little in the way of conversation? It was true she seemed to have an excessive interest in clothing—or at least in talking about clothing—but why should that matter? Lucy Kittridge was breathtaking and charming—and she *did* resemble a kitten, albeit a wicked one. Gabriel could—and had more than once—imagined her being something of a tigress when it came to the sensual part of marriage. But no matter how appealing such thoughts might be, Gabriel suspected the magnificent Miss Kittridge would not be pleased to find herself saddled with another woman's child. No, marrying Miss Kittridge was not in his future.

Lord. He couldn't think about that right now.

He took out his watch and frowned: the girls had been gone far too long for the mere mending of a hem. What had Eva gotten up to now? He sighed and made his way toward the ballroom exit. It was time he take his chaperoning duties seriously and go find his sister and her annoying friend.

"You're angry with me for suggesting Gabe dance with you, aren't you, Dru?" Eva asked from behind her, having to trot to keep up with Drusilla's longer—and angrier—stride.

"Of course I'm not mad," she lied, tossing the words over her shoulder. "Oh my, there is a dreadful crush, Eva. We'll never get in." They both stared at the women thronging the room that had been set aside for wardrobe catastrophes and critical gossip sessions.

Drusilla glanced around. "Come," she said, leading her friend away from the noisy, crowded chamber.

"Where are we going?" Eva asked as a footman leaped forward to pull open a door.

"To the conservatory, where we can sit down and rest a few moments." The door closed behind them, and the sudden hush in the corridor made her voice sound loud. She spoke in a softer tone. "We can fix your hem and take a few moments of peace and quiet."

"There is a conservatory?"

"Yes, I believe it was one of the first of its kind in the city."

"How do you always know about such things?"

"It's no secret, Eva. I read about Abingdon House long ago, in a guidebook to fine London houses." Her lips twisted into a self-mocking smile. "Little did I know I would one day be allowed to actually set foot in this holiest of holies." Dukes did not, as a rule, invite the daughters of tradesmen to their houses. But they occasionally made exceptions for the very wealthy ones, especially if they had five unwed younger sons.

And of course Eva had been invited; she might have madness in her veins but she also had a dowry that was greater than most other aristocratic misses as well as august connections that went all the way back to before the Conquest. It was ironic that two of the Season's greatest prizes were also its biggest lepers.

Drusilla chewed her lower lip and hesitated. "I believe it is this way," she said, taking a short corridor that led to the back of the house. There were candles in the sconces, but not enough to indicate this was a part of the house intended for ball guests. Drusilla didn't care. She needed some peace and quiet to recover from her brush with Gabriel Marlington, just as she always did.

She had hoped protracted exposure to him this Season would eliminate her more severe reactions to him, but her attraction had become stronger, rather than weaker, the more she was exposed to him.

Drusilla opened the door at the end of the hall, and they both froze and stared: it was a magical place, a huge room constructed from hundreds of panes of faceted glass.

"My goodness," she whispered, stepping inside. Outside, it

was a rare night in London when even a few stars were visible, the moon surrounded by silvery wisps of clouds.

"It's fabulous," Eva said, her head tipped back as she gazed through the plate glass above their heads. "And it smells *divine*."

It did. It smelled of fresh earth, citrus from the potted trees, and a dozen kinds of flower.

"This is *so* much nicer than that stuffy ballroom." Eva extended her arms and spun in a circle, laughing, her white muslin billowing around her, its tattered hem dragging.

Drusilla opened her reticule, which held more items than most people's medicine chests—it was her way to always be prepared for any emergency—and rooted for the small paper with pins.

"I'm dizzy," Eva said in a breathy voice, landing with a thud beside Drusilla on the stone bench.

"Let's see the damage, Eva."

Eva swiveled on her bottom and put her feet across Drusilla's lap, flopping back onto the bench. Drusilla couldn't help smiling; Eva behaved like a girl half her age—unaffected and childlike. She'd always been this way. When they'd been at school together, most of the other girls had either teased Eva or avoided her entirely, put off by her wild and unpredictable behavior. It was true that a person could never guess what Eva might do in any given situation; she seemed to lack the filter other people were born with.

Of course, those same girls had taunted Drusilla, too, albeit for different reasons. She was a merchant's daughter, a girl with the smell of the shop about her.

Dru and Eva had been inseparable almost from the moment they'd met each other at Miss Barnstaple's Academy for Young Ladies.

Eva had made school not just bearable for Dru, but enjoyable. But then, between their third and fourth years, Eva had become ill and not returned to school. That last year without

Eva had been miserable. As had her first two Seasons without her friend.

Eva should have had her first Season last year, but she'd taken a long time to fully recuperate. Drusilla knew her friend had made the most of her illness, hoping her parents would forget about a Season altogether. But this year she'd been forced to make her debut at the grand old age of nineteen, almost twenty.

Drusilla placed the last of her pins in the ripped hem and examined her repair work.

"This will not last long if you are not careful," Drusilla warned her friend.

"Careful? Do you mean with all my dancing?"

Eva was so lovely it was hard to believe she lacked for dance partners, but Drusilla knew it to be the truth. Her friend's unpredictable and unconventional behavior appeared to frighten off potential suitors as much as the rumors of madness. She didn't help her situation by sitting in corners with Drusilla.

Eva took a deep breath and swung her feet down, stood, and lifted the hem of her skirt to examine it. "As good as new," she pronounced. "Are you ready to return to the ballroom?"

Drusilla wasn't. This room was far too magical to leave, but . . . "I suppose I'd better go check on Aunt Vi and—"

Eva laid her hands on Drusilla's shoulders and smiled down at her. "You stay here and take a few moments to rest. I'll check on her."

Drusilla gave her friend a dubious look. "Are you certain?"

"Quite."

"But it will be supper and your brother will wonder what has become of you."

"I'll tell him all is well after checking on your aunt, and then I'll return and we can enjoy this beautiful, magical garden together until after supper, when we can ask Gabriel to take us home. Is that not an excellent idea?" Eva looked hopeful. She was constantly seeking ways to either get out of *ton* functions entirely or leave early. Drusilla knew she shouldn't encourage Eva's behavior, but . . .

"Promise you won't go anywhere, Dru?"

"I promise, just—"

"Good—then I'll be back soon." Eva spun and headed toward the door at an unladylike trot.

"Don't forget to check on Aunt Vi first," Drusilla reminded her.

Eva did a clumsy pirouette, stumbled, and then laughed before pulling open the door. "I shan't," she called out, and then disappeared.

Well, that was Eva: unable to behave like a lady no matter how often she'd been disciplined in school. Drusilla envied her friend her carefree nature and her ease when it came to doing exactly what she wanted—no matter the consequences.

She glanced at the spot Eva had just vacated. Why not? Why was she always so proper? It wasn't as if anyone was ever watching her. Eva had stretched out on the bench without a care in the world. So could she.

Feeling as naughty as if she were displaying her garters at Almack's—not that she could ever hope to secure a voucher for that venerable establishment—Drusilla lay back on the bench and balanced her reticule on her midriff. She closed her eyes and forced her tense body to relax in this unusual position.

Pictures of Gabriel Marlington immediately formed behind her eyelids. She grimaced. Why must she be afflicted with this stupid infatuation? Could there be anything more pitiful than a homely wallflower yearning for an arresting, attractive Corinthian? Because that was exactly what Gabriel Marlington was. Even with her dismal knowledge of male pursuits, Drusilla knew he rode, shot, fenced, and boxed superbly.

And then there was the way women behaved toward him.

A groan of frustration slipped from her, and she bit her lower lip. They say eavesdroppers never hear good about themselves, but in Drusilla's case, she never heard anything good about Gabriel when she listened to the conversations of others. Oh, it was nothing too horrid—he didn't torture animals, nor was he cruel to small children—but he was, it was loudly whispered, a slayer of hearts.

It appeared that tales of his wickedness only made women wilder for him. Even smart women like Drusilla were not immune to such charm and male beauty.

She'd pondered her obsession with Gabriel Marlington for *years*, long before she'd heard tales of his mistresses—*plural*—or seen the amorous widows stalking him, or watched him bewitch one woman after another.

Drusilla was not, in the main, attracted to bright and shiny objects. She'd always believed that if she ever did marry, it would be to a man who was kind and gentle and devoted to the same causes as she was. Not that Gabriel was not kind and gentle—at least to his family. And apparently the Kitten.

Thinking about Gabriel and the Kitten was like abrading her soul with a cat-o'-nine-tails. How could a person make themselves stop wanting something they could never have?

She punished herself by envisioning them together.

Yes, some sage inner voice praised her flagellating behavior, *that is the way—face your fears head-on and you will conquer them.*

Drusilla pictured them dancing—waltzing—together. She didn't have to imagine it because she'd seen it times beyond counting. Separately they were perfect; together they were almost too perfect to look upon.

Next, she pictured them *kissing*. She'd seen people kissing more than once. Oftentimes the more fortunate people—the beautiful people—believed they were unobserved at the balls, routs, and picnics that comprised the Season. They should have realized the walls had eyes. Or, to be more precise, the wall-*flowers* had eyes. And what else did they have to do with those eyes but watch those around them?

Thankfully, Drusilla had never actually seen Gabriel and the Kitten kissing. She knew the Kitten had probably schemed to orchestrate such a thing, but Gabriel—for all his wild ways with widows and actresses—was the very image of propriety around maidens.

Still, Drusilla could imagine them embracing, his powerful shoulders sheltering the Kitten's delicate frame, his hands, elegant and strong, one splayed on the small of her back, the other cradling her head like a priceless and fragile object. His lush, sensual lips—lips that were almost as expressive as his brilliant, flashing eyes—pressed against the Kitten's perfectly bow-shaped mouth.

The horrifying image shifted in her mind's eye, and Drusilla smiled dreamily at the new picture: *her* in Gabriel's muscular arms.

She let her body relax on the unforgiving marble bench and enjoyed the mental image. What a rebel she was, sprawled on a bench in a conservatory during a ball. Alone. She was wicked and her aunt would scold her if she found out.

She sighed, telling herself to get up—to go back and join the bouquet of wallflowers—but her eyelids were so heavy . . . so heavy. And it was so peaceful . . . so . . .

"What have we here?"

The low voice penetrated her dozy state at the same time that something warm touched her cheek.

"A sleeping beauty," the same voice murmured. "Not the one I was looking for but you will have to—"

Drusilla's brain awoke from its slumber, and her eyes flew open to find a face looming over her. She shrieked and jerked into an upright position—or at least tried to—slamming her forehead into his nose.

"Oww, dammit, that bloody hurt!" Her assailant staggered back

Drusilla tried to sit up, but her legs had somehow become tangled in her skirts and she began to slide off the bench, her fingers scrabbling to grip the smooth stone, her other hand stupidly clutching her reticule rather than participating in her rescue.

Powerful hands clamped on to her shoulders. "Quit your bloody squirming or you'll land on your head."

Moonlight slanted across his face, and Drusilla gasped and jerked away. It was Lord Godric Visel—a handsome, sneering libertine who'd never had a second to spare for her in the past.

"Unhand me," Drusilla demanded, jerking away and then sliding off the back side of the bench in the process.

"Bloody hell." He caught her up in his arms before she could fall, lifted her, and then dropped her onto her bottom with an undignified thump. "There." His hands steadied her. "Will you quit already, Miss Clare? I'm only trying to—"

And then, suddenly, he was gone.

Chapter 3

Even when he'd been at war with his brother Assad, Gabriel had not felt such hot, unadulterated rage. He'd often heard the saying "to see red" but hadn't believed it until now. Not only was he seeing red, he was *feeling* it. He was swelteringly, brain-cracklingly hot.

The suppressed emotions of the past months boiled over, the memories of untold slights and jabs he'd silently endured from Visel without capitulating to his desires to either plant the man a facer or meet him at dawn.

"What the bloody hell do you think you are doing?" He forced the words through his clenched jaws. "Well?" he demanded, and then realized he was gripping Visel's neck far too tightly and loosened his hold.

The earl's mouth was moving, but Gabriel could not hear the words. He leaned closer.

"I thought it was your mad sister stretched out on that bench and I was going to—" The words were hardly a croak, but they acted like fuel on an already raging fire.

Gabriel banged the man's head against the thickly leaded panes, setting the rectangles of glass chattering like hundreds of teeth.

"You bloody bounder," he snarled.

Visel's mouth stretched into a leer, his eyes bulging, his nostrils flaring—and he *laughed*; the bastard *laughed*.

Gabriel was vaguely aware of a hand on his shoulder.

"Mr. Marlington? Please! *Gabriel*, you must *stop.*"

He glanced from the hand to its owner. Miss Clare was not her usual neat-as-a-pin self. Her hair had come down in several places and silky brown spirals framed her usually supercilious face. Her gray eyes were round and her pale cheeks had bloodred slashes of color that made her appear lively and quite pretty.

Gabriel shook off the bizarre observation.

"Are you all right?" he asked, only slightly loosening his grip on Visel, who was trying to break free, snorting and snuffling like a pig hunting truffles.

"Yes! Yes, I'm fine. *Please*, he didn't hurt me. You must let him go before you kill him."

Gabriel looked from her to his captive, who stared at him with fury-filled eyes. Why did this man *hate* him so very much? He shook his head at the pointless thought and shoved Visel away while releasing his grasp on his neck.

The earl staggered to one side and then plopped down on the flagstone floor like a piece of rotting fruit falling from a tree. His attractive face was an ugly, splotchy red, his lips almost purple, and his bulging, bloodshot eyes made him resemble a bloated rockfish pulled up from a great depth. The scent of stale alcohol filled the air.

Gabriel felt, rather than saw, Miss Clare sway beside him, and he turned just in time to slide an arm around her. Some part of his brain made the unexpected—and unwanted—observation that she felt soft and womanly beneath her ugly, prim gown.

"Steady on, Miss Clare," he said to the top of her head, holding her shaking body against his.

She muttered something into his shoulder.

He turned slightly and slid his other arm around her waist; he told himself it was only to hold her upright "What was that?"

"You might have killed him."

He gave a humorless chuckle. "Hardly. Please, hold on to me if you fear you might faint, Miss Clare."

She turned until she faced him, gazing up at him through huge pupils, her hands resting lightly on his shoulders. "I'm so sorry, I was foolish. I—I shouldn't have been here."

Gabriel agreed, but there seemed no point in saying so. "Where is my sister? She told me she was coming back here."

"I don't know." She sounded much better, much calmer, and much more herself. Gabriel watched in fascination as her cool, competent expression put itself together right before his eyes.

"Can you stand unassisted?"

"Yes, I—" She stopped, cocking her head. "What was that?

It took Gabriel a moment to understand what she meant. It was like the susurration of waves on a beach. But some primitive part of his brain must have known even before he spun around: It was the sound of people whispering. Lots of people.

He shoved Miss Clare behind him and stepped between her and the small crowd that had assembled in the doorway, but he knew it was too little, too late: Everyone would have seen them with their arms around each other. At least a dozen heads bobbed in the entrance, men and women, their eyes darting from Visel to Miss Clare to Gabriel.

Nobody spoke.

He glanced down. Visel was scooting sideways like a crab fleeing an incoming wave, the slick heels of his dancing shoes skittering as he tried to gain a foothold on the smooth floor.

The man was having entirely too much difficulty controlling his person, and Gabriel realized he was drunk—very drunk.

"Dammit!" Visel swore, pushing back against the glass and scrambling awkwardly to his feet, his breathing an audible soughing in the near silence of the conservatory. His heavy-lidded eyes slid from Gabriel to Miss Clare, his brows pulling together over his nose until they resembled a solid blond hedge. He opened his mouth, but another voice interrupted whatever he was going to say.

"Dru? Gabe?" Eva was pushing through the bodies blocking the doorway as if they were a bothersome thicket of weeds. "What is going on?" She sped toward them in her heedless, headlong way, her blue-violet eyes round with shock as she stared at the swaying form of the earl. "What have you done?"

Visel's too-pretty face screwed into an ugly sneer. "Well, if it isn't Mad Mary herself—come to rescue the barbarian bastard and the shopgirl, have you?" He laughed. "I think you're too late for that, sweetheart."

Gabriel's body moved toward the other man before his brain knew what he was doing. But this time Visel was expecting him and met him head-on.

"You are *drunk*," Gabriel grated between clenched jaws as they grappled with each other, well matched in size and strength if not in sobriety.

Visel's choked laughter filled the conservatory. "I might be, but I'd say the same things sober, Marlington. What are you going to do about it?"

Before Gabriel could answer, Visel twisted one arm out of his grasp and swung wildly. His fist clipped Gabriel's jaw hard enough to send a cascade of stars across his vision, and he lost his grip on Visel's other arm. He lunged toward him just as several hands landed on his shoulders.

Gabriel ignored the frantic voices behind him and the violent handling, his eyes locked with Visel's. The earl straightened up and pushed his sweat-damp blond hair from his forehead, his eyes narrowed to slits.

At least four sets of arms tightened around Gabriel's arms and shoulders and held him steady.

Visel walked up to him, close enough that the hot, sweet stench of alcohol made Gabriel flinch. Close enough that he could see the almost mad glint in the other man's eyes. "You assaulted me, Marlington; I demand that you meet me for this."

"No!" Eva and Lady Drusilla yelled in tandem.

The men ignored them.

"Let him go," Visel snapped at Gabriel's captors.

The hands fell away, and Gabriel heard the shuffle of feet as they quickly moved out of range.

Gabriel took a card from his coat pocket. "Here is my direction. Viscount Byer and I share the house. He will receive your man." He flicked the small rectangle at the earl, and Visel flapped clumsily to catch it.

He stared across at Gabriel with a hatred that should have left him scorched to a cinder, a fanatical expression of glee on his face. "Finally," he said, and then shouldered past Gabriel and strode toward the exit.

Finally? What the devil did *finally* mean?

"Noooooo!" Eva's anguished cry snapped Gabriel out of his daze. Luckily, Drusilla had her arms wrapped around the much smaller woman or she would have attacked Lord Visel.

Visel cut Eva an unpleasant smile but didn't pause. The crowd parted to let him through and then dispersed more quickly than rats exposed to daylight. No doubt they were sprinting back to the crowded ballroom to spread the word. Gabriel needed to get his sister and Miss Clare out of here.

"Where the devil is your aunt?" he asked Miss Clare.

Eva answered. "I just spoke to Mrs. Peel," she said, her eyes wide, shocked—frightened. "She is quite ill, but I think she—"

"She is *very* ill." Miss Clare's cool, quiet voice cut through his sister's words like a blade. "She takes a potion to fight most of the pain, but it can become quite bad at times."

Gabriel threw up his hands. "Then why is she *here*, at a ball, engaged in such frippery? If my mother had known, she would have engaged somebody for you both."

Miss Clare pursed her lips. "She is here because it is her *wish*, Mr. Marlington. We are all the family we both have, and she does not want me to be alone." She swallowed hard. "Although now I can see I might have made a terrible mistake giving in to her." This last part was spoken more to herself. She looked up. "I thought Eva and I were perfectly able to care for ourselves."

Gabriel snorted, even though he knew recriminations were not helpful. "Yet here you were. Alone. And you, Eva? Why were you not here with Miss Clare? You left me almost a quarter of an hour ago." He flicked Eva a scalding glance.

"I'm sorry, Gabe. It's not Dru's fault." Eva reached out and took his arm, and it was all he could do not to snatch it away. "I'd just left Mrs. Peel, who wanted me to fetch a—"

"We don't have time right now. Word of this will reach your father's ears before we set foot in the door." He glanced at Miss Clare. "I'll take you back to your house on the way."

"She's staying with me tonight, Gabriel—at Exley House."

Gabriel squeezed his eyes shut and muttered every vile curse he knew. She was under the marquess's roof? That meant she was his lordship's responsibility—or Gabriel's, by extension. His stepfather and mother would strip the hide off his back, and they had every right to do so.

The door to the conservatory opened, and Mrs. Peel entered with two other women. She raised a narrow, pale, shaking hand to her mouth when she saw her niece. Gabriel thought she might collapse then and there.

The other women, however, were alert and watchful, like avid, sniffing bloodhounds scenting a kill.

"Come," Gabriel said to the girls, ushering them toward the entrance. "Let's get you out of here while we can."

Chapter 4

"The French have a phrase for what I am experiencing right now, Gabriel."

Gabriel heaved a sigh. "Would that be déjà vu, sir?"

The Marquess of Exley was, indeed, looking remarkably similar to the last time Gabriel had seen him in this room, a little over two months earlier—when his stepfather had asked him to escort Eva and her friend about during the Season. But there was one important difference: this time they were not alone.

"Tsss!" Lady Exley hissed.

The sound sent a flicker of amusement across the marquess's usually emotionless face. "Perhaps you might be more articulate, my dear?"

Gabriel's mother ignored her husband, instead gazing up at Gabriel in a way that made him feel as if he were seven years old. And then she made it worse. She reached up and cupped his face in both hands. His mother was an exceptionally small woman and had to stand on her tiptoes.

"Oh, Jibril, how did this happen?" She asked the question in Berber, the language of his father's people, which just went to show how upset she was. They'd not spoken Berber since their days in Oran.

"The same way this kind of thing always happens, Mother." Gabriel answered in English, not wishing to have to repeat the entire conversation a second time for the benefit of his stepfather.

She released him and spun on her heel, marching to her husband, acres of emerald silk dressing gown billowing behind her like the wake from a very small ship.

"You must do something, Adam—say something to Visel's family. Is he not the Duke of Tyndale's heir?" She stopped beside the marquess's chair and rubbed her hip against his hand, which lay on the upholstered arm.

Gabriel quickly looked away from their point of contact. His mother was an expert when it came to manipulating the seemingly unmanipulable Marquess of Exley, and no weapon was beneath her—especially not her body.

The marquess took his wife's hand and raised it to his mouth, the lingering kiss causing Gabriel's mother to sway closer.

Good. God.

Gabriel cleared his throat, and they both turned his way, their pupils huge, as if he'd interrupted them in some kind of drug-induced pre-rutting daze.

The marquess was the first to recover his wits. "You'd better sit, darling. Over there." He pointed to another chair when it appeared his wife might crawl into his lap.

Gabriel's ears became hot at the marquess's endearment. But at least his mother sat. Exley turned to him again, his face no longer indulgent but hard and dangerous. "What happened?"

"I didn't instigate this duel, my lord. Visel did when he molested a defenseless woman and then challenged me." Gabriel hesitated, considering his next words. "He's been goading me for months—almost as if he is obsessed with me." He felt like a fool for saying that, but it didn't make it any less true. "I have no idea why, but I have the feeling we would have met each other one way or another."

The marquess's eyelids dropped to half-mast. "I see."

Lady Exley shook her head. "But, my love—"

Exley directed a deceptively mild look at Gabriel's mother, but it was enough. She sucked in a breath and bit her lower lip. The only other person who'd been able to silence her so quickly was Gabriel's father, the sultan. But *everyone* had obeyed his father, and for obvious reasons: Sultan Hassan had exercised complete and uncompromising authority over all his subjects.

Gabriel wondered what threat the marquess held over his wife? Knowing the two of them, it was probably something physical and revolting. Gabriel hastily put all thoughts of his mother and her husband and their private business from his mind.

The marquess studied him as if he were an insect on a pin. And not a prepossessing one, either. "You could have done nothing less tonight," he said after an uncomfortable pause.

Gabriel began to smile.

"At least not once your sister and Miss Clare had been allowed to wander from the ballroom, unaccompanied."

Gabriel's smile died before it could reach full maturity; his stepfather was correct. If he'd been paying attention, he would have accompanied them or at least located their chaperone. He certainly should have gone searching for them far earlier.

"It is my fault, Adam," his mother said. "I noticed Mrs. Peel looking unwell the last few times I saw her, but Cousin Rebecca needed to go to my aunt's and could not chaperone the girls, and I, of course—" She waved a hand over her bulging midriff.

"Blame does not matter now, Mother."

She smiled at Gabriel but the expression was sad and strained. "You are correct, Jibril. It does not matter." His mother was the only person who still used the Arab form of *Gabriel*, and the sound of his once-familiar name left an ache in his chest.

Lord Exley cleared his throat. "I understand the rumor is that you were meeting Miss Clare, and Visel interrupted you?"

Gabriel had to laugh; the *ton* was bloody amazing. Even before they'd made it to the foyer at Abingdon House, Gabriel had heard the rumors flying.

"While we know that is not the truth, it does not signify—the truth never matters." The marquess's wry tone reminded Gabriel that Lord Exley knew about the power of rumors from personal experience. "You understand what must be done, Gabriel?"

Gabriel's mother took one of his hands before he could answer. "I know your heart was elsewhere, but when something like this happens, you must do the correct thing."

He smiled down at her and squeezed her hand, not in the mood to disabuse her of the belief that he'd fallen in love with the Kitten, and then turned back to the marquess. "Yes, I understand what has to be done."

"You'll make your offer kindly, my son?" Lady Exley asked, gripping his hand.

"I shall be as kind as I am able."

Gabriel didn't bother mentioning that he somehow doubted Miss Clare would receive his offer well, no matter how kindly he put it.

Drusilla stared out the window, even though there was nothing to see other than the winking of streetlamps and the occasional carriage.

"It's all my fault," Eva said for at least the fiftieth time.

Drusilla had stopped arguing an hour ago.

"What if he dies?" Eva wailed.

Drusilla turned to her friend. "Eva, come sit by me. Please?" she added when the other woman did not cease her relentless pacing.

Eva slumped down beside her, her hands twisting and twisting the royal blue silk of her dressing gown. Just looking at her friend was enough to rob Drusilla of breath. She was achingly gorgeous and yet utterly unaware—or uncaring—of her beauty.

Drusilla put an arm around her and drew her close, resting her cheek on her soft almost-black hair. Something about Eva de Courtney brought out the mothering instinct in her—even though they were close in age. Eva had a family who obviously loved her, but she always seemed so . . . waifish, so alone. It was ironic that Drusilla, the one with only one aunt, was the more secure of the two.

"What if he dies, Dru?"

Drusilla squeezed her harder. "Your brother was a warrior before he turned seventeen, Eva."

"Yes, but Lord Visel was a soldier for *years* and has only returned from the War recently. We don't know *what* kind of man he is." She paused. "Well, other than an atrocious libertine And the Duke of Tyndale's new heir."

Drusilla absently stroked Eva's hair as she considered the new earl, a relative newcomer to London society. Godric Fleming, the current Earl Visel, was often intoxicated, madly reckless, and exceptionally mysterious.

He'd surfaced when the Duke of Tyndale's son died last November in a freak carriage accident. All of London had been curious to meet the duke's new heir, his eldest grandson, a man who'd been away at war for over a decade.

"We don't even know if it will be pistols or swords," Eva said. She grabbed Dru's hand and squeezed hard enough to make her wince. "Oh God, Dru. What if Gabe is so angry he chooses pistols? What if Visel is a crack shot? What if Gabe kills Visel and has to leave England? What if—"

Drusilla gave Eva's shoulders a gentle squeeze. "Stop borrowing trouble, Eva. We don't know anything yet. It's possible one of them will apologize and—"

"Never! And what did Gabe do that he needs to apologize?" she demanded, not waiting for Drusilla to answer. "And Visel? He challenged my brother—he would hardly apologize for *that*. Besides, I think this is exactly what Visel wanted. I think he's been trying to goad Gabe into a fight since they met. You know what I mean, Dru—you've seen it yourself. He's been needling Gabe since he first saw him two months ago."

Drusilla *had* noticed Visel's behavior but had chalked it up to yet another oddity of male aggression. After all, the recently arrived rake was not the only man who appeared to enjoy digging at Gabriel Marlington. Men seemed to dislike him as much as women found him captivating.

Eva shook her head. "I don't understand it."

"Understand what?" Drusilla asked.

"Why Visel hates him so much."

"Because he is different, I suppose. That is how some people are, Eva. They're afraid of people who are different, and they hate that fear in themselves—especially men." She gave Eva's hand a reassuring pat. "Your brother was a warrior, Eva. If Visel is fortunate, then his pride is the only thing that will suffer in such a confrontation." Drusilla ignored the fact that Visel had been a warrior, too. "Worrying about men and what they will or will not do is as useful as grasping at shadows. They'll do what they want, whether we women dislike it or disapprove it." She could have added that both men in question were even more unpredictable than average.

Eva sniffed and gave a watery chuckle. "You are right, of course. Gabe will thrash him." She sat up and met Dru's eyes, her own red-rimmed from crying, which made Drusilla feel like even more of a beast since she had not shed so much as a tear for the man who'd come to her rescue. She couldn't help herself—she felt far more angry and guilty than grateful. Because all she could think about was the fact that she'd not only met *her* fate in that conservatory, but she'd condemned Gabriel Marlington along with her.

Eva was too impetuous to have realized what tonight meant, and Drusilla did not want to be the one to tell her. She'd wait until the summons came. Who knew, perhaps there would be a miracle intervention and she'd be saved.

You want it. You want him more than life itself, her conscience accused. *It's Gabriel who will be punished, not you.*

Drusilla knew that was true—there was no denying it. She couldn't even console herself with the argument that he would gain possession of her money. After all, the Kitten was wealthier, more beautiful, charming, and everything else a man could want. And now he would have to settle for plain, tall, gawky, and surly Drusilla.

There was a light tap on the door before a maid poked her head into the room. "Your presence is requested in the drawing room, Miss Clare."

Eva stood, but the maid shook her head. "Lord Exley said only Miss Clare, my lady."

Drusilla forced herself to smile. "I shall be fine, Eva."

"I could come—Father would—"

"No. You should wait here. But thank you for the offer."

"Very well. But, please, send for me if . . ." She shrugged. "Well, if you have need of me." Eva threw up her hands. "If anybody has need of me."

Lord and Lady Exley and Gabriel awaited her in the drawing room. Gabriel was looking out the window, his hands lightly clasped behind his back.

The marquess gestured to a chair across from his wife. "Please have a seat, Miss Clare."

Drusilla had always been a little frightened of Eva's father. Not that she believed he would hurt her, but rather because he was so very . . . perfect.

Lady Exley fluttered toward her in the graceful way she had and settled beside her on the settee, taking Drusilla's hand in her much smaller ones. She was dainty and tiny and as perfect as her husband. She was also quite pregnant. Guilt welled up in her at the trouble she'd caused them all by embroiling Lady Exley's son in a duel because of her foolish actions.

Gabriel came to sit across from Drusilla, his face unreadable. "How is your aunt, Miss Clare?"

"She feels dreadful, of course. And responsible. But I refuse to hold her to blame. I knew she was ill, but I also knew it meant a great deal to her to be involved with this Season. I should have put my foot down when I saw how much these late evenings took out of her, but—"

Lady Exley chafed Drusilla's hand reassuringly between hers. "You did not want to make her feel rejected or redundant because you are kind. We understand that, Drusilla."

Drusilla glanced at the two men, both of whom looked as if they were very far from understanding such a decision. But they were men, rulers of their domains, not women who must depend on the kindness of others.

"Would you like to wait until your aunt is well enough to join us?" the marquess asked.

She shook her head. "I understand the matter is somewhat . . . urgent. She's already indicated to me, on the ride from the ball, that she understands the gravity of the situation." Drusilla did not relate what her aunt—the guardian of her trust—had actually said: that she would approve the union between Gabriel and Drusilla and advise the other trustees to do likewise, a necessary step according to the terms of Drusilla's father's will.

At least if she wished to accede to her fortune before the age of thirty.

"She's given me permission to speak for myself, my lord. Of course, I have men of business to see to my affairs, so . . ." She let that hang, not wishing to state the obvious: that she would be well represented when it came to the marriage contract.

Lord Exley traded a look with his stepson, who nodded.

"I'm sure you're aware of the scandal we are facing, Miss Clare?" Gabriel's voice was subdued, but clear.

"Yes. I am r-ruined." She swallowed, amazed at how difficult it had been to say so little.

"Not ruined," Lady Exley chimed in, but then bit her lower lip after a sharp look from her son. "I am sorry, Jibril. Perhaps you would like some time to speak together alone?"

Gabriel looked at Drusilla. "Would you like me to ring for your maid?"

"No, that will not be necessary."

The marquess helped his wife to her feet. "We shall give you a few moments' privacy." The door clicked softly shut behind them, and they were alone.

Chapter 5

Gabriel wasn't sure what he'd been expecting—eyes red-rimmed from crying? He should have known better. Miss Drusilla Clare was not a woman to be overset by much—apparently not even a forced marriage to a man she openly despised.

She gazed across at him, her face pale but composed.

"I am sure you know what tonight means?"

"I know my reputation is ruined and I will be ostracized. Unless . . ." She let the sentence dangle.

Her pale face blushed wildly, and Gabriel wondered what she was thinking.

She chewed her lip and then blurted, "It doesn't seem fair that you should be punished for saving me from my foolishness, Mr. Marlington."

Gabriel had been thinking the same thing, but it was hardly politic to say it. "I would be honored to marry you. I would—"

She laughed and the sound was bitter. "Please, we both know that is a lie. If you had any intention of marrying at all this year—which I doubt—it would have been Miss Kittridge you would have honored."

Gabriel met her cool gray stare and realized her obsession with bluestocking causes was not the only way in which she differed from other young women. Miss Clare did not like her truths to be sugarcoated. So be it.

"While it is true we might not be each other's first choice for marriage—"

She snorted.

Gabriel ignored the flare of irritation he experienced and continued. "I'm afraid we are the *only* choice we have."

She eyed him shrewdly. "There is another way."

Hope flared in his breast. "And what is that?"

"If you give up the duel, I'll release you from any obligation to marry me."

It was Gabriel's turn to snort. "I'm not sure you understand what has happened, Miss Clare. Visel has attacked a woman in my care—" She opened her mouth, but he raised his hand. "Yes, you *were* under my care. Not only has he insulted you, but he was unpardonably cruel to Eva. He has, in short, exhibited behavior no gentleman should tolerate. But the most compelling reason for our nuptials is the rumor currently making the rounds: that you and I were trysting in the conservatory and Visel interrupted us—hence my behavior toward him. If he'd not challenged me, ma'am, I would have challenged *him*."

Drusilla *did* know about the rumor that had, amazingly, been in circulation before their carriage had even come for them. "But Eva knows the truth. She's our witness and would say what really happened."

"Please, Miss Clare. I think you know that would never wash. Whether there is a duel or not is irrelevant: we must marry."

She pursed her lips, her expression not entirely convinced. Her eyes flickered back to his, and her cheeks turned a becoming shade of pink. "I'm a very wealthy woman, Mr. Marlington. I could carve out a solitary existence of sorts and weather this scandal alone."

"You could," Gabriel admitted. He waited for her to think through her suggestion.

"But it would make life difficult for you, wouldn't it?"

He gave her a wry smile, and she glanced away.

"Difficult is not the word I would use, Miss Clare. My reputation—such as it is—would be in tatters for debauching an innocent female under my care and then abandoning her. And then there is Eva. My sister loves both of us and she is loyal beyond reason, beyond self-preservation—to a fault, in other words. She would never shun you or give up your friendship—no matter how society regarded you. I'm not sure there is a chance of her ever marrying, but if there was, that chance would diminish if she maintained her association with you."

Rather than argue the matter—which Gabriel had expected—her shoulders slumped, and she nodded. "I understand."

Gabriel began to get to his feet, but her voice stopped him.

"If I agree to marry—will you give up the duel?" She was staring down at her clasped hands rather than at him.

Gabriel chuckled, and her head jerked up.

Her flush, which had receded during their discussion of Eva, flared with a vengeance. "I am pleased to entertain you, sir."

"You are a like a hedgehog with me, Miss Clare. You always have been. No matter what I say or do, your spines come out." He cocked his head, curious about this woman who would soon be his wife. "Do you really hate me so much, ma'am?"

She opened her mouth, closed it, and opened it again.

Gabriel waved his hand. "Never mind; it does not signify. To answer your question, no, I will not apologize to Visel for any reason, ever. Does that put paid to that idea?"

Her jaw was so tight it hurt merely looking at her. A wave

of pity washed over Gabriel, and he gave her a gentle smile. "I'm aware I'm hardly the husband of your dreams, Miss Clare. But—"

"As difficult as it might be for you to believe, Mr. Marlington, I am no schoolroom chit whose head is stuffed with nothing but *dreams* of marriage. In fact, it would be fair to say thoughts of marriage hardly penetrate my mind at all."

Gabriel grinned at this very Miss Clare–like flare of spirited defiance. "No, that is not difficult to believe. So you were not dreaming of marriage. Well, neither was I, truth be told, yet here we are. I advise you to do as I am and look on the positive side, Miss Clare."

"And what side would that be, exactly?"

"We will salvage what remains of our reputations and make a life together, just as others have done in our position from time immemorial. I think you will also find your position as a married woman is much freer than an unmarried one. As Mrs. Marlington you may pursue your"—he waved his hand in the air—"causes, and what have you, with far less interference."

"Except from you, that is."

He raised his eyebrows. "I beg your pardon."

"I might pursue my *causes and what have you*"—she spoke the words in an accent that was a surprisingly good imitation of his own—"with more latitude. But I pointed out that *you*—as my lord and master—would be able to curtail my activities."

He laughed. Life might be irritating with Miss Clare, but it certainly would never be boring.

"You are correct, Miss Clare. You will be my wife and, therefore, subject to my will under the law. Does that really concern you?"

She huffed out a puff of air. "Does it *concern* me? No, Mr. Marlington, it *terrifies* me."

Gabriel frowned, his amusement draining away. "Whatever for? Do you really think I am such an ogre?"

Her mouth flattened into a remarkably straight, tight line. "You don't want to know what I am thinking."

"Oh, but I *do.* Please, enlighten me." Gabriel crossed his arms over his chest and told himself to be calm. After all, he would be with this woman for the rest of his life. She was not a garden-variety miss, but a woman of sharp wit and piercing intelligence; it behooved him to treat her with a little patience. Surely they could find some common ground?

He would begin practicing such patience right now. "Well?"

Drusilla wanted to bang her head on the arm of the settee. Why had she even raised this topic?

She looked into his captivating, no-longer-laughing eyes. "Whether or not you are an ogre is utterly beside the point. Why should I have to give control over my person to any man—ogre or saint? Why should it not be *you* who is subject to *my* control and will?"

The way his mouth fell open was comical. *"What?"*

"I said—"

He held up a hand. "No, I heard you. I merely do not take your point."

"Of course you don't."

"You wish to be my master in this marriage." The flat way he spoke the words told her all she needed to know what he thought about *that.*

"I did not say that."

He inhaled deeply, his fine nostrils flaring, and assumed the expression of a man who was forcing himself to stay calm in the face of overwhelming provocation. Drusilla had seen this same expression on men's faces whenever they did not meet with instant agreement from a female.

When he spoke again, his voice was cool. "Are you worried I will beat you? Lock you away in the country? Commit you to Bedlam? Because I can assure you, Miss Clare, even if you do not take *my* word that I would never do such things, you can certainly agree that my mother would never permit any harm to come to you."

Drusilla knew that, of course. But she could not tell him what she *truly* feared: that she would be married to a man she loved who would never love her. That she would have to suffer in silence while he took lovers. Already she had suffered knowing he kept not only one mistress, but several. Watching him court Miss Kittridge and flirt with countless widows who pursued him had been painful enough when she had no claim on him. What would it be like if he was her husband? It would be agony.

But she could hardly say any of *that*, could she? So she said nothing.

He continued. "And then there is Eva. I ask you this, Miss Clare—can you imagine my sister sitting by quietly while I did villainous things to you?"

A choked laugh broke from her at the notion, and his eyes widened.

"What?" she demanded, immediately suspicious. "Why are you looking at me that way?"

He pushed out his full lower lip and slowly shook his head from side to side, his expression bemused, his eyes never leaving her face. "It is nothing."

Drusilla stared at him hard, looking for answers. All she found were more questions. Why was she arguing? Just to save face? Well, she'd probably never manage that feat. He was watching her with a speculative look she found annoying—yet also invigorating.

"What about you?" There, how would he enjoy it if she turned the tables?

"Me?"

"Yes, *you* have said nothing about your own concerns when it comes to this marriage."

"I have none," he said.

"I believe you are lying."

That made him laugh. "Only you, Miss Clare—only you would call me a liar to my face."

They held each other's gaze for a long moment. Drusilla would have given her entire fortune to spend five minutes inside his beautiful, mysterious head, even though it would most likely be a painful experience for her. Already the blend of emotions inside her was bewildering. The knowledge that he would soon be her husband was, like a rose with thorns, both delightful and painful. She could never, ever, ever let him see either emotion.

She gave him an arch look. "You are taking a bride with the stink of the shop, Mr. Marlington. It is an association that will not endear you to the circles you are accustomed to move in."

"Such matters hardly concern me. Besides, my connections will make any concerns irrelevant." He gave her a mocking smile. "Although you probably find that difficult to credit."

"I am fully aware of your *connections.* And how will His Grace of Carlisle feel about your marrying a cit?"

"My grandfather will support whatever decision I make."

Drusilla somehow doubted that.

"And we already have the support of my stepfather and mother who are—" He hesitated, a slight smile curving his lips. "Well, unorthodox but not without powerful friends and influence of their own. Come, what else should I be concerned about?" he prodded.

She chewed her lip, trying to think of something else—*anything* else—that might save her from a lifetime of unrequited love.

When she remained mute, he gave a dry, humorless laugh. "I thought as much."

Drusilla glared at him. "What?"

"It is not *my* concerns that worry you, but your own, Miss Clare. Does the *ton's* reaction to our marriage really cause you such anxiety?"

"Of course it is not the *ton* that concerns me, Mr. Marlington."

"Then what is it? Is it my background? The fact I am not wholly English?" Her face heated at his suggestion, and his pleasant smile shifted into one that was distinctly *un*pleasant. "Ah, so is it the fact my father was the infamous Sultan Hassan?" She opened her mouth to deny it, but he didn't let her. "You must tell me if that is the sticking point, Miss Clare, because there is not a thing in the world I can do about my parentage, even if I wished to. My father might have done bad things, but he was my *father* and I loved and respected him. I will not refute him any more than I already have by abandoning my country, my name, and my people." He cocked his head. "Or perhaps you cannot see yourself married to a man who once practiced a religion most in this country would view as heathenish?" He paused, and then launched one last salvo. "A man who was raised to expect more than one wife?"

Drusilla bit the inside of her mouth hard enough to taste metal.

His laughter dripped disdain. "Ah, so that is it—the English preoccupation with harems."

"I'm afraid I don't find that to be a laughing matter."

"Trust me, Miss Clare, neither do I." He gave her a hard look. "Is that your concern? That I will keep a harem hidden away in our cellar or attic?"

"Of course not!"

"Perhaps you were not aware, Miss Clare, but when I

moved from Oran—from my home—to England, I not only changed the pronunciation of my name to make it more palatable to my new countrymen, I also changed my religion and my way of life. I changed *everything* to live in this country, Miss Clare. Believe me, my right to have more than one wife was the least of the many things I gave up."

"But that is what you were raised to expect, was it not?" She stopped, bit her lip, and then blurted. "Are you sure you can be satisfied with only one wife?"

He leaned toward her with eyes that had suddenly become heavy lidded. "That question is one only *you* can answer, is it not? Will you be able to keep me satisfied, Miss Clare?"

She gaped, and he took advantage of her tongue-tied state to pursue another tack.

"Enough about me and all the wives I will have to forgo if we marry. What about you, Miss Clare? Is all this resistance about me? Or is it about what *you* will have to give up?"

"Me?" Her voice was several octaves higher than normal.

"Yes, you. Is there perhaps somebody *you* might have to forgo?"

"Somebody?"

He *tsk-tsk*ed. "A lover, a sweetheart: some man you were hoping or planning to marry?"

"Of course not."

"Why *of course not*?"

"I am not a proponent of the married state."

His forehead wrinkled and he shook his head, his expression weary. "You have lost me, Miss Clare. Utterly and completely."

Gabriel's head was beginning to hurt.

"I am a follower of Mary Wollstonecraft's."

Gabriel had heard the name, of course. One could hardly avoid hearing it in Miss Clare's presence—generally at least one time an hour, not that he had ever paid attention to the actual substance of her lectures. He had some vague notion of the Wollstonecraft woman—some radical female who had taken lovers, had children outside wedlock, and tried to kill herself when abandoned.

"I see," he said, not seeing at all, but hoping that would be enough to head off any tedious conversations about the rights of women.

Miss Clare's eyes narrowed. "You don't see anything. You don't even know what I'm talking about."

Gabriel sighed and lifted his hands in surrender. "Guilty as charged."

"You've not listened to a word I've said to you over the past four years, have you, Mr. Marlington?"

"That is not true. I've heard you speak many times on Mrs. Woll—" He frowned. "Wollkenstonen—"

"Wollstonecraft, Mr. Marlington. *Mary Wollstonecraft*. I've no doubt you've *heard* me speak of her, but it's apparent you've never listened to the actual words."

Gabriel did not argue, hoping that might end the conversation. Besides, it was true—he hadn't paid her railing any mind.

But it appeared Miss Clare did not need his participation to carry on an argument.

"She was a woman who claimed that women have an existence beyond that of their relationship to men. A woman who advocated that women are human beings with a right to education rather than merely an *appendage* of some man. A woman—"

Gabriel held up a hand. "I beg your pardon, I was not aware I was arguing that women are *not* human beings." He frowned. "As for education—"

"It does not signify at this moment, Mr. Marlington. Forgive me for clouding the current issue."

He hated to admit it, but his head was spinning a little.

"Returning to what you've just said: I am aware of the way things are; I know a woman needs the protection of a man's name in situations such as this." Her lips twisted into a bitter smile. "I understand that we must marry, no matter how repellent the concept."

Gabriel gaped in stupefaction. "Are you *trying* to be insulting, Miss Clare?"

She cocked her head and squinted. "No—why would you say that?"

"Is it my person you find *repellent* or something else about me?"

"Oh." Her cheeks darkened. "Well, perhaps *repellent* was not the correct word."

Gabriel waited for her to choose another word, but whatever she saw on his face made her look away.

He studied her while she fiddled with the seams on her gown, his mind bucking against the inevitable like a wild, unbroken horse resisting a bridle. What kind of life would he have with a wife who found him repellent? Good God. An entire lifetime spent with a woman who disliked him. He shook his head. Still, what other choices did he have? None.

Something occurred to him. "Is this about your money, Miss Clare? About the fact you have been hounded by every gazetted fortune hunter in Britain? Are you worried I am forcing the issue of marriage to get my hands on your money?"

She did not look up. "I know you are not marrying me for my money."

The misery in her voice made him cringe. She truly loathed him. Or the institution of marriage. Or marriage with *him*. Whatever it was, he could not in good conscience force himself on her.

"I propose a compromise."

Her head swung up, her silky brown brows arched.

"We could have a temporary betrothal."

The muscles in her jaws flexed, but at least she did not fly off into a pelter. "Go on."

He shrugged. "There really isn't much more to it than that. Once I have dispensed with Visel, you could repudiate me and our betrothal. You could say you changed your mind. It hardly matters—nobody will ask you for an explanation."

Her mouth tightened and her eyes narrowed until they were chips of gray stone. "You would have me wait until you fight a duel to defend my honor to *jilt* me."

Gabriel gave an irritated hiss. "I just *said* that *you* would refute *me.*"

She crossed her arms over her generous bosom, the action momentarily distracting him. He didn't believe he had ever considered her body before—he'd always been far too busy defending himself against everything that came out of her mouth. She was tallish and tending toward plumpness, at least from what he could see of her in the concealing gown she was wearing. Gabriel swallowed. She had a most impressive bosom.

"Mr. Marlington."

He wrenched his eyes from the bodice of her homely gown and looked up to find her rather plain features a fiery rose, her eyes snapping. She also sounded like a person who had repeated the same thing more than once. "I beg your pardon?"

"I *said* that jilting you will make me not only an outcast, but a laughingstock."

Her words were like the fine strands of a spider's web—just like so many of the things English people said and did and expected. Gabriel might have lived here over five years, but he still had no idea as to their more subtle meanings much of the time.

He crossed his own arms in a mockery of hers. "I'm afraid you will have to explain this to me. After all, you know what an unlettered savage I am."

She did not bother to refute his words. "If we announce an engagement and then break it off, it will be clear to anyone with a teaspoon of sense that you merely offered a fake engagement in order to pursue this asinine duel."

Gabriel felt as though she'd slapped him. *"Asinine?"* he asked in a voice that did not sound like his.

Her smile was . . . insufferable. "Asinine."

"I was *defending* you."

"And so you did—you stopped him, for which I am extremely grateful. But this?" Her gaze flickered over him in a dismissive and highly insulting manner. "This duel is nothing more than a monument to your inflated sense of masculinity."

Gabriel knew his mouth was hanging open, but he didn't care.

"You think to engage in your manly pursuit, to end this sham betrothal, and then to continue on your way, leaving me a pariah."

"What?" he bellowed. "I suggested this to *spare* you from the indignity of having to marry me. Of having to marry a savage—of having to marry at *all* when it is something you find so utterly *repellent*."

"I would ask that you not raise your voice to me, sir."

Gabriel clamped his jaws shut so tightly he thought he might have cracked a tooth.

Her expression became even more contemptuous. "As for sparing me? Please. Do not bother to offer the protection of your name in the first place if you are only going to add insult to injury with this . . . this . . ." She threw up her hands. "I don't know what to call it."

Gabriel's head throbbed and his eyes felt strange—sweaty and hot—and he couldn't seem to settle on a collection of words that made any sense. Never, *ever* had anyone spoken so slightingly, so *insultingly* to him. If she had been a man . . .

But she was not a man—she was the woman who would soon be his wife. And she sat there looking so condescending, so superior, *so . . . English*. Fury addled his brains and fueled his mouth.

He pointed at her, knowing full well how rude the gesture was and reveling in her widening eyes and frowning lips more than was probably normal or healthy.

"You sit there on your . . . your"—a phrase from the nursery rhyme his twin nieces incessantly recited echoed through his head and Gabriel spat it at her—"*tuffet*."

She opened her mouth, but Gabriel was only warming to his task.

"Yes, on your *tuffet*—and you judge me, when I am only trying to spare you. Perhaps you might turn your keen sense of observation on yourself, Miss Clare. Perhaps you might ask *yourself* what you were doing alone in that conservatory without—"

She leaped up and Gabriel met her halfway, closing the distance between them with one long stride.

"Don't. You. Dare." She punctuated her words with her finger—poking him hard in the chest between each word. Her own chest heaved, the heat of her body against his scorching. Her eyes were narrowed slits of gray as sharp as the edge of a sword. "Don't you dare blame me for that drunken rake's unforgiveable actions."

Gabriel stared down at her; the slight tremor in her chin gave away something of the tumult that must lie beneath her bravado—not to mention making him feel like a cruel, insensitive, and selfish brute.

Which of course brought to mind his father.

Gabriel had known, even as a boy, that Sultan Abdul Hassan had been a man with a notorious temper—a temper like

Gabriel's, not that his mother didn't have an impressive temper, herself. But the sultan had coupled his temper with absolute power, and he had wielded that power without any check. His father's harsh behavior had been something Gabriel never wanted to consider when the sultan was alive; after all, he was his father and Gabriel had loved him. But that did not mean Gabriel ever wished to *become* him.

Although the sultan had shown him nothing but affection and indulgence, it had pained Gabriel to see his father did not love or honor his mother. But such had been the way of things in that household. Only when he was older did he understand that not all households operated as the sultan's had. Again, it had been his mother who had disabused him of his ignorance. She'd caught him with one of the servants—one of the many women who'd angled at Gabriel since he was barely thirteen. By the time his mother caught him, he was no callow youth as he'd been when a woman three times his age took his virginity. No, by the age of fifteen Gabriel had been an arrogant young man who'd bedded dozens of women and believed his father's people were his possessions: the women to serve the urges of his body, the men to follow his orders without question.

His father, the women of the harem, everyone around him, none of them except for his mother had challenged him in that belief.

They'd had their first argument the day she caught him with a harem servant, and Gabriel still shuddered to remember it.

"Debauching one's servants is the act of a weak and despicable man, Jibril. That girl might have knelt for you but remember that she cannot say *no* to you. These people who serve our needs are like slaves." Her face, which had always shown him nothing but love, had gone hard. "As *I* am a slave. And you are inflicting yourself on people who will not say no to you—never let yourself think otherwise—even when they may appear willing."

Those words rang inside his head as Gabriel looked down at Miss Clare, a woman who had been compromised by an arrogant, selfish, thoughtless young man tonight and would now be forced to give all power over her person to another man: to him.

Shame mingled with myriad other emotions that had been surging and roiling inside him ever since he'd entered the conservatory and encountered Visel and Miss Clare. But it was not Miss Clare's fault he was trapped. It was neither of their faults. Yet he was behaving as though it was.

He exhaled and nodded. "You are correct, Miss Clare, and I apologize for even daring to imply that you are somehow culpable in this mess. Please, forgive me."

The moment stretched before she gave an abrupt nod.

She was, Gabriel realized, for all her self-sufficiency and outward strength, deeply shaken by the incident this evening. And his ill-conceived suggestion had not helped.

"I accept your generously tendered offer of marriage. You needn't get down on your knees and do the pretty for me, Mr. Marlington." She sat with her hands folded in her lap, her expression lofty and martyrish: like a Christian about to be sacrificed to the lions.

Gabriel took a good look at his wife-to-be and tried not to shiver. Oh, she wasn't unpleasant to look at—at least not her features. While it was true she wasn't pretty, she had a desirable body—lush and womanly—and he already knew he would enjoy touching her. But she was a cold, judgmental woman, and he came away from all their encounters feeling as if he'd been weighed and found wanting. In short, she was not the sort of wife he would have chosen for himself, but then he was not the man she wanted, either.

A fleeting picture of Lucinda Kittridge flickered through his mind, but he banished it. That was over.

He dropped to one knee and reached for her hand. She started but did not pull away.

Something about looking up at her from this unusual angle made his actions feel more real. "I know you don't want me to *do the pretty*, but I would like to demonstrate my regard for you by proposing properly. You would do me a great honor by becoming my wife, and I give you my word that I will always strive to deserve your trust and regard."

Her jaws worked, as if she were testing and discarding responses. "Thank you, Mr. Marlington. I accept your offer."

He raised her hand to his mouth, kissing the back of it even though he knew such things were not done. Her fingers tightened for a moment, and then she drew away, as if even his smallest touch disgusted her.

Gabriel stood, swallowing his dread; he'd better become accustomed to her disdain and loathing. He knew reserved English ladies did not seek passion in their husbands' arms, and Miss Drusilla Clare was even more reserved than most. He pushed the disturbing thought aside.

"The marquess will assist me in procuring a special license. If you do not object, we can be wed the day after tomorrow." Gabriel did not bother to spell it out for her: that by marrying before the duel, she would have the protection of his name if he were not to walk away from his meeting with Visel.

Her expression softened slightly. "That will be acceptable to me. Will we live here, at Exley House . . . after?"

"My stepfather has already offered us a small but well-appointed house on Upper Brooks Street." The marquess had actually insisted on giving Gabriel the house as a wedding gift.

As much as he'd wanted to reject such a generous gift, one did not say no to the Marquess of Exley.

Gabriel realized she'd asked a question. "I beg your pardon, my lady?"

"I said *I am not without means.*"

"Means?"

"My aunt and I live in the house my father built here in London."

Gabriel had seen the house in question, a gothic monstrosity. While that didn't bother him so much, it did bother him to think of living on her bounty.

"Are you fond of the house? Do you wish to live there?"

"No. My father built it while I was away at school, so I only stayed there during the holidays and, of course, since leaving school." She hesitated. "If you don't care for it, we will have plenty of money to acquire or construct our own lodging."

Gabriel's face heated. "I am no fortune-hunting fop below the hatches, Miss Clare. I can house my own wife." Even without the marquess's generous gift, he had ample means. The Duke of Carlisle was a wealthy man and Gabriel was his only grandson; the duke had been most generous.

She opened her mouth—no doubt to utter some emasculating pronouncement, but he made an abrupt chopping motion with one hand, surprised and pleased when the gesture worked.

"Your money is your own—I will take none of it."

"But—"

"There is one thing you should know about me right now, Miss Clare. I do not argue once I have made up my mind."

Her eyes narrowed dangerously. And, by God, Gabriel felt a slight chill. "Neither do I."

He barked a laugh. "Excellent, then we shall rub along famously—and with very few arguments. Now, after the wedding we shall stay for the remainder of the Season to dispel any residual scandal. We can attend balls, be seen at the theater—" He shrugged. "Whatever is necessary."

She remained quiet, her gaze serious and steady, which made him uneasy. And feeling uneasy made him irritated. What the devil was it about this woman—hardly more than a girl really—that put him on edge so? He was a man with a decade's worth of experience with war, death, and women, but she made him feel like a callow youth.

"What about the wedding?" she asked, jarring him from his uncomfortable musing.

"Ah, yes, the wedding." Gabriel cleared his throat, which seemed to have filled with his heart and lungs. *God. Married.* And to a woman who loathed him. Still, men of his class were not expected to limit themselves to one woman for the rest of their lives. In England a man would have one wife, one woman to give him children and comfort him in old age and infirmity. But most of the married men he knew either kept a mistress or conducted affairs. He could always keep Giselle and Maria and no one would look sideways at him—well, no more than they already did.

For some reason Gabriel found the thought of such a dual existence vaguely depressing.

He let his gaze linger over his wife-to-be's body—a body that would be his in only a few days. Surprisingly, his groin grew heavy at the thought. His physical response was not what he would have expected; after all, bedding a woman who hated him was unlikely to be a satisfactory experience.

"Mr. Marlington?"

He met her gaze. "Hmm?"

"You were saying, about the wedding?"

"My mother and the marquess have offered to host a wedding breakfast for us."

"That is very kind of them, Mr. Marlington."

"Perhaps you might call me Gabriel as I am to be your husband in less than two days' time."

"Of course . . . Gabriel."

She did not invite him to do the same, but then Gabriel did not expect it. Miss Drusilla Clare had never made her disdain for him a secret. And now this woman who could barely countenance looking at him or speaking to him would be his wife. If he survived his duel, of course.

Chapter 6

Drusilla discovered that escaping her Aunt Violet—whose health had rallied at the prospect of a wedding, no matter how rushed—her prospective mother-in-law, and Eva was more difficult than escaping Coldbath Fields Prison.

But it was imperative that she get away. The twice-monthly meetings of her charitable group—the Society for the Practical Application of Wollstonecraftian Ideals—were often the highlights of her week, and she hated to miss one. Besides, she needed to tell her small group that she would be the first of their number to violate their own principles and enter the married state. And then she would need to tell them that she'd be leaving town after the Season, something she'd not done since settling into the London house after finishing school.

Drusilla squirmed to think of her friends' reactions. She'd formed this group almost three years ago, its membership comprising only seven people including her—four women and three men, all of them except one from the merchant class. The last member to join—barely half a year ago—had been a young man from the aristocracy, although only the youngest son of a baronet. Still, it gave them all hope that if one man from the ruling class could see the merit in Wollstonecraft's writings, there would be others.

As Drusilla hurried along the damp sidewalk, her maid struggling to keep pace, she reminded herself, yet again, that she would be married tomorrow—that she would be Mrs. Gabriel Marlington. She had reminded herself of that fact at least once every five minutes since his proposal, and it still had not stuck.

And then she had needed to remind herself that the morning after her marriage, she might very well be a widow.

Drusilla groaned at the ridiculousness of it all.

"Miss Dru?" Fletcher asked breathlessly, trotting along beside her. "Did you say something?"

"I will want you to wait for me in Hatchards, just as usual."

Her maid's silence was most speaking.

"It will only be an hour, Fletcher. There will be plenty of time to get back to the w-wedding preparations." Even speaking the word was difficult—what would being married to him be like? What would the *wedding* night be like . . . ? She slammed the door shut against that thought: it would come soon enough.

"But Miss Dru, it is only tomorrow and—"

"Fletcher."

The older woman heaved a long-suffering sigh. "Very well, miss."

Good. So that was done.

Drusilla dreaded the discussion she was to have with her small group—especially Theo. Although it had never been spoken of openly, it was understood their membership would live up to the beliefs set out in Miss Wollstonecraft's writings and they would eschew marriage. And now she was the first of their number to break that vow. She was, in other words, a hypocrite. No matter how often she told herself she was being forced to marry, her heart sang at the notion of becoming Gabriel Marlington's wife.

You are getting exactly what you have yearned for, a smug little voice inside her said, bringing with it a vivid image of the man she would be marrying.

She was abandoning her principles with hardly a backward glance.

Drusilla flushed at the undeniable truth as Gabriel Marlington's fierce features and powerful, muscular body flashed through her mind, the image making her female parts behave in a most distracting manner. It would hardly do to become so bothered—so physically stimulated—at even thinking the man's name. Not that the sensation was anything new. She'd been a quivering lump of fool for him since she'd first laid eyes on him. She recalled the day with crystal clarity.

She'd been visiting Exley Castle for the first time. Her aunt had been over the moon that she'd been invited to the country home of a marquess. Gabriel had been down from college with his idiot friend, Lord Byer, the oldest student in the history of Oxford. Or so Drusilla had heard.

Eva and Drusilla had been out riding—her friend was a far better equestrienne than Drusilla would ever be—when they'd come upon two horses, bridleless and cropping grass.

"That is my brother's horse—the other is Byer's." Eva had sprung from the saddle before Drusilla could even comment. "And look—" She held up what was indisputably a pair of breeches and grinned. "Let's take their clothing."

"*What?*" Drusilla had shrieked.

"They're swimming, although it looks like only one pair of breeches are here. I'll sneak down to the pond and grab the other pair. If we take their clothing, they'll have to walk home naked. Or . . ." She chuckled evilly. "Would they *ride* home in the—"

"Yes, yes," Drusilla had said, not wishing to hear any more about her friend's brother in an unclothed state.

But Eva had already disappeared through a gap in the trees.

"Eva? *Eva?*" There was no response. Drusilla had walked her mount back and forth, unwilling to dismount because there were no nearby rocks or fallen logs to serve that purpose. That was all she needed, to be caught without her horse when—

"Eva!"

An answering laugh came through the trees a second before Eva burst through the foliage and tossed an armload of clothing at Drusilla, startling both her and her horse.

"Run, Dru! Run! They're right behind me." She'd already caught up her horse's reins and was trotting toward the trail as quickly as the heavy skirt of her habit would allow.

Drusilla's mount had pranced nervously, refusing to obey her clumsy urging. "Eva, come back!"

And then *he* came through the foliage. And stopped, facing her.

Drusilla had been able to do nothing but stare. His body had been wet, drops of water glinting in the light like tiny crystals, his torso and arm rippling as he reached up with one hand to push his overlong hair from his forehead. Drusilla's eyes had behaved as if they'd had minds of their own, and she'd become fixated on his hips, on the tangle of dark auburn curls, on the—

"Miss Dru?"

"Hmm?" Drusilla looked around, suddenly aware she'd come to a stop.

Fletcher was looking at her, her brow wrinkled. "Do you want to cross now?"

They were paused on the street corner, an urchin lingering hopefully, a scraggly straw broom clutched in one hand.

Drusilla nodded, and Fletcher took a coin from her reticule and gave it to the boy when they reached the far side.

"Is aught amiss, Miss Dru? You look quite flushed."

"No, no, nothing is wrong. Just a lack of sleep, I expect."

"*Hmmph.* You'd be better off getting in a few hours' rest before tonight than gallivanting around." They were to have a family dinner at Exley House. Lord Exley's other two daughters were too far from London to return in time for the wedding, but there were still scads of cousins, uncles, aunts, and—of course—his grandfather, the duke. On her side there would be only Drusilla and her Aunt Vi, provided her aunt didn't wear herself to a frazzle before tomorrow morning with the whirlwind of wedding preparations.

It would, no doubt, be a tension-filled evening. Still, though Drusilla had never met the others who would be there tonight, she liked Lady Exley very much and loved Eva, who was her dearest friend. But Lord Exley? She shivered. No, he was not a comfortable man. And a duke? She shivered again. And the sisters of a duke? More shivering.

And Gabriel? Well, he gave her shivers of a completely different sort. He was far too good-looking for any woman's peace of mind, and he'd made his opinion of Drusilla plain years ago. To him she was nothing more than a dowdy nuisance to be tolerated because of her connection to his sister. If disaster hadn't befallen them, he doubtless would have been betrothed to Miss Kittridge at the end of the Season. Two perfect people together, as it should be. They would certainly have had the most gorgeous children . . .

"Miss Clare?"

Drusilla looked up to find Theo Rowland standing only a few feet away. She knew his lodgings were in one of the many bachelor dwellings that were not far from Piccadilly.

"Good afternoon, Mr. Rowland." Drusilla's lips curved into a genuine, welcoming smile.

"What a delightful surprise it is to find you here."

Drusilla cocked her head. "A surprise? But today is Thursday."

"Yes, but—well, I wasn't certain you were still coming." Theo gave her hand a gentle squeeze before releasing it.

"Why?"

A red stain spread across his pale cheeks. "Well, because of last night."

Drusilla's mouth dropped open in what she was sure must be a singularly unattractive expression. "You heard?"

He grimaced. "I'm afraid all of London has heard by now."

She didn't know what to say—why hadn't she guessed as much? He was, after all, related to a baronet even if he did not mix in *ton* company. And there were always the papers. Just because she didn't read the scandal sheets didn't mean others didn't. She glanced around, looking for the rest of the group. "Are we the first to arrive? Are we early?"

"Er, about that . . . I'm afraid you might be angry with me."

"Whatever for?"

"When I heard what happened last night, I took the liberty of sending word to the other members and told them you probably would not come today."

"Oh." Drusilla tried to hide her disappointment and irritation. He *had* taken a liberty, but there was nothing to be gained by pointing that out. Instead she said, "I was so looking forward to seeing everyone." She realized how rude that sounded and smiled at Theo. "Not that I'm not very happy to see you, Theo."

"I apologize if I overstepped."

"No, of course not—how could you? It is *our* group, not just mine."

"I only did it for your own comfort." He was sounding a little sulky.

"Yes, of course, Theo. It will be fine."

"And it is only for a week—you will see them all at the next meeting." He hesitated and then asked, "Unless—surely you're not leaving London because of this?"

Drusilla realized they were still standing on the sidewalk. She turned to Fletcher, whose disapproval rolled off her in almost visible waves. "Come back for me in half an hour, Fletcher."

Her maid did not move. "But—" Her eyes slid to Theo, the message clear: there was no meeting; why was she staying?

"Half an hour," Drusilla repeated.

She waited until Fletcher stomped away before turning to Theo and shaking her head. "You know how protective she is."

"And with good reason," Theo said, opening the door to the quaint tea shop where they usually met with the other members. The group focused on helping powerless people who could not help themselves. To that end, they'd endowed four women's homes in London and an orphanage in Brighton, among other things.

From the very first, Drusilla had felt a kinship with Theo. He was a man whose dedication to the plight of women—especially poor women—was as fervid as her own. The fact that a man from the aristocracy could care for something other than drinking, gaming, and horses had been a revelation. In the half year he'd belonged to the group, he had facilitated the establishment of three new women's homes, all in other large English cities. It had been Drusilla's hope to visit these new endeavors this fall, which was when Theo said they would be operating and ready for inspection. And now what would happen to all their fine plans?

Oh, Gabriel had said she could go on the same as ever, but she suspected he would draw the line at her traveling the country to inspect poor houses—especially in another man's company.

"Hello, Miss Clare, Mr. Rowland. I've held your regular table."

Drusilla smiled at the woman who hurried out from behind the pastry counter and led them to the table in front of the bow window where they usually sat. It was just past one o'clock and the small tea shop was bustling.

"I'm afraid it will only be we two, today, Mrs. Tilly."

"It is a pleasure to have you," the older woman said. Drusilla would order some sweets to be delivered to make up for the shortfall they created by taking the best table for only two people. It was unfortunate it was in front of the bow window, but it was not as if she were doing anything wrong by meeting an acquaintance—even a male acquaintance.

They ordered tea and pastries and chatted about the weather until the tea had arrived and been poured, and biscuits distributed.

Theo, ever sensitive to her moods, laid a hand over hers. "It was my brother who told me what happened at the Abingdon ball; he was there."

"Ah," Drusilla said. Theo was so different from most other aristocratic men she'd met that she always forgot about his connections.

Theo scowled. "Visel is a cad and has always been an embarrassment to our family."

"Your family?"

Theo's cheeks reddened slightly. "He is my cousin—on my mother's side."

"Oh. I had no idea." How uncomfortable. She looked at her friend and wondered what he'd heard. "What—"

He squeezed her hand. "Don't let what he said concern you. You are my dearest friend, Drusilla, and far more important to me than my idiot cousin, whom I've not spoken to in years. He's been away on the Continent for a good part of that time, and since his return he's been something of a—well, never mind. You should relax and have some tea. You are as wound up as a top." He made a *tsk*ing sound. "I can't say I'm terribly surprised after what I heard—"

The last thing Drusilla wanted was to hear just how the brief encounter had swelled into something shocking or more grotesque.

"I am to be married," she blurted.

"*What*?" His hand clenched hard enough to make her bones hurt.

She sucked in a breath, and he glanced down, loosening his grip. "Lord, what a brute you must think me."

"Of course, I don't. You are merely shocked, and, I daresay, more than a little disappointed that I am to abandon our principles and enter a marriage after resisting for so long."

"I can't believe the duke would allow it," he muttered.

Drusilla's face heated at his response; she wouldn't have expected snobbery from a man she considered a friend. "His grandfather can hardly expect to dictate whom he marries," she snapped.

The strange expression on his face flickered and his eyes seemed to come back into focus. "Oh, Dru! I'm sorry. I didn't mean that the way it sounded. I just meant the duke is known to be terribly high in the instep."

Drusilla frowned, only slightly mollified by his comment.

"Tell me what happened."

"You know what happened." She felt her face heat, which only angered her. Why should she blush? She had nothing to be ashamed about. "Surely you can see that I have no choice now but to marry? It is either that or live my life on the fringes of society." She shrugged. "While I don't care if I'm never invited to another ball or rout, I hardly wish to become an outcast."

"No, of course not," he echoed, his voice faint, his eyes rather wild as they flickered around the room restlessly.

Drusilla felt a sudden surge of affection for him. "You are taking this almost as hard as I am," she said.

He gave a rather high-pitched laugh. "Oh, I'm sure everyone in the group will be equally concerned on your behalf, Drusilla."

"How fortunate I am to have such loyal and caring friends." She squeezed his hand. "Thank you, my friend." He gave her a look of confusion. "For understanding just how difficult this is for me—how this goes against all our principles."

His smile was tight and he looked nothing like his usual self. "Of course, yes, of course. I'm sure you are feeling this violation of your principles most horribly."

Well, that seemed rather a strong way to put it, but Drusilla decided not to correct him. "While it is not what I'd planned for myself, marriage is the only way, Theo."

"Yes, marriage." He pushed the fingers of one hand through his hair and shoved back a few somewhat lank brown curls that had fallen over his forehead. He shook himself and looked up at her. "But, Lord! What a cad I am being. Never mind all that, how are *you* faring after this heinous ordeal?"

Drusilla was tempted to ask just what he'd heard but decided against it. "Oh, the incident itself was not so horrific, Theo. I am made of sterner stuff. I refuse to allow a—" A shadow passed in front of the bow window and stopped. Small hairs on the back of her neck—which she'd never really noticed before—stood on end.

Theo turned toward the window as the shadow persisted. "I say, what's this nosy bloke all about?"

Drusilla knew before she looked who it would be.

Gabriel felt like rubbing his eyes with his knuckles, or perhaps closing them and then opening them again, hoping the bizarre vision would be gone.

He leaned closer to the window and stared. No, it was not

a hallucination; it was real—she was still there. It really was his betrothed holding another man's hand. And that man was glaring at Gabriel as if he were some sort of street rubbish.

Gabriel looked at Drusilla and met her haughty stare. *She* was looking at him as if he were street rubbish, as well.

He pivoted on his heel, strode to the shop door, and almost tore it off the hinges. The clatter of bells filled the little room with shrill, almost hysterical ringing. He felt, rather than saw, dozens of eyes upon him as he closed the short distance between the door and his fiancée.

The man had released her hand but was now standing, half hovering in front of Drusilla as if to protect her. From *him*, Gabriel could only assume.

"Miss Clare. What a surprise. I would have assumed you were busy today." His mouth twisted into a mocking smile and his gaze settled on her hand, gloveless and limp and now alone on the table. "But I suppose you *are* busy, just not with wedding preparations."

Her companion took a step toward him. "And just who—"

She laid a hand on the other man's forearm, her gaze still on Gabriel. The casual gesture—that easy touching of another man—sent fury thundering through him like a herd of stampeding horses. His hands clenched so tightly that the pain brought him back to himself: thrashing this man here and now would not be wise for about a dozen reasons. Besides, he had no wish to air such private feelings in public. He would have time enough to deal with this—and *her*—later. For the remainder of his life, as a matter of fact.

"This is Mr. Marlington, my fiancé. Gabriel, this is Mr. Rowland, a . . . a friend of mine."

"Fiancé!" Rowland shouted.

Drusilla, Gabriel, and every other patron in the shop stared at the man, who appeared as though he was already regretting his outburst if his dark, ugly red flush was anything to go by.

Drusilla frowned at her companion. "Yes, Theo, I told you I was getting married."

The man—*Theo*—shook his head. "But I thought it was to Visel—"

Drusilla shuddered, her face a mask of distaste. "Never."

Gabriel almost smiled; at least there was somebody she found more repellent than him.

"But I asked you about the duke and you said—"

"Mr. Marlington's grandfather is the Duke of Carlisle," she said flatly.

"Oh," the other man mumbled, looking a bit wild around the eyes.

Gabriel stared down at him, his brain not obeying his orders to focus; instead dozens of thoughts were zinging through his head. Most frequent were graphic suggestions as to what he should do to the man across from him for having the audacity to sit with his betrothed in public and fondle her hand.

Mr. Rowland was a slender man, and Gabriel knew he could break him in half without effort. The aggressive way he was eyeballing Gabriel demonstrated more clearly than words that while Drusilla might consider them merely friends, *he* had other ideas.

She gestured to one of the empty chairs around the table with an unsteady hand. "Won't you sit with us?" Her face was as emotionless as ever, and Gabriel felt a sudden sense of heaviness, of . . . depression as he looked into eyes that left him feeling chilled. He would spend his life with a woman who had no emotion, no passion, and certainly no liking for him. On the contrary, here she sat the day before her wedding, holding hands with another man.

He almost laughed out loud: he would marry a woman in love with another and live out his days in a country where his face and name would forever make him an outcast.

Some part of his mind pointed out that he was behaving in

a dramatic, self-pitying manner, and he shook himself and forced an appropriate expression onto his face.

"Thank you for the invitation, but I'm afraid I cannot stay. I have business to attend to." He gave her a significant look. "Wedding matters, you know."

She inhaled sharply, but did not speak.

Gabriel dropped an abrupt bow. "I shall see you tonight at dinner, Miss Clare." He didn't bother speaking to the man but turned and left.

Once he was outside, he stood in the shop doorway and glanced left and then right. Now what the devil had he been doing? Where the hell had he been going? He cursed under his breath. Rather than look like an utter pillock, he turned left and continued on past the bow window, this time not looking inside.

He walked a good five streets before he recalled just what it was he was supposed to be doing. In his pockets were three gifts—two of them parting presents. He'd not given much thought to his amorous arrangements, but his mother—the nosiest and bossiest woman in the world—had cornered him early this morning after he'd finished speaking about settlements, dowries, and a dozen other matters with Drusilla's *three* men of business. While it had been entertaining to stun the three men with his disinterest in her fortune, the exchange had still put him in a foul mood.

And then his mother had pounced on him the moment he'd returned to Exley House to discuss a few matters with his stepfather. She'd dragged him into the library, forced him into a chair, and then stared at him.

Gabriel had massaged his temples. "What is it, Mother?" he'd demanded when he could take it no longer. He'd been tired from lack of sleep, irritated from the mind-numbingly tedious meeting, and there were still a half-dozen matters to deal with—such as meeting with Viscount Byer to see if he'd received a visit from Visel's second. But the duel was a far from his most pressing concern.

Namely, that he was filled with a sense of impending dread: he would soon be married. His life stretched before him, years and years of furtive couplings in dark rooms until she was breeding. Although he wondered what the point was? He was no scion of some great house in need of an heir. He was simply a man without a country who was now living on the bounty and charity of his family. He was—

"Jibril, you are not paying me any mind!"

He looked up to find the marchioness staring down at him. "Yes, Mother, I am here and listening. What is it?"

"You must discharge your mistresses." Her eyebrows descended to form a surprisingly threatening frown. "*All* of them."

Gabriel was a man of four and twenty, but his mother still had the power to rob him of breath. He could have ended the conversation right then if he'd disclosed that he'd already made up his mind on the matter. But that was none of her concern, and the last thing he wished to do was engage in an in-depth conversation with his mother about mistresses.

Instead he'd rested one glossy booted ankle on his knee and asked, "What do you know of such things?" But then he raised his hand in a halting gesture. "Never mind that question—I do not wish to know the answer. It is a testament to how exhausted I am that I would even ask such a foolish thing. No, the better question is, *Why* you have decided it is your place to broach this subject with me?"

She paced in front of his chair. "Because you are your father's son and were raised with far different expectations from other English gentlemen, I have not commented on your amorous arrangements."

Gabriel considered reminding her of the dozens of times she'd not only commented, but actively meddled, in his *amor-*

ous arrangements, but he'd decided it would only prolong their conversation. So he clamped his jaws shut, letting her run her course.

"I've seen how women of all ages fling themselves at your head, so it does not surprise me that I hear of your exploits almost daily. Indeed, I believe you've almost *charmed* the *ton* with your shocking behavior, especially your notorious arrangement with the two French actresses."

Gabriel examined his fingernails.

"You might have been raised with certain marital expectations, but you are English now."

His jaw hardened and his head whipped up. Their gazes locked, but Gabriel did not speak. So she continued. "You cannot marry this young girl and maintain mistresses. It will crush her spirit and poison any chance you might have for happiness."

His face heated, which only irritated him more. He raised his eyebrows in the haughty fashion he'd seen Exley employ to suppress pretention. "Rubbish, Mama. *English*men keep mistresses all the time."

Instead of being suppressed by his eyebrows, she whirled on him. "Tsst!" She grasped the arms of his chair and brought her face uncomfortably close to his, until he was pressed flat against the chairback. Her eyes were the most startling shade of green, far lighter than his own. It had always been difficult to look away from his mother when she focused her not-insignificant will on him.

"You must listen to me, Jibril."

The fan of deep lines that radiated from her eyes caused an uncomfortable tightening in his chest: his mother was getting old. She'd been the cornerstone of his life—the one person to believe in him, to love him, and to support him, no matter what he did or how he failed—for as long as he had been alive. Hardly more than a child herself when she'd given birth to him, she had fought tooth and nail for him and she'd supported his goal of seizing his father's faltering empire when the sultan had died. He loved his mother with all his heart. But he also knew she was the devil herself when it came to getting her way.

"You are only allowed one wife under English law, Jibril."

It took everything he had not to roll his eyes. "Yes, Mother, I understand that."

"I do not think you do."

He threw up his hands. "Why don't you say your piece? Because I know you'll not stop hounding me until you've done so."

She smiled, sat on the arm of his chair, and took his hand. "I've had an unhappy marriage and a happy marriage, Jibril. I can tell you, in all truthfulness, that a happy marriage is much better."

"That does not surprise me."

"You have not chosen each other, that's true, but she's an intelligent, comely girl and love isn't something you stumble into; love is something you build."

Gabriel did not bother telling his mother how much his prospective wife actively disliked him. Instead he said, "I'm entering into this marriage with the best of intentions and—"

"Bah!" She flicked one hand, "*The best of intentions*. What is that? You must enter into it with an open heart. You must look at intimacies with your new, young wife as the first step in a lifelong commitment to each other and to joy."

Gabriel's head became so hot it felt like it might explode. "Fine, I am entering it with a joyous and open heart and mind."

She'd squeezed his hand so hard the bones shifted. "You are my eldest son and I love you beyond life itself. But—" Her eyes clouded and she looked, for the first time he had ever seen her, defeated. "But you are also your father's son and he has left his stamp on you." She held his hand pressed between her much smaller ones. "Although there was no love between us, I have rarely spoken ill of your father."

"That is true."

"But I must do so now. You view women as—well, you view them as a sultan would. That is to be expected, given where you grew to manhood, but you live here now."

He disentangled himself and got to his feet. "Putting aside your ridiculous assertion that Englishmen somehow treat Englishwomen so much better than the treatment women receive in *my* country, is it your point that I am an Englishman in England who should behave in the English manner? Because I *have* grasped that, Mama. Believe me—I know who I am *not*. I would have thought my behavior over the past five years might have proved that to you. I've changed my name and abandoned my people—*everything* that I was is now behind me. I am English." His voice had risen, which only bothered him more. "Now, I must go."

She caught his arm before he could make his escape.

"You will do the right thing, Jibril. I know you will."

Oh, if only his mother knew just how many wrong things he'd done lately and how he was—most likely misguidedly—trying to make them all right.

He snorted as he recalled the uncomfortable exchange. His mistresses were the least of his problems.

Besides its not being any of his mother's concern, Gabriel was hardly enthusiastic about breaking off a mutually satisfactory association with a beautiful, passionate woman—or *women*, as the case may be—so that he might enter into marriage with a wife who at this very moment sat holding another man's hand.

Irritation roiled with something else—surely not jealousy? No, *fury* was more like it—inside his chest.

Such loose behavior might be the norm between English husbands and wives, but Gabriel was not English. At least not in *that* way. He'd never liked the way Englishwomen went about uncovered and exposed to other men's eyes, and he liked it even less now that his wife-to-be was one of those women. Drusilla would soon learn that he would not permit hand-holding with other men—or holding of anything else—once she was his.

Perhaps he should tell his mother to go and deliver her speech about extramarital lovers to his *wife-to-be* instead of him. He snorted and shook his head, diverted at the image of *that* conversation.

Gabriel had been so caught up in his own thoughts he'd walked halfway across London without even noticing; here he was already at Giselle and Maria's.

Their maid greeted him at the door. "Miss Maria is not here, Mr. Marlington. She's gone out with Sami. Only Miss Giselle is here."

Gabriel was relieved to find Giselle alone. He could speak with her first and Maria later. While he cared for both women equally, it would be easier to say what he had to say individually.

"I'll see Miss Giselle," Gabriel said, pulling off his gloves, tossing them into his hat, and handing both to her.

She showed him to a small second-floor parlor and went to fetch her mistress.

Gabriel had met Giselle almost three years ago, right after he'd first seen her perform onstage. She'd been in a minor part then, but she'd shone, and Gabriel had found himself with flowers in hand, waiting at her door the very next night.

At the time she'd just been starting out and could find only small roles. She lived with Maria, her childhood friend, fellow actress, and—unbeknownst to Gabriel at first—her lover.

While it had been Giselle who'd first attracted his notice, he'd quickly become fond of both women, who also seemed pleased with him.

At first he'd believed Giselle had encouraged his interest to divert attention away from her relationship with Marie—or that the two women had needed, like so many other actresses, a wealthy protector. When Gabriel had raised the subject, they had let him know—in their blunt fashion—that he was not their first male lover. That admission had effectively quashed any erroneous notions he'd had of being their savior in that way, but he'd still insisted on leasing this house—citing his own comfort rather than their safety as the reason—to get them away from the collection of rundown rooms where they'd been living.

Word of their arrangement was bound to get out, and it had. As much as it titillated the jaded palate of the *ton* to imagine what went on in their notorious pied-à-terre, the relationship the three of them shared was remarkably domestic in nature.

Having grown up among so many women, Gabriel was comfortable with them.

At least some women, he corrected as he lowered himself onto the settee in the cozy sitting room—not, apparently, his wife. Unlike his English counterparts, the notion that two women could love each other—even physically—had not shocked him. Perhaps that was a flaw in his character or the result of being raised by a woman who possessed a pliable notion of sensuality and love.

And so they'd enjoyed their comfortable union for over three years. He would hate to end it, but he knew—deep down—that he would not wish to maintain the liaison once married.

He probably should have told his mother as much, but it was none of her concern.

The truth was, Gabriel had hopes—although not particularly high ones—that he and Drusilla might find a way to rub along together. And if they did not? Well, he would reevaluate his decision at that point.

The door opened, and Giselle made her entrance as only an actress could.

"How delightful to see you, Gabriel," she said in her charming French accent, offering her cheeks for his kisses.

Gabriel took both her hands and held them out to her sides. Giselle Fontenot was small—only a few inches taller than his mother, but her exceptionally lush hourglass figure, full pouting lips, and bedroom eyes had rightfully earned her the title of the French Pocket Venus.

Today her generous curves were wrapped in an apricot silk peignoir trimmed with chocolate lace, and it made her golden curls appear burnished and rich.

"How is it that you can work until midnight, play until dawn, and yet look so fresh, Giselle?"

"Flatterer." She pushed him down onto the settee, lowering herself beside him. "You have been busy, I hear?"

Gabriel scowled. "Just what the devil have you heard?"

"Perhaps one part the truth, nine parts exaggeration? You know how word of scandalous happenings spreads fast."

"What did you hear and from whom did you hear it?"

"Maria saw Visel and his cronies when they came to an opening night party—I was not there."

"And he was talking, was he? That surprises me." As much of an irritant as Visel had been, Gabriel had never believed he was the type to have a big mouth.

"According to Maria, Visel said nothing. It was one of the other men—a man who was somewhat the worse for wear."

"Visel wasn't drunk?" Gabriel asked. He had certainly seemed well on the way during their scuffle. Perhaps the prospect of a duel had sobered him up?

"Maria only said he was quiet, as he usually is." She took his hand and placed her delicate palm against his, absently examining the difference in size. "He does not seem the type to run with that crowd of louts. I believe he is more of a lone wolf beneath the reckless and outrageous veneer he has cultivated."

Gabriel believed she was correct. "He appears to harbor a good deal of enmity toward me."

"Yes, it certainly seems so." She cocked her head. "Have you had many dealings with him? I thought he only recently returned to England a short while ago?"

"Yes, only a few months—six at the most, after years in the army." And then he came to London with the sole intention of annoying and persecuting Gabriel. Or so it seemed.

Gabriel's gaze was on her fingers, which were slender, soft, and delicate against his own much broader hands.

"Tell me what really happened last night? There was a girl, I think?"

He smiled at her. "You know I cannot speak of such things, Giselle."

She gave him a playful nudge. "You are such an honorable man, *mon amour*. Surely you can tell me who this girl is?"

He supposed that would not hurt—since she was soon to become his wife. "Her name is Drusilla Clare. She is a close friend of my sister's."

She slanted him a look. "Ah, she is a good girl, then?"

Gabriel ignored that question. "We are to be married, tomorrow."

Her hand tightened, but her expression did not change. "That is what Maria and I suspected. I am so sorry, Gabriel. I know you had become quite fond of Miss Kittridge. We both believed you might ask her to marry you before the Season's end."

Gabriel did not feel inclined to confirm such a statement

even if there might have been some truth in it. He was to be married to Miss Clare and hardly wished to begin their union by dishonoring or embarrassing her by admitting to a regard for another woman.

Instead he asked, "Where are Maria and Samir?"

"Sami was getting restless so Maria took him out."

Gabriel frowned, and Maria squeezed his hand. "He is safe—you look so worried."

"Did they take—"

She laughed. "Yes, they took Daniel with them."

Gabriel *was* anxious at the thought of Samir wandering around the city without him—even if Maria or Giselle was with him. He'd worried about the women going out unattended, as well, although they'd teased him, pointing out that both of them came from the stews of Paris and had survived.

Gabriel might be an Englishman now, but he'd spent his first seventeen years in a place where women and children rarely left the safety of the palace—and when they did, they were never alone. He felt compelled to protect those in his care and didn't mind if others viewed his concern as excessive.

Maria and Giselle had allowed him to employ Daniel, a brawny footman, and had also agreed to use him whenever they went out. Gabriel slept better knowing that. He wondered if he should hire somebody else—just for Samir. What if Maria wished to go somewhere and—

Soft lips kissed his temple and he looked up.

Giselle was smiling. "Quit worrying."

He would like to, but did people ever stop worrying about their children? He supposed that must be part and parcel of being a parent: worrying.

"Where did they go?"

"Maria took him to see the beasts—to the show at Astley's."

That made Gabriel laugh. "Again?"

"Marie told him she would take him if he stopped pulling Bonbon's tail." Bonbon was Maria's ancient, fat, ill-tempered poodle.

"That little rascal. You know that is where I took him before I went to Brighton."

She slipped her fingers into his hair and massaged the back of his neck, making him groan with pleasure. Her small hands were remarkably strong.

"He is a clever little boy who knows how to get his way—just like his father, I suspect. How did things go in Brighton?"

Her second hand joined the first, and Gabriel closed his eyes, letting his head fall back.

"I don't really know. Captain Delacroix of the *Batavia's Ghost* told me there was no word of Samir's family—of his grandparents. He spoke with Sami's uncle—Fatima's eldest brother, but—" Gabriel did not wish to share everything Delacroix had told him during their brief visit. Especially when he did not know what he thought about all of it himself.

He opened his eyes and looked at Giselle. "How has Sami been?"

"He still misses his mother, of course, and I've heard him cry in the night. But I think he might miss you more, Gabriel—especially when you were gone over a week."

"I understand why he would miss Fatima, but how can he have become so attached in only a few months?"

She gave a sinuous, Gallic shrug. "Blood calls to blood."

Gabriel didn't bother correcting her. Instead he pondered his soon-to-be wife's reaction to having a five-year-old child living with them.

"Will you send him away now that you are getting married?" Giselle asked, as if she were reading his mind. "Maria and I adore having Samir here—we would love to have him stay."

"That is kind of you, Giselle. But I know his mother would have wanted him to be with family. Until I can find the rest of Fatima's family—*if* I can find them—I will keep Samir with me. I'd hoped Captain Delacroix would have better news, but he is waiting for one of his men to return from Oran. The city is in a state of chaos right now." A lot of that was Gabriel's fault, but he had no desire to discuss what had happened in Oran with anyone—not even Giselle, his lover. "If we're able to find any of Fatima's sisters or brothers, then Samir should be with them—it was Fatima's wish. Her family is well respected, and there will be plenty of other cousins for him to grow up with—it is what he is used to."

"And if your captain does not find them? Or if he learns that all your sister-in-law's family have died?"

"Then I will bring him to live with me on the country estate my grandfather gave me."

"When will you hear from this captain again?"

"I don't know. My guess is that all of Fatima's family will be hiding in the mountains if they managed to escape the city." The English navy's attack on Oran had left thousands fewer casualties than their assault on Algiers. Unfortunately, Gabriel's brother Assad and his wife Fatima had been among those who were killed, leaving their only son an orphan.

Giselle nodded, gently stroking his nape. "Will you leave him with us until you find out—now that you are getting married?"

Gabriel chewed his lip. Giselle and Marie were taking care of the boy as his bachelor chambers were not the sort of place for a child. He'd been planning to take Samir to the country right after the Season ended and stay there with him until he received word about Fatima's family. But, of course, that had been before last night. He could only imagine the stern Miss Clare's reaction when he confronted her with Samir. He would not wish to take the boy if his new wife was cold or cruel to him. At the same time, he would not shun Sami to appease Miss Clare.

Gabriel knew he could tell his mother—indeed, he *should* have already told her—and bring Samir to her. He'd kept the information from her because he'd wished to make the decision without her meddling. But now . . . ? Well, she would take the boy in an instant.

But he was not yet ready to make that decision.

He kissed Giselle's hand. "I don't know what I'll do, my friend. But he'll stay with you until the end of the Season as we've already decided. He's already suffered enough upheaval, and I don't wish to change our plans at this point."

"I will miss him, Gabriel." Her eyes glistened with unshed tears.

"I know you will." Gabriel pulled her to him, holding her familiar body in a tight embrace. "You need a child, Giselle. You and Marie both—you were made to have children."

She sighed heavily against him, and he heard a delicate sniff. "I would have liked to have yours, Gabriel. But I know . . ." She trailed off.

Gabriel was grateful she'd not completed the thought. He knew the two women desperately wished for children, but he'd never felt right about being a father to a child he could not claim.

She disentangled herself from his arms and moved off his lap. "But what of this duel?" she asked, wiping her eyes with a scrap of lace that mysteriously appeared, before reclining against the plush velvet cushions that spilled over the settee. "It is to be swords, I hope?"

"Hmm?" he asked, hoping his vague response would communicate his unwillingness to discuss the situation.

She shook her head, her lips pursed. "Very well, I see the way it is—it is *man's* business and you will not discuss it."

Gabriel smiled.

"But at least tell me one thing."

He raised his eyebrows, unwilling to promise an answer before he knew the question.

"Please tell me you are not going to kill him, my love."

He chuckled and took her hands, bringing them to his lips. "You never know—I might."

Her mouth puckered into a disapproving moue. "But then you would be forced to flee to the Continent."

He kissed each of her knuckles. "I could live out my life as a card sharp."

"But you do not like cards."

"Then perhaps I might have to make my way seducing the bored wives of wealthy men and living off their largesse."

"Mmmm, yes—a cicisbeo. Now *that* I can see you doing." Her full lips curved, and she brought their linked hands to her mouth, where her tongue darted out, licking the sensitive skin between his fingers.

Gabriel's cock sprang to life at the suggestive gesture and he groaned. "You could make a dead man hard, Giselle."

She laughed. "Come, Gabriel, you are hardly dead—just betrothed." She lowered their clasped hands to her lap. He drank in her voluptuous beauty, which masked a sharp intelligence and wicked imagination, before dropping his head against the plush velvet headrest of the settee, closing his eyes as the image of his wife-to-be elbowed her way into his mind.

Giselle fiddled with their joined hands, brushing the sensitive skin on the back of his hand against her silk-covered thighs in a most distracting manner. "I have not seen this Miss Drusilla Clare; is she so ill-favored? Or is it that your affections are with Miss Kittridge?"

Drusilla Clare's intelligent gray eyes, frowning lips, and generous bosom clothed in an unflattering gown flashed into his mind.

"She is an attractive young woman," he said, realizing he spoke the truth only after he'd uttered the words. He ignored Giselle's second question entirely. Miss Kittridge—and whatever there might have been—was no longer a subject he cared to think about. Had he loved her? He did not believe so. But perhaps he could have grown to love her. He had certainly *lusted* for her—had envisioned bedding her. But that was true about many women.

"Is she stupid—this Miss Clare?" Giselle's voice pulled him from his thoughts.

"No, she is very clever." Perhaps too clever.

Giselle brushed her lips over his knuckles yet again, her hot breath making his groin ache. "And she is rich, no?"

"Yes, she is very wealthy." Gabriel had learned only a few hours earlier just how wealthy his new wife was.

"*Mon dieu*, Gabriel! I would marry her myself, if she would have me."

He laughed. "Yes, Miss Clare is attractive, intelligent, and possessed of great wealth, Giselle. It is not the lady herself I have trouble with," he lied, hardly wanting to cast aspersions on his wife-to-be. At least not anywhere but in the privacy of his own mind. "It is the institution of marriage I was hoping to avoid."

She made a dismissive sound. "What a fib. You've been considering marriage—both Maria and I have heard people talk of you and the Kitten."

"You never mentioned it," he said, wishing to avoid the subject.

"Not around you."

"Ah, so that's how it is. I'm the one who is left out in the cold. I always suspected as much."

Her eyelids lowered and her mouth curved into a wicked smile. "Maria and I would never leave you out in the cold."

Gabriel tried to ignore the swelling brought on by her suggestive stare. He didn't have time for such things today, no matter how much he might need such *things*.

He turned the subject. "Anything you heard—about *any* young lady—was just idle speculation by gossips. Trust me, I had no plans to marry anytime soon."

"You men—you are all the same, behaving as if marriage is an appointment with the gibbet. I expected more from you."

"Lord, Giselle, you sound just like my mother."

"I will take that as a compliment—I understand she is a remarkable woman."

Talking about his mistress with his mother had been bad enough; he did not want to talk about his mother with one of his mistresses. "Why do you expect more from me, Giselle?"

"Because you are not English. You are a man of the world."

"I have lived in North Africa and England; that is hardly the world."

"Yes, but you were raised to expect an early marriage from a young age, were you not?"

He had been, although that changed in an instant when his father died and his betrothed had married his brother. He shrugged, not wishing to discuss the complicated subject of Fatima.

"In any case," she said, reading his mood correctly and leaving the topic behind, "your experience is enough to know there is more than one way to"—she hesitated—"to skin a cat. I believe that is the English saying?"

"How the devil would I know—it certainly sounds dreadful enough to be an English saying."

Her hand tightened. "We've wandered from the point."

"What *was* your point, *cherie*?"

"You know you are not my first male lover."

"Nor are you my first female lover, Giselle. Come," he said, pulling her closer, her lush, responsive body melting against his like hot wax from a candle. "Out with it, my dear. What is it you are trying to say?"

Her expression became serious. "You are the only man Maria and I have met who has accepted what we feel for each other without either being threatened, treating us as unthinking vessels for nothing but pleasure, or acting as if we were depraved."

Gabriel had nothing to say to that—he had no idea how other men thought about their lovers or what they did with them. It was a private matter that he'd never had any interest in discussing with another man—even with somebody as close as his friend Byer; although he knew his friend was intensely curious about his arrangement with Giselle and Maria.

"I see you are looking skeptical, but it is true. Most men only want a woman like me to open her mouth if I use it for something other than talking. You—" She traced a fine scar on his chin. "Well, you are different, and for the life of me, I cannot understand why. After all, you are the son of a man who kept women by the hundreds sequestered for his pleasure."

"Well, not by the *hundreds*."

"You know what I mean." She reached up and brushed back his hair before lowering her cool hand to his jaw. "You were raised with the expectation that one day *you* would have that many women. Yet you have always been a friend to us, the only lover who has asked about *us*, where we are from, what dreams we have, what *we* want. I can only assume this is the work of your famous mother—a woman who has lived more in one lifetime than most have in ten."

"Ha. Infamous is more like." He flushed under her warm regard, and she chuckled, skimming his jaw with her knuckles, her smile turning impish.

"You are a wonderful lover and friend and we will miss you dearly." She slid her arms around him, straddling his lap.

"What? Are you tossing me out already?" Gabriel wrapped his arms around her, flexing his hips beneath her spread thighs.

She chuckled at what she felt. "Mmm, I believe your mind is on other things, Gabriel."

"Perhaps." He lowered his mouth over hers, and her lips opened without hesitation. For a moment he lost himself and his problems inside her, stroking into her, reveling in her hot, sweet taste.

But then he recalled he'd not come here for this. He sighed and pulled back, smiling into her sky blue eyes. "I have a gift for you, my dear."

Her brows arched. "Oh? I thought this was my gift?" She stroked his groin, and Gabriel groaned, laying a hand over hers. She was making this hard for him, in every sense of the word.

"Very well," she said with a shrug, giving him a wicked smile.

"Witch," he muttered, shifting and trying to adjust himself into a less painful position.

"If you've brought me something, I hope you brought something for Maria and Samir."

"I am not a fool, Giselle. My coat pockets are stuffed like a sneak thief's. You can give my gifts to the others."

"You won't wait for them?" Her eyes flicked upward—toward the bedchamber she shared with Maria, and which they both shared with Gabriel when he visited.

"I cannot indulge myself, as much as I might need and want to." He shook his head, his regret unfeigned. "I probably should not have come today but—"

She squeezed his hand. "You wanted to tell us in person."

"Yes." He gave her a gentle push. "Now go fetch everything from my coat pockets—yours is the inlaid box."

She returned with the three packages and then sat on his lap to open her gift.

Her eyes widened when they saw what was inside the box. "Oh, Gabriel, they are splendid."

"Not as splendid as you. Put them on."

She removed the earrings already in her ears, looking at him as she did so. "This is a farewell gift, I think?"

Was it? He'd certainly come with that intention in mind. But after seeing his fiancée clutching another man's hand, he was no longer so sure.

Gabriel frowned at the petty thought. Was that how he would begin his married life? Engaged in an immature and spiteful battle of wills with his wife? He ignored Giselle's question, instead pulling her toward him and lowering his mouth over the swell of her breast, breathing in her familiar scent. He would miss her companionship and affection even more than her beautiful face and luscious body. "You are a goddess," he told her in French.

She took his face between her hands and tilted it up to kiss him. "Thank you for the delightful gift, Gabriel. Thank you and—"

"Hush," he ordered, kissing away whatever it was she was about to say and then gently holding her at arm's length. "I need to ask you something, Giselle."

"I know what you will ask—you want me to see that Samir gets back to his family if your ship captain manages to locate any of them . . ." She gave a slight shake of her head, as if rejecting something too painful to consider, and added, "And if you do not come away from the duel."

"Yes. It is very important to me. I've left all the information you will need in a sealed envelope with Byer, to be delivered to you along with instructions if they do *not* respond."

"What of your mother?" she asked gravely.

"I've written a letter for her, as well." Because he was too bloody cowardly to speak to her right now. He told himself he did not wish to inflict additional worry upon her when she was so close to her lying in. But that was a lie. He was a coward.

"We shall see to Samir's well-being, my friend."

The relief that coursed through him told him that fear for the boy had been no little part of the stress he'd been carrying. "Thank you."

She squeezed his hands so hard they hurt. "It's over between us, isn't it?" Tears spilled down her cheeks, and he kissed them away.

"Yes, Giselle, it is."

"Will you still come visit—even after Samir gone?"

"You know I will. You and Maria will always be my dearest friends."

"I'll miss you, Gabriel, but I'm proud you will give yourself to your marriage with a whole heart—it's the right thing to do."

Gabriel wondered if his new wife would feel the same way.

Chapter 7

Drusilla stared at her reflection and grimaced. She looked wrecked—absolutely, positively wrecked. Dark smudges beneath her eyes—which were heavy and bloodshot from lack of sleep. She'd been too nervous to eat at dinner last night. The atmosphere around the marquess's table had been so genial and normal it had felt . . . dreamlike. Or nightmarish, rather.

"You look lovely, Dru."

She started at the sound of Eva's voice, meeting her friend's gaze in the mirror. Drusilla forced a smile.

"You're not frightened, are you?" Eva asked.

What could she tell her friend? That she was terrified of her feelings for her brother? That she'd loved and wanted Gabriel with a fierceness that had almost paralyzed her since the first moment she saw him?

"I'm not frightened," she lied.

Eva chewed her lip, clearly agonizing over something. "I know you and Gabriel have sometimes rubbed each other the wrong way—"

Drusilla snorted at her friend's understatement.

Eva took her hand. "*And* I know he can appear . . . imperious—"

"Because he *is* imperious."

"Very well then, because he is imperious," Eva conceded. "But he can also be very caring, kind, and protective." She shot Drusilla a direct look, making her feel like an ungrateful shrew—because that was how she was behaving. Here was a man who'd not only fought for her honor, but was marrying her and would soon be putting his life at risk for her.

"I know he's kind, Eva. He's also been a savior to me—twice. I appreciate what he is doing. I only wish he didn't have to do so *much*, to sacrifice himself for me."

Even her friend could not argue with her words: Gabriel Marlington *was* sacrificing himself. If he was going to offer for any woman this Season, it would have been Lucinda Kittridge and everybody knew it. It was mortifying to know he would now be forced to settle for Drusilla.

Luckily the door opened, and Lady Exley and Aunt Vi entered. The marchioness stopped in the doorway and smiled.

"Oh, Drusilla, you do look lovely."

Aunt Vi kissed her on both cheeks in an unprecedented display of affection. Neither her aunt nor her father had been given to physical warmth, and she guessed what her aunt was mostly expressing was relief. Dru didn't blame her aunt for looking relieved to have shed the burden of finding her a husband. No doubt the older woman had believed she'd be chaperoning Drusilla until the end of her days.

"You look very fine, Drusilla. Your father would be so happy for you today."

"Thank you, Aunt Vi. How are you feeling? I hope you'll not overexert yourself."

Her aunt squeezed her hands. "Don't worry about me, please. I want you to enjoy your special day."

Drusilla swallowed down a hysterical bubble of laughter. Her special day? Enjoyment was the last thing she expected from this day.

The marchioness enfolded Drusilla in a warm, tight embrace, her hard pregnant belly pressing against Drusilla in a way that made her realize she might be in a similar condition before too long. That was the wrong thought to entertain; it left her feeling weak, woozy, and unaccountably hot. And . . . eager.

Lady Exley then held her at arm's length and laughed up at her. "Good, you have some color in your cheeks—no doubt because you are horrified at me for touching you so familiarly." Drusilla opened her mouth to protest, but the vivacious woman waved it away. "You will learn I frequently act before I think. The marquess says it is part of my charm." She waggled her eyebrows, making everyone laugh before she turned to her stepdaughter, who returned her embrace with enthusiasm.

"And you, my wonderful daughter," Lady Exley said, examining Eva with keen eyes and making a *tsk*ing sound. "You must be the loveliest young woman in all of England, and you get prettier every day."

"Oh, Mama." Eva squirmed under her stepmother's affection, but Drusilla could tell she loved it—and Lady Exley.

The tiny redhead leaned close to Drusilla. "We ladies are all too fine for our menfolk, but such is the way of things." She squeezed Drusilla's arm. "You must not tell my son I said that. Jibril believes he is the most beautiful, perfect creature alive, thanks to his doting mama."

Drusilla could have told her, in all honesty, that she agreed. Yes, she could have said that easily. But she would have followed her declaration with weeping and the mortifying confession that she was about to marry a man with whom she was madly in love and who actively disliked her and wanted to marry another.

Fortunately, she kept her tongue behind her teeth.

Lady Exley chattered all the way down the stairs, into the drawing room where the rest of the small party waited, not stopping until the carriage arrived at the church perhaps a quarter of an hour later. The marquess watched his wife through slitted eyes the entire time, a half smile hovering on his cruel-looking mouth.

Aside from greeting her, telling her she looked lovely—a valiant lie—Drusilla's bridegroom hardly said a word. He sat across from her and looked out the window, his expression like that of a man in a tumbril on his way to Madame Guillotine. As always, he was gloriously handsome. Her dress was a pale blue, and he had donned a dark blue coat over a gray silk waistcoat, fawn pantaloons, and glossy Hessians. The wedding was to be quiet and informal, so both he and Drusilla looked little different than if they'd been going for a walk in the park.

It did not disturb her to have a small wedding. After all, she had never planned to marry. Even so, part of her wished she'd possessed the courage to invite the members of her small circle, no matter that marriage went against everything they'd always stood for.

But she'd worried that, like Theo, they would have given her disapproving looks for joining the ranks of those who spent their lives frittering away time and money on the selfish pursuit of pleasure. An activity that would no doubt comprise the majority of her life henceforth.

Thinking about Theo brought back memories of their surprising—and rather unpleasant—discussion after Gabriel had left.

"My God, Drusilla—that man is—is, well, he is a barbarian. He is one of those responsible for terrorizing Christians in the Mediterranean, for ransoming captives—for *raping* Englishwomen." He'd paused in order to let the full horror of his words sink in. "He is a *slaver*, Drusilla. Surely you cannot think to marry such a man."

Rather than cause her to feel shame, his words had angered her. "You are doing nothing but rumormongering, Theo. Mr. Marlington had the support of Baron Ramsay, a man famous for his hatred of the slave trade. I find it hard to believe Lord Ramsay would countenance slavery, don't you?"

Theo had shrugged that off. "Perhaps everything you've heard about Ramsay is mere *rumormongering*, as well."

"Mr. Marlington's sister, Lady Eva, assures me my fiancé was fighting for a new future for his people—one that didn't rely on slavery."

"Of course she does; she is his *sister*. Besides, everyone knows she is—"

"Theo."

He'd lifted his hand in a gesture of placation. "I am sorry, I shouldn't have said that." His expression said he thought otherwise. "Even if what she says about her brother is true, the man was reared in an environment where women were less than things, not even worthy of taking the sacrament of marriage for. It is said his father had over a hundred—well, one can't call them wives." He stopped and eyed her.

Her lips had twisted into an unpleasant smile. "Oh, and Englishmen behave so much better toward women? It is more civil and pleasant to marry one woman and keep others as mistresses, is it? Or to behave like the Regent, who married that poor Fitzherbert woman and denies it whenever it is convenient for him?"

He'd opened his mouth, looked into her eyes, and then shut it. Drusilla had just *known* he'd been about to mention Gabriel's notorious union and thought better of it.

But then he'd veered onto another subject. "You know his mother was never—"

"Do not, Theo. Do not say what you are going to say."

Drusilla had been stunned by the force of her anger. "These people are to be my family. And the woman you are about to disparage survived unthinkable conditions."

Theo's pale face had darkened. "You're correct, Drusilla. Please, forgive me. In my zeal to convince you, I've behaved badly." He'd taken her hand again, but this time she'd pulled it away; his touch hadn't been nearly as comforting after he'd exposed his prejudice. "You do not need to marry him to save your reputation—marry me, instead."

Drusilla had been flabbergasted by his desperate expression and passionate tone. But she had been even more shocked by her immediate, and visceral, response to his offer: she did not *want* to marry Theo. The truth—the painful truth—was that she *wanted* to marry Gabriel Marlington. Drusilla wanted *him*. And, at the end of the day, she didn't care if he loved another woman. She knew such a thought doomed her to a well-deserved life of misery. But she simply did not care. Meanwhile, she'd needed to come up with a response that didn't crush her friend.

"I—I can't, Theo, although I do appreciate your offering to sacrifice yourself and—"

He'd seized her hand again. "It is no sacrifice, my darling. I have a confession to make—I've loved you almost since we first began working together. In my eyes, you're the perfect woman. Together we might—"

She'd yanked her hand away. "Theo, please recall where we are."

He'd glanced round the teahouse, as if only now noticing they weren't alone, and hung his head. "Forgive me—I've behaved like a fool. It's just that I'm terrified our good work will now stop." When he'd looked up, his eyes had been anguished. "And as to the other . . . Well, I *do* hold you in high regard, Drusilla—the highest. Together we would be such a marvelous team. We could continue your plans and even expand them.

We could establish houses for poor women and children in every town and city in Britain. I *love* you, Drusilla, and I—"

She'd leaned back in her chair, deeply uncomfortable with his declaration and not wishing him to repeat it. "I'm engaged to be married, Theo. Please say no more on the topic."

His cheeks were flaming red. "Yes . . . of course. I'm so sorry. Can you forgive me?"

"Of course I forgive you. And even though I will be married, I'll never abandon our work, Theo. You should know that. Marriage will free me from the economic constraints I've lived under." She didn't want to directly mention her father's will, but just about everyone in London knew the conditions. "I will now have more resources than ever to put toward our cause."

"I do know that, Dru. And I'm sorry. It's just—"

"Just what?"

"Well, Marlington, he will be your husband. Are you certain he won't—"

"He's taken nothing in the marriage contract, Theo."

His jaw had dropped. "*What?*" he'd demanded in a skeptical tone. Her displeasure must have been clear on her face because he'd made a swift recovery. "Do remember, Drusilla, that as your husband, he'll have complete authority over you. What if he decides your work is not suitable or appropriate?"

The question had irked her, but she could see why Theo would be concerned, given all the work, time, and effort he had put into the various projects. "He will not interfere."

"But—"

"I won't discuss such private affairs with you, Theo. He is to be my husband and our marriage is our own concern."

He'd behaved with far more circumspection after that, and they'd discussed two of the recent projects he'd been overseeing.

"Miss Clare?"

The carriage had stopped, and Gabriel was waiting to help her out. He was looking up at her, his hand outstretched, his beautiful face unreadable. In less than an hour he would be her husband.

She swallowed hard and took his hand.

Viscount Byer and a small clutch of other guests—mostly Lady Exley's family if the hair color was anything to go by—had just arrived and were greeting one another outside the church.

Drusilla was introduced to her husband-to-be's terrifyingly proper grandfather, the Duke of Carlisle, as well as a dizzying number of cousins and aunts and uncles. She became weak with relief when they all followed Lady Exley into the small church and left her alone with Eva and Byer. She didn't have much of an opinion of the viscount, who appeared to spend his time drinking, gaming, womanizing, engaging in foolish bets, and becoming the oldest student in Great Britain.

Byer examined Drusilla through an ornate quizzing glass as they stood waiting in the narthex. Gabriel and the marquess had gone to meet with the vicar, and the other guests were taking their seats, almost filling the tiny church.

"You're looking lovely this morning, Miss Clare." Byer's voice had the bored, languid quality of an exhausted fop. He wore rings on every finger of his hand but one: the ring finger on his left hand.

Before Drusilla could answer him, Eva burst out laughing. "Lord, Tommy, you put on such a horrid show with your wretched glass." She punched him in the shoulder hard enough to make him wince.

He rubbed his arm. "Proper young ladies do *not* punch proper young men."

"But we are neither of us proper, are we?" Eva countered,

twisting her gloves—which were already grubby—into a tight spiral with both hands. "Tell me, did you ever manage to sell that wind-sucking mare of yours?"

"To which horse are you referring, my child?" Byer turned his glass on Eva, but she just grinned up at him and then poked him in the abdomen with her wad of gloves.

He coughed and dropped his glass.

"That dreadful roarer you bought from Lord Buckingham."

Byer looked pained. "Such cant does not become a young lady," he said repressively.

Eva laughed, unrepressed. "I shall take it that is a *no*. Next time you're in the market for cattle, you'd do far better to allow my brother to choose for you, or, better yet, bring me along to Tatt's."

Byer rolled his eyes, but Eva was looking over his shoulder.

"Ah, there you are, Gabe. Are you ready for us?" she asked.

Gabriel was accompanied by Lord Exley, who'd offered to give Drusilla away. Just thinking the words made Drusilla want to scowl: *give her away*. As if she were a parcel or a jar of calf's-foot jelly or a bundle of old rags. Drusilla would have preferred walking alone to accompanying the intimidating marquess but declining his offer had seemed the wrong way to begin her new life.

"Ah, Marlington—at last," Byer said, "Come and save me from your sister."

Gabriel ignored his groomsman and cut Drusilla a quick glance and, surprisingly, a reassuring smile. "Are you ready?"

She nodded, not trusting herself to speak.

Gabriel turned to Eva. "You and Byer will come with me."

And so Drusilla found herself alone with Lord Exley.

"Miss Clare?"

She looked up from her clenched hands. "Yes, my lord?"

"You are pale—do you feel well?"

His solicitousness surprised her. "Just fatigued from lack of sleep, my lord."

"Yes, it has been a whirlwind. As I am standing in place of your father, I want to ask if you are quite certain of this? It's not too late to change your mind until the vicar pronounces you man and wife."

Drusilla found the energy for a smile somewhere. "I do not wish to change my mind, my lord." No, what she wished to do was change who she was—or her appearance, to be more precise. The shallow, vapid desire shamed her. Although she had occasionally wished she were prettier, it had been years ago, when she was a young girl. But tonight, Gabriel Marlington would come to her and—

"I'm pleased to hear you wish to go through with the ceremony, Miss Clare," the marquess said, his cool tone mingled with amusement. "I'm afraid my wife would beat me black-and-blue if I walked down that aisle without you."

Drusilla laughed at the image of the tiny marchioness beating her terrifying husband. The marquess stared down at her, his strange crystalline eyes seeming less cold, but his expression as unreadable as ever. "That's better, my dear; you no longer look as though you might faint."

"My lord?"

"Yes?

She hesitated. "Do you know if . . . well, the duel . . . Is it still—"

"Nothing has changed."

She swallowed. "I'm sorry this happened."

"I know you are. I'm sorry you had to endure such treatment at the hands of a man who is supposed to be a gentleman. But I'm proud Gabriel was there to assist you." His message was clear: Lord Exley would do nothing to stop the impending meeting, nor did he wish to discuss its particulars with a mere female.

Music flooded the tiny building, and the marquess held out his arm. "Are you ready?"

Drusilla was as ready as she would ever be. She took his arm, and they entered the church.

The wedding breakfast was almost at an end and Gabriel felt his stomach clench—a sensation that was not so dissimilar to going into battle. Except the thing that was causing him anxiety was not potential harm to his person, but the unavoidable knowledge that he was now a married man.

He looked at his wife, who was seated between his stepfather and Byer. The marquess had finished eating and was dangling a glass between his fingers, his eyes—where else?—on Gabriel's mother at the far end of the table.

Byer was saying something to Drusilla that was making her frown. Gabriel caught the word—*Wollstonecraft*—and gritted his teeth. Good God. Byer would be baiting her. Wouldn't that be bloody helpful! Byer could get her all worked up, and Gabriel would have to deal with the results. He would throttle the man.

Yesterday, after speaking to Drusilla, he'd spent some time with Eva, who had told him a bit more about his wife. He'd already known about her obsession with Wollstonecraft and her "improving" societies, but he'd not known the true extent of her donations to charities and worthy causes.

Gabriel had also learned she was alone but for her ailing aunt. This year marked her third Season, and she'd received only one offer in spite of her enormous dowry. Well, he'd experienced firsthand her methods of driving off suitors, hadn't he? He'd always assumed—it now seemed wrongly—that social awkwardness accounted for her behavior. Now he knew she deliberately repelled men in order to avoid offers of matrimony. And Gabriel had forced her into marriage.

Her charitable work was impressive—she was no dabbler

doling out moralizing tracts, but a woman who poured thousands of pounds into housing, medical care, and apprenticeship programs.

One thing that should make her happy was that marriage to him meant the entirety of her fortune was now at her disposal and she could pursue all the causes she chose.

Gabriel could only hope she did not view *him* as yet another project awaiting her *improving* efforts—however unworthy he might be. Something poked him hard in the side, pulling his thoughts away from his wife, and he turned.

He smiled at his sister. "I hope you don't poke all your dining companions in the ribs, Evil."

She gave him a stony look, refusing to be charmed. "I want to know about this duel."

Gabriel groaned. What a bloody nuisance it was that Visel hadn't kept his mouth shut with females present and delivered the challenge later, as a normal, intelligent man would have done.

"Eva, you know I will not speak of this so do not tax me. This is nothing that—" A snatch of conversation—the words spoken in a tone of asperity—drifted across the table toward him, drawing his attention away from his sister.

". . . what possible difference could it make to you if women were to receive the same educational opportunities as men, Lord Byer? Or are you concerned a woman might best you if she were allowed to sit exams at Oxford?"

Before the viscount could answer her charge, the Marquess of Exley burst out laughing, causing all conversation at the table to come to an immediate halt. Every eye in the room was riveted on a man Gabriel had never actually *seen* laugh in all the years he'd known him.

The marquess appeared not to notice the effect of his laughter and was wiping the corner of one eye with his napkin, shaking his head.

"Good Lord, Byer, if I were you, I would give my tongue a holiday." Exley turned his icy stare on Miss Clare. "My new daughter has already pinned your ears back. I should hate to see what damage she does if you continue to offer yourself up for fodder."

Byer being Byer—which was to say good-natured—he laughed and lifted his glass.

"Thank you for saving me from myself, my lord." He turned to look at Gabriel. "To your new wife, Gabriel—a woman who is not only lovely, but also formidable."

The rest of the table, including Gabriel, lifted their glasses and the various conversations resumed. Gabriel cut a glance at his mother, only to find her gazing lovingly down the length of the table at the marquess.

Gabriel shook his head. He was happy for his mother, of course—life could not have been easy for her with the sultan—but it was a trifle mortifying when one's own mother behaved like a besotted debutante after almost six years of marriage.

Marriage.

The word echoed in his mind like the banging of a judge's gavel. He'd not even been married six *hours* and already he was fatigued. Thinking about tonight was causing him more stress than thinking about tomorrow's duel. Especially after his mother, once again, had poked her nose into his business.

She'd pulled him aside the moment he'd arrived at Exley House and dragged him into the nearest room, which had been the music chamber, a room that went almost entirely unused by his family as not a single one of them could play the piano without making dogs howl.

"Sit," she'd ordered.

Gabriel had sat. Really, what was the point of arguing with the woman? Not for the first time did he think that if his mother had been fighting against Assad for control of the sultan's empire, she would have won quite handily.

"Have you given thought to tonight, Jibril?"

He had only stared. Surely she was not—

"You will be bedding a virgin. Have you ever done such a thing?"

Gabriel's mouth had been open, but that hadn't meant he could force any words out of it.

She gave him a knowing look. "Ah, I thought not. Virgins are different from the women you usually—"

"Stop." The word had been a hoarse squawk. He'd stood, holding up one hand, as if that might hold her in check. "Just stop. I am not having this conversation with you, Mother."

"But, Gabriel, you must—"

"No."

"You do not wish to make her cry, do you?"

That had caught his attention. *"What?"*

She nodded, her expression sage. "Yes, virgins must be handled . . . delicately."

He'd not believed his face could become any hotter nor his head pound any harder. "What kind of beast do you think I am, Mother? One who would roughly debauch an innocent?" He shook his head, cutting her off before she could respond. "I do not need your advice when it comes to the proper care and handling of . . . of—" He scraped a hand through his hair and glared upward in slack-jawed amazement, as if the entire interaction were the ceiling's fault. "I cannot believe I am having such a conversation with my own mother."

She'd grabbed his arm. "Be gentle and patient, my son, as I know you can be. She is—" Gabriel had actually been interested in what "she is," but, for once, his mother had censored herself. Instead, she'd patted his arm. "I know you will do the right thing."

Gabriel looked across at his wife now—his *virgin* wife—and thought that perhaps he should have swallowed his qualms and listened to his mother. After all, it was true he knew nothing about innocents, nor could he clearly recall losing his own virginity. Sexual encounters had been part of his life from the age of fourteen, and he'd enjoyed them and so—he hoped—had most of his lovers. To be honest, women had flocked to him, and he'd never really given much thought to sexual encounters and what, if anything, they meant other than pleasure.

In Oran, Gabriel had been well aware it was not his irresistible person the women pursued, but the power he represented. And after his brother Assad had fallen from favor and Gabriel had been elevated to most favored? Well, more women had pursued him than there were hours in the day. They all would have known a sultan would never marry any of them, that he would take only a pure woman to wife. But they would have been promoting the interests of a younger sister or cousin or maybe even a daughter. Had he taken control of the sultan's faltering empire, he would have gone about filling the vast seraglio with virginal women. After all, having male sons—and lots of them—was what insured the continuation of his family line.

Of course, when Assad had seized control, that had changed in a heartbeat.

Gabriel frowned at his thoughts: Now was not the time to be thinking of such things. No, he should be thinking of his virgin wife and not the life he'd left behind.

Gabriel's eyes flitted around the table. This was his life now; these people were his family—all the family that remained to him. Even before he'd fled Oran in disgrace, his war with Assad had scattered and divided their vast number of stepsiblings. There was nothing back there for him. He no longer had to tell himself that a dozen times a day, but the yearning for his old life still hit him—sometimes with a violence that took his breath away. Today made him think about the life he might have had—and the one he now faced.

Gabriel looked at his new wife. Her expression reminded him of the Sahara: one did not always see movement in the desert—not until it crept up and surprised you.

Chapter 8

Drusilla hadn't seen inside the town house where she would live with her new husband. There simply hadn't been time before the wedding. But her clothing and possessions had been packed, and Fletcher had taken care of moving everything.

The house wasn't far from the huge mansion where she'd lived with her father, and then, after his death, with her Aunt Violet, who would now make her home with Drusilla, so she could see to her care.

Drusilla had been glad to leave the monstrosity, and the first instructions she would give to her man of business, now that the property was hers, was to sell the house and everything in it. The house had never been home. Indeed, her father had constantly built or purchased bigger houses as his wealth increased. A poor lad from St. Giles, he'd seemed to feel it was the only way to keep track of his progress.

Drusilla had hated all those cold, empty, cavernous houses. She immediately liked this cozy town house far better. It looked like many others from the outside, but within it was warm, intimate, and decorated with taste and elegance.

The ride from Exley House had taken only a few minutes,

and she and Gabriel had hardly exchanged a word. She wondered if he was thinking about tomorrow morning. The wedding ceremony would have been strange enough in itself, but the overhanging threat of his duel—the complete unreality of eating, drinking, and celebrating when he might very well die tomorrow—had left her feeling as if she'd suffered a hard knock on the head.

A dozen servants waited inside the small foyer and trailed down a hallway that must lead to the kitchens. Drusilla recognized her two favorite footmen among the servants and reminded herself to thank Fletcher later for thinking of such matters.

"This is Parker and Mrs. Parker," Gabriel said, introducing her to the man dressed in the sober suit of a butler and a woman swathed in black bombazine.

Mrs. Parker dropped a curtsy and Parker bowed low. "Welcome, Mrs. Marlington."

"Thank you, Parker, Mrs. Parker."

The butler introduced the members of Drusilla's staff, but when Mrs. Parker opened her mouth—no doubt to offer to show her to her room—her husband spoke.

"I shall give Mrs. Marlington the tour," Gabriel said, dismissing the servants. He turned to her. "It's far smaller than what you are accustomed to, I'm sure." He continued before she could offer any comment. "There's a small parlor on this floor, behind the stairs, and the kitchens are down the corridor."

He gestured toward the staircase that led up one side of the foyer, and Drusilla preceded him up the stairs.

On the second floor were a pretty blue sitting room, a small library already partially stocked with books, a dining room with an adjacent drawing room, a retiring room, and a study. The third floor held bedrooms.

Gabriel opened the door at the end of the hall. "This is the mistress's quarters." The rooms beyond were smaller than those at her father's house, but they were beautifully decorated in shades of fawn, gold, and chocolate brown.

"And through here"—he went into her dressing room, which was already full of her possessions, and opened another door—"are my rooms."

Drusilla peered into the room, but didn't enter. It looked like a mirror image of hers, but decorated with dark green and antique gold. His valet was busy filling the drawers of a tallboy, but stopped and bowed.

"This is Drake, my valet. Drake, this is Mrs. Marlington."

The valet uttered the correct pleasantries, and Gabriel shut the door, leading her back to her sitting room.

"You must be very tired," he said, his own eyes shadowed.

Drusilla pulled off her gloves and tossed them onto the nearby table. "I didn't sleep well last night."

He came to stand before her, close enough to put his hands on her shoulders. Drusilla started at his touch, and he immediately removed them.

"I wanted—"

"I didn't—"

They both spoke at the same time, and then stopped, cutting each other embarrassed smiles.

"Please," Drusilla said, feeling like a fool for jumping at the mere touch of his hands on the fabric of her dress. "What were you going to say?"

"I wanted to say that I hope we can both find happiness in our marriage. I'll do everything in my power to make certain you do not regret your decision." The look that accompanied this declaration was almost shy, and Drusilla recognized nothing of the arrogant young man in his hopeful expression.

"Thank you," she said softly.

"I interrupted what you were going to say."

"It wasn't important."

He hesitated, as if he were going to inquire more deeply, but then seemed to think better of it.

"There's ample time for you to rest before dinner. Is there anything you need? Shall I send up Mrs. Parker?"

"No, Fletcher will see to my needs. Thank you."

"Excellent. Then I'll see you in a few hours." He bowed and turned to leave.

"Mr.—ah, Gabriel."

"Yes?" He stopped and turned.

"About tomorrow. I was—"

His pleasant expression hardened. "I'd hoped I'd made it clear that I don't wish to speak about this again, Drusilla."

Her name on his tongue sent a shock of surprise through her. His accent seemed more pronounced when he said her name. Foolishly, she wanted to hear him say it again. And again. That desire was overborne by the irritation she felt at being silenced by him.

"And I do not appreciate being quieted like a child, *Gabriel*."

His lips—those full, shapely lips she saw in her dreams—curved into a smile that was without amusement. "I'm not treating you like a child; I'm treating you like a wife."

"You promised me you wouldn't lord your status of husband over me."

"You believe *this* is an example of me lording something over you?" He gave a humorless chuckle. "Oh, you're sorely mistaken, my dear Mrs. Marlington." He shook his head while Drusilla tried to ignore the sudden awareness that flooded her body at the sound of her married name.

Drusilla crossed her arms. "Why am I not surprised that you won't live up to your word of not even two days ago?"

She'd hoped to anger him, but he just smiled. "I promised I wouldn't beat or confine you. But I did *not* promise that I would permit you to interrogate me or run roughshod over me, or turn me into some kind of squeaking worm of a man who—"

"Worms don't squeak."

He blinked. "I beg your pardon?"

"You said you wouldn't permit me to turn you into a squeaking worm of a man. Worms don't squeak. Perhaps mouse is the word you were searching for?"

He stared, arrested. And then he took a step toward her. The hairs on the back of her neck rose up, but she refused to step away.

"I stand by my word that I shall never cause you physical harm." His voice was soft, but that just made the words sound menacing.

Drusilla wanted to yell at him, to tell him that he'd been causing her emotional agony that was almost physical in nature from the first moment she'd met him.

But he could *never*, *ever* know such a thing. She could *never* disclose how it would tear her apart be married to a man she loved, but who would never love her. And she could *never* tell him how it would kill her by inches to watch in silence while he took lovers. It would be agony; if it did not actually kill her, it would make her wish she were dead.

No, she could never say those things.

Drusilla realized he was waiting for some response. She pursed her lips and raised her eyebrows, a silent challenge to his bid for authority.

He frowned, the skin over his high, sharp cheekbones darkening with displeasure. "I will protect you and treat you with respect, but you will not rule me, Drusilla. This business of the duel is no concern of yours, this—"

"You're fighting because of *me*. How can it not be my concern?"

He muttered something in another language beneath his

breath and released the door handle before striding back to her. "I'm fighting this duel because Visel challenged me. *Me.* If he had not been such a drunken fool, he would have waited until there were no women about—he would have confronted me in private. But he is an idiot, so now the entire world—including you, my sister, my mother, and every other female in England—is privy to my business." One of his eyebrows cocked, and he stepped close enough that she could feel the heat of his body through their combined clothing. His shockingly green eyes narrowed. "That still does not mean I will discuss the matter. That means—"

There was a soft knock, and Parker opened the door. His gaze slid between Drusilla and Gabriel, and he froze like a hare startled by a bright light.

"What is it, Parker?" Gabriel asked curtly.

"This just arrived for Mrs. Marlington, sir." He came forward with a salver.

Gabriel took the note and handed it to Drusilla without looking at it. She recognized the handwriting as belonging to Theo and shot what she knew was a guilty look up at her husband. His lips curved in a sardonic smile.

Parker lingered.

"Was there something else?" Gabriel asked.

The butler cleared his throat. "The messenger was instructed to wait for a reply."

"Is there a reply, *my dear*?" His expression and tone were light, but his green eyes had taken on the color of a killing frost over the new growth of spring.

"No, thank you, Parker."

Parker disappeared almost before the words were out of her mouth.

Gabriel eyed her from beneath lowered lids. "Perhaps you might like to discuss your letter with me? Who sent it? What information it contains?" He paused, the silence threatening, his smile growing—but only more cynical. "Or perhaps you wish to tell me what answer the messenger was waiting for?"

Drusilla stood frozen, the letter clutched in her hand, memories of Theo's accusations against Gabriel and his wild, frantic pleading still echoing in her mind. She hated to think what words the distraught man might have written on these pages, but if Gabriel insisted on reading the letter, she knew she would have to give it to him.

He gave a bark of humorless laughter. "No, I thought not. That letter is your private *affair* so I will not pry. Perhaps you might extend me the same courtesy when it comes to my own private matters?"

Drusilla swallowed, trying to think of a way to reassure him she was not carrying on some romantic intrigue behind his back—even though she was receiving hand-delivered missives from another man on her wedding day. The same man her new husband had seen holding her hand yesterday. She winced at what he must be imagining. She opened her mouth, but nothing came out, her wits scrambled by his proximity, not to mention the situation. Besides, who knew what drivel Theo had written on these pages? She could hardly assure her husband it was harmless when it might not be. So she merely nodded.

His eyes burned as he leaned lower, until she could feel hot breath on her cheek. "Oh, and one other thing. Your correspondence is private, Drusilla, but I would caution you to have a care in your dealings." His eyes glinted, and she *knew* that *he* knew who had sent the letter. "Yesterday you were not my wife; today you are." The planes of his face were hard and merciless, making him look more like a falcon than ever. "While I wish you to be contented and to thrive in our marriage, I will not tolerate infidelity or intrigues—"

Drusilla gasped. The hypocritical *nerve* of the man. She opened her mouth, but he gave her no opportunity to speak.

"If you think to shame me, *wife*, know that I will react both swiftly and punitively. And also know that *you* will not be the one I punish. Do we understand one another?"

Fury and something else mingled within her at his blatant display of masculine dominance.

She ignored the unknown emotion and seized on the fury, giving an ugly laugh. "Thank you for telling me in such barbaric terms who is the master in this marriage. I never expected any less from you—regardless of what you promised when you proposed; nor does your hypocrisy surprise me."

Drusilla swore she heard a crack of thunder at her words.

Impossibly, he took a step closer, his body emanating volcanic heat. "How relieved I am to hear neither my barbaric nature nor hypocrisy surprises you. It also pleases me that you understand whose hand holds the whip in this marriage. Let us hope you do nothing to make me use it." His lips twisted into a cruel smile at the sound of shock that slipped out of her. "Now that you understand what our respective roles are—mine to give orders and yours to obey—I expect this will be the last time we shall have to discuss this particular subject." Behind his barely restrained anger, Drusilla thought she saw something else: Had she wounded him? Or at least wounded his pride?

She dismissed the thought. So what? She didn't care. After all, he'd wounded her over and over for years with his flirtations and careless, blatant amours.

"So what are you *ordering* exactly? That I end my association with Mr. Rowland?"

"Not at all, my dear. I am only telling you what will happen if you do not."

Drusilla's eyes widened as he stared down at her, his face carved from stone. Good God! Did he mean he would call the other man out just for being her associate? Was this what she could expect? A husband who would kill any man she spoke to? Who would—

"You've had little rest these past few days, Drusilla, so I will leave you to sleep tonight. I'll have your dinner brought to you and shall satisfy my own appetite elsewhere." His cold green gaze flickered over her, dismissing her—letting her know that going without bedding her was not a hardship—the words *satisfy* and *appetite* and *elsewhere* ringing in her head.

"Sleep well," he said, turning abruptly on his heel. And then he was gone. Her husband. A stranger, and now a hostile one.

He was leaving her alone—on their wedding night? She stared down at the piece of paper, reeling at her husband's cold dismissal.

And why do you think he is leaving, you little fool? her conscience goaded. *He was behaving toward you in a courteous and generous manner until you began questioning him about the duel. And what man would like to see his wife receive a missive from another man on their wedding night? How would* you *like it if he'd received a missive from his mistress in front of you?*

Drusilla ground her teeth. Why had she let him provoke her into combative, shrewish behavior? She'd suspected the letter had offended him, and yet she'd pushed him even further instead of simply admitting Theo had become rather hysterical. Instead of reassuring Gabriel, which was what *she* would have wanted if the situation were reversed. Drusilla stared at the door—should she go after him?

And say what? Will you tell him the letter is not *from Theo? Will you let him read it? Will you beg him to stay? Offer him your body? Tell him that you have been thinking about what would happen tonight for the last forty-eight hours? Perhaps even for the last five years? That you could have married Theo if you'd wanted, but instead you wanted* him*—a man who clearly wanted another woman, a* *beautiful, wealthy woman that he can now never have thanks to you? Is that what you will tell him, Drusilla?*

She groaned, staring at the crumpled letter and cursing its sender. Why would Theo do such a thing? He must know she was married already and that this was her husband's house. Why?

The letter felt heavy in her hands and the temptation to merely throw it in the fire was strong. But her fingers had a will of their own, and they broke the seal and exposed the contents.

Gabriel had not been this furious even when he'd been banging Visel's head against the wall. How dare this Rowland creature send a letter to *his* wife on *his* wedding day?

You went to your *mistress's house the morning of* your *wedding,* some bloody-minded voice in his head pointed out.

I went to see Samir, to explain why I would be scarce for the next few days.

Perhaps she is merely discussing yet another of her tedious charities with the man? Perhaps the letter is nothing more than a report on spending?

"Ha!" Gabriel wrenched open the door to his library, his vision red. "Then why the devil didn't she just tell me so?"

His bellow startled a shriek out of a maid who was dusting a bookshelf, and she shot toward the door without being dismissed. Gabriel heard a soft click behind him as he went to stare out the window and impose some order on his chaotic thoughts.

The library looked out over a small garden, its flowers, hedges, and little winding path charming. The whole house was charming—not that he'd had anything to do with it. His stepfather had won the place in a card game, and then he'd proceeded to do what he always did: fix the property and either sell it, allow the family of the gambler a life estate, or lease it for some purpose or other.

Given the size of the dowry his wife had brought with her, they could have set up housekeeping anywhere short of St James's Palace—although Prinny might even lease them *that* since he was pockets to let.

It was bad enough taking houses from his mother's husband or an allowance or country estate from his grandfather. But taking money from a woman who hated him—and who might even have some lover waiting in the wings? No, that would be unbearable.

His fingers gripped the wide window frame until his knuckles whitened. He was behaving like a child. He knew in his gut that his bride was still an innocent and would not be unfaithful to him with another man—at least not physically. If anything was going on between her and the milksop she'd been sitting with in the tea shop, it was the sort of tragic, gothic tale the Minerva Press cranked out—and which his sisters adored.

He shouldn't care what she was doing or whom she was doing it with, but he did.

"Blast and damn." Gabriel closed his eyes and took a few deep breaths. He had no interest in living a life of turmoil and tension. Their union was permanent, and he was not a child to rail against reality. He would need to sit her down and try to find common ground—try to overlook their differences and find something in which they both shared an interest.

But not tonight. Tonight he was tired, impatient, and irritable. Bedding his virgin wife in his current condition would certainly lead to tears.

He turned from the window and went to his desk. Other than a pen knife, a few quills, and empty ink vials, there was only the leather-wrapped packet from his grandfather, His Grace of Carlisle.

He opened the deed, even though he'd stared at it for a good hour last night.

"This was a property that came to your grandmother through her mother," the duke had explained when he'd spoken to Gabriel in Exley's library last night after dinner. Even after five years, Gabriel was not quite sure what to make of his proud, distant grandfather. The Duke of Carlisle was a famous stickler for propriety whose sensibilities had taken a battering since the day his daughter returned to England six years earlier. Gabriel knew the duke couldn't have been happy about his own appearance a year later: a bastard grandson with a notorious connection to corsairs But—and Gabriel had to credit the man—the duke had made certain he would never want for money or security.

"The estate is called Sizemore Manor—is between Exham Castle and London." His Grace had given Gabriel one of his distant, wintery smiles. "So it will have the added advantage of being near the marchioness," he said, seemingly unable to refer to his own daughter by her name. "And yet not too close."

Gabriel had almost laughed at what the man had left unspoken. Yes, he loved his mother, but it would not do to live too close and have her constantly in his pocket, offering nonstop advice to him or, God help him, to his new wife.

The duke had continued, as unsmiling as ever. "It comes with a pretty piece of farmland which has always supported the property with some to spare. It has been unoccupied, although Abermarle has periodically stayed there during the summer." The Marquess of Abermarle was Gabriel's uncle, his mother's only brother and the duke's heir. He was a studious, bookish man who was a great disappointment to his father. The duke was a skilled rider to hounds, a crack shot, and a skilled political orator who was a close associate of the Regent and had long been part of the Carlton House set. His son, Cian, preferred solitude to socializing, history to hunting, and privacy to politics. Gabriel liked the quiet man, although he had spent very little time with him.

Gabriel unrolled the packet of information and studied it. There were drawings of the houses, additions, and outbuildings and also a survey of the land. It was near the coast but far enough inland to have plenty of fertile land worth farming. It was a modest-size manor house with perhaps ten thousand acres, most of it divided into tenant farms with a smallish plot reserved for the home farm.

A detailed plan of the property was included, and Gabriel felt a frisson of pleasure as he examined it. A stream, a small lake, even a little wooded area. It would be the perfect place for a boy to run wild. Samir could have a pony and explore and grow up without all the dangers Gabriel had faced as a boy: poison and assassination plots and the stomach-curdling jealousy of his half brothers' mothers.

Yes, he could take a property like this and make even more of a success with it, just as he'd done for his father when the sultan sent him out to one of his holdings once he'd turned fifteen.

Gabriel could still recall the day he'd left home. His mother had been desolate and Gabriel, himself, had been more than a little concerned about leaving the only home he'd ever known. But leaving the palace and going to one of the Sultan's palaces to prove himself was a sacred rite of passage for a royal heir.

And of course there had also been the lure of Fatima to ease his homesickness. Her family had once controlled the al-Kamat palace but her father had been relegated to acting as the sultan's vizier after Abdul Hassan had seized the property over a decade earlier.

Al-Kamat was where Gabriel had been when his father died and Assad assumed the sultanate. Gabriel had been lucky to escape with his life when Assad made a secret deal with Fatima's father: the return of his palace and lands for his support against the sultan's chosen heir. And his daughter's hand, even though Fatima had already been promised to Gabriel.

Gabriel had been over one hundred miles away from Oran when his friends—the men who'd supported him since he was a boy—sent a small contingent to tell him of his father's death and his mother's disappearance and to help him to safety. His life had changed forever that night, but he hadn't known the full extent of those changes until weeks later. His sixteen-year-old self had been arrogant to a fault, believing all he had to do was return to Oran and summon his people—that they would rise up and support him without question.

Instead, it had been the beginning of a year-long civil war within their tribe. That's how his father's people had always viewed themselves: as a Berber tribe rather than an Arab nation. They had nominally accepted Arab and Ottoman customs, habits, and religion, but they remained, first and last, Berber, even hundreds of years after they'd been conquered.

Gabriel turned his mind from the past and focused instead on the plans before him: his new life and this new property. The Season would be over soon, and they would leave the city. He'd been looking forward to going to Sizemore Manor with Samir—before. Perhaps his new wife would rather go to Brighton and continue the endless round of balls and assemblies? He would speak with her. If she wished to stay in Brighton, they could rent her a house and he would spend his time at Sizemore. After all, it was a marriage of convenience. They might as well arrange it to *be* convenient.

He doubted his wife would find Samir's existence convenient. Gabriel winced at the thought of that particular conversation. Whatever he decided, he had a little more than a month to say it.

He rolled up the papers and put them away. It was always possible he would never see this property—that he would die tomorrow morning.

Strangely, that thought did not cause him any worry or concern. Perhaps that was because his life had contained so many other, more real dangers. Heading into a desert skirmish with fifty men, going up against his brother's army—better armed, better fed, probably better trained—had stripped him to the bone and left him raw. Meeting the nephew of a duke in the park at dawn? It seemed about as dangerous as a visit to Almack's. Not that he would know, never having been invited to such an elevated gathering. According to his friend Byer, whose mother had dragged him to balls at Almack's for almost a decade, the place was the culmination of every man's greatest fear: a Tattersall's for men. Where marriage-mad mamas inspected and selected the prospects with as much ruthless expertise as a man chose a mount.

"It's a dashed nightmare," Byer had complained more than once. "Women inspectin' your teeth, trying out your paces, reviewing your bloodlines. You're lucky, Marlington—that will never be your lot in life."

And it hadn't been. He'd skipped the inspection period and had jumped straight into the traces. He ground his teeth. Thinking of marriage only made him think of his wife, and he didn't want to do that right now. Gabriel hated to admit it, but he was more than a little jealous as to what her hot-eyed swain had sent her on their wedding day.

"Fool," he muttered, focusing on more important matters. Like this meeting with Visel. He'd seen the man fence at Angelo's. He was not bad with a sword, but Gabriel was better. He had practiced with his stepfather over the past few years, and the Marquess of Exley had been accounted one of the best swordsmen in Britain in his youth.

No matter how certain he might be of his skill, Gabriel couldn't help recalling his last conversation with the Marquess of Exley, which had taken place just this morning while the women were preparing for the small wedding ceremony.

"Dueling is not only a matter of skill. Sometimes the outcome is a matter of odds, probability—*statistics*," the marquess had said.

Gabriel cocked his head. "I beg your pardon?"

"Cardano, Pierre de Fermat, Pascal, Huygens, Laplace." Exley frowned when Gabriel continued to look blank. "What did they teach you at Oxford?" He waved a dismissive, elegant—and, Gabriel knew—lethal hand. "Never mind. The point is, you've enjoyed good fortune thus far. That will become less of a certainty if you continue to engage in such dangerous activities."

Gabriel bristled at that. "Good fortune and no small amount of skill, I would like to think."

"That is true; you are a superlative hand with both pistol and sword," Exley agreed mildly—since he was the one who'd honed and polished Gabriel's skills in both areas. Gabriel tried not to preen at this rare praise from a man all of England considered one of the most proficient at both. "However, all good things come to an end. Sometimes a less skilled opponent can surprise you. Sometimes"—his features hardened—"the outcome depends upon nothing but chance. After all, a clock that stands still is sure to point right once in twelve hours."

Gideon frowned. "I beg your pardon, sir. A clock that—"

Exley rested his fingertips against each other and stared at Gabriel over the steeple of his fingers. "I'm going to do something I rarely do: repeat myself. I advise you to heed me well." His tone was neutral, but Gabriel could see by his calm, implacable stare this would not be over until Exley finished saying what he had to say. Well, he owed the marquess the courtesy of listening.

"I am listening, my lord."

"You will eventually either run out of luck or your skill will fail you or your opponent will have more skill, or your opponent will be so . . . clumsy you might inadvertently cause more damage than you intend or even, God forbid, kill somebody."

Gabriel agreed. Still . . . "That never happened with any of your duels, and you had four—three more than me."

"That is correct."

He had not needed the older man to spell out his meaning. While Gabriel might think that engaging in swordplay with Visel would be like whipping a puppy, he knew he shouldn't make the mistake of viewing the duel with complacency: No outcome was ever certain. Especially not when your opponent was as irrational as Visel appeared to be. The man hated him—and had their situations been reversed, Gabriel knew Visel would have chosen pistols.

Gabriel fiddled with the shaft of a quill, stroking the barbs first one way, and then back, as mystified as ever about Visel and his unreasoning hatred toward him.

The last thing Gabriel wanted to do was administer a thrashing tomorrow. Not only was it tedious, but the man deserved more than just a beating for what he'd said to Eva and had done—or at least for what he'd tried to do—to Drusilla. But Gabriel couldn't let his mind roam down that particular avenue. Not unless he wanted to be on a packet to France tomorrow evening.

The truth was that he would have given in to his bloodthirsty urges in a heartbeat if it were not for his mother and sisters—and now his new wife and Samir, of course. But his half brothers were all dead, and the half sisters he'd grown up with were married and scattered across North Africa, lost to him. What remained of his family was here in England. Not only that, but he'd committed himself to Drusilla and owed her a chance at a respectable life. He had no desire to make himself a fugitive—not for a second time in his life. And it would break his mother's heart if he were banished from England as a murderer. And what of Samir? If none of Fatima's family claimed the boy, he would need a home and security. Dragging him back to Oran, where there was nothing for either of them, was beyond foolish.

No, he could not kill Visel. And he'd better watch out that he didn't underestimate the man and meet his own untimely end.

Gabriel tossed the quill onto the desk and stood. He'd go and find Byer and do what he'd told Drusilla: leave her to rest. No doubt she would appreciate his absence and enjoy having the evening to herself and her dream lover.

Chapter 9

Drusilla was pretending to eat dinner—alone—in the cavernous dining room. She had rung for a servant upon hearing her husband depart. The last thing she would do was cower in her room on her wedding night. So she'd ordered dinner to be served in the dining room. And now she was regretting it.

Parker entered the dining room. "I beg your pardon, madam, but Lady Eva is here to see you"

Drusilla lowered her fork. "Right now?" she asked stupidly.

Parker ignored the foolish question and inclined his head.

"I will see her—where is she?"

"I put her in the first-floor receiving room to wait, ma'am."

She tossed her napkin onto her almost untouched plate and stood. "I'm finished with dinner."

Eva was waiting in the tiny parlor, examining a watercolor of a horse that hung beside the room's only window. And she was wearing breeches, a claw hammer coat, a caped driving coat, a mangled neckcloth, and the smallest—and grubbiest—pair of top boots Drusilla had ever seen.

"Eva! Why are you dressed that way? What if somebody should see? I can't—"

Her friend's unusual blue-violet eyes flashed. "Gabe went out, didn't he?"

Drusilla flushed. How mortifying. Was there some sort of town crier who went about London communicating such information? *Hear ye, hear ye! Gabriel Marlington leaves his wife alone on their wedding night!*

"Yes, he went to his club for dinner. How did you know?"

Eva scowled and ignored her question. "Have you two had a row?"

"No."

"Then why is he behaving like a nocky boy and leaving you to dine alone on your wedding night?"

This was not a conversation Drusilla wanted to have. "Where do you learn such words, Eva? I can't imagine—"

"Oh don't, Dru. Just—" She flapped a hand in wordless irritation. "Just don't."

Drusilla sighed, too tired to argue. Instead she strode toward the bellpull. "Fine, Eva, I won't. Now, why don't you remove your hat and cloak and take a seat. I shall ring for some—"

"I know when and where the duel will be held."

Drusilla froze, her hand outstretched but not quite reaching the pull. "What?"

"I found out an hour ago."

"But how?"

"Drake—he's Gabe's valet, you know—came by to see Ellie, one of the parlor maids." Eva gave her a quick, searching look. "That is how I knew Gabe had gone out for the evening."

Ah yes, the silent network of servants who lived among them.

"Anyhow, Drake and Ellie are walking out together." Eva paused, her brow wrinkling. "He is at least fifteen years older than she and so stodgy and boring. I can't understand what Ellie sees in stuffy old Drake, can you?"

Drusilla gave up on the idea of tea and took a seat beside Eva. "Will you please finish what you were saying?"

"Oh yes—the duel. Well, I was down by the kitchen when—"

"Oh, Eva. You know you should not be eavesdropping." Her friend had gotten into trouble more than once at school for lurking and listening. It was such an unappealing habit, not to mention Eva had heard unpleasant things about herself more than once. But who was she to lecture her friend on behavior after the letter she had received earlier?

Not that Eva appeared to mind the gentle scolding. Instead of being contrite she laughed. "Gabe calls it *Evasdropping*." Her lip trembled and her beautiful face seemed to collapse in on itself. She grabbed Drusilla's arm with small hands sheathed in York tan gloves. "I am so frightened for him, Dru. I know he's done this before—but that was different because I didn't learn about it until *after*."

Drusilla knew exactly what she meant.

"I believe he's more skilled than Visel, but mistakes and accidents do happen and . . ." She swallowed a sob. "Lord, I'm just so afraid for him."

So was Drusilla, but she didn't think admitting to her fear would help matters. She opened her mouth to soothe her friend, but Eva was not finished.

"I can't stand the thought of him being there alone."

"He won't be, Eva. He will have Byer with him."

"Oh, Byer." She shook her head, dismissing the viscount with barely a thought. "I want to go."

"What?"

"I want to be there. Do you want to go with me, or not?"

"Eva—"

"What? Why are you 'Eva-ing' me and looking at me that

way? He is your husband now, Dru. Don't you care what happens to him?"

"Of course I care."

"Don't you want to be there—to know what happens?"

Dru hesitated a moment too long.

"You do—I can see it in your face. I knew you did."

Drusilla heaved a sigh. "I *would* like to know what happens."

Eva squealed and grabbed her, but Drusilla shook away her hands and gripped Eva's shoulders, giving her a slight shake.

"Listen to me."

Eva stilled.

"I said I would *like* to go but I cannot."

"But . . . why not?"

"I promised him, Eva."

"You promised him you would not watch his duel?" She sounded understandably skeptical.

"No, I promised I would respect his privacy."

"But this is *not* private—everyone in London knows about it by now."

"That may be true, but that doesn't mean he wants everyone in London to be watching tomorrow morning."

"You don't *understand*, Dru. Visel is . . . well, he's been following Gabe."

"What?"

Eva nodded, her color heightening. "Yes, he's up to something—something more than just this duel. He's—"

Drusilla held up a hand. "Wait. How do you know he is following Gabriel?"

Eva stared at her for a long, silent moment and then admitted, "Because I've been following *him*."

"My God, Eva!"

"I *knew* you would respond that way. You needn't worry—he's never noticed me."

"Why would you do such a thing?"

"Because he's been acting hostile toward Gabe all Season. I thought he might try to harm him. And it turned out I was right, didn't it?"

Drusilla ignored the question. "So why didn't you tell somebody? Why would you come to the conclusion that following him was wise?" She allowed her gaze to travel over her friend. "Is that why you are wearing these clothes? Have you been going about dressed like this? What would happen if your father—"

"I did not come here to discuss what I've been wearing or doing. Are you going to come with me tomorrow, or not?" Eva looked remarkably like the terrifying Marquess of Exley, her beautiful features as cold and distant as the Scottish Highlands.

"I told you, I cannot."

"But he will never *know*."

The next half hour saw a repeat of this conversation, but with Eva finding new and creative ways to couch her argument. They went around and around and around.

Eva wasn't the only one arguing; Drusilla had her own demands.

"You must promise me you will not go, Eva."

Eva's derisive laughter told her what she thought about *that* suggestion.

Drusilla stared at her friend and carefully considered her next words before she released them.

"I will tell Gabriel what you are going to do unless you give me your word you will not go."

Eva's jaw dropped, and a series of small, disbelieving sounds came out of her mouth before she leaped to her feet, the hem of her greatcoat swirling around her boots. "You *wouldn't*."

Drusilla's face was hot and her heart felt as if it were being squeezed by a giant fist, but she could not back down. "Yes, I would."

"But—but I came here to share this with you. It is a . . . a sacred trust between sisters."

It was like having a knife twisted in her chest. "I know you came here to share this, but he is my *husband*, Eva, and I owe my first allegiance to him. Even without asking him, I know he would not want you there. And he would be furious with me if I concealed your plan from him."

Drusilla had always known Eva had a terrible temper, but she had never been the focus of it before.

"So, you are married now and our friendship is nothing? Is that how it will be with us?"

Drusilla tried to take Eva's hand, but she jerked away.

"No, don't try to placate me." Her mouth twisted into a sneer. "There was a time—only *yesterday*, I believe, when we were as close as sisters—no, *closer*, because my sisters and I never shared as much as the two of us have. But now I see that is over. I tell you things in confidence, and you tattle on me." She barreled toward the door, her billowing coat brushing against a side table and sending a small crystal bowl to the polished wood floor. The sound of shattering glass made her spin around.

"Eva—"

"Don't worry," she said, her eyes glittering with unshed tears. "I won't be going tomorrow morning—I won't force you to betray my confidence." She paused, her hand resting on the door handle, and then turned, her expression spiteful. "Oh, and since we are now embracing this new code of *honesty*, I should tell you that Gabe did not go to his club—he went to see his mistress. Or perhaps I should say mistress*es* as he keeps a lovers' nest for all three of them." And with that she was gone, not bothering to close the door, leaving it swaying gently on its hinges.

Drusilla felt as if she'd just been run over by a mail coach. Her friend's final words rang in her ears. She shook her head. Of course she'd known about his scandalous liaison with the two actresses. But she'd hoped he'd not gone to them tonight. Had she really believed he would end his relationships because he was married? This was what men did. Drusilla's own father—a commoner and of the merchant class—had kept a mistress, the truth of which had emerged only at her father's death when Drusilla had encountered the woman, a rather plain, small, mousy female, at her father's grave. But of course her mother had died long before then, so it was not the same thing at all.

Gabriel, apparently, would not wait for her to die before taking a lover—*two* of them. Drusilla slumped down in her chair and lowered her head in her hands. Perhaps she should just sleep here tonight? Who would care?

Nobody.

She groaned. No, it was bad enough all of London knew her husband had abandoned her on his wedding night for his mistresses. The last thing she needed was to set the servants abuzz with more pitiful behavior.

Drusilla was so exhausted she could barely raise her feet to climb the stairs. Fletcher was waiting in her bedchamber.

"Ahh, there you are, Miss Dru. I've laid out your nightgown."

"I want my pink flannel."

"Oh, ma'am, surely not that old thing? Why I—"

"Pink. Flannel."

Even in her barely aware state, she could register Fletcher's disapproval. Too bad. The last thing she intended was to get dressed like a sacrificial lamb, only to find there was to be no sacrifice.

* * *

Gabriel had known it would be bad, but he'd somehow not expected it to be this bad. Half the *ton*—the male half—was crowded into White's, with more drifting in every minute.

"Everyone is here except Visel," Byer drawled.

"Good God," Gabriel muttered, shaking his head. "That is all we would need to make this farce complete."

The other man chuckled.

"I'm glad you find this so entertaining," Gabriel snapped.

Byer was as impeccably—if outrageously—dressed as ever, even though Gabriel knew he couldn't have slept more than a wink last night. It seemed Visel's second had shown up at Byer's lodgings not long after Gabriel and the girls departed the ball two nights ago. And, of course, last night there had been the dinner and an evening of revelry afterward.

Yet somehow Byer looked as fresh as a daisy.

"How the devil do you manage it?" Gabriel asked, aware the rest of the room was listening so hard to their conversation the only audible sound was the distant buzzing of a fly.

Byer raised his brows slightly, as if to do more was too much effort. The man had looking bored and lazy down to an art form. But it would be foolish to underestimate him, no matter how foppishly he liked to dress and behave. Gabriel had fenced and sparred with him since the first week they'd met at Oxford, two outcasts thrown together in a bastion of elite snobbery: Byer was a lethal man, a wolf in sheep's clothing—or at least a wolf in the clothing of a feckless, no-longer-so-young pink of the *ton*.

Thomas, Viscount Byer, had been born the youngest of four brothers. The Byer family was perhaps the only *ton* family more notorious than Gabriel's.

His eldest brother had run off with the Earl of Graythorpe's wife when Thomas was still at Eton. Although Byer never said so, Gabriel knew he would have suffered dreadfully at the hands of the other boys—especially Graythorpe's twin sons, who'd been in his same form.

Byer's brother and Lady Graythorpe had been headed to Italy when their ship ran afoul of the French navy, and everyone on board died.

His middle brother, the next viscount, died less than a month after coming into the title. His death had been even more ignominious than his elder brother's: he'd been engaged in a horse race—in which both contestants had ridden their mounts backward—and had died instantly when his horse ran into a stone fence. His opponent had suffered only the loss of one leg.

The third Viscount Byer had been neither a libertine nor reckless. He had, however, been something of a gambler. And a very bad one. In the end, he'd taken the coward's way out of the mess he had made and shot himself in the head with a dueling pistol, but not before he'd lost everything that hadn't been nailed down or entailed on the viscountcy, leaving Byer, the new viscount, with a mountain of debts.

Byer had been at Oxford when his last brother died—just a few months before Gabriel left to come to London this year. His friend left Oxford after spending almost seven years there, never having actually studied or attended a lecture that anyone could recall. Or really even been there most of the time. Byer had spent more time at his random mistresses' houses or sponging houses or other, unknown, places than he ever had in the quarters they'd shared.

Since leaving Oxford, Byer had gone about town with his usual care-for-nobody air. But Gabriel was not fooled. His suave, jaded, and sophisticated best friend had lost his heart to Eva years ago—not that his sister seemed to notice. Nor, Gabriel suspected, would she want Byer's heart—or any other part of him. Eva was a person even more averse to marriage than most men of his acquaintance. She'd known Byer almost five years and viewed him as a brother. He suspected that if she ever fell for a man, it would not be the seemingly lazy, languid, and foppish viscount.

Shouts and yells pulled Gabriel from his musing, and he saw a familiar face pushing through the crowd of onlookers.

Byer sat up straighter in his chair as Visel strode toward them, accompanied by two other men.

"Ah, it would seem His Grace of Tyndale has finally taken an interest in his heir's activities."

Something about his friend's voice made him turn. Byer's face was hard, his usually lazy smile nowhere to be seen.

"This should be interesting," Byer said under his breath just before Gabriel got to his feet.

The duke was a very old man—at least in his eighties—and as thin and sharp as a rapier. His blue eyes were clouded with age but his expression was as haughty as a king's.

The younger of the two men accompanying Visel stepped toward them and bowed.

"Good evening, Endicott," Byer said.

Geoffrey Endicott—Visel's second—ignored his greeting, turning instead to the duke. "Your Grace, may I introduce you to Mr. Gabriel Marlington." His voice was unnecessarily loud.

Before either Gabriel or the duke could respond, Byer chuckled, his sleepy gaze flickering from Endicott to Tyndale to Visel and then back. "My goodness, Endicott—trying your hand at the dramatic arts, are you?"

Endicott flushed, Visel looked bored, and the duke ignored them both and stepped forward, his eyes on Gabriel.

The crowd was frozen—neither servants nor patrons bothering to hide the fact they were openly listening and watching. This meeting—or whatever it was—should have taken place elsewhere, somewhere more private, but Visel, or perhaps the duke, must have wanted it this way.

The duke lifted a plain gold quizzing glass and examined

Gabriel through it. Gabriel suspected the ancient man was one of the few people in the room who needed his glass. The only sound in the club was that of half a hundred men breathing.

His Grace finally dropped his glass and pronounced, "You bear a remarkable resemblance to your grandfather."

"So I've been told."

Tyndale's thin, bloodless lips flexed into a frown. "I paid a call at your house, expecting you would be there," he said in ringing tones. "But—as you were not at home on your wedding night, my grandson deduced you would be here."

The murmur of voices made Gabriel realize he'd probably need to leave the country before he would ever live this down. The duke, however, seemed impervious to the stir he was causing.

"I've accompanied my heir to put an end to this foolishness. Visel claims he was merely keeping the girl from falling off a bench when you attacked him."

Gabriel looked at the earl, who gave a slight shrug and cocked one eyebrow as if to say, *Go ahead, argue with an old man if you must*.

Gabriel said nothing and waited for the duke to say what he'd come to say.

Tyndale studied him with eyes that were a flinty pale blue. "Visel also told me he attempted to kiss the girl."

Gabriel just stared.

The duke's mouth flexed into a grimace of resignation. "I see. So you are prepared to duel over a kiss that never happened." It was not a question.

"A kiss with a woman who is now my *wife*." The air in the room hummed with the sound of whispering and tension. Gabriel ignored it and continued. "And then there is the rumor that grew out of that encounter. A rumor your grandson conceived in order to destroy a young woman's reputation." Gabriel felt, rather than heard, Byer sigh beside him.

The tissue-thin skin that stretched over the duke's sharp cheekbones reddened and the man's eyes narrowed. For a moment Gabriel wondered if *he* was going to slap a glove in his face, too.

But, to his surprise, the duke turned to his heir. "Lord Visel has something he wishes to say." His voice was as dry and cold as the desert at night.

Visel met Gabriel's eyes, and—for once—Gabriel could read no message in them, not even hatred.

Byer held up one beringed hand. "Gentlemen, would you not like to retire somewhere more, er, private?"

Visel cut him a humorless, dismissive smile. "It makes no odds to me *who* hears it."

Byer's eyebrows shot up. "Well then. Please go on."

"I would like to apologize for my behavior in the Abingdon conservatory, Marlington."

The room buzzed as if from a sudden infestation of crickets.

Gabriel waited.

The corners of Visel's mouth curved ever so slightly. "My actions were not those of a gentleman."

The small room—overstuffed with warm, sweating, drinking male bodies—exploded with exclamations, and men started pushing through the crowd toward the exit, no doubt eager to be the first to spread the word.

But Visel was not yet finished. "And, of course, I would like to apologize for any misunderstandings I might have inadvertently perpetrated." Visel watched him with the intensity of a man studying a scientific experiment. He knew, as Gabriel and every other man in this room knew, that to refuse such a public—albeit bizarre—apology would be unthinkable.

"I accept your apology, Lord Visel."

The duke nodded. "You are magnanimous, Marlington." His voice could hardly be heard in the din. "The best thing for all involved will be to put this behind us as soon as possible.

Tomorrow night is Lady Renwick's ball. I propose we publicly acknowledge each other and bury the hatchet. The evening after that we will attend the theater, the last night of the current production. I know Lord Exley keeps a box."

Gabriel felt a muscle in his jaw jump. Yes, his stepfather kept a box: at the same theater where one of his ex-mistresses was currently performing.

"Yes, he does."

"We can meet under the eyes of three-quarters of the *ton,* and that should put paid to the worst of the scandal. The sooner this dies down, the better it will be for all of us, Marlington, especially the ladies involved."

Visel had not taken his eyes off Gabriel while the duke spoke. He did not look like a man who had just apologized—or, at least, he did not resemble a man who felt any remorse.

Quite the contrary. As ever, Gabriel could feel the hatred emanating from him.

When Gabriel had first moved to Britain, the ill will had mystified him; how could men who'd never met him, or spoken to him, hate him?

How naïve he'd been back then: how foolish not to realize that men would hate him not simply because of who he was, but because of *what* he was. These men—English aristocrats—who considered themselves the highest level of society, behaved no better than a pack of stray dogs encountering another stray, or a train of camels when a new member was introduced. In fact, they behaved worse. Because camels and dogs would eventually accept the new member, until, one day, you would not be able to tell them from the others.

These men would never accept him. That was what men like his stepfather and his grandfather would never understand. Gabriel did not need to look for fights: they would come looking for him.

"Gabriel?" Byer asked.

He realized the duke was waiting for his response. "You are correct, Your Grace. The sooner this is forgotten, the better."

"Until tomorrow, then." The duke gave a sharp nod and turned.

Visel paused before following him, nodding his head slowly, his smile never reaching his eyes. "Until tomorrow, Marlington." And then he, too, was gone.

Men flowed from the room like bilge water from a scupper. At any other time, Gabriel would have been amused by his contemporaries' behavior. But he was not in a mood to be amused tonight.

"Well," Byer said.

Gabriel turned to his friend. "Well, indeed."

"What do you think that was all about?" Byer asked, dropping back into his chair and picking up his half-full glass, his lazy gaze drifting over the nearly empty room.

Gabriel snorted softly, both body and mind worn down and exhausted. "I have no idea." Visel's flat, intense stare flickered through his mind. "But whatever it was, I believe it's far from over."

Chapter 10

After the emotionally draining episode with Eva, Drusilla had expected to fall asleep the moment her head hit the pillow. Instead, she'd lain awake in bed, staring at the connecting door between her suite and Gabriel's. It seemed to be moving, breathing, expanding—just like a living thing. But she knew that was her imagination. It was just a piece of wood—a silent, unmoving piece of wood—that separated her room from her husband's dark, empty chambers.

Her body was exhausted but her mind ran on like a tedious play—a play that enacted the same few scenes over and over: Gabriel's face when he'd seen Theo holding her hand at the tea shop, his expression of fury earlier in the evening when Parker had delivered the letter, and Eva's final, hurtful words.

She'd woken at five but was determined to wait until six to ring for hot water and Fletcher.

Meanwhile, she paced.

Where was he? Facing Visel in a field somewhere? Was one of them already injured or—

The sound of feet—boots, to be more precise—passed her door. A moment later she heard a door close somewhere nearby. Gabriel?

She tiptoed across the room and placed her ear against the dressing room door: the murmur of men's voices—no doubt Gabriel and his valet, Drake. After an eternity she heard his door close again and soft footsteps recede down the corridor. A sliver of light shone beneath the door. Was he preparing for his duel? Or had he just returned? Either way, she could take it no longer. Drusilla swallowed a couple of times, controlled her ragged breathing, and then tapped on the door before she could lose her nerve.

There was a pause, and then the door swung open.

His expression was cool, but not hostile. "Drusilla. You are awake early."

Drusilla's eyes were immediately drawn to his body. Oh. Dear. God. He wore a red-and-black Chinese silk robe, the red the same dark, burning coal color as his hair. He'd not bothered to tie the sash, and it hung open, framing his nude, muscular, and magnificent torso. He still wore black pantaloons but his feet were bare. Her mouth flooded with so much moisture it threatened to drown her.

"How may I be of service?" His vivid green eyes glittered as he took in her worn dressing gown and the old pink flannel beneath. She had not purchased either garment for appearance, but, rather, comfort. And right now she was wishing she had thought to change before knocking.

He cocked his head, and she realized he was waiting for her to speak.

Her eyes darted around his room—there did not appear to be anyone else. "Do you have a moment?" Her hot face, she knew, would be as pink as her gown.

He stepped back. "Please, come in. I have only just arrived."

"I know—I heard you. I was w-waiting for you."

His eyebrows rose, his expression haughty. "I see. Have a

seat," he said, gesturing to the two chairs in front of the dormant fireplace.

Drusilla sat while he went to the narrow console table that held a single decanter. When he turned to her, she saw that he'd tied his robe shut.

He lifted the bottle. "Would you like a glass?"

"Isn't it a bit early?" She sucked her lower lip into her mouth and bit it, wishing she could take back the judgmental words and tone.

He smiled. "For me it is late." He poured a glass.

"What is it?" she asked.

"It is a wine that comes from the region where I was born. I have an associate who brings several cases for me whenever he comes to England."

"Oh. But—"

"But?" he prodded.

"I thought alcohol was prohibited by your religion."

He looked arrested. "You know about Islam?"

"A little."

"And how is that?"

Drusilla swallowed, wishing like mad she'd not opened her mouth to begin with. If she told him why she—

But it was too late and understanding dawned on his handsome features, his stern mouth flexing into a smile. "Ah, I see."

"You see what?"

"You have been *researching* me, have you?"

Yes, but she was hardly going to admit that. "Perhaps not all English people are as ignorant of other religions and cultures as you suppose."

He laughed. "What an unexpected sense of humor you possess."

Drusilla reminded herself that she hadn't come here to argue. "I would have a glass of your wine," she said, hoping to move past the uncomfortable moment. "Just a little."

He nodded and poured a second. "You are correct about the prohibition against alcohol. But there are some Muslims who . . ." He turned to her. "Well, shall we say who *bend* the rules." He handed her a glass and took the seat across from her.

"And you are one of them?"

He swirled his glass, an undecipherable expression on his face as he considered the garnet liquid. His words, when they finally came, were not what she expected.

"Visel has apologized. There will be no duel."

"What?" Her hand shook badly enough to slosh wine over the rim. It landed on the rich wool of the carpet and lay beaded on top.

They both stared at the spill without speaking.

Drusilla set her glass on the end table with a shaky hand and pulled her handkerchief from the sleeve of her dressing gown, using it to clean the wine from her hand.

"Visel came into White's—he and the duke, both. He made a rather, er, public apology. Not only for his behavior, but for the untrue rumor that spread directly after the altercation." He sounded bemused.

Drusilla was torn between amazement at Visel's behavior and joy that Gabriel had been at White's, not with another woman. But, of course, he would not have been at White's until now, would he? He could have gone to those women after, or before, or—

"I can see you are astonished, Drusilla."

Drusilla could have told him he did not know the half of what she was thinking. "Weren't *you*?"

His lips twisted. "Yes, very much so."

"So you were not expecting it?"

He gazed into space and shook his head slowly. "No."

"But—but you accepted his apology?" Good God, please say *yes*.

His eyes flickered back to hers, and he smiled—this time with genuine amusement. "Yes, Drusilla, I accepted his apology."

She could listen to him say her name all day—and all night—long. She kept that mortifying observation to herself.

"Was his apology, er, unusual behavior?"

"Very—especially in a place as public as White's. Which was packed to the teeth, by the way. As if the *ton* was expecting something like this to happen," he added musingly.

Her eyes darted to his pantaloons, and quickly back up. "Are you going to tell your mother?"

"I've already paid a call on my mother and stepfather."

"Lady Exley must have been frantic."

"She'd calmed down by the time I saw her." He saw Drusilla's questioning look. "I sent a message to Exley House last night, directly from White's. I did not wish her to worry herself into a state all night. A woman in her condition needs rest—sleep."

But he hadn't bothered to send a message here—to Drusilla. Did he not think she would worry? Probably not after their argument over Theo. She nodded, not trusting herself to speak, but he must have noticed something in her face.

"I would have sent you a message as well, but I assumed you would already be catching up on much-needed sleep."

"Yes, that is true. I fell asleep almost before my head hit my pillow," she lied, forcing down the hurt. "I'm sure your mother was relieved."

"Ha! She had forgotten her relief by this morning and commenced chastising me the moment I entered her chambers." He shrugged and then took a drink of wine before turning his attention—and his gorgeous green eyes—back to her. "But none of that matters. What matters is that it is over. There is nothing we can do about the incident, but at least people are not laboring under the misapprehension that I, er, *defiled* you in the Abingdon conservatory."

Drusilla dropped her gaze, her face heating at the word and what it meant—not that she had any personal knowledge of *defiling*. Even now that they were legally married, Drusilla remained perfectly . . . well, *filed*.

"We shall attend the requisite functions and face down the curious stares, and, I daresay, your reputation will be as pristine as ever by the end of the Season."

She looked up at his words, a dreadful thought hurtling out of the recesses of her mind. He was staring at her, his smile gone, his gaze speculative. He'd stopped speaking, but the words were pouring off him all the same.

"We needn't have married, after all, then." Her voice was thin, reedy. She cleared her throat and tried again. "Visel's apology would have cleared either of us of any inappropriate behavior. After a brief period of awkwardness, we could have gone on as we were."

He shrugged, the gesture smacking of fatalism. "There is no point in dwelling on such things, no matter how much either of us might regret it. We must do our best to move away from all this—to put it out of our minds."

His cool, uncaring stare acted like fuel on a fire and her mouth opened and words started to flow.

"I do hope you are able to bear up under your *regret*."

He frowned, and she could tell he was struggling to keep his temper.

Good. She was glad—childishly so, she knew—that she wasn't the only one who was angry.

"You know that is not what I meant, Drusilla."

As it happened, she *did* believe he'd not meant to be insulting, but the knowledge—the certainty and the guilt—that he must bitterly regret the marriage he'd been shoehorned into—burned into her like the most caustic acid, dissolving her tenuous restraint in the process. She was being unfair, but she could not bring herself to be otherwise.

He met her hostile stare with a weary smile. "I know things might appear rather dire now, but our lives will not always be so dramatic or hectic. Things will settle, and we will get back to the way we were."

"I'm sure *you* will."

He put down his half-finished glass, his gaze sharpening. "What do you mean by that?"

"I mean exactly what I said. I doubt you will let marriage change your life, will you?"

"I would have you speak plainly, Drusilla." His puzzled expression infuriated her all the more.

"You cannot really be asking me that? I'm sure all of London knows where you went last night."

More wrinkles joined the ones already on his forehead. "To White's?"

"You weren't there *all* night, were you?"

"No, I wasn't." He shrugged. "What of it?"

An ugly laugh slipped from between her tightly clenched jaws. "What of it? What *of* it? You threatened me not so subtly last night about what would happen if I were to take a lover, but I suppose the same does not apply to you? Men may have lovers and mistresses aplenty, but a woman must sit at home and endure the ignominy in silence."

Comprehension dawned, and he sat back in his chair. "Ah, you wish to know where I went last night—or you believe you already know—while you were home reading missives from your paramour?"

"That's—"

He raised a hand, his lips curled into an unpleasant smile. "No. You have said enough. Let me address your comments, *my dear*. Yes, you are correct. It *is* a different situation for a man than a woman when it comes to the taking of lovers. Part of that is because a man cannot bring a surprise home to his wife nine months later."

Her face heated at the vulgar innuendo, but she refused to be cowed. "I beg to differ, sir. A man can bring home *little surprises* to his wife at any time."

His eyebrows leaped up. "And what do you know of such *surprises*?"

She gave him a look of scorn. "Please, such matters may not be spoken of in polite conversation but they are common knowledge, not to mention a very common fear among married women. A woman always pays for her husband's indiscretions one way or another."

"You sound as if you speak from experience."

"You know what I mean."

"Yes, I do know what you mean—and I also happen to agree with you."

She snorted in disbelief.

Gabriel continued, undaunted by her scorn. "I do know, but I would enjoy hearing you elaborate on the subject."

"That is not going to happen."

He shrugged. "Well, perhaps some other time. But for right now, you may rest assured you shan't pay for my *indiscretions*, my dear."

Her heart leaped at his words. Did he mean he'd stop taking lovers? Her lips parted. "What—"

"You see," he said, his eyes narrowing to dangerous slits. "I have always worn a sheath when I am uncertain of a lover." She stiffened at the word *lover* and the sensual way it rolled off his tongue. But that other word?

He noticed her hesitation and gave her a superior smile. "I'm not shocking you, am I? You gave me cause to believe you are a sophisticate."

"Of course I am," she snapped.

"Really? Because I thought you looked confused. Was it the word *lover* or the word *sheath*?"

She clenched her teeth hard enough to crack walnuts. "I know what the word *lover* means, Mr. Marlington."

"Ah, so it is the word *sheath* that is in doubt. Let me educate you: a sheath is a supple, impervious tube which a man places over his—" He glanced down at his lap, his eyebrows raised. "Well, I shouldn't like to be vulgar—which word do you prefer? Breeding organ? *Membrum virile*?"

Drusilla sucked in a noisy breath, and his smile grew.

"Yes, I see you understand. In any event, Englishmen call them French letters." A wry smile twisted his lips. "But the French call them English hats. Amusing, don't you think—that such national animosity would carry even into the area of bed sport?" He didn't wait for an answer. "I use them so that I neither leave any little *surprises* behind nor take any away with me when engaging in my numerous *indiscretions.*"

A sound of muffled fury slipped out of her before she could stop it.

He cocked his head. "What was that?"

"You . . . you . . ." Drusilla could find no words. How *dare* he speak to her about such things?

"Oh dear, it would seem I overestimated your sophistication."

Anger, mortification, and something else—jealousy?—pounded her like waves hitting the shore. She shot to her feet. "You have certainly overestimated my tolerance for vulgarity."

He stood. "Leaving so soon, my dear?" he called after her as she stormed toward their connecting door. "By the way," she heard him say as she went through, "we are expected at Lady Renwick's ball tonight. Make sure you wear your prettiest gown."

She slammed the door with all her might, but the sound of his laughter—though muffled—was still audible through the thick wooden door.

* * *

Gabriel shook his head at the still-vibrating door, poured himself more wine, and then returned to his bedchamber and stretched out on his bed, balancing his half-full glass on his chest. Lord, but he was tired. He closed his eyes, his body heavy yet tense, willing himself to rest. For a moment the velvety blackness was all he could see, but then visions of his wife's furious face thrust aside the curtains of darkness.

He opened his eyes and groaned.

He should not have provoked her. Or let her provoke him, more accurately. And certainly not regarding such unseemly topics as mistresses, diseases of the sexual organs, and sheaths. He should have told her that he had already parted ways with his mistresses—even though he'd seen her holding hands and reading missives from her mooncalf of a lover on their wedding day.

Gabriel could tell her that he'd stopped bedding Giselle and Maria, but she'd never believe it when he continued to visit their house, and he knew word of that would circulate. He could move Samir, but that was hardly fair to the boy. No, he refused to take Samir from the comfort and security of their home only to put him—where? Here? In this house of discontent and dissension? No. Samir would stay with Giselle and Maria until it was time to remove to the country.

His jaws ached and his tired brain reeled from the oddly invigorating encounter. As to the rest of his behavior—his inability to resist taunting her—yes, it was wrong of him to shock her sensibilities. In reality, he'd been rather surprised she'd not heard of a sheath. Didn't she spend her time with charities for impoverished women? What better use of her funds than to promote sheaths and the concomitant reduction in disease and unwanted children? He took a sip of wine and decided he probably should not raise such a question to a well-bred English lady.

What was it about Drusilla that made him behave like such

a brute? Perhaps it was the prudish expression she wore whenever her eyes landed on him? It made him wonder what stories she'd heard of him. Obviously she'd heard of Giselle and Maria. He snorted. Who hadn't? The subject of his amours seemed to fascinate the *ton*.

As for the scores of married women and widows who pursued him? Those rumors seemed to take on a life of their own, regardless of the fact he had never bedded a married woman. The notion of cuckolding another man was repulsive to him. He had enjoyed liaisons with a few widows, but hardly the number he'd read about in the various betting books and none since his association with Giselle and Maria.

"You are an exotic creature, Gabriel. You might as well become accustomed to the amount of attention you attract," his friend Byer had said when Gabriel once complained about the erroneous gossip. "Whether you are doing the things people think or not, they will still speak and wager about them."

Byer was correct: the *ton* was determined to find his behavior notorious, no matter what he did. The fact that he'd been in a monogamous relationship—albeit with two women—for three years seemed to count for nothing.

He finished his wine and placed the glass on the nightstand, pressing the tips of his fingers into his temples, willing his eyes to close, his brain to slow, his body to go to sleep.

His body refused to obey.

"Damn it!" Gabriel considered ringing for Drake, but decided it was too much of a bother. He swung his feet off the bed, yanked the sash of his robe, and tossed it aside before going to the now-cool water in the ewer and pouring it into the basin. A quick, cold wash woke him but did not make his brain any less fuzzy. Well, it wasn't as if he had to do anything mentally strenuous today. While he was up and awake, he might as well visit Samir. He would enjoy seeing what the boy made of the gift he'd left with Giselle—a brightly colored top that depicted alternating illustrations of cages and animals. When it spun, it created the optical illusion of the animal in the cage.

Gabriel had become quite skilled at choosing gifts for young children. His three half siblings were aged five and three. And of course his mother had yet another child on the way.

He pulled a fresh shirt over his head as he considered the subject of children—not that he would ever get one on his wife at the rate they were going.

He flopped onto the bed and pulled on his boots, cursing himself for acting like an ass toward her. He was tired, but that was no excuse. He would go out, see the boy, swing by the jewelers, and fetch something for his wife—a bride's gift was what such things were called. He should have done so already, but it had seemed wrong to buy his wife and mistresses a gift at the same time.

Gabriel shook his head at the idiocy of that concern as he shrugged into a waistcoat and pushed his hair off his forehead. Tonight would be difficult, but once they'd been seen in public receiving Visel and Tyndale, the furor would die down.

With the duel out of the way, he could concentrate on making something out of this marriage they'd both been forced into. He didn't wish to live in constant conflict with her. He would make more of an effort from now on, no matter how much she tempted him to misbehave and taunt.

Chapter 11

Today it was Maria who was home and Giselle who had gone out. Luckily, Samir was in the nursery, finishing his breakfast.

Maria was already in the gold-and-blue sitting room when the maid ushered Gabriel in.

She stood and reached out both hands for him. "Gabriel! How lovely to see you. I was so sorry I missed your visit."

"I missed you, too," he said, kissing her on both cheeks and then lowering himself onto the dull gold silk of the bergère settee beside her. Whereas Giselle was blonde, voluptuous, and blue-eyed, Maria was dark, slight, and possessed eyes of such a dark brown they looked black. She was not pretty in the traditional sense, but the colors, cuts, and designs she chose for her clothing, along with her short, almost boyish dark brown curls, made her a delectable combination. Both women had that panache Frenchwomen possessed when it came to knowing how to dress and turn themselves out.

Today she was wearing an exceptionally plain and simple white muslin day dress, which perfectly set off her velvety olive skin and rich brown hair. She smoothed her small hands over her skirt and cut him a curious look, her dark eyes twinkling.

"Gigi told me some rather surprising news when Samir

and I came home from our journey—and then I heard even *more* surprising news last night when I stopped briefly at Mr. Kipling's house."

Gabriel cocked his head. "I didn't know you were in his latest production at the Drury. I thought you were still at the Little?" The Little Drury Lane was a theater that was far less prestigious than its namesake but offered more regular parts for Maria's range.

"Last night I stepped in for Mary Clemens, who swelled up like a balloon after some bad oysters."

"Ahh, so you played alongside Giselle?"

She nodded, a big smile stealing across her usually serious features.

"I'm sorry I missed it." He loved to see both Giselle and Maria onstage together, which happened only rarely.

She eyed him slyly. "I understand you were participating in some rather grand theater yourself last night."

He groaned, but recounted the bizarre episode for the third time. Just as he was finishing, there was a knock on the door, and Samir came charging into the room, flinging himself onto Gabriel.

"Jibril, Jibril!" His voice was muffled because he'd shoved his head into Gabriel's armpit.

Gabriel laughed and looked up at the waiting nurse, who was smiling indulgently from the doorway. "Thank you, Mrs. Banks; we'll ring when we need you."

She nodded and quietly closed the door.

Gabriel held the squirming little body at arm's length. His hair, curly and dark brown with glints of gold and red, was ruffled up as if he had rolled down the stairs on his head.

"You are burrowing like a desert owl, Samir."

That made the little boy giggle, his hazel eyes pushed into crescents by his plump cheeks.

"I think you have missed me," Gabriel said in English.

"I went to see the *namur*," he said, using the Arabic word for tiger. He spoke in a charming blend of Arabic and French, but very little English. Gabriel spent a part of each visit teaching him English words, and Maria and Giselle did the same.

"What sound does a tiger make?" he asked.

Samir bared his teeth and gave a creditable imitation of a roar.

Maria cowered back on the settee. "You are so fierce that you are frightening me, Sami."

The boy laughed.

"It is naughty to scare ladies and then laugh," Gabriel chided him—and then commenced to engage in a roaring contest, until Maria put an end to it.

"You are two boisterous tigers," she said. "I think perhaps you need to take a walk and expend some of your ferocious energy." This second part was for Gabriel, who grinned and took the hint.

"Come, Samir. We are being banished. Go fetch your coat and hat from Mrs. Banks and meet me in the entry hall."

The little boy hooted and sprinted for the door.

"No running," Gabriel called after him.

He and Maria listened to the thunder of small feet, shaking their heads.

Gabriel picked up the cushions they'd scattered during their play and pushed back his hair, which was no doubt as mussed as Samir's.

"He is such a wonderful boy, Gabriel. How could you bear to let him go?"

He'd been hoping to get out of here today without anyone asking such questions. He shook his head and flopped down onto the settee.

"It is not about what I want, Maria, but what will be best for him. Right now I don't know what that is."

She brushed his jaw with the back of her hand. "Poor Gabriel. You've had a rather trying year, haven't you?"

Gabriel thought about the wreckage that was now his father's palace and shook his head. "I've had a much easier time than many others."

Maria and of course Giselle were two of the very few people who knew about his last trip to Oran and why he'd gone. She kissed his cheek and changed the subject.

"And now you are a married man."

He sighed; this topic wasn't much better. But to avoid it was cowardly, not to mention an injustice to his new wife.

"I must tell her about Samir, Maria—but what do I tell her when even I do not know the truth?"

"I cannot answer that—I do not know her. But I do know well-bred English ladies do not usually accept their husband's offspring by their former lovers."

Gabriel knew that, too. It would be an insult to Drusilla to expect her to live with his by-blow. But it would be an insult to Samir to make him live anywhere else. Regardless of their actual relationship, they were still family. He groaned. All of this would not have been a problem but for blasted Visel goading him into this marriage. He kept such thoughts to himself.

"Tell me," he said, "how does one broach such a conversation with one's new spouse? Over tea and toast? Dinner?"

Maria laid her head on his shoulder, her small body a comfort beside him. "Perhaps after you've made love to her and she is sated and sleepy and malleable?"

Gabriel tried to imagine such a sight as a sated Drusilla Clare—well, Drusilla Marlington now—but could bring to mind only her furious face from this morning. Still, if he couldn't imagine her sated, that was entirely his fault, wasn't it? He should have gone to her last night instead of storming off like a child. But he would go to her tonight. This could not drag on.

He took Maria's hand in both of his. "What would you want—if you were my wife? Would living with a child who was not your own be unbearable? Would you find it a crushing stigma?"

She turned her head, until her chin was resting on his arm. "I am not the right person to ask, my love." Her dark eyes were soft and caressing. "Stigma? Embarrassment?" She gave a throaty chuckle. "You know I care nothing for such things. Life is fleeting and precious; wasting time worrying about pleasing strangers is foolish. As to my feelings on such a matter? Well, I do not seem to feel jealousy like other women or men." She lifted one shoulder in a gesture that was ineffably French. "I have always believed I have enough love to share. I don't need to ration it among the people I care for or hold it close." She gave him an arch look. "If I could share my beloved Giselle with you, I certainly would not begrudge the child of a lover or spouse their own parent—especially when the child was conceived long before we even met."

He kissed her forehead; she was correct. Both she and Giselle had more self-assurance than almost anyone he'd ever met, male or female. Gabriel knew the number three was a difficult number when it came to lovers: a dangerous triangle. But not once in the years they'd been together had there been any jealousy or hurt feelings or competitiveness among the three of them. Was that unnatural? He smiled to himself at the question—there was no denying the rest of the *ton* viewed the arrangement as unnatural.

Perhaps the word he was searching for was *unusual*. Lovers did not usually like to share. He knew his mother and Exley would never share each other. Gabriel had been raised with the expectation that he would eventually have several wives and that *they* would need to learn to share *him*, but never the other way around. He knew relations in his father's harem had never been easy. Some of the women had waged war against one another—a few even resorting to murder to get what they wanted. But he did not think any of his father's wives had been jealous of his father's affection, only jealous of his favor and on whom he bestowed it.

To be truthful, Gabriel knew he could not share a woman he loved with another man; Samir's mother had been an excellent case in point. Perhaps that was wrong of him—especially since he had expected females to accept such behavior from him. It might be wrong, but it was a simple truth.

"We would be overjoyed to keep him, Gabriel."

Maria's voice pulled him out of his memories, and he smiled at her. "I know you would, and this is a loving household. But if he can't be with his mother's family, then he should be with me: I am his family."

"So you will tell her?"

Yes, he would tell Drusilla, and the sooner, the better.

The sound of little feet followed by a slower pair roused him from his reverie, and he disentangled himself from his erstwhile lover and stood.

"Jibril!" Samir called when he realized Gabriel was not waiting in the foyer.

Maria chuckled as Gabriel picked up his hat and gloves. "You'd better make haste as the young master sounds short-tempered. Where will you take him?"

Gabriel pulled on his gloves. "It seems like a nice day for an ice, don't you think?"

Chapter 12

Drusilla had a lot of time alone to think.

First she paid a brief visit to her Aunt Vi, who was staying in the old house for a few weeks to supervise the dismantling of the household before the property was offered for sale. Drusilla had tried to convince her to move with them to the new town house, but the older woman had been adamant.

"You are a newly married couple, Drusilla; you need some time together," her far-too-thin aunt said when Drusilla issued the invitation. "Besides, now that you have a husband to escort you, I believe I will rest for the remainder of the Season and retire early to Bath. You know Maisie has invited me to stay the summer with her and her niece. It shall be pleasant."

Maisie was a distant cousin whom Violet had always been close to, and her niece was a girl not yet out of the schoolroom. No doubt her aunt would enjoy Bath's more gentle entertainments, which only the young and old seemed to truly relish.

After leaving her aunt she considered paying a call on Eva, but her friend's furious, hurt face flashed in her mind's eye, so she left that visit for tomorrow—or maybe even the day after. Besides, she would see Eva at the Renwick ball tonight.

Thinking about the ball made her think about her clothing—a pastime she rarely engaged in. But she was no longer an unwed wallflower; she was the wife of a handsome, sought-after man. It behooved her at least not to shame him when she went out in public. A dress flashed into her head—it was a gown she knew had been made and then not been paid for. She'd seen it at Maison d'Hortense when she'd gone with Eva to pick up a new white muslin to replace a dress her friend had ruined with some food item or other.

"You should buy that," Eva had told her when she'd noticed Drusilla eyeing it.

The gown was a deep shade of teal, an unusual blue-green silk that had made her fingers twitch to touch it. She loved colors and fine fabrics, but she tended to order more serviceable clothing. It wasn't only her academic reservations concerning finery, but also the fact so many people had nothing—why did she need a hundred gowns that she would wear only once? And so she wore her simple gowns many times. She kept the minimum in her dressing room, giving away an old gown whenever she bought another and keeping her selection of clothing sparse. Sparse enough to drive her maid to distraction. But now . . . didn't she have some duty to her husband? A duty to not always appear the dowd?

Oh, she was so weak; she was just lying to herself. All she wanted was to make him see her—not as an object of pity he'd needed to rescue, but as a desirable woman.

A new dress is hardly likely to do that. You will not be different—only the dress.

Drusilla did not want to *become* a different woman, but she wouldn't mind *looking* like a more attractive one. Surely there was no sin in wanting to make the most of the gifts one had?

Perhaps the gown was still available?

* * *

Fletcher had just finished with Drusilla's hair and was securing her small pearl drop earrings when the door to her dressing room opened and Gabriel entered. Drusilla had to pull her eyes away from his powerful body, which she had often imagined bestride some stallion charging through a desert, but which also looked every bit as natural in stark white-and-black evening clothing, his hair glowing like a banked fire.

He met her gaze in the mirror and smiled. "Good evening, Drusilla." His eyes drifted to Fletcher, who was fiddling with something in her jewelry case.

"You may go, Fletcher. And you needn't wait up tonight."

The maid left without a word, her cheeks flaming.

Gabriel came to stand behind her, their gazes locked.

"This is a new gown, I think? Or at least I have not seen it before." His expression was one of surprise and it immediately put her on the defensive—but not as much as his admission that he might have noticed what gowns she wore, which left her feeling almost light-headed.

"I thought this color was more suitable for a married woman than white. I am not profligate when it comes to clothing. Or at least I hope not. I saw this last week when I was out with Eva and thought it was an unusual color." She stopped, her cheeks also an unusual color.

He looked amused by her babbling. "It is a lovely color and you look very fine." His eyes dropped to the snug, low bodice, a bodice that was moving up and down more quickly than was normal. "You have very beautiful skin—like a pearl." His eyes lingered on her breasts, which were mounded over the top of the bodice. Her breasts had always embarrassed her. They were large—far too large for her small rib cage, and she usually did her best to reduce the appearance of their size. But this gown had already been cut, and there was nothing Madame Hortense could do to create a more modest neckline. And of course one did not wear lace fichus with ball gowns.

He looked up and caught her with lips parted in shock. She closed her mouth.

"It was your skin which made me think of this for you."

She saw he was carrying a rather large jewelry box.

"This is a belated gift to thank you for agreeing to be my wife."

Drusilla's hands shook when she took the box, and she stared at the lovely inlaid patterns on the lid rather than her husband's face. She was no stranger to jewels, even though she didn't wear most of them. Her father had lavished them on her, and there was a king's ransom in the safe. But this was different. Gabriel had picked out something for her?

She flipped up the lid and gasped. "Oh."

He chuckled and she looked up. "Is that a good *oh*? Or a bad *oh*?"

"It is a very good *oh*. These are so lovely."

His cheeks darkened with pleasure. "I am relieved to have selected something you like. Here, let me help you put them on." He reached into the box and removed the five joined strands of pearls that were held together with a gold clasp inlaid with diamonds. His long, elegant fingers were intensely masculine against the creamy, silky pearls.

"The jeweler called this a choker." She stared at his hands as they hovered over her shoulders and then lifted the strands against her throat. "Not only do they look lovely with your skin, but I knew this design would be flattering to your neck, which is long and elegant."

Her breath froze in her chest. She wrenched her eyes up to his, but he was looking at the clasp he was fastening, unaware of the impact of his words. It was pitiful to experience such crippling pleasure at such a minor comment. But only her aunt and father had ever complimented her appearance, and they'd made just the obligatory "you look pretty" type of comment she knew was not true. But a long, elegant neck? She turned her head slightly as he continued to fiddle with the clasp. Yes, she *did* have a rather nice neck—why had she not noticed before?

"There," he said, his gaze turning back to the glass, his mouth curving into a genuine smile. "They suit you." He absently caressed the jewels, his fingers grazing her skin, his pupils flaring. They stared at each other, and Drusilla realized she wasn't the only one whose breathing was uneven. His gaze dropped back to the box.

"Remove your earrings and put these on," he instructed in his usual arrogant style. She decided to forgive him for it this time and did as he bade her. Each earring was a pearl dropped from a large solitary diamond, the design simple and extremely elegant.

"Thank you. I—I like both gifts very much." Drusilla knew the dress and jewels didn't transform her into a diamond of the first water, but she did look her best.

His expression turned serious. "It will be uncomfortable tonight. We will have to acknowledge Visel."

"I understand."

"It is probable he will ask you for a dance."

"I assumed he would."

"And you are prepared?"

His concern warmed her. "I will be fine."

He laid a hand on her shoulder, his body hot through the fine silk of her sleeve. "I will be there to support you—should you need me. And our family will also be there."

Drusilla was still struggling with the words to thank him when he turned away. She resolved to thank him at some point tonight. She wanted him to know she appreciated his gesture and regretted the friction between them. Yes, she would tell him so tonight.

He returned, holding a long wisp of teal gauze. "This is your wrap?" She nodded, luxuriating in the brushes of his warm fingers as he arranged the silky fabric over her shoulders.

"There," he said, lowering both hands lightly onto her shoulders and studying their reflection.

In the mirror was a young couple. He was a creature of masculine perfection, and she—while not beautiful—was a not-unattractive woman with a graceful neck and beautiful skin now stained with a fetching blush.

Drusilla smiled at him, and his eyes widened. Did she really smile so rarely?

He held out his arm. "Shall we go slay the dragon?"

Gabriel held out his hand to his sister. "Will you honor me with a dance, Evil?'

She lost her surly look and rolled her eyes, her exquisite features illuminating the room like a flaming branch of candles.

"You never tire of that, do you, Brother?"

"Tormenting a younger sibling is one of life's true pleasures."

She laughed, and they took their places for the waltz. Gabriel could feel the tension in her hand and body.

"What is wrong?" he asked.

She glanced up, worrying her lip so hard it made him wince. "What makes you think anything is wrong?"

"You haven't said a word to Drusilla—not through dinner and not on the carriage ride here."

She shrugged, her eyes restlessly sweeping the room.

"Eva?"

Her unusual blue-violet eyes narrowed. "Honestly, Gabe, just leave me be. You get to do whatever you choose—engage in swordplay, keep mistresses—and I am allowed no say in my life, not even when it comes to my own private thoughts."

Gabriel could not believe it. "What the devil do you know about my mistresses?" he demanded in a low voice.

"No more than anyone else in our circle."

He swore in Arabic, and she lifted her eyebrows, making him remember he'd taught her most of the words when he'd been young and foolish. Well, younger and more foolish.

"Do people have nothing better to do than carry tales about my doings?" he demanded.

"Not when your *doings* are so very wicked."

He snorted.

"Besides, what do you care? It's not as if anyone does anything to stop you. Just imagine how annoyed you'd be if you were *me*. And here you are, grilling me like the Inquisition, as if even the contents of my head are not my own." Her voice rose as she repeated her earlier complaint. "It hardly seems fair that I'm not even allowed to keep my thoughts to myself."

"Keep your voice down," he said. "People are staring."

"Oh, shut up, Gabriel. And quit asking me questions. You know I need to count while I dance."

Luckily the music commenced, and they could concentrate on the dance. Eva had not been jesting: she *did* need to count. She was one of the worst dancers he had ever seen. How a woman who was such a superb equestrienne could be so clumsy, Gabriel would never know.

She stared down at their feet, her lips moving, as he guided her out of the way of a white-haired couple who moved in perfect concert and with enviable ease. He let his gaze wander over the dancers, easily picking out Drusilla, who was dancing with Exley. The marquess was an excellent partner who probably made any woman appear graceful, but Gabriel could see Drusilla was an accomplished dancer. He realized he'd never had a waltz with her. Indeed, they'd danced no more than a handful of times, and those usually under duress. Tonight, when they'd danced the opening set, had been the first time he'd partnered her out of interest rather than a sense of obligation, but it had not been a waltz. He grimaced at his past behavior. He'd allowed their childish rivalry and bickering to deter him from doing his duty as a gentleman and now—

Eva made a guttural noise, and Gabriel followed her gaze: Visel had appeared. The duke was not in sight and the younger man appeared to have arrived without his usual band of cronies. He stood beside his hosts, who were speaking and smiling at him while he surveyed the ballroom, as if looking for something.

"They say Visel is mad."

It was Gabriel's turn to stumble. *"What?"*

Heads turned in their direction at his expostulation, and Gabriel leaned closer to Eva and lowered his voice. "What the devil are you talking about?"

"I heard he has the male hysteria."

He was momentarily nonplussed, and then: "Who told you that?"

"What does it matter who told me? Is it true?"

Gabriel looked at the man in question, as if careful study would somehow help answer her question. The war hysteria? He supposed it was possible. Visel had fought for over a decade, and Gabriel knew the toll war could take. While he'd not engaged in the vast battles on the Continent, he'd lived with war for almost a year after his father died. His desert campaign against his brother had been on a small scale, but the strain of around-the-clock conflict wore on men—it had certainly worn on Gabriel.

Was that what was wrong with Visel and why he mindlessly persecuted Gabriel? Was the man suffering some mental trauma and Gabriel just happened to be the unfortunate individual his fixation had settled on?

"Look. He's staring at you, Gabriel."

Visel had left his hosts and come into the ballroom. He was

indeed turned in their direction although he was too far away to see his eyes.

"Perhaps he is staring at you, Eva. You are quite beautiful, even though you refuse to admit it."

She didn't seem to hear the compliment. "Are you sorry he apologized?"

"Of course, I'm not sorry. Did you think I *wanted* to fight him?"

"I don't know. Did you?"

He would like to beat the man black-and-blue, but he didn't want to kill him. Eva didn't need to know that. "No."

She made a skeptical humming sound, which he ignored.

"I'd like to fight him myself," she said when he failed to comment. "With swords rather than pistols so I could make it last a good, long time."

Gabriel could believe it; his little stepsister was fierce. She would have made a good man, and he'd often thought it was a pity she'd been born a woman. And such a beautiful one, at that.

"Are you angry at Drusilla?" he asked, not interested in discussing the subjects of Visel, war-induced hysteria, or duels.

She held his gaze for a long, stubborn moment before speaking. "Not really, not anymore."

"Well then I do wish you'd patch up whatever it is that is bothering you, Eva. Haven't we all endured enough emotional turmoil these past days to last us the rest of the year?" He recalled too late that ironic sarcasm was not the best approach to use with Eva.

Her body stiffened under his hands, and she glared fire up at him. "You aren't my father, Gabe, so quit behaving as if you are."

"I would if you'd quit behaving like a child," he retorted.

"Look who's talking. You still engage in duels."

Gabriel took a deep breath, counted to ten, and tried again.

"Drusilla has had a difficult time of it, and I'd prefer not to have her upset yet again."

"Perhaps you should have thought of that before you left her alone on your wedding night to go gallivanting about town."

Gabriel gaped.

She didn't look away, but a red stain was creeping up her neck.

"What the devil are you talking about, Eva?"

"You were obviously at White's, since Visel found you there and apologized to you—didn't he?"

Her reasoning was unassailable, but somehow he thought that was not the whole of it.

"I don't wish to argue with you, Eva."

"Then don't."

He studied her beautiful, rigid profile and sighed. When she was in one of these moods, it didn't matter how much a person cajoled her: she wouldn't leave her irritation behind until she was ready. Luckily the music indicated the dance was about to end, so he could drop the matter, telling himself a dance floor was hardly the place for a discussion of such a subject—and certainly not with his mercurial sister.

They returned to where Lady Exley sat with several other married women. Gabriel thought his mother was looking rather pale and cursed the need to drag her out in such a condition. Although she would deny it, each pregnancy seemed to be harder than the last. But she'd insisted on being here and also attending the theater tomorrow night.

"I can offer my support for these two appearances, Jibril," she'd said when he'd tried to argue. Gabriel had looked to the marquess, but Exley had, surprisingly, agreed.

"I don't like it, either, but we need to provide a unified front. And these are the two events you've discussed with Visel. We should all be there."

So, here she was, wan and exhausted, but at least she was sitting.

"Can I get you something to drink, Mama?"

Her gaze flickered over his shoulder, and she smiled. Gabriel knew who was behind him before he even turned.

"Thank you, Jibril, but you may see to your wife and sister."

Drusilla went to sit beside Eva while the marquess came toward his wife, exchanging a glance with her that appeared to contain entire conversations. "Lemonade, my dear?"

"Thank you, Adam. I would love a glass." When he turned to go fetch her drink, she gestured Gabriel closer. "We will slip out during supper, Jibril."

"You needn't stay, Mama. The first rush of fascination is over. People are beginning to lose interest. Eva can stay with us and I will bring her home. We will be fine."

"I know *you* are fine, my son, but how is Drusilla? This cannot be easy for her."

"No, but she is a strong woman." He smiled. "Like another woman I know."

Again her gaze flickered over his shoulder, but this time her smile was cool rather than melting. The hairs on Gabriel's neck rose as he turned.

"Ah, and this must be Lord Visel," the marchioness said, her tone like an arctic cold front.

The tall blond man flashed her a smile of genuine amusement as he took her hand and bowed low over it. "And *you* must be the famed Lady Exley." He lowered his mouth over her gloved hand but—wisely—did not touch it with his lips. Even so, Gabriel bristled at the sight of this man touching his mother.

As if sensing the incipient violence, Lady Exley pulled her hand away, cutting Gabriel a mildly repressive look.

"You are even lovelier than I'd heard, my lady." Visel didn't appear to notice his mother's frosty expression. Instead, his eyes moved on to Eva and Drusilla. "Lady Eva, Mrs. Marlington, please let me take this opportunity to apologize for my behavior the other evening."

Drusilla eyed him with a cool, unruffled stare that made Gabriel proud. "I'm ready to put the entire affair behind me, my lord."

"As am I," Eva added, her face almost dangerously composed. Gabriel felt a twinge of apprehension as he looked at his sister's tight expression, but Visel's smile only grew.

"You are indeed generous in your forgiveness. I hope it extends to a dance with each of you? Perhaps the next set, Mrs. Marlington?"

"I'm engaged for the next set but free the one after that."

Visel nodded and turned to Eva, his air expectant.

"I only have the supper dance free, my lord."

Gabriel knew that was a lie. In fact, it would surprise him if there was even one slot filled on her dance card. What was she *doing*? By dancing the supper set with Visel, she was dooming herself to dining with him.

The earl grinned as if well pleased. "I'm honored." He dropped a bow, cut Gabriel a glance that was sharper than a razor, and took himself off.

Just as at White's, it was not until the conversation was over that Gabriel realized just how quiet the ballroom had gone around them.

Drusilla was glad to be sitting down. The confrontation, although clothed in civility, had been the most tension-filled minutes she could remember.

Seeing Visel and Gabriel a mere foot apart, and under the bright light of the chandeliers, had made her realize the men were almost physical equals. If Visel was a hair taller, then Gabriel was a little stockier. The men had reminded her of an animal trainer she'd gone to see when she was a girl. The man had exhibited a mongoose and a cobra, the animals such inherent enemies they'd been frozen with ire—until one of them had struck, moving faster than the eye.

She'd had the same feeling tonight—although it would be difficult to say who was the cobra and who was the mongoose.

"Drusilla?"

She pulled her gaze away from Visel's departing back and looked up into the concerned face of her husband.

"Are you committed for this set?"

She shook her head. She'd only told Visel the next set because she knew she would need some time to prepare her wits.

"Would you like to take a stroll on the terrace?"

She stood immediately. "Yes."

The way the crowd parted told her everyone had been listening and watching the exchange with Visel. The murmur of voices right now was like the hiss of the surf as the gossip made its way to the far reaches of the ballroom.

"Ah, this is pleasant," he said, once they stepped from the sweltering room. He glanced down at her. "Would you like me to fetch your wrap?"

"No, the air is lovely."

"Shall we follow the lanterns? They seem to have been placed out here for that purpose." He led her down the steps into a sizeable garden, following behind several other couples, most of whom would need to remain within sight of their chaperones. The hedges had been trimmed and shaped to form a series of concentric circles with breaks, the inner circle containing a huge fountain that held pride of place. It was flanked by stone benches, the colorful lanterns more sparsely spaced on their wrought iron holders. It was . . . romantic.

He led her to a bench, and she sat while he propped one

foot on it and leaned over his bent knee until their faces were not far from each other. The nearest lantern had a blue glass cover, and the cool light bathed his handsome features in silver and made him seem as distant as the moon.

"That was not so terrible," she said, uncomfortable with his silent regard.

"Yes, but you've still to dance with him."

"Just one dance, and that will be the end of it."

"Hmm. I meant to ask you sooner—are you free for the supper dance?"

"But—" She bit her lip, not wanting to say the next words.

"But what? Surely you cannot be thinking a man cannot ask his brand-new wife to have supper with him?"

She couldn't help smiling at his arrogant tone. "It will be our second dance this evening."

He shrugged. "You are free? And if you are not, you can disappoint the other gentleman."

She shook her head to hide the joy leaping inside her. "You are incorrigible. Do you always get your way?"

He gave her a smoldering look. "Always."

Drusilla felt as if she'd been brushed with fire. He was flirting with her—just as she'd seen him flirt hundreds of times with other women over the past few months. But now he was flirting with *her*, even though he did not need to expend the effort. She was his under the law to treat however he pleased; he did not need to charm her to bed her.

She realized he was still staring at her in a way that seemed to consume her. In fact, she'd rejected two offers for the supper dance earlier—unheard of for her—hoping he might ask "Yes, I am free."

He nodded, taking her acquiescence for granted. Drusilla tried to work up some outrage, but found she couldn't. After all, it was a dance with her he was arrogantly commandeering—how could she dislike that?

"Why do you think Eva would give Visel the supper dance?" he asked, changing the subject.

"I've been wondering about that myself."

He cocked his head. "And you cannot ask her?"

She opened her mouth, and then closed it again.

"Come, Drusilla, why are you two out of sorts with each other? I asked her, but she would not tell me. She is in ill humor tonight—I don't envy Visel his supper with her. If he is not careful, he will end up with a fork in his forehead or a plate of food in his lap."

"She is very angry at me."

"I gathered as much. You don't wish to tell me why?"

"I will tell you if you demand it, but I would rather not."

He straightened at her cool tone and clipped words, lowering his foot and stepping back, the intimacy between them gone as suddenly as it had come. "You are under no compunction to share your thoughts or secrets with me."

He didn't sound any different, but Drusilla knew her words had hurt him. She reached out and touched his hand, and he glanced down at her, his eyebrows arched, his expression proud and haughty.

"I didn't mean to repulse you. I would like to tell you, but I would ask you not to speak of it to anyone else."

"Of course, what you tell me is in confidence."

His posture was stiff and he was frowning, and she realized she'd impugned his honor yet again: gentlemen did not carry tales. Lord, would she ever get this right?

"Eva came to me with the location and time of your duel. She wanted me to go and watch with her." She decided to leave out the matter of Eva's clothing *and* her Visel-related espionage.

He sucked in a noisy breath and let it out along with a few harsh-sounding words in Arabic. He pinned her with his gaze. "I take it you said *no*, hence the argument?"

She hesitated, and he sat down beside her. "Go ahead. I will not speak of this to Eva or my parents."

"I threatened to tell the marquess if she went alone."

He grimaced. "Ah, I see why she is so angry."

"Should I not have done so?" she asked, her tone sharp.

He smiled. "Shhh. You remind me of a creature we have back home."

"I look like a *creature*?"

"*Tsk*, my precise wife, you did not listen. I said you *remind* me of this creature, not that you look like it. It is called a porcupine—you have heard of it?"

"Yes, of course, an animal with some sort of spines?"

"They are covered in sharp quills; it is their defense mechanism—they display their quills when threatened." He rubbed the top of her hand, his thumb warm through the fine kid glove. "You do the same with me—you always have." He leaned in and breathed into her ear. "Why do you display your quills? To scare me away?" She sat frozen as he stroked from her hand up her leather-sheathed forearm, not stopping until he reached the place where glove met skin just above her elbow. She shivered with pleasure.

"I do no such thing." Her voice was breathy and not her own.

"Mm-hmm, you do." He brushed her lobe with his lips as he whispered, "Put down your quills, Drusilla. I would like to come closer and touch you."

She stiffened. "But—but somebody might *see* us."

"We are married—kissing, and more—is permitted." His mouth caressed the sensitive skin of her neck, and she sucked in a noisy lungful of air. The sound acted as some sort of catalyst, and he slipped a hand around her nape and turned her to face him, his other hand at her waist, his lips moving across her jaw until they reached her mouth, where he began to feather kisses.

"So soft," he whispered, the words hot against her skin.

She was breathing loudly, her soughing, uneven gasps drowning out even the stridulation of the evening insects.

"I like kissing and touching you far better than fighting with you, Drusilla." He paused, nibbling her jaw, an area she'd never thought of as particularly sensitive. Until now. "Do you like me touching you? Kissing you?"

She swallowed convulsively, not trusting herself to speak.

He pulled back and she opened her eyes, but he did not release her. Instead, he studied her with huge pupils and stroked her cheek with his thumb. "I want you." His nostrils flared. "I *desire* you. I want to make you my wife. Tonight I will come to you." His voice had lost its usual smooth, low timber, and it made her heart thrash and swell: he wanted her.

"Yes," she said, the only word she could manage to squeeze out. But it was enough.

He lowered his mouth over hers, the hot tip of his tongue tracing the seam. He nibbled her, licked her, sucked her—she lost track of what he was doing, until his tongue slid between her parted lips. Drusilla started.

"Shhh," he murmured, kissing and nibbling her lower lip. "Let me inside."

Her head spun at his words and the tone with which they'd been uttered.

She opened and he slid inside, his tongue stroking hers, teasing a response. Drusilla was hesitant at first, but his low growl of encouragement made her bolder and she accepted his invitation to explore. She gloried in his taste, smell, and texture, and invaded him more deeply and with growing confidence. When she took his tongue between her lips and sucked, he groaned, his arm tightening around her, making her realize he'd been feathering touches up and down her side, his hand hot against the silk of her gown.

He kissed her once more and then pulled slowly back.

When she opened her eyes, she saw that his were black and

heavy lidded. His lips seemed fuller and redder, and his breathing was uneven and labored.

He gave a slight shake of his head, his smile gentle as he tucked a straying curl behind her ear. "Drusilla." His voice pulsed with . . . something.

His other hand continued its caressing while they held each other's gazes. Never had she imagined she would see such an expression on his face: he *wanted* her.

He sighed, leaned close, gave her a brief kiss, and then stood, turning away to make some adjustment to his clothing before turning back and holding out his hand.

"Come," he said, "let us get the next few hours over with and then we can scheme some way to get out of here early."

When they reentered the ballroom, Drusilla was stunned to find that life was still moving on as usual. How could that be? Out in the garden the earth seemed to have altered—or the air had thinned, or her body had begun to float away, or *something*.

He *wanted* her. Gabriel Marlington, the perfect star always beyond reach, wanted *her*. The knowledge left her breathless, as if she'd been dropped suddenly from a great height. He wanted her.

"Ah, it appears we returned just in time," Gabriel said, leaning down to whisper in her ear, the intimate gesture causing a tightening that began in her chest and shot down to the place between her thighs. So *this* was what it was like not to be a wallflower? To be with a handsome man? She cut a furtive glance around the room beneath her lashes and saw female eyes trained on her with envy.

"Mrs. Marlington, I believe this is my set?"

They turned to find Visel behind them, his arm extended. Gabriel squeezed her hand and released her.

Lord Visel's blond good looks were angelic, but the expression in his celestial eyes was hard: he was not a happy man.

They took their positions, his gaze never leaving her. "How are you enjoying married life thus far, Mrs. Marlington?" He did not speak loudly, but the words would have reached those around them, all of whom were behaving as if their ears weren't stretched to capacity to listen to this most fascinating of conversations.

Drusilla realized he was trying to discompose her, expecting her marriage was not a happy union.

She gave him what she hoped was a smug, self-satisfied smile. "I find that it suits me very well, my lord."

The music began, and it was a few moments before he could respond. They came together, and he bowed over her hand before leading her into formation, the two of them side by side.

"I'm very pleased to hear that, Mrs. Marlington. I'm afraid I inferred—from your husband's presence at White's on your wedding night—that matters between you might be rather . . . unsettled."

Drusilla stumbled slightly. *How dare he!*

"Is aught amiss?" His question was solicitous, but the glint in his eyes was avid.

They broke the figure and she was spared from answering. It was just as well, because she pulsed with fury. Her face was hot and she could only hope she was not glowing like a lighthouse beacon. Plainly he was trying to make mischief, and that should have made his behavior easier to dismiss. However, the fact that Gabriel *had* left on their wedding night merely provided grist for people like him.

Any hope that her anger would go unnoticed was dashed when they next came into contact.

"I can see my comment upset you," he said in a low voice, gracefully guiding her into the turn. "I didn't mean to, but I seem to be making a dreadful hash of my apology." His mobile, shapely lips were turned down at the corners, giving the appearance of contrition. Drusilla knew better.

She ignored him, hoping he would shut up. Unfortunately, he either did not notice or did not care.

"It's just that . . . well, I feel somewhat responsible for what has happened to you—for your marriage to Marlington."

"You take quite a lot upon yourself, sir."

He smiled at her chilly tone. "It is the guilt, you see. If only I could be sure of your happiness." He hesitated, as if he were indecisive, and then said, "But that is not my place—I beg your pardon. Besides, I can see you are both putting on your best face."

Drusilla followed his gaze to where Gabriel was dancing—with the Kitten. All the joy she'd felt earlier drained away like liquid down a funnel. The two beautiful people were laughing as they danced, their movements easy and confident, as if they'd danced together a hundred times before. Which Drusilla knew they had, because each time she'd seen them was etched into her soul.

"I shouldn't worry," Visel said, interrupting her agony. He wore an expression of regret that seemed genuine. "Neither of them appears heartbroken."

Drusilla met that comment with the stony silence it deserved.

"Tell me," the earl said, the next time the dance brought them together, "how are you enjoying being part of such a big family?"

The innocuous question aroused her suspicion, but she could hardly ignore a direct question. "Very much, thank you."

"I was surprised to learn that even Mr. Marlington's family from Oran managed to make an appearance at your nuptials—I didn't see the boy's parents, just Mr. Marlington walking with the handsome little fellow in the park."

Drusilla stared. "I beg your pardon?"

Visel's eyes became wide, and he grimaced. "I'm devilishly sorry, ma'am—it seems I—dash it!" He bit his lip, and Drusilla fumed through the next several minutes until they were once again close enough to speak.

"I apologize, ma'am. I must have mistaken Marlington for somebody else."

Only by sheer force of will was Drusilla able to lift her eyebrows and give him a cool smile, once again saved by a break in the dance from having to respond.

Just what was the man up to? Whatever it was, Drusilla knew it involved mischief.

Chapter 13

Gabriel had hoped to sit with Eva and Visel at their supper table, but there were no places available when he and Drusilla made their way through the crowd into the area set aside for dining.

Instead, unfortunately, Lucinda Kittridge saw them looking about for seats and sent her companion over to fetch them. He wanted to groan. He had already engaged in one heated interaction with her this evening—in the middle of the bloody dance floor. Tonight seemed the night for that. She'd taunted him about Drusilla so relentlessly that he'd finally been forced to point out how unbecoming her jealousy was.

That had made her beautiful, jewel-like eyes fly open. "*Jealous?* Of—of *her*?"

Gabriel had bristled at the scorn in her voice. "Have a care, Miss Kittridge. That is my wife you are speaking of."

The remainder of the dance had passed in false laughter and smiles.

"Lucy would like you both to join us," Lord Deveril said, his soft, peach fuzz–covered cheeks flushing as he extended the invitation. Gabriel could just bet she did. No doubt her plans would be unpleasant.

Still, what else could he do but say, "We would be honored," and nod at the younger man, whom he'd played cards with on several occasions. Deveril was a shy, spindly, and pockmarked young fellow, but he would inherit an earldom one day: no doubt the reason he was Lucy's partner for the supper dance.

Gabriel felt Drusilla stiffen beside him at the invitation and looked down as he followed Deveril. Her face had the set, superior expression he had always associated with her in the past—not the sweet, soft, almost affectionate look she'd given him in the garden. A sudden insight struck: this was her mask—for those times she felt insecure, it must be. How had he been so foolish not to notice? She was far cleverer and more interesting than the kittenish Miss Kittridge—even if her tongue was also sharper—but the other woman was, undoubtedly, far more physically beautiful, so it must be insecurity about her appearance. But then she was best friends with Eva, a woman even more lovely than Lucy. Perhaps it was something else?

Gabriel drew her arm closer, feeling an overwhelming urge to protect her wash over him. It surprised him—and surprised her, if her quick glance was anything to go by.

Lucy and another couple—people whose names Gabriel could not recall—were already seated when they arrived.

"Mr. and Mrs. Marlington," Lucy gushed, her remarkable blue eyes flickering from Drusilla to Gabriel. "I told Deveril that I absolutely *must* have the *ton*'s newest couple at my table."

Gabriel waited until Drusilla was seated before taking Lucy's hand and bowing over it, ignoring the almost painful squeezing of his fingers such a delicate hand could inflict. "What a dark horse you are, Gabe. I was just telling Deveril that I had no idea you and Drusilla were such fast . . . friends."

Gabriel ignored the unconcealed dig. Instead, he smiled. "I

think I speak for both myself and my wife when I say thank you, Miss Kittridge."

Her laugh—a sound that was truly heavenly, even though he now knew it held nothing but thwarted anger—filled the air like chamber music. "Oh please, we were Gabriel and Lucy before—I do hope that won't change now that you are married?" She cut Drusilla an arch look.

Drusilla returned her look with a slight, almost contemptuous twist of her lips. "Indeed no, Miss Kittridge. Rest assured that Gabriel's name remains the same; only my surname has changed."

Gabriel bit back a smile.

"How you must dislike that, Mrs. Marlington." Lucy was looking at Drusilla with a notch of concern between her luminous eyes.

Drusilla blinked. "I beg your pardon?"

"Changing your name—isn't that something your heroine, Mary Wollstonecraft, advocated? That women should not have to take their husband's names?"

"No thank you," Drusilla said to the footman who'd arrived to pour her a glass of wine. She turned back to Lucy. "I must say I am pleased, Miss Kittridge. I did not know you'd read Miss Wollstonecraft's books."

Lucy frowned, the expression a petulant moue. "But I haven't."

"Ahh." Drusilla's features were arranged in an expression of patient understanding.

Gabriel's face ached from suppressing a grin. His wife was a mistress of subtle but oh-so-effective snubs—who should know that better than he? Even so, being the focus of the Kitten's claws could not be enjoyable.

Gabriel laid a hand on her forearm. "Will you come help me select our supper, my dear?"

She flashed him a look of gratitude and anger mingled with fierce pride. But it was replaced in an instant by cool, imperturbable acceptance taking its place. "I should be pleased to."

Gabriel took two plates from the hovering servant. "I will do the heavy lifting if you choose for us."

"You trust me to select your food?"

"It is a weighty burden, I know. I trust you are up to the challenge?"

"You'd better behave, *Mr. Marlington*, or I'll fill your plate with nothing but pilchards."

Gabriel's stared in mock horror. "God no—they can't have such horrid things here, can they?" She laughed, as he was hoping she would. "Who the devil told you I loathed pilchards?" he asked, holding out both plates for lobster patties.

"Eva frightened you with one," she said, placing two on each plate. "Several times, if I recall."

"I take great offense at the word *frighten*, ma'am."

"Oh?" She gestured to a platter of thin slices of ham, and he nodded. "And what word would you use, sir?"

"*Menace*, or perhaps *brandish*. Yes, definitely *brandish*."

"One *brandishes* pilchards?" She was openly grinning as she put a cluster of purple grapes on each plate.

Gabriel nodded, transfixed: Lord, she was a bloody siren when she smiled.

He realized she was waiting for a response and gave her an exaggeratedly lofty look. "Yes, it is most assuredly brandishing. It is a little-known fact, but pilchards were at one time offered along with pistols and swords. Thankfully, that barbaric practice has been discontinued."

She made a choking sound, the tongs she was holding shaking with her suppressed laughter.

Gabriel was foolishly pleased to have made such a serious

woman laugh with his silliness. "Oh, please, some of those strawberries, Mrs. Marlington. Yes, that big one fits just nicely on my plate—no, no—do not try to take it for yourself."

She laughed outright.

"I know that is what you were thinking, ma'am, and I must say I'm disappointed you would try to cheat your lord and master out of the finest bounty," he chided.

She responded by piling a half-dozen more berries on his plate, and it was his turn to laugh. "Enough, enough—you've got me on my knees—I beg for mercy."

They'd reached the end of the buffet, and she laid aside the serving fork and glanced up at him, her eyes glowing. "Hmm," she said, her look arch. "You are not on your knees nor do you sound like you are begging, to me."

He leaned close and whispered in her ear, "Would you like to have me begging on my knees, Drusilla?"

Her cheeks blushed furiously, but she coolly retorted. "I *know* Miss Kittridge would. Preferably while crawling over burning coals."

Gabriel laughed.

As he accompanied her back to their table, Gabriel felt a sense of hope for the first time since this debacle had started.

He realized that Drusilla's dry playfulness must be one of the qualities Eva prized in his new wife. That shouldn't have surprised him; after all, a mutual appreciation of the absurd was something that had drawn Gabriel and Eva together from the first time they'd met. It seemed Drusilla was a kindred spirit. Why was it that he'd taken so long to see this in her—her light, witty, and amusing side?

Unfortunately, her laughter had dissipated by the time they returned to the table.

The following half hour was filled with barbs so finely

honed the average person would be unlikely to recognize them as such. Even so, the atmosphere at their table was underlaid with a tension even the witless Deveril and the other young couple could not fail to miss. As for Drusilla? How she kept her cool in the face of Lucy's incessant attacks was a mystery. Gabriel soon realized Miss Kittridge was anything but a kitten. In fact, he would compare her to a tigress—one who'd been thwarted and did not relinquish her prey without a struggle.

Her behavior was not only astonishing, it was fatiguing and annoying. Just what did she hope to achieve by such a display? He was already married; making a spectacle of their prior attachment could only make Drusilla uncomfortable and embarrass him. What she ought to be doing was sitting with Visel and working her wiles on him. Which made him recall his sister.

While Lucy prodded and poked, Gabriel tried to keep an eye on the table where Eva sat with Visel and two of his cronies and their partners. Of course, he could not hear the conversation, but he could see by Eva's rather fierce expression and the flushed faces of their tablemates that she was probably behaving as badly—if not as subtly—as Lucy.

Lord, what an evening.

At least his mother and the marquess were not here to witness the small dramas being played out. They'd left just before supper.

"You needn't concern yourself with Eva, Jibril," his mother had said as she and Exley prepared to leave. "Elizabeth is here." Elizabeth was his great-aunt on his mother's side, a matronly woman who'd launched five daughters of her own. "She will see that Eva returns home tonight."

"Are you sure Aunt Elizabeth is up to the challenge?" Gabriel had asked, not entirely jesting. Even with all her experience, his aunt was no match for Eva when she went on a tear.

As she was showing dangerous signs of doing with Visel this evening.

But his mother had merely patted his hand. "Go home, Jibril." She'd given him a sly smile. "You are a newlywed."

Her laughter had followed him even after he turned away and left her with the marquess. His mother was relentless.

Chapter 14

Tonight Drusilla permitted Fletcher to dress her in the finest nightgown she owned. But even that was not much to look at. She supposed she should purchase new bedclothes now that she was a married woman. Wasn't that what women did? Wore attractive negligees?

Drusilla shuddered at the thought of putting on such a garment and presenting herself to her beautiful husband.

The evening had been unpleasant in parts—especially supper—but her time in the garden with Gabriel and their silly banter at the buffet had made all the uncomfortable bits of the ball melt into insignificance.

He wanted to make this marriage work. He was almost . . . courting her. She just needed to suppress her insecurities, raging jealousy, and suspicious, judgmental nature.

I need to stop and think before I speak. She knew that—impulsiveness had always been her worst fault. And when you coupled that with a swift and rather barbed tongue, it led to poor results. And with Gabriel it always led to arguments. Tonight she would be different. She would—

A light tap on the door made her spin around. He was in

the open doorway between their dressing rooms, once again wearing the deep red silk robe. But, unlike this morning, she saw no pantaloons beneath it.

He lifted his hands to reveal a bottle and two glasses. "I brought my last bottle. Would you care for a glass?"

"Yes, please."

He smiled at her while his hands worked on the cork. "Do you like the wine? Or are you merely being polite?"

"Both."

He laughed. "You are a diplomat."

She smiled like an idiot.

He brought her a glass and gestured to the seating area. "Shall we sit?"

Her legs were wobbly and she was grateful for the opportunity to gather her wits. At the same time, she was anxious to get this awkward part of their lives over and done with. Still, she could hardly say such a thing.

"I think tonight went well," he said, taking a sip of wine.

"So do I. We shall see them again tomorrow?"

"Yes, His Grace indicated he would be occupying his box, which was his way of letting us know he would pay us a visit." He shrugged. "Of course, he did not come tonight, so who knows?" He cocked his head at her. "What is it?"

"What is what?"

"I think you want to say something, but have decided against it."

"Am I that easy for you to read?"

He just smiled.

"I was wondering why Visel seems to dislike you so much. I couldn't help feeling he might have apologized, but he was not really sorry."

"I agree. He seems to be driven by something. Tonight Eva suggested perhaps he is a victim of male hysteria."

Drusilla considered that while also considering the matter of the little boy the earl had mentioned. She decided to leave that be—at least for the moment. Instead she said, "Well, he was away a long time—a decade, I believe. But how would his war experience manifest itself into hatred of you?"

"I don't know. It was Eva's notion. I personally think he simply hates *what* I am more than *who* I am. But come," he said, setting down his glass and standing. "That is enough talk of Visel."

Drusilla stared as he came toward her, his body far more masculine and imposing in a robe than it appeared fully dressed.

He held out one hand. "Come here."

Drusilla stood, but her legs seemed to have grown roots into the floor. Moving her feet the few steps toward Gabriel was one of the most difficult things she'd ever done. He waited, patient and expectant. His lids had lowered over his eyes, giving him the look of a sleepy predator. His chest, she was pleased to note, was rising and falling faster—although not as fast as hers.

When she stepped within reach, he grazed her jaw with the back of his hand, the gentle touch making her jump.

"Shhhh," he whispered as he lifted her hand to his mouth and kissed the tips of her fingers with a lingering sensuality.

Drusilla made a noise unlike any that had ever come out of her mouth.

He chuckled softly. "What was that?"

"Uhmnph."

His smile turned to a grin. "That is what I thought you said." He released her hand and slid both of his beneath her jaws, his thumbs caressing her cheeks and brushing over her lips.

He looked at her through green slits. "I know it is said that there is some pain the first time, but I will see that you experience great pleasure—you trust me, don't you?" He continued his distracting exploration of her face, her chest rising and falling faster with each gentle stroke of his thumb over her lower lip.

She nodded. She'd never stood so close to him. She'd always known he was broad chested, but he seemed to surround her with his body. And his eyes. Lord, just looking at them made her feel faint. A thousand shades of green shot through with gold, his eyelashes like soot—all except the very tips, which were a surprising reddish gold. He took the glass she still clutched in her hand and set it down before turning back to her.

"I wish to see your hair down."

A shock went through her body as if he'd yelled, and his lips, full and shapely, flexed into a gentle smile.

"You are so nervous. Is it me?" His gaze flickered over her, and her heart clenched. Was she behaving like a lovelorn girl? Was that what he thought he saw?

"No, it is not you."

"You're afraid of what will happen tonight?"

"Not . . . afraid, but perhaps—" Perhaps what? She didn't even know herself what she felt—how could she describe it? "A little anxious. But I do not wish to stop." The words came out in a garbled rush. "I understand my duty." She expelled a careful breath. "I know what a wife owes her husband."

His eyebrows jumped up, and his white, even teeth flashed briefly. "Does your duty include letting down your hair?"

The playful question left her speechless, so she nodded.

He removed her cap, his full lips pulling down at the corners as he stared at it and then tossed it to the floor. "I do not care for that." His dark eyes met hers. "My sisters and mother do not wear such things. Why do you?"

Drusilla had no idea why. She'd been raised by her aunt and governess, both of whom had made it plain that a virtuous woman covered her hair. But she could hardly say that as it would imply his mother and sisters were *not* virtuous and—

"You are giving such serious thought to the matter." His mouth twitched, and that was when Drusilla noticed the small freckle just on the curve of his upper lip. She had a mad urge to reach out and touch it, to—God save her—taste it.

"You have beautiful hair and I would like it to be unbound when I come to you."

His words rocked her, sending shock tremors through her body. The realization that they would do this again and again made her stomach quiver and the area below tighten, the sensation that echoed outward so intensely pleasurable she felt ready to slide to the floor in a boneless heap.

She began to lift her hands, but he shook his head.

"I will do it." He turned her around, her back to his front, and she felt his hand moving on the heavy braid that hung down her back. "Hold out your hand."

Her hand shot out before her brain had approved the gesture. "Do you never say please?"

He gave a soft laugh and placed the ribbon that had held her braid in her hand before lightly grasping her shoulders and pulling her back, hot breath fanning her neck. "I will say *please* for you, my wife." He kissed her beneath her ear, and Drusilla swayed, grateful his hands and body were propping her up. She'd had only one glass of champagne and had barely sipped her wine at supper, but she felt as though she'd come unmoored from her body.

"It is like fine silk," he murmured behind her, his low, intimate growl vibrating through her back and shoulders.

"It is too c-curly and impossible to control."

"And my sisters complain theirs is too straight." He began

to unbraid the rope of hair. "This must be a heavy crown to wear." He combed out the braid with his fingers and kissed her temple again. "A crown for my queen."

She swallowed; she should say something—anything—but she was empty of words and thought. His chest was warm and hard against her shoulders; had he moved closer, or had she?

He spread the froth of curls over her shoulders. "Would you like me to tell you what I am doing? Do you wish to know what is happening?" He buried his face in her hair, his nose pressing against her throat as he inhaled deeply. "Or would you like me to shut my potato hole?"

A laugh broke out of her at the unexpected words.

"That's better," he said, the words a caress against her skin. "This is not serious business; this is pleasurable business." He inhaled again. "Mmm. You smell delicious." His voice roughened. "I wonder how you taste." He flicked a tongue over her, and she jolted. "You taste of flowers," he whispered, his mouth leaving a chain of hot kisses that encircled her throat like a warm embrace, his words turning her legs to jelly.

He wrapped his arms around her waist and pulled her against the hot length of his body, nuzzling her neck. "Can you feel how much you excite me, Drusilla?" He pressed against her, and she felt the truth of his words. He turned her and held up her chin to look in her eyes.

She couldn't stop swallowing—her mouth seemed to be producing an unprecedented amount of saliva. And looking at him made her eyeballs hot—actually made her vision blur and waver—as if she were staring through steam from a boiling pot. His body was big—far bigger than he looked in his clothing. She'd seen him nude once before, of course, but he had been a mere boy—seventeen or eighteen. He was a man, now, and there seemed to be muscles on top of muscles, surrounded by more muscles.

His skin was a velvety bronze and heat was coming off him in waves.

"Will you touch me? Put your hands on my shoulders?"

Drusilla jumped at the sound of his voice, forgetting this broad expanse of chest belonged to an actual man. She reached out shaking fingers, the silk of his robe smooth and hot. Her heart pounded—so madly and loudly she just knew it must be obvious by looking at her. He made a low humming sound and leaned closer, just like a dog pushing closer for a pet.

That was it: she would just think of him as a big dog. She'd never *had* a big dog, but there were loads of them at Exham Castle. They were always lolling all over the place, underfoot, on furniture. The marquess and his family apparently enjoyed them.

He stepped even closer, and her arms slid around his neck, her body pressed tight against his. The soap he used was unusual—a blend of spicy smells she could not identify. It evoked images of amber and exotic music and perfumed smoke.

"Are you sniffing me, Drusilla?"

She hadn't thought her face could become any hotter. "I-I'm sorry."

His hand came beneath her chin and tilted her face up again.

"Don't apologize for your curious nature." His mouth was stern. "You needn't be ashamed of anything you wish to do—anywhere you wish to touch, or have me touch. It is only we two together, and we should feel comfortable to explore each other's bodies." His mouth flexed into a smile. "That is part of the joy of becoming one."

This close to him, Drusilla could see the red-gold hairs that broke through the skin.

His eyebrows jumped up, and his teeth flashed. "What is it, my wife?"

She gaped as if only now realizing what the brief blur of a ceremony had meant: He was her husband. He was *hers*. A shock went through her body at the wonderful, frightening, amazing thought.

His lips, full and shapely, curved into an oddly gentle smile. "I want you, Drusilla—I want to bed you."

She knew she should say something—anything—but she was empty of words and thoughts. Besides, her throat had constricted. It was a miracle any air was getting through; words would not have a chance.

She nodded jerkily, and he kissed her again.

"If I do anything you do not like, you have only to ask me to stop. Is that understood?"

Again she nodded.

He laughed softly into her hair. "Where is Miss Clare—what have you done with her? Why isn't she here to scold me—to hector me?"

"I—I don't know," she answered foolishly, staring at his feet.

"Look at me, Drusilla."

She realized, as the seconds ticked past, that he was not going to speak or move until she obeyed.

"That's better." He slid his hands around her throat, his thumbs resting on her jaws while his fingers massaged the taut cords of her neck.

"I'm going to remove your gown. I want to look at you—at all of you."

"But—"

His fingers paused at the fastenings that ran from her neck to her waist. "Yes? Remember, you may ask questions or tell me to stop at any time."

"Is that, er, well, necessary? My aunt said—"

"I can guess what your aunt said. No, nudity is not necessary, but I would like to see your body."

Drusilla felt positively woozy and closed her eyes. "Oh." She gulped. "Why?"

"Because it would give me pleasure to look at you—to touch your skin, all of it."

"Uh."

"Is that a yes?"

She nodded.

His fingers resumed their journey, his featherlight touch almost imperceptible on first her dressing gown and then her nightgown.

"Do you want a child, Drusilla?"

Her eyes snapped open.

He was smiling, and his gaze flickered from her eyes to her chest. When she looked down, she saw the soft fabric was gaping open. Her breasts were still concealed, but she saw, with horror, that her nipples had hardened, as if she were cold. But she wasn't cold . . .

"Drusilla?"

Oh, yes. He'd asked her a question. "Wh-why do you ask if I want a child?"

"Because I know you did not wish to marry. I'm in no need of an heir and there are ways to lower the likelihood of conception."

She wanted to ask—with all her person—if this was what he did with his mistresses. And did he have any children already? But luckily she could not force out the words.

Instead she stared up at him, his gaze mesmerizing her.

He smiled when she didn't answer. "We can utilize a sheath, if that is what you would prefer." Her face heated at his intent look—and she knew he was recalling the last time they'd discussed the subject, and how that had ended. When she said nothing, he continued. "It is no guarantee that I will not put a child inside you, of course, but it will reduce the chances."

He continued his distracting stroking, his high, sharp cheekbones tinted with pink; Drusilla realized he was excited. By her. Never in her life had a man looked at her like this. She knew, deep in her bones, it was an expression she would do almost anything to see again, and again.

"I love children." She swallowed, finding thought difficult with his proximity, her near nudity, with . . . everything. "It is true I never expected to have them."

"Oh? Why is that? I think Mary Wollstonecraft had children, did she not?"

Drusilla's lips parted. "Yes, she did. But how did you—"

"I am not so savage or ignorant as you might think, Mrs. Marlington. I might have glanced at the good woman's writings once or twice, if for no other reason than to have artillery when next we met."

Drusilla could only gape. He had thought about when they would see each other and imagined what he might say? But that was what *she* had always done with him. Why would he do such a thing?

He caught a spiral of hair and wrapped it slowly around his finger, his eyes tracking the motion.

"You never answered my question." He kept his gaze on his hand, which allowed her to force out the words that boiled and bubbled inside her.

"I very much want children." Her voice shook and she sounded hoarse, rough . . . desperate.

The muscles seemed to shift subtly beneath the skin of his face, and his expression became almost . . . austere. He released the curl and pulled her close, lowering his mouth over hers.

He stroked her tightly pressed lips with the tip of his tongue. "Open for me, *ya helo*. I want to taste you, Drusilla."

She parted her lips, as she had earlier, in the garden, and he made a low humming sound, all the while stroking, kissing, nibbling.

The feel of his tongue on her teeth, her gums—it should have been revolting. It was not.

He wrapped his arms around her waist and pulled her against the hot length of his body. "I'm going to undress you now." It did not sound like a question, but he paused, and she knew it was.

She nodded, her face hot and no doubt as red as a boiled lobster. His questions, as kindly meant as they were, required her to speak, or at least respond. And the things he wanted her to say . . . oh, they were improper and embarrassing and, ultimately, frightening. Frightening because her body was pulling her toward him—toward the edge—without any approval from her mind.

He began to lift both the robe and nightgown from her shoulders, his eyes on hers as he released the garments and they fell to her feet like a silent waterfall. And then she stood before him, naked.

His gaze dropped, and he sucked in a harsh breath, his eyelids heavy. "You are a goddess."

She reeled from his words, one hand going to her mound, the other arm across her breasts.

His expression was fierce and filled with want; he reached out and traced the underside of one breast, and she could not contain her groan.

He took her face in both hands, his expression gentling. "Go, lie down on the bed, and I will extinguish the lights." She hesitated, and he kissed her again, his lips and tongue sliding over hers in a way that was becoming, if not familiar, at least no longer shocking.

She opened without being asked this time, even kissing

him in return, the tip of her tongue darting into his mouth just as he pulled away.

He released her and went to snuff the candles.

"Do you always extinguish the candles when you do . . . this?" Drusilla asked.

He paused. "No. But I do not wish to mortify you on—"

"No, I want—"

They both waited to hear what she wanted. But she had no words, and her tongue seemed to have gone to sleep.

"I shall leave them." It wasn't a question, but she nodded.

"But I am going to disrobe and am not wearing a nightshirt. Do you wish to see me?"

Oh, she did, she did. Her memory of that brief glance all those years ago was like a favorite blanket, worn and handled again and again until it was frayed around the edges from overuse.

"Yes."

He led her to the bed and lifted the bedding. Drusilla crawled beneath, grateful beyond words to be covered.

"Have you seen a man before?"

"I saw you," she blurted.

His hands froze on the sash of his robe and he frowned. Drusilla realized he'd forgotten the incident—an incident that had been so very life changing to her had meant nothing to him. But then he'd been seen by women dozens if not hundreds of times, hadn't he?

She swallowed the thought, as unpleasant as one of the draughts her old nurse used to mix up at the sign of the first sniffle.

He laughed and nodded, his grin releasing a mad fluttering in her chest. "Ah yes, the time Eva stole our clothing." His eyes narrowed but his smile did not dim. "You recall that, do you, my peeping wife?" His hand moved low over his abdomen, to where the silk bulged, and his palm rubbed over the hard ridge.

Drusilla's body clenched in response.

"I don't believe I was displaying at my finest that day." His fingers wrapped around the ridged silk, his hand stroking absently as he gazed at his memory.

She had no idea what he meant and didn't care. She couldn't take her eyes from the sight of his hand, the veins prominent and the muscles of his wrists and forearms defined, clutching something that looked monstrously big.

"Look at me, Drusilla." Whatever he saw on her face made him chuckle again and take a step closer to the bed. "Give me your hand . . . *please*."

She extended the hand that was not holding her propped up.

His fingers were long, nimble, and dark against the pale skin of her wrist. He was openly amused, but when he placed her hand over the silk-covered ridge, his smile dropped away and he hissed.

Drusilla's fingers tightened, and he shuddered. She pushed herself up, not caring when the blankets slipped away. She dragged her fingers lightly up his length, transfixed when he shivered.

His chin tilted down, and it was Drusilla's turn to suck in a noisy breath; the expression on his face was one of fierce hunger. She closed her shaking fingers around his girth, and his eyelids fluttered but did not close.

"God, yes . . . just like that."

Drusilla looked at her hand and blinked: yes, he really was as big as he felt.

His hand covered hers and tightened. "Like so." He squeezed far harder than she would have believed comfortable, and stroked, from root to tip. He groaned, repeating the motion several times before removing both their hands.

Drusilla frowned. Why had he taken her hand away? She'd just begun to—

"Will you remove my robe?"

She looked from the intriguing bulge to his taut, expectant face and swallowed yet again as she reached for the sash with fingers that trembled with anticipation, rather than fear. A quick tug and the fine fabric slid open. Skin like silk stretched over muscles that were impossibly sculpted and defined. Auburn hair lighter than that on his head dusted his chest, with darker curls at the base of his . . .

"Oh."

He made a sound of amusement. "Oh, indeed." His fingers threaded into her hair, and he tilted her face upward. His lips had thinned and were curved in a tight smile, his green eyes black. "Do you like what you see?" His gaze dropped to her throat as she swallowed. And then swallowed again.

"Yes." The word was a dried husk and his pupils flared.

"Let me in beside you."

She scooted away from the edge of the bed, and the mattress moved as he lowered himself.

"Ahhh, that feels so good," he said, stretching out on his side, facing her. Lines of strain radiated from the corners of his brilliant eyes, and the grooves that ran from the side of his nose to his mouth seemed to be deeper. She recalled he'd not slept for at least a full day, and an unexpected wave of tenderness washed over her.

She pulled the covers up over them both, and he smiled. "Thank you for protecting my modesty."

Her face heated at his gentle teasing. "You are so tired. Are you sure—"

He stroked her hair, shaking his head. "I'm not too tired for this. I am *never* too tired for this." His hand slid lower, over her jaw, resting at the pulse point on her throat. "I want to be inside your body."

She stared.

His hand caressed her side, his thumb lightly grazing her breast, making her shudder. He leaned forward, pushing aside the blankets and exposing her, his lips finding one of her painfully hard nipples. He rolled her onto her back while he knelt over her, straddling her on his hands and knees, his mouth never stopping its teasing, licking, kissing.

One hand lowered over her belly and circled softly, the way she had often rubbed one of the many kitchen cats over the years. She caught her lower lip between her teeth, trying to bite back the sounds spilling out of her as he stroked and petted; no wonder cats made that purring sound.

And then his fingers slid lower.

He lightly grazed the swell of her midriff, not stopping until he reached her mound. Drusilla's hips quivered, making her realize she'd lifted them off the bed and was thrusting toward him. He parted her curls with a finger, and her body shook as he stroked between her lips.

He continued his caressing, applying a bit more pressure with each pass, her hips straining more and more.

He groaned, the sound one of near pain. "So hot and wet."

His words caused the ache that was growing between her thighs to throb.

His finger circled her entrance, lightly probing, but not breaching her. She spread her thighs as she pushed toward him, willing him to touch her . . . *there.*

But he chuckled and teased.

"Please."

He paused, making her realize she'd spoken her thought aloud.

"What was that, Drusilla? I did not hear you."

She could see by his wicked, wicked smile that he was lying.

She didn't care.

"Please," she begged, frustration and want overwhelming shame.

"Please what?"

But she couldn't form the words.

His finger slid to the apex of her thighs, lightly brushing a spot so sensitive her hips bucked. "This?"

A guttural cry slipped from between her lips when he stopped.

She screwed her eyes shut. "*Please*, Gabriel." The words were almost a sob.

"Shhhh, *ya helo*. I want to make you suffer, but you beg me so prettily." He chuckled evilly. "I'll give you what you need." His fingers began to move in languid but rhythmic circles.

Drusilla almost wept with gratitude, her hips pulsing and pushing against his hand so hard the blankets began to slide back. She didn't care. Her body was shaking and quivering as it had when she'd once been in the grip of a violent fever.

"Look at me, Drusilla." He stared down at her, his jaw tight. His finger stroked gently against her entrance and he gave a grunt of what sounded like frustration. "You are tight." He pushed harder, and her entire body clenched against the slight invasion. His pupils flared until his eyes went black. "So very tight." This time he pushed and did not stop. Her hips tilted to accept him, and he slid into her until his knuckles rested against her swollen flesh, his thumb stroking between her lips, touching her *there*.

He began to move in and out, his thumb occasionally, maddeningly flicking her core. His smile grew fierce and demanding as he pumped her deeper, harder, the sounds of her wetness unnaturally loud in the quiet of the room.

Drusilla shook her head from side to side; it was too much, too much.

"Too much," she breathed out.

He leaned low and tongued one of her aching nipples. "Should I stop?"

"No!"

He laughed and then sucked her hard as his hand resumed its rhythm.

Drusilla's thoughts fractured and broke into a thousand insubstantial pieces. Every muscle in her body clenched, as if to hold back the mad, pounding surge that originated from his hand. The sensation was elusive and engulfing—but trapped behind some barrier within her. Her body strained toward . . . something. Something just beyond her reach . . .

And then the dam broke.

Somebody yelled—her?—and she clutched at him, as if to hold on, but nothing could stop it and she went over the edge of awareness.

She was shuddering in the aftermath of her climax when he knelt over her, lowering his mouth over hers. They kissed as she floated, their tongues tangling—almost dancing—until he began to thrust into her, his suggestive motions causing her to tighten with anticipation.

Drusilla had believed she couldn't bear even one more sensation, but then his thick crown pressed against the entrance to her body.

"Will you take me?" he whispered, nudging her swollen flesh with his blunt hardness.

She thrilled at his words. "Please."

He pushed gently but inexorably, until he breached her. It was nothing like his finger; not even like two fingers.

"Breathe, sweetheart."

Drusilla realized she'd been holding her breath and took short, sharp mouthfuls of air, her heart fluttering like a trapped and frantic bird as he came deeper, deeper—

Oh God . . . when would it end?

And then he flexed the powerful muscles of his hips and thrust, seeming to break through some barrier before fully sheathing himself. Her body struggled to accommodate not only the hard length, but his thickness.

"I am sorry, Drusilla. That was the worst of it."

The thrill of pleasure she felt at his rough and ragged tone lessened the discomfort. And then she realized there *was* no more pain.

Her womb was heavy and full: his big body penetrating, stretching, and dominating hers. The invasion was as raw and primal as nature and she reveled in his mastery: she never wanted him to leave.

When he began to pull out, Drusilla clutched at his taut, corded waist, her fingers slipping on his slick skin. "No. Don't—don't leave."

His body shook against hers, and she realized he was shaking with suppressed laughter.

"Don't worry, darling, I won't be gone long," he promised, his breath hot against her temple as he settled onto his forearms, the muscles of his back rippling beneath her hands. His hips began moving, filling her yet again, the sensation becoming desirable—almost addictive. Her body jerked, and it was his turn to gasp as she tilted her hips to accept him even deeper.

His muscles went rigid beneath her hands as he thrust. "Yes." The word was a sibilant hiss. "Take all of me."

She spread her knees wider, opening herself and earning a murmur of approval as he withdrew and invaded, withdrew and invaded.

His skin was velvety and damp from exertion. His broad, powerful shoulders tapered to an unbelievably tight collection of muscles at his waist. And his bottom . . . It was her turn to moan. And then his hips began to drum, driving her into the bed with the force of his thrusts.

His body began to shake and she knew what was happening because she'd just experienced something very much like it. It thrilled her to know she could bring him a similar pleasure. His pounding became brutal—savage—and it ripped away what was left of her breath. Gone was the gentle, careful lover; in his place was a man who employed his body like a weapon—like a battering ram.

She drew up her knees and tensed her muscles, a bolt of intense pleasure shooting through her.

He gave a guttural cry, plunged himself hilt deep, and held her in a crushing embrace. The only part of him that moved was buried deep inside her, pulsing within her and filling her with the warm wash of his seed.

"Drusilla." The word was a sigh.

She wrapped her arms around his narrow waist and held him close as the aftershocks of pleasure rippled through his body. The only sound was their ragged breathing, his slick, hard form pressing her into the mattress, crushing her. It was delicious. She could die happy.

For the first time in years—as long as she could remember—she was content. Utterly content.

Unfortunately, her contentment didn't last long.

He pushed up onto his forearms, his face slack, his green eyes dazed. "I'm sorry. I'm crushing you." He rolled to the side, his body abandoning hers and leaving her feeling bereft. She yearned to pull him back down on top of her. But her mind advised caution . . .

Drusilla was still embroiled in the internal debate when strong hands took her by the waist and turned and positioned her until her back was tightly nestled against his front, his hard, lightly furred chest pressed tight to her shoulders and spine. A heavy arm slid around her ribs, his hand curving possessively around one breast.

He gave a deep animal sigh of satisfaction and his thumb brushed her nipple, making Drusilla bite her lower lip to keep from making her own animal noises.

And then he fell asleep.

She lay stiffly in his embrace, listening intently as his breaths became as regular as the waves on a beach.

How could he possibly sleep? She was more awake than she'd ever been in her life. She was in a bed, unclothed, with Gabriel Marlington: the man of a thousand fantasies lying beside her. Never in a million years had she dared to hope for this—to hope for a night when he treated her not just like a wife, but like a lover—almost as a friend during that horrid supper.

A child might be forming even now as she lay in his embrace.

Tonight he'd behaved toward her as if he could imagine no other wife—as if he were *pleased* to have her in his arms. Did that mean he—she cut off the thought before it could even sprout. He was simply making the best of their arrangement. He was a gentleman and would not let her know what he was really feeling—which was most likely that he'd never have needed to marry her at all if he had waited only another twenty-four hours. And that he'd probably been looking forward to doing *this* with Lucinda Kittridge instead of Drusilla.

She jolted, the image of Gabriel doing what he'd just done to her with the beautiful Lucinda was like a mallet blow to her temple.

Gabriel twitched in his sleep and his arm tightened, his hand brushing her nipple again and turning her liquid inside. She squeezed her thighs together, thrilled but alarmed at her body's immediate response to him. It was wonderful but . . . terrifying. When had she ever wanted somebody so much? Never. The truth was, this marriage was exactly what she'd wanted. But for him? She swallowed against the gorge rising in her throat. Drusilla was not his first choice—or even on his list of choices, most likely. He'd been forced into proposing.

He muttered something in his sleep and pulled her tight, his breathing hot and regular against her neck. It was delicious torture to lie in his arms.

Something tickled her cheek, and she reached up, stunned to find her skin wet. Tears. How was it possible to be so happy yet so miserable at the same time?

Chapter 15

Drusilla woke to an empty bed.

Bright sunlight was streaming through the windows and the clock on the nightstand said it was ten thirty.

She sat up abruptly. Ten-thirty! She blinked the sleep from her eyes and glanced around her room, frowning.

The door opened, and Drusilla squeaked, yanking the tangled sheets up around her naked chest.

"Ah, the sleeper has awakened." Gabriel stood in the doorway, a large tray in his hands as he shut the door with one foot.

He came to a halt, an amused expression on his face.

"What—when?"

He laughed and set the tray down on the foot of the bed before fetching her discarded dressing gown and holding it open for her.

Drusilla looked from his hands to his face to her hands, which clutched the sheet up around her breasts.

"I'll close my eyes." He demonstrated and Drusilla scrambled out of bed, thrusting her arms into her dressing gown and then spinning around.

He was grinning down at her. "I didn't say I'd *keep* them closed."

She was too mortified to chastise him. Although why she should worry about what he was seeing this morning when he'd certainly seen everything she had last night . . .

"I've brought you breakfast in bed." He gestured to her, and she climbed back in the warm bed, bolstering herself up with cushions and sitting against the carved mahogany headboard.

Drusilla looked down at the delicious assortment he'd brought. "But this is only food for one."

He arranged the tray on her lap, his hands brushing her body as he positioned the blankets, the fresh clean smell of his damp hair teasing her nostrils, his proximity . . . dizzying.

"I've already eaten and ridden in the park while you slumbered. There," he said, smiling down at her. "Comfortable?"

She nodded, her face hot beneath his solicitous stare. He was so beautiful and virile and irresistible in the light of day; it was difficult to look directly at him. So she turned her attention to her tea and fussed with the pot.

He pulled a chair up next to the bed and lowered his elegantly clad body.

"You should have woken me," she said, not taking her eyes from her cup and saucer.

"I did—several times last night. Or don't you remember?"

Her head whipped up, and he laughed at whatever he saw on her face. Her cheeks flamed like a torch and—to her utter amazement—her lips curved into an answering smile.

"There, that's better." He motioned to the pot. "Fletcher said you preferred tea at breakfast rather than chocolate."

"I am not fond of chocolate."

His eyebrows shot up.

"You find that odd?"

"Eva and Melissa will drink as much as you give them, and my mother takes it in the morning *and* the evening. I don't believe I've met a woman who does not care for it."

Drusilla did not want to consider what other women he might be thinking of. Instead she took a sip of the dark, steaming liquid and closed her eyes in bliss.

The sound of his chuckle made her open them again.

He wore an indulgent—almost affectionate—expression. "I don't think I've ever seen anyone enjoy tea quite so much."

"I cannot think straight until after my first cup," she admitted, picking up a triangle of toast and nibbling one corner.

"Ah, so if I wish to be the victor in a dispute, I should call on you before you break your fast?"

She took another sip. "I sincerely doubt you need to ambush me before breakfast to triumph over me in a discussion."

He grinned and sat back, crossing his arms. "Oh?"

"Well, at least not in *all* matters."

"You must tell me what areas you mean, and I will apply myself to studying."

She snorted, and he threw back his head as though she had struck him. "That was a cruel blow, Mrs. Marlington. Do you doubt your husband knows how to study?"

The word *husband* caused a dull ache to pulse between her legs and she had a flash of his face above hers, his features not playful and smiling but taut, hard, and intense as he thrust into her, his body buried deeply inside hers . . .

She swallowed convulsively and set down her cup with a shaking hand. "I'm sure you know *how* to study, but I'm not sure you actually did so."

"Ah, so precise. That is a characteristic I greatly admire in you, my dear." Drusilla tried not to preen at what was probably not an actual compliment. "I'm afraid you are correct. Books and studying are not my strong suit." His eyelids lowered and his nostrils flared, his mouth pulling up into a smile that was suggestive and wicked. "I prefer more physical pursuits."

Drusilla felt woozy. "Er."

He leaned forward. "Here, let me top up your tea."

She watched his hands, entranced by their strength and beauty and the memory of them on her body, *in* her body. It was beginning to be an effort to breathe and she was grateful when he sat back.

Her eyes flickered over his clothing—skintight buff pantaloons molded to his thighs, a forest green superfine coat that followed the contours of his powerful shoulders so lovingly it might have been cast from his body. He wore Hessians rather than top boots. He was not dressed for riding but in the clothes of a man who was paying calls.

Drusilla looked up from her thorough inspection of his body to see humor glinting in his eyes, his expression that of a man who was accustomed to female homage and comfortable with it. She was torn—alternately wanting to tear off his clothing and drag him into bed with her and wanting to beat him with a big stick for turning her into such a besotted slave.

Drusilla was not a violent person and the images—both images, actually—disturbed her.

He picked a speck of something from his sleeve. Drusilla could not get enough of his elegantly shaped, long-fingered hands. Yet again she was flooded by memories of how those hands had touched, opened, entered, caressed . . .

"If you continue to look at me like that, you will never leave this bed, Mrs. Marlington."

She glanced up and met his darkened eyes, his slightly flaring nostrils telling her he *knew* what she was thinking.

Drusilla opened her mouth, but had nothing to say.

His sinful lips curved. "Ah, I have rendered you speechless. I would wager that is not a common occurrence."

"No," she agreed with a breathless laugh. "But you seem quite, er, adept at it."

He eyed her from beneath lowered lids. "I look forward to showing you just how adept."

Her entire body responded to his look like a well-trained

pet. Only one night and already he knew how to command her with a look.

The realization horrified her. She was . . . pathetic. He was not in love with her. If not for the incident at the Abingdon conservatory, he would still be happily pursuing the Kitten. What must he think now that he realized he'd not needed to marry Drusilla, after all? He was a gentleman, so he would never show his true feelings, but she could imagine them. He was a beautiful man who enjoyed beautiful women and was now stuck with *her*.

We should make the best of things. His words echoed in her mind.

She lowered her cup with a clatter. "Would you be so kind as to ring for Fletcher?"

As dismissals went, it was less than subtle. His face—taut with passion only an instant before—tightened with something else.

A notch of concern appeared between his eyes, and he leaned forward. "Is aught amiss?" He laid a hand on hers, and Drusilla started and snatched away her hand as if she'd been burned. Her violent movement set the dishes clattering on the tray.

His eyes widened slightly as he sat back in his chair, his expression changing so rapidly she could not identify all the moods.

Drusilla opened her mouth to say . . . something, but—

He stood, his face a beautiful, impassive mask. "I apologize for keeping you. I shall send your maid directly." He dropped an abrupt bow and turned away.

Frustration at her horrid, awkward behavior was thick enough to almost choke her. Once again Drusilla opened her mouth, this time to call him back—to stop him, to apologize, but what could she say? *I'm sorry I am behaving stiffly, but I love you madly and have done for almost five years. I know you are proba-*

bly in love—or at least were considering marriage—with somebody else, but I cannot be sorry you were forced to marry me. Even though I know it is hopeless, I am in danger of losing myself completely and becoming your creature. I never want to leave this bed if you are in it. When you touch me, I lose what little control I have. I adore and—

He stopped, his hand resting on the door handle. "Oh, incidentally, don't forget we are joining a party at my stepfather's box tonight. There were also a few invitations waiting below. I'll have Parker bring them up and leave it to your discretion to sort through them and decide which are best." He turned without waiting for a response, and the door shut with a soft click.

Drusilla looked down at her tray, her hunger having vanished as quickly as her happiness. Why did she have to do this with him? Why?

Self-preservation, you fool. He bedded you last night because he is your husband. If you think that means anything beyond the mere physical act—that he will leave whatever mistress or mistresses he most likely has and become your devoted lover—you are a bigger fool than I believed.

Drusilla knew her relentless inner critic spoke the truth. Gabriel Marlington was the epitome of masculinity. He fenced, shot, rode, and made love like a man who'd had plenty of practice in all those activities. Why would she ever think he would stop his pursuits—either dueling or taking lovers—for a drab plain Jane like herself? It was already going to be agonizing the first time she heard gossip of his amorous exploits. How much worse would it be if she fell into the belief that she was somehow special to him—that what they'd done together last night was just for her, for them.

"You are such a pitiful fool," she whispered through clenched jaws. "Such a fool."

* * *

Gabriel wished it had been some other production—or some other cast—at least when it came to two members. But it was what it was. He'd known Giselle would be onstage, but Maria's presence had surprised him. The way things had been going, he supposed he should have expected that both his mistresses—*ex-mistresses*—would be performing for his wife.

His family had arrived at the theater only a few moments before the curtain rose; the evening would be tense enough without drawing matters out by engaging in the pretheater promenade.

As for dinner? Gabriel had declined an invitation from his mother to dine at Exley House, instead dinning at home with his wife for the first time. It had been a polite but stilted affair, Drusilla behaving as if their night of passionate lovemaking had never happened.

Gabriel was mystified and more than a little irritated. Why must the woman be so awkward? They'd come together last night, they'd found pleasure in each other, and they'd not engaged in a single argument.

But that didn't appear to suit the new Mrs. Marlington.

Thankfully his mother, stepfather, Eva, Byer, and two crazy spinster friends of the marquess's were already present when they arrived, so he and his wife didn't need to make more awkward conversation. The entire theater had paused to watch them enter the box, and Gabriel knew that would continue for the rest of the evening.

Drusilla wore the same stiff, proud expression she'd worn this morning when he'd brought her breakfast. Who knew what went on behind that mask? Certainly not Gabriel.

She was seated between Gabriel and the marquess. Eva must still be mad at her and had not, as far as Gabriel could tell, spoken to Drusilla once since they'd arrived. In fact, his usually boisterous sister appeared rather subdued.

Hmmm, that did not bode well for somebody.

It was not the most relaxed of evenings. Visel was present—as was Tyndale. Both had conspicuously come to pay their respects during the break. If that wasn't enough, Lucy had come by with Deveril. She'd made up to Gabriel in a shameless way, touching him and treating him as if he were an object that belonged to her. There was nothing he could do as she chose to carry out this exhibition in their box, in front of his wife and half the *ton*.

Gabriel thought the theater manager would have done better to charge tickets to watch Exley's box than to watch the actual production.

Not that Giselle was not at her best.

She was powerfully gripping in her role as Regan. And Maria performed her much smaller role with the usual flair. Gabriel would have preferred not to bring his wife to watch his former mistresses, but Tyndale had been the one to ask that they be there.

Tonight the need to see and be seen with Visel had been more important than who was on the stage.

While Tyndale watched the production from a box almost directly opposite Exley's, Visel watched from the pit. Gabriel was certain the farcical nature of the arrangement was fueling at least some of the attention they were receiving.

He felt Visel's gaze more than once during the evening—when the other man wasn't watching either Maria or Giselle. Gabriel was not stupid. Visel's message was clear: the gorgeous actresses were available, and he would do his best to have them. Visel was, he supposed, an attractive specimen. Certainly the women of the *ton* seemed to flock to him, although that could be his position as a duke's heir rather than his person. Gabriel thought the man was unbalanced and did not trust his public apology in the least. Still, there was nothing Visel could do to hurt him, so there was no point wondering what he was up to.

Gabriel found the other man's actions amusing rather than annoying. If he thought to make Gabriel jealous, he was certainly engaging in futile behavior. While he had no idea what Giselle and Maria might do, he was positive that inviting Visel to become their lover while Samir was living in their house was not going to happen.

Samir.

The name brought a poignant blend of pleasure and pain. He'd gone to see the boy today after his wife had tossed him from her chamber. Each time he visited, he found it more difficult to leave him. There was a perfectly good nursery in their London house and Sizemore Manor had a huge schoolroom and nursery. Apparently some ancestor of his grandmother's had enjoyed a large brood and an entire floor of the house had been given over to children's quarters.

He'd been optimistic about broaching the topic after his first night with Drusilla and had planned to bring it up today.

Just thinking about last night made him stiffen. God. She'd been so responsive. He shouldn't have used her so hard her first night but she'd looked at him with such . . . *hunger.* Gabriel was not a believer in false modesty; he knew women found him appealing and he was no stranger to lustful looks. But the way Drusilla had stared at him when he'd taken off his robe? It had done something to him. He could only assume it was the knowledge that this was his wife—she was *his* and he was *hers*. It was different from the feelings he'd had with lovers, even Giselle and Maria. He'd always known what the three of them had wasn't permanent; they loved each other far more than they did him. Last night had been different—special. But then there had been this morning . . .

He felt a sharp jab in his side and looked over to find Eva staring up at him. He raised his eyebrows at her.

"Why does he keep looking up here?" she whispered behind the protection of her fan.

Gabriel didn't need to ask whom she meant. "I don't know."

"Those are your mistresses, aren't they?"

"What?"

Heads turned in their direction—including Drusilla's—at his expostulation, and Gabriel leaned closer to Eva and lowered his voice. "What the devil are you talking about?"

"I'm not stupid, Gabe. That's one of them—the beautiful blonde down there. Regan. And that's the other one—playing the servant girl."

"Who told you that?"

"What does it matter? Is it true?"

How did this keep happening to him? Why were the women in his life so curious about his personal matters?

"Well?"

"*Ex*-mistresses."

"Good. Anything else wouldn't be fair to Dru."

Gabriel turned his body to look at her. "Oh? And you are so interested in being fair to her, are you? Is that why you've been shunning her?"

Her lips thinned, and she turned back to the stage, staring as if she'd never seen a more fascinating production in her life.

So, he guessed that answered *that* question. He shook his head; wasn't there enough aggravation in their lives? Did he have to deal with feuding women as well as a nosy mother and a mad, antagonistic possibly war-traumatized earl, and repairing his and his wife's damaged reputations before this disastrous Season was over?

The sound of clapping pulled him from his thoughts. The play had ended; it was time to go home.

Drusilla paced. Would he come to her?

His words from last night, *You are a goddess,* came to her unbidden and made her belly tighten.

She tried to consider his statement objectively. Would he have said such a thing if he had not meant it? And the expression on his face when he'd uttered the words. Lord. Just recalling the hunger in his eyes sent desire licking through her body. No, it had not been a lie. At least not in that moment, in that moment he had believed her desirable.

But then she'd behaved like a shrew. Not only that, but she'd seen the two women reputed to be his mistresses tonight: they were both beautiful.

When she'd realized whom she was watching onstage, she'd been furious—and *glad* she'd snubbed him this morning. But then she'd recalled it was not Gabriel who'd made tonight's arrangements. He hadn't looked pleased or relaxed, and she'd seen that it was all he could do to greet Visel and Tyndale with a smile: he'd been as tense as a coiled spring.

No, he'd not been the one to orchestrate a mess like this evening. That realization didn't eliminate her jealousy, but it did make her feel relieved to know he did not enjoy situations that caused her discomfort or embarrassment.

Fletcher set her ivory hairbrush down on the dressing table. "Will that be all, my lady?"

Drusilla looked at her reflection. She'd left her hair down, just as he'd requested. Fletcher had not commented when she'd said she didn't want either a cap or a braid, but the knowing look in her eyes had made Drusilla blush.

Her dark curly hair glowed from brushing, the heavy mass striking against the plain white lawn of her nightgown. Her cheeks were flushed and her eyes sparkled. She should have felt embarrassed, but instead all she felt was expectant. And aroused.

"That will be all, Fletcher."

She was too anxious to get into bed, so she went to her dressing room and took out her favorite dressing gown—the one she'd put on the night they'd gotten married. As she tied the sash, something crinkled in her pocket. She took out a folded piece of paper: the message from Theo. She had forgotten all about it after reading it. She opened it:

Dear Drusilla:

I apologize for my behavior today. I do hope you will forgive me and chalk it up to my extreme shock and disappointment. I am sorry I made you uncomfortable and wish you every happiness in your new life. I hope we can continue to work together. I am making excellent progress on all three establishments and would hate to think I've jeopardized the future happiness of untold women with my foolish behavior.

Lastly, I hope we shall continue to meet on Thursdays but will understand if you feel you can no longer work with me.

Respectfully yours,
Theo

She *had* been angry with him—not so much for his behavior at the tea shop, but for his ill-advised message and how it had appeared to Gabriel. She frowned. She realized she had done more to offend Gabriel this morning than Theo's letter had done the other night.

Although she'd been angry at the time, she had already forgiven Theo. He'd been repentant and nervous, eager to apologize. She could understand that. She felt as if she should apologize to Gabriel and had agonized over the words she would use. But he'd been gone when she'd finally come downstairs and hadn't returned again until it was time to dress for dinner.

And dinner? She grimaced. Today's awkwardness was all her fault. She glanced at the clock—it was not quite midnight. She decided to pen a brief message to Theo and let him know all was well and forgiven.

That took less than ten minutes, so she riffled through the pile of invitations and selected a few she'd decided they should accept. She wrote brief responses to all of them, which only took another fifteen minutes.

Where was he?

She pulled the bell and gave the letters to the sleepy-looking footman who answered her summons. "See these go out first thing in the morning, please."

Alone again, she crept toward the dividing door. All was silent on the other side. Perhaps he'd already gone to bed?

Drusilla leaned against the doorframe and chewed her lip. She should apologize. He'd come in peace this morning—even bringing her breakfast—and she'd recoiled from his affectionate behavior as if she found his touch repulsive. Not only had she flinched away from him, she'd behaved like a tongue-tied fool after. Why should he come to her, expecting such a reception?

She took a deep breath, arranged her hair over her shoulder, and knocked.

And waited.

And waited.

She'd just turned away when the door opened.

It was Drake. "Can I help you, ma'am?"

The man's demeanor and voice were as mild as milk, but Drusilla couldn't help imagining he regarded her with disfavor. "I was looking for Mr. Marlington."

"He has gone out, madam."

Drusilla cocked her head. "Out?"

"Yes, madam."

She opened her mouth to ask when he would return, but then she saw something in Drake's eyes she *did* recognize: pity.

Heat washed over her face, and she nodded. "Thank you. Good evening, Drake."

"Good evening, madam." He shut the door and left her alone.

She stood in the dressing room, staring blankly at the door.

He had gone out without saying anything to her. Two out of three nights of marriage. Drusilla had opened her mouth a dozen times to apologize for her coldness toward him this morning, but something had always stopped her—her pride, most likely.

She groaned and turned away from the door, which seemed to silently reproach her. Why did she have to be so prickly? Today could have been the beginning of a whole new life. How would she have liked it if she touched him and *he* flinched away as if she were repulsive?

And she'd had an entire day to explain her awkward behavior. All she'd needed to do was say she was shy about physical affection in the harsh light of day—which was no more than the truth. He'd been pleasant to her this evening, not cold but a little reserved. Even so, he'd made an effort to ask her about her day and to compliment her on her gown. She'd sat in muted agony, unable to respond naturally to his conversational gambits because of her stupid inability to open her mouth and *speak*.

And now he'd gone out.

Chapter 16

Perhaps it was the strain of the last few days, or even the past six months—or maybe the lack of exercise—but Gabriel was far too restless to go to bed. Nor was he feeling calm enough to deal with his wife just now. He promised himself he would not make this a habit—leaving her, especially without any explanation—but he simply did not have the patience for yet another baffling interaction with her. Nor did he wish to see her expression go flat and hostile as it had this morning. What had happened? One moment they'd been laughing and chatting—almost flirting—and the next her face had become rigid and she'd recoiled from him as if he were a poisonous serpent. He probably would have overlooked her behavior and persisted with his overtures of friendship if they'd not had such an emotionally draining few days. But he was too fatigued for more dramatics tonight.

It would be a good night to sleep alone. Tomorrow was a fresh, new day and he always woke with optimism. But tonight . . . well.

Gabriel had enjoyed making love to his wife last night and had looked forward to seeing her this morning. It had shocked him to realize that he was the only one of them prepared to be pleased with their marriage and forget how it had begun.

His young wife—he'd been surprised to learn—was a sensual, passionate woman in bed. But outside a bed? The barriers she had erected between them had been clear in the bright light of day: They were high and well fortified. She disliked him—or at least disapproved of him.

Gabriel shook away the thoughts, alternately feeling enervated and restless as he walked the darkened streets. When he'd been a boy, he could walk for hours and never see another soul. His father's palace was on the outskirts of Oran. To the north and west was the ocean; to the south, the foothills and mountains and endless expanse of the Sahara.

London was, naturally, nothing like it. But after midnight the streets were quieter, the carriages and wagons no longer clogging every thoroughfare; clerks and vendors and park saunterers were home in their beds, at least most of them. While it was true pedestrian traffic was sparse—a few servants scurrying out on errands and young men moving from one entertainment to the next—the city by no means slept.

He considered going to Byer's, but he found he didn't wish to speak to his friend, either; he didn't wish to speak to anyone. What he needed was time alone to think—especially about all the things he'd been avoiding. Things like his last trip to Oran—the trip only a handful of people knew of and which he'd avoided thinking about since he'd returned to England; things like bringing Samir down to Devon this summer. Every day he became more attached to the little boy. He was beginning to believe he could not relinquish him even if one of Fatima's brothers or sisters sent a letter saying they would take him. And what if—

"Well, well—what have we here?"

The voice cut through his thoughts like a machete. Gabriel

had to blink to clear his mind's eye of disturbing images, but he knew whom it belonged to before he turned around.

He stared at Visel with disbelief. "Did you follow me?"

The other man laughed. He still wore his theater clothing and looked the epitome of an unruffled English aristocrat out for an evening of entertainment. But all was not serene beneath his unrippled surface. As usual, Gabriel sensed a lethal whirlpool of hatred, fury, and something like a lust for vengeance churning within the other man.

Visel was watching him with an intensity that was combustible. What was he looking for? And what the hell was he doing so close to Gabriel's house—which was only a few streets over?

"I was not aware we were neighbors," Gabriel said when the other man did not answer his first question.

Visel smiled. "I don't live nearby." He gestured with his chin to the street ahead. "I was visiting a friend not far away from here, on Gray Street."

Gabriel didn't believe him for a moment.

"What are *you* doing out so late?" His blue eyes glinted. "Away from your new wife so soon after your wedding?"

Visel's grin was annoyingly insouciant and it was all Gabriel could do not to plant the man a facer. Instead he tightened his grip on his emotions—he refused to let Visel push him into another situation he did not want.

"How reassuring it is to know you care so much about my doings, Visel. But perhaps your time would be better spent on your own affairs."

His blond eyebrows jumped. "Perhaps you are correct—I can't decide whether I should spend my time consoling Miss Kittridge or keeping my lovelorn cousin from doing anything foolish."

Gabriel blinked. "Your cousin?

"Yes, Theodore Rowland is my cousin—although once removed." He cocked his head. "Didn't your wife tell you that?"

Gabriel was nonplussed. Rowland was Visel's *cousin*? Did Drusilla know that? She must—she'd certainly appeared very well acquainted with the man. Why would she not have mentioned that the man he was dueling was a cousin of the man she'd been holding hands with? It was not a critical piece of information to withhold, but he couldn't help feeling it epitomized their marriage.

He felt Visel's scrutiny. The air between them was as thick as a swamp—a swamp of volatile emotions. Visel appeared driven to make trouble any way he could—although Gabriel did not know why. That Visel was so transparent about his mischief-making did not make it any less dangerous or effective. Still, Gabriel did not think there was anything to be gained by drawing out this exchange. Quite the contrary. He was beginning to believe Visel *was* mad, as Eva appeared to think.

So he shrugged. "Your relationship to my wife's friend makes no difference to me," he lied.

Visel chuckled. "You're too busy with your other family to care for such matters."

Gabriel froze. "I beg your pardon?"

"Why, the boy, of course." He grimaced. "Damned and blast! I didn't realize the matter was a secret—I'm afraid I might have said something indiscreet to your wife." Visel's wide-eyed innocence was underlaid with avid glee.

So Visel had seen Gabriel with Samir. Well, he shouldn't be surprised. After all, it wasn't as if he was doing anything to hide the boy—he just hadn't decided how to handle the child's future. It would have been nice for the matter to remain quiet for a bit longer, but it really made no difference. Although he *was* curious why Drusilla had said nothing to him. Was this the reason for her prickly behavior? But, no, Visel had been indiscreet at the ball—which had been *before* their night of lovemaking.

Gabriel shook away the pointless speculating and looked at Visel; he had no intention of letting the other man know he'd needled him. He would take the subject of Sami up with his wife, as he should have done before now.

He gave Visel an abrupt nod. "I bid you a good evening."

Visel wasn't quick enough to hide his surprise—or the flash of angry disappointment—at Gabriel's sanguine reaction. It was almost as if he'd followed Gabriel with the hope of generating another disagreement—perhaps another duel, or a confrontation of a more immediate nature.

The back of his neck prickled as he walked away. Visel's dislike of him was almost tangible. The primitive part of his mind—the animal part that had saved him countless times in his war against Assad—strained for any sound and prepared to repel Visel's attack.

But the only footsteps he heard were his own.

By the time he reached Upper Brooks Street, he was loose-limbed and exhausted. And also more than a little expectant when he saw his wife's windows were still lighted. He stared up at her room for a long moment before making his decision. Visel was nothing but a troublemaker and he should ignore whatever it was the man had been trying to imply. Indeed, his hatred of Gabriel probably meant he was willing to say anything. He refused to let the other man come between him and Drusilla.

He would shave himself since Drake would be in bed, and then he would pay his wife a late-night visit. The notion made him smile. Yes, he would try again—and keep trying, until she grew to accept him.

When he went to open the front door, he found it locked, which was when he recalled he'd sent the servants to bed when he'd left. And forgotten to bring his key.

"Idiot," he muttered beneath his breath. He looked at his watch: it was past two. He'd go around back and see if the door to the sunroom was unlocked. If it wasn't, then he'd have to wake up a servant.

The narrow alley that ran beside the house was dark and he had to walk slowly. The servant's entrance was at the rear of the house and the journey was treacherous it was so dark. He would tell Parker to hang a lantern outside the door and leave it all night. A person could break their neck in this gloom and the last—

"—all right, Dru. I understand. I do."

Gabriel froze as a dark figure came out through the door in the high wall that led to his garden. What the devil?

The shadow stopped just outside the wall. "I shall see you on Thursday?"

Gabriel took a quick step back into the servant doorway, his hand clenching so hard on his walking stick it cut into his skin. He recognized the voice even though he'd only heard it once before.

Whomever Rowland was talking to—Gabriel's *wife*, apparently—spoke too softly to be heard.

"What's that you say?" There was another long pause: "Well, just once more, then—for old time's sake. I know, me too. Thank you, Dru." He shut the garden door and then turned—not in Gabriel's direction, but toward the small stables that served the house. Rowland didn't even hesitate before opening the door into the building and closing it softly behind him, behaving for all the world like a man who was comfortable in his surroundings.

Gabriel leaned back against the servant's door, his brain refusing to admit what his eyes and ears had just witnessed. She was meeting a man she'd held hands with, a man he'd asked her not to see again—in their back garden, at two in the morning.

It was bloody amazing.

He stalked back around to the front door and rang the bell, coming to a boil as he waited. It was Parker who opened the door, and he was wearing his nightcap and a red plaid robe.

"I am sorry, sir. The evening footman said you'd dismissed him earlier and I took him at his word."

Gabriel forced himself not to shove past his servant and thunder up the stairs to his wife's room.

"He spoke the truth, Parker. I forgot my key." He dropped his cane into the brass holder, tossed down his hat, and began yanking off his gloves.

A few letters were scattered on the salver, and one caught his eye. He turned his head to read the direction: Mr. Theodore Rowley.

Gabriel froze, his right glove only half off. His heart was pounding in his ears and his neck and back had become so tight—so tense—the muscles actually *hurt*.

He glanced up to find Parker looking at him, his gaze in the flickering candlelight . . . knowing. "You may go back to bed, Parker."

"Thank you, sir. Good night."

Gabriel waited until the older man turned the corner before looking at the letter. So, he had gone for a walk and she had not only had a secret meeting with her lover but she'd written him a letter, too?

He flung his gloves onto the table before picking up the letter, turning it round and round in his hands. The temptation to open it tore at him more violently than gale-force winds. It was his right to know whom she was corresponding with and what she was saying. As her husband *everything* she did was subject to his approval.

Gabriel suddenly envisioned himself lurking in the dimly lighted foyer, furtively reading his wife's private correspondence like some sneak thief.

He tossed the letter onto the salver, snatched up the candlestick, and headed for the stairs. He took them two and three at a time, already composing the things he would say to her. He had told her he'd not tolerate a continued liaison with a man she was apparently accustomed to holding hands with and meeting in their back garden. Now she could deal with the ramifications of her willful, thoughtless actions.

He flung open the door to his room, startling Drake so badly the older man dropped a pair of boots he'd been carrying to the dressing room.

"What the devil are you doing still awake?" Gabriel snapped, slamming the candlestick down hard enough that it sheared a sliver of wood off the inlaid console table.

Drake's eyes jumped from Gabriel to the table, back to Gabriel. He opened his mouth.

"Never mind," Gabriel said, sliding a hand beneath his cravat and ripping it from his neck so viciously the fine fabric made a friction burn on his skin. He flung the wrinkled linen onto his dressing table and began unbuttoning his coat, his hands shaking with barely restrained violence.

"Mrs. Marlington was looking for you, sir."

Gabriel stopped, arrested. "When?"

Drake swallowed, his Adam's apple bobbing in a way that Gabriel might have found amusing—if he didn't feel like such a monster for terrorizing the poor man. He pushed the air noisily from his lungs.

"I apologize for snapping at you," he said, tossing his coat to Drake. His valet caught the garment and nodded, the slight flush over his cheekbones telling Gabriel the apology, as terse as it was, had pleased him.

"She was looking for you about two hours ago, sir."

"What did you tell her?"

"Only that you'd gone out."

Gabriel lowered himself into his dressing room chair, his boiling anger gone as suddenly as it had seized him, cold fury taking its place. So, she'd been doing proper reconnaissance before making her plans and inviting her lover.

Drake came to remove his boots. "I just fetched some hot water, thinking you might be back soon," Drake said, turning one boot in his hand and looking for flaws before setting it down carefully and removing the other.

Gabriel grunted, his brain pulsing.

Drake glanced at the connecting door to his wife's room. "Would you like me to shave you?"

He considered his reflection in the mirror. Candlelight glinted off the tiny hairs that grew fast enough that he had to shave twice a day. He ran his knuckles over his jaw. Did he want to see his wife? He'd been so certain a mere moment earlier, but he'd look a damned fool rushing in there like a jealous husband, wouldn't he? Besides, he'd wanted to shave because he'd been planning to take her to bed. Now he wanted to throw her out of the bloody house. She could go to her lover, by God.

Gabriel realized he'd become excitable just thinking about speaking to her. No, talking to her in such a mood would be catastrophic.

He met Drake's eyes in the mirror. His valet was a perfect example of his breed, and his expression was as unreadable as the dark side of the moon.

"Not tonight, Drake. I'm for bed."

Her husband did not greet her with breakfast.

Drusilla had heard him return home last night—terrifyingly soon after Theo had left. Just thinking of the idiot's ill-conceived visit made her stomach churn with nausea.

What would have happened if Gabriel had seen him on his way back? Good God! What if Gabriel had been *here*?

She *knew* the answer to that: Theo would be standing in Hyde Park at dawn with a pistol in his hand a few days hence.

She'd shivered at the thought.

Where had Gabriel gone for such a short time? He'd not been away above a few hours. He could have visited his mistress—*mistresses*—she corrected, gritting her teeth. But she somehow doubted that.

Yet he'd not visited her, either. She'd waited and waited for him to come to her last night, although she could hardly blame him for staying away after her shrewish behavior. She'd waited even after the light between their dressing rooms was extinguished—for over an hour. Even after she'd gone to sleep, she'd done nothing more than thrash and twist and turn until the bedding formed a tight spiral around her body.

So she'd given up on sleeping and gotten out of bed at dawn, waiting impatiently until it was a civil hour to summon Fletcher. She was dressed in her nicest morning gown and in the breakfast room before eight.

Only Parker was inside when she arrived. "Good morning, Mrs. Marlington."

"Good morning, Parker." She hesitated. "Has Mr. Marlington already eaten?"

"No, ma'am, he has not returned from his morning ride. Can I bring you some tea and toast?"

She smiled at the fact that her preferences were already well known. "Yes, thank you."

A freshly ironed paper sat at the head of the table, giving her hope he might join her. She was just finishing her toast when she heard the distinctive sound of boots in the hall. She closed the paper and set it aside.

He stopped in the doorway when he saw her. "Ah, Mrs. Marlington. I didn't expect you would be up or I would have bathed and changed first. I smell of the stables."

He was ruffled and sweaty, his dark brown top boots dusty: he looked delicious.

"Please, do not delay your breakfast on my account," she said, and immediately cringed at her cold tone and hastened to add, "Indeed, I would like it if you joined me."

His eyebrows shot up, but he entered the room. "Very well. A pot of coffee, Thomas," he told the footman hovering beside the door.

The servant left, and Gabriel went to the buffet. When he turned back to the table, she saw he had a full plate.

He spread a napkin over his lap, his expression distant, reserved. Gone was the affectionate, teasing, and amorous man of yesterday. He must have noticed her eyes on his mountain of food. "Riding always works up an appetite."

"Do you ride every morning?" she asked, latching on to the innocuous topic.

He cut into a slab of ham. "Most mornings."

The breakfast room was silent but for the sound of cutlery on crockery.

He met her eyes, his own unreadable, while he commenced to methodically consume the contents of his plate.

Drusilla's face was hot, and she knew she must be red and splotchy. She took a sip of tea, cleared her throat, and tried again. "I hope you don't mind, but I accepted an invitation to dine at Exley House."

He swallowed, took a drink of coffee, and wiped his mouth with his linen before saying, "Very well," and resuming his meal.

She could tolerate it no longer. "I wanted—"

Parker entered with his pot of coffee and cast a look at Drusilla's empty plate. "May I bring you anything else, ma'am? Perhaps another pot of tea?"

"Thank you, no. I shall float away if I drink a second pot."

Parker looked ready to hover, but Gabriel said, "You may leave us, Parker. Thomas, we shan't need anything else."

Drusilla looked from Parker's receding back to Gabriel. What was going on?

He laid down his silverware and pushed away his unfinished plate. "I was going to wait until later today to speak to you, but I would rather do so now if you have a few minutes to spare?"

"Yes, of course." A chill shot up her spine at his cold, polite tone.

"What I am about to say will no doubt surprise and displease you. However, it cannot be helped."

Drusilla stirred a bit of milk into her final cup of tea and waited, her body becoming tenser by the second.

"I have a son."

Her spoon clattered against the porcelain teacup and her head whipped up. He was looking at her with that haughty, distant expression she was beginning to hate.

"I b-beg your pardon?" The words came out a croak. She cleared her throat. "Did you say you had a *son*?"

"Yes."

She stared at him, looking for signs of . . . anything. But he was as readable as a brick wall.

"He is not yet six and his name is Samir." He watched her closely, and she couldn't help wondering what her face looked like; what was he seeing? "When we move to the country at the end of the Season, I intend that he will go with us—that he will live with us at Sizemore."

Drusilla suddenly recalled Visel—and his sly questions about Gabriel's family—did *he* know about this? He must; that *must* have been what he meant.

Dear God—was the child one of the French actresses'?

The room was quiet but for the ticking of the longcase

clock behind her and the faint sounds of street noises. He took another sip of coffee. She had to ask—*had* to.

"And his mother?" Her voice broke on the last word, and she felt her face heat. "Will she be living with us, too?" She hadn't meant to say that.

His high, sharp cheekbones flushed. "His mother is dead." His grim expression told her that was all she'd get out of him on that subject.

She swallowed—something she seemed to be doing constantly—her mind beginning to function again, beginning to whir, in fact. No, the child could not belong to one of his mistresses. She had been foolish. If the boy was almost six, Gabriel could not have been much more than a boy himself when his son was conceived. In fact, he must have been in Oran and—

"He is only recently arrived in England and he does not speak English very well. He is, however, conversant in French."

"He is in London?"

"Yes."

"But . . . where is he?"

His nostrils flared slightly. "He is with friends for now."

She looked down at the table, to where her hand was turning her unused fork over and over and over in place. If the boy wasn't at Exley House or here—where was he? Drusilla could not bring herself to ask.

"He has a nurse he is fond of and she will come with him. The schoolroom and nursery at Sizemore are both remote from the rest of the house. He will be close enough for me to see him as much as possible, but not so close as to cut up your peace."

His words rendered her mute. Did he really *mean* what he'd just said? Could he believe she was so . . . cold?

"I know this is unconventional, but it is likely he has no other immediate family, and—even if he does—I wish to keep him with me."

Drusilla stared down at the fork.

He had a child. A child he loved enough to insist on bringing him into their home. He was not asking her permission; he was telling her.

"I hope your silence does not mean this will present a problem for you?"

She looked up, bristling at his haughty expression and commanding tone. How dare he drop such a bomb on her and expect a quick and thoughtful response?

How *dare* he assume the worst of her only because of her silence?

"And if it was a problem, Mr. Marlington?"

His handsome features shifted into hard, haughty lines. "Then you would have to learn to overcome it. My son will live in my house."

Drusilla held his stare, so furious at his high-handed ways and insulting assumptions she felt she might go up in flames. Who was he to believe her so cruel and unfeeling? She released the fork, folded her napkin, and set it beside her plate. "Was that all you wished to say to me?"

His jaw flexed. "No, that is not all. I saw you sent a letter to Mr. Rowland last night."

Drusilla's jaw sagged. Was that the only thing he'd seen? Oh God, please don't let him have seen Theo.

He nodded, as though she'd said something. "I thought I had made my desires on the subject of Mr. Rowland clear." His words were clipped, his tone as sharp as a blade.

"I beg your pardon?" she said, even though she'd heard him perfectly well.

He put his napkin beside his plate, the action mirroring hers. "I am going upstairs to change, bathe, and then get dressed. And when I come down again, I will pay a visit on Mr. Rowland." She sucked in a breath and he smiled. "His direction was on the envelope, you see."

"Wh-what are you going to do?"

"I'm going to tell him what I hoped *you* would have told him—that I don't want him talking to my wife. I am going to tell him this will be the last time we speak of the matter. The next time, we will let pistols do the talking."

"But . . . but this is *outrageous.* He is not my l-lover." She paused to catch her breath, her face scalding at the word. "He is part of a group I formed to provide assistance to the poor and needy."

His expression was implacable. "Either he leaves the group, or you do."

"This is a group to administer money to *charity*," she repeated.

"If you wish to manage charity endeavors with Mr. Rowland, you may do so through the proper intermediary, your man of business." He hesitated, a harsh expression on his face. "Unless he, too, is a man you hold hands with in public?"

The reality of what was happening had finally begun to seep in, like rainwater into hard-packed soil: he was forbidding her to see somebody—a man.

She shook her head slowly from side to side. "No. You cannot do this."

His mouth shifted into an unpleasant smile, and he sat back in his chair, resting his hands loosely over his flat midriff.

"I assure you, I can. And I will."

She sputtered. "He is not my lover."

"I am pleased to hear it."

"This is draconian! You think you can control whom I see and whom I befriend?"

"Yes." The hard glint in his eye sent a shiver of fear up her spine.

"And what about you?"

"Me?"

"Yes, you. Do I get a say about whom *you* see?"

He chuckled, appearing genuinely amused.

"Why are you laughing? That was a serious question."

He leaned toward her, his face as hard and pitiless as the falcon he so resembled. "Then here is a serious answer: no."

"So you may keep as many lovers as you want and I can do—"

"Nothing." The glint in his eyes was mean—hurtful. "And you had better accustom yourself to that fact."

Her hands were shaking, and she clasped them tightly together. "Why are you acting like this?" she said, disgusted by the pleading in her voice. "I have done nothing wrong. Why are you behaving this way? I thought you said you wished to—"

He shot to his feet and shoved back his chair so hard it skittered across the smooth marble and clattered against the sideboard. She sprang to her feet, her mouth hanging open.

"What did you think, tell me? You thought I wished to make something of this marriage? Whatever gave you that idea? A single evening of sex? A pot of tea in your bedchamber?"

Drusilla's head spun. Had it only been yesterday when he'd been so kind to her?

"Yes, only yesterday," he said, making her realize she'd spoken out loud. His lips became thin, his expression one of barely repressed fury. "Before I saw Rowland leaving through our garden gate last night."

Drusilla grabbed the back of the chair to steady herself.

"Ah, yes. Now I believe you understand."

"It is not what you think, Gabriel." Even to her ears, the words sounded weak.

He strode toward her, not stopping until he loomed over her. "You know what I think?"

She could imagine. "No," she whispered.

"I think you could have come to me last night and told me

of his visit—or even this morning. Or perhaps you could have sent him away in the first place, told him you refused to see him at any time, but most *especially* at two o'clock in the morning. You wouldn't even need to speak to him to tell him that—we keep servants for that purpose. But what did I see?" He did not wait for an answer. "The moment I am out of the house, the two of you come rushing to each other—lurking together in the dead of night. Two conspirators—two *lovers*—meeting in the dark." He leaned even closer, until she could clearly see the shards of green and gold, his pupils mere pinpricks.

Drusilla saw no trace of the man she'd flirted with at the Renwick ball, the man who'd defended her against the sharp claws of Lucinda Kittridge, the man who'd said such lovely words and done such intimate things to her.

The knowledge that much of this was her fault came crashing down on her. She had rejected his kindness yesterday and last night had met a man he believed to be her lover in his garden. *That* at least she could straighten out.

She laid a hand on his arm, which was as hard as steel beneath the fine wool of his coat. "Please, *Gabriel*."

His lips tightened, but he did not snatch his arm away.

"I am *not*—"

"I had hoped we could make something of our lives together. I had hoped we might build something out of the mess Visel created for us. But now I see I was just a fool." His eyes brimmed with disgust, disappointment, and something else—regret?

"I will not be made a cuckold, Drusilla. I will kill Rowland before I allow that to happen." He turned from her and strode toward the door.

Drusilla could only stare in mute horror as he swung open the door and slammed it shut behind him. Leaving her alone with the mess she had made.

* * *

Gabriel kept seeing her white, shocked face. Her huge, terror-stricken eyes.

"So what?" he said aloud, although there was only himself to answer. He turned to the grimy hack window and stared out onto the street, trying to block the image from his mind. He'd only done and said what she deserved. He felt like a fool for having tried to make an effort to salvage their faux marriage. He had ended his relationship with two women he liked very much; he had forgiven her incessant slights; he'd swallowed his regret at being forced into a lifelong union with a woman not of his choosing and had entered into their marriage with an open mind even after she picked at him and picked at him and looked at him as if he were lower than the dirt on her shoes. Even when he had caught her holding hands with her lover after they were betrothed.

And this was what he received in return: his wife meeting with a man who clearly held intentions toward her—in his very own garden!

He'd gritted his teeth until his jaw ached. The hackney slowed and then stopped. A glance out the window told him he was nowhere near Rowland's lodgings. The vent opened.

"Sorry, gov, but there's a bleedin' mess in the road."

Gabriel opened the door and looked ahead. A wagon filled with barrels appeared to have collided with a mail coach.

Gabriel hopped out and flipped a coin up to the driver. "I shall walk."

"Aye," the bent old man muttered, "I might join ye."

He decided to leave the main street, which was rapidly devolving into chaos. It would take a little longer and he would come out a few streets behind the square where Rowland kept lodgings, but, to be honest, Gabriel was in no hurry.

He was in a devil of a mood and didn't trust himself with

the other man. Not only did he not wish to kill anyone, but he'd look a terrible fool getting into another duel less than a week after his last one.

Another image of his wife's stricken face flickered through his head.

"Dammit to hell," he muttered, ignoring the startled look of a pair of young men who just happened to be passing.

Perhaps she'd not been doing anything improper with Rowland. In the garden. At two o'clock in the morning.

Gabriel gave a brief, scathing laugh and stopped at a busy street to wait for a coach to pass.

What if the only thing she'd felt guilty about was being caught? a caustic inner voice demanded. *What if she had an explanation but you wouldn't stop long enough to hear it?*

Gabriel handed a penny to a young street sweeper, who scampered off, and gestured for an older woman dressed in the clothing of a governess to precede him. She nodded primly and followed the urchin.

Once across, he took a right and then an immediate left into a mews that led to the square. He was stopped at an unexpected split in the narrow alley, wondering which way to turn, when a voice he recognized came from up ahead.

"Dammit, Theo, what the devil could you have been thinking?"

Gabriel experienced a distinct déjà vu: Hadn't the same thing happened to him less than twelve hours ago?

Not exactly the same: this time two men stepped out of a doorway onto the cobbles. Once again Gabriel sidestepped back into the other alley, peering around the corner.

Visel had stopped and was looking down at his boot, which he was cleaning on a metal scraper embedded between cobblestones for that very purpose.

Gabriel couldn't see the other man's face as he appeared to be locking the door.

"I've told you to put an end to whatever it was you've been scheming with the woman," Visel said, his tone that of a man who was delivering a familiar lecture. "You were just to go there, be seen by him, and *leave*. Trust me, I will pay you enough to make it worth your while."

The second man turned to the first, and Gabriel wasn't surprised to see it was Theodore Rowland.

"But I merely need two more signatures, Godric." Rowland was speaking in a whiny, snively voice that made Gabriel's foot twitch to kick him.

Visel gave his boot one last scrape and frowned down at it before turning back to the other man. "I don't give a damn what you need. Just do what I bloody tell you." He set off down the alley without waiting for an answer. "Don't get in the middle of this, Theo. This is about more than just money."

"I know, I know," Rowland said in a placatory tone, his voice becoming fainter. "There is Marlington. I understand. But I don't understand why—"

Gabriel couldn't hear the rest of what he said and there was no chance of following the two men without being seen. He watched until they turned onto the square and disappeared from sight. No doubt they were headed to Rowland's rooms. Gabriel went to the door Rowland had locked and saw through the cutout that it led to some stalls and a small covered courtyard; a shared mews.

He turned to stare at the empty alleyway, as if that might give him some answers to the questions whirling around in his head.

Just what the devil was Visel up to now and how did it involve Gabriel?

He took a deep breath and released it slowly while staring down the empty alley. He knew one thing: he could not go to the man and tell him to stay away from Drusilla—at least not until he knew what it was Rowland and Visel were up to.

He couldn't confront him, but he'd damned well keep an eye on both of them.

Gabriel's head had begun to ache. Just what was going on?

Nothing came to mind—nothing at all.

The only thing he knew for certain was that Visel and Rowland were up to something and, whatever it was, it involved Gabriel's wife.

Chapter 17

Drusilla paced the three rooms that comprised her domain, back and forth. Back and forth. She'd had Fletcher dress her for dinner and then dismissed her. The last thing she wanted was a witness to her mood.

Her mood: That was inaccurate. The truth was she was having *moods*. Her moods were swinging from one extreme to another every few minutes. She had been as taut as a spring since breakfast, and the day had been a miserable blur.

She could not bear it.

One minute she was making plans for escaping Gabriel. She could run away—to Europe, now that the war was over, or even to America, where nobody would know her. She certainly had enough money to do such a thing.

But there was her Aunt Vi.

The older lady was too ill to travel and Drusilla knew she wouldn't wish to leave England even if she could. Her aunt was visibly excited about moving to Bath at the end of the Season. So that would mean Drusilla would need to leave alone. It was not ideal, but the option was available—if things became too unbearable.

Thanks to Gabriel's generosity with their marriage contract, she was in full control of all but a portion of her money—the money set aside for any children.

Children.

Even if she remained in England, it was likely they would never have children. At least not together.

She pressed her cool hands to her hot cheeks but did not slow her pacing.

Was she jealous he had an illegitimate child? Drusilla had examined her conscience on the question at least a hundred times. The answer, she was sure, was no. That had relieved her—it would have been unbearable if she'd been petty enough to blame an innocent little boy for his situation. She was, however, angry at Gabriel and the irresponsibility of his action. His son would have to bear the stigma of illegitimacy his entire life.

Drusilla knew how Gabriel struggled with the label in England. Of course, he'd been something of a prince in his own country—surely where this child had been conceived—so probably the specter of illegitimacy had not been an issue. Besides, his father had been a sultan—the ruler of his people. No doubt it was like England, where it was prestigious to be the bastard child of a king.

She could never be happy that Gabriel had had many other lovers and had even had a child by one. But the fact that he could believe she would take out her anger on an innocent child? That she would believe the boy should be raised anywhere but with his father? What kind of monster did he think she was?

Drusilla stopped in front of her dressing room mirror and stared at her reflection, searching for whatever it was in her face that would make him believe she could act so cruelly toward a child.

All she saw was a woman with purple circles beneath her eyes from lack of sleep. Her pale skin—skin he had praised as beautiful—broadcast her exhaustion as plainly as a torch on a moonless night.

But that wasn't all.

Nasty thoughts pushed up like weeds between cobbles: *What about the rest of what he said, Drusilla? What about that? What about those two mistresses who* must *have the boy right now? What does a man* do *with two women at one time . . .*

"Oh, stop!" she cried, slumping onto the padded bench in front of her dressing table and dropping her head into her hands. It ate at her that he would not introduce her to his son, that he would keep the child with . . . Drusilla could not say the words out loud even though the women were indelibly etched in her mind after the play she'd been forced to watch. Jealousy and anger surged again at the thought of being forced to watch his mistresses. She told herself it was not his fault—he'd not been the one to arrange the evening. It had been the Duke of Tyndale. The thought should have calmed her, but her anger was joined by hurt, and that was much harder to forget or ignore.

She could not live this way. If he planned on flaunting his multitudinous affairs, she would—

"Drusilla?"

She looked up to find Gabriel standing in the opening, dressed for dinner. She must have been so distracted she'd not even heard him come in.

"I knocked, but there was no answer." He sounded as emotionless as he looked. "Are you ready?"

She stood, her legs watery. "Could we take just a moment?"

He hesitated, but then stepped back and gestured to his room. Drusilla followed him though the dressing room, bedchamber, and into his study. It was very similar to hers, but decorated in soothing shades of brown and forest green. Two overstuffed leather chairs faced each other in front of the dormant fireplace.

"Please, sit."

Her pulse was pounding in her throat and she hoped he did not see it. "I wanted to explain something to you."

He raised his eyebrows and crossed one black pantaloon-sheathed leg over the other.

"It is about Mr. Rowland."

His lips tightened, but he did not speak.

"I did not know he was coming last night." She chewed her bottom lip. "I had forgotten all about the message he sent the night of our"—she broke off—"well, the message he sent the night we were married. I'm afraid that with everything else, it slipped my mind." She ignored his skeptical look and rushed on. "The message was still in my dressing gown." Drusilla held the paper, which she'd folded into a tiny rectangle, in her palm and offered it to him. "Please, read it."

While he unfolded and read the letter, Drusilla smoothed her skirt. The gown was one of her favorites, although it was nothing particularly special. The color, a pearly off-white, was accented with a navy-blue sash that ran beneath her breasts, somehow managing to make them look far less conspicuous. It was probably old-fashioned and too modestly cut, but she believed it suited her generous figure.

She heard paper rustling and looked up to see him refolding the letter.

"When I found and read the letter, I sent him one in return—a letter saying I forgave him, but that he should no longer send me messages or attempt to meet me in private." She swallowed, needing to prepare for this next part. "Apparently he was anxious that he'd not received a response. So he came here last night and delivered a note to Thomas and then waited in the garden." She took a deep breath and exhaled. "I told him the same thing I said in my letter. Additionally, I told him it would be better if he left the group entirely. He asked to attend one more meeting and then agreed he would leave."

Gabriel handed her the letter, his face still shuttered.

Drusilla could not tolerate the silence, the suspicion, no matter that she might deserve it.

"Do you believe me?" She held her breath while he stared at her—*into* her.

"Yes, I believe you."

Drusilla dropped her head and closed her eyes, concentrating on breathing. She thought she might faint she was so relieved.

"I am glad you told me this, but I am also curious." She looked up. "Would you have done so if I had not confronted you?"

Her face heated, but she wanted to be honest. "I would not have spoken of the matter."

To her surprise, he gave a dry chuckle. "Well, at least you are truthful."

"The reason I would not have told you is that I couldn't believe you would credit such a story as true." She laced her hands together and then unlaced them. "I hope you don't mind that I've allowed him to come to one last meeting."

He shook his head, his eyes dark and serious, but his expression was no longer as hard as granite.

"And I want you to know that I have done as you said and have written a letter to Jenkins to explain about the work Mr. Rowland began in Birmingham and Leeds. He responded to say he would put one of his men on it immediately." She exhaled a gusty sigh. "I should have done this from the beginning. But I was so excited about the notion of setting up more houses."

He stood, closing the distance between them, holding out his hand and helping her to her feet.

"There is one more thing."

"Oh?" He went still, as if he were girding himself.

"It is not more bad news. I just wanted to say I am pleased you will bring your son to live with us."

His hand tightened almost painfully on hers, and she winced.

"I'm sorry." He released her.

"You didn't hurt me." She forced herself to meet his eyes for her next words. "I told myself not to be insulted by what you said at breakfast—that you believed I would protest the fact you wished to be near your own child. I told myself you were thinking I possessed the sensibilities of a lady of the *ton*. But the truth is, you married a hardheaded woman of the merchant class. And also a woman who is concerned about the plight of the weak and dispossessed. What kind of a person would I be if I wished my husband to abandon his own flesh and blood?"

"You *wish* for him to live with us?"

Drusilla gave a small huff. "Of course I do, Gabriel. He is your son—conceived before we met—how could I be angry about such a thing?" She did not tell him she was jealous of the fact another woman had carried his child; there was no point. "I love children and I am eager to meet him."

"Even though he is not legitimate?"

Drusilla gave him an arch look. "That's hardly his fault, is it?"

He flushed under her critical stare but then surprised her by smiling. "No, it is not." He offered her his arm. "Come," he said, "the carriage is waiting."

If Drusilla was hoping he would explain his son's origins, she was to be disappointed. Still, she felt more optimistic about them—certainly about their ability to communicate when they both put their minds to it.

Perhaps they might learn to make something of their marriage, after all.

The truce between Gabriel and his wife was a delicate one but it strengthened over the coming days.

Like any *ton* couple, they went out every night, attending the mad whirl of routs and balls that occurred as the Season drew to an end. Unlike other *ton* couples, they attended many of the *same* functions. It was unusual for a husband and wife to socialize so often in each other's company, but Gabriel knew his new wife did not have a broad social circle. Besides, he found that he enjoyed accompanying her. In addition to being a very clever woman, she also possessed a well-developed sense of humor and had a keen eye when it came to evaluating her fellow man.

They often returned home near dawn, said goodnight, and did not see one another until the following evening, when it was time to do it all over again.

During the day they lived almost separate lives.

Drusilla spent a great deal of her time with her aunt and paid a few calls. She sometimes went shopping, although he did not think she was in any way as profligate as his sisters and mother when it came to clothing.

Gabriel had considered offering to go shopping with her, himself. Her clothing was . . . well, it was not always flattering to her rather voluptuous figure.

But of course he made no such offer.

Instead he saw Samir each day and rejoiced in the opportunity to get to know the boy. He also went to his club, rode in the park with Eva and Byer—Drusilla had still not offered to join them—and even accompanied the marquess when his stepfather visited one of his newly acquired properties.

Her friendship with Eva appeared rather stilted but at least the two women were talking. As for their own interactions, Gabriel had found the few times they were alone together to be agreeable. Dinner, which they usually ate at home, had been much more pleasant and enjoyable since the evening of their "talk." They spoke on general subjects and avoided any of those topics that had caused trouble in the past. Gabriel never asked about what transpired at her charity group meetings, and she did not ask him how he spent his days.

They lived the life of a newly married young couple, with one notable exception: Gabriel did not go to his wife's bed.

It was not that he did not desire her—quite the contrary—nor was it because he had not forgiven her for their past disagreements. He bore no grudges and he had enjoyed their one night of lovemaking—*very* much—and found that she grew increasingly appealing with each day that passed.

But she was an enigma to him and he was in no hurry to make love to her and find himself slapped down the following morning. Besides, he'd decided it could not hurt to take some time and get to know her outside the bedroom.

As often as he told himself that noble reason for avoiding Drusilla's bed, he probably wouldn't have been able to stay away from her for ten days if he'd not been spending his evenings elsewhere.

Ever since seeing and hearing Rowland and Visel together, he'd been spending most nights after she'd gone to bed prowling around their house or the area where Visel and Rowland appeared to live. Because he couldn't watch everywhere at once, he'd brought Byer in on his problem—not that he was sure what the problem *was*.

It had turned out to be a good idea to bring in his friend

as Byer seemed to know everything about every member of the *ton*, no matter how obscure.

Gabriel had gone to meet the viscount at White's the evening after he'd seen Rowland and Visel outside Rowland's lodgings.

"You might as well tell me what you know about the two of them," he told his indolent friend, who'd been waiting at the club when Gabriel arrived.

Byer's eyebrows shot up. "The last time I tried to say anything, you told me you'd rather gargle glass than discuss Visel."

"And I would. Unfortunately, I don't have the luxury of ignorance. Back then I believed he was going to disappear from my life. Now I fear I shall never be rid of him."

"Very well, I shall tell you what I know, which is not very much. Visel and Rowland are cousins, although I did not know they were close. But if you saw them together twice in as many nights—in such odd places as your mews and outside Rowland's lodgings—obviously they are closer than I believed," he mused, tilting the glass of brandy back and forth in front of the light.

"I know as little about Rowland as I do about Visel," Byer admitted. "He is from the poorer branch of the family. I believe he was schooled at his father's country manse—I recall his having a dozen siblings." Byer shrugged and waved his hand as if dismissing the poorer man. "Now Visel . . ."

"Yes?" Gabriel prodded.

"Visel is older than I, of course. He was in my brother Kenneth's form. They weren't mates, but I recall his mentioning Visel when he went off to war." He shot Gabriel a mocking smile. "Kenneth was mad to join up, but my father refused to cough up the dosh to buy him a pair of colors. He was destined for the Church, you know. But I am digressing. I think Visel was several rungs down the ladder when it came to inheriting his uncle's dukedom. If I am not mistaken, Tyndale's son and at least two of Visel's elder brothers stood between him and the dukedom when he joined the army." He stopped and took a sip, savoring the mouthful and clearly in no hurry to continue.

"What happened to the brothers?"

"They died. They'd gone over just before Napoleon escaped Elba. They went en masse to celebrate the end of the war and visit Visel, who'd been bedbound for months from a life-threatening injury." Byer gave Gabriel an odd look. "Their ship was attacked on the journey over and their captain—a man who'd been in the navy—gave fight instead of trying to outrun their aggressor."

Gabriel shook his head in disbelief. "They were attacked between here and Calais?"

"No, they didn't take a packet. Visel was someplace smack in the heart of Spain. Apparently they deemed it faster to go through Gibraltar rather than overland." Byer paused. For the first time in Gabriel's memory, the talkative man did not seem interested in talking.

"Out with it, Tommy."

"It was a corsair ship that sank theirs." He shot Gabriel a flat look and then threw back the remains of his glass, grimacing at the burn. "Everyone on board was either killed when the ship sank or taken prisoner."

Gabriel had a sick feeling in the pit of his stomach. "Who was onboard?"

"All of them—every single member of his immediate family decided to pull up stumps and go see him. You know how things were just after the war—people were giddy with the end of the seemingly endless conflict. The French had been vanquished—what danger could there be?"

"Who?"

He took a deep breath. "Mother, father, two brothers—one with his wife and child, and a younger sister."

"My God. *Seven* people. His entire family wiped out?"

A mist of red covered Byer's sharp cheekbones. "Not the sister or the second eldest brother. But by the time the duke sent a man with ransom money, the brother had died and the sister was nowhere to be found."

Gabriel closed his eyes and dropped his head into his hands, the sense of guilt crushing. He knew it was irrational: he'd fought to end his people's dependence on slavery. He had never dealt with slavers and had argued more than once with his father that slavery was not only immoral, but that it was the way of a bygone era.

No, he should not feel guilty—he'd done nothing. But he probably knew the people who had—he was probably even related to some of them. People who'd killed Visel's entire family.

He shook his head and looked up at his friend. "That is why Visel hates me—he blames *me*. Why didn't you tell me this before?"

"Because I knew you'd get that look on your face: the one you are wearing right now. The one you were wearing when you came back from Oran this last time."

"What look is that?" he snapped.

"As if you'd like to put a pistol to your head." Byer leaned forward. "What happened to Visel's family is not your fault, Gabe."

"Where did the ship take the prisoners?"

Byer shook his head.

"Tell me, dammit!"

Four men at the nearest table turned at the sound of his raised voice. Gabriel got hold of his frazzled emotions. "Just tell me."

"Oran."

Gabriel groaned. "Good Lord. Why don't I recall reading about any of this?"

"It was small news compared to Napoleon's escape. People were in a state of shock and paying attention to the resumption of war—not the sinking of a ship. As for Visel's sister? Well, the duke has impressive connections and made sure the story was not spread—on the chance the girl could be ransomed."

"How the hell do *you* know about it?"

Byer just gave him a stony look. This wasn't the first time Gabriel had wondered what his friend was really up to when he hadn't been in their shared lodgings at Oxford. That there was more to Byer was apparent—Gabriel already knew that—but he suspected the man kept even deeper secrets hidden beneath his lazy, foppish façade.

"So, Visel wants to make me suffer because somebody else—quite probably one of Assad's captains—killed his family."

"You are the only one left to punish."

Gabriel knew his friend was correct—no matter how mad or illogical it was. "Then why did he apologize and call off the duel?"

Byer's face flushed, and he shifted in his chair.

"What? What is it you are not telling me?"

His friend shook his head. "No. If I tell you, you'll kill the man."

Gabriel took a deep breath and let it out slowly. "I will not. I give you my word."

Still Byer hesitated.

"Byer—"

"All right, all right." He raised his hand. "But I'll need another glass for this." He waved to a waiter and held up two fingers.

"I didn't ask for that," Gabriel said.

"No, but I think you'll be glad you have it."

"Will you just get on with it?"

"Visel apologized that night because he'd already gotten his revenge. Not only was he pleased about breaking up your budding romance with the Kitten, but he felt you'd been doubly punished by being forced to marry Miss—" Byer grimaced.

Gabriel stared. "Go on."

"Dash it, Gabe—why must you make me say it? Fine." He went on before Gabriel could answer. "Visel said it was punishment enough to be forced to marry a woman like Miss Clare."

Gabriel stared at Byer without seeing his friend. His blood boiled, but not just with fury at Visel. No, words always hurt the worst when there was a grain of truth to them. And it was the unfortunate truth that he, too, had viewed marrying Drusilla as a harsh punishment.

"I told you that you wouldn't like it," Byer said, pulling Gabriel's thoughts away from his shame.

No, he didn't like it. In fact, he burned at the insult to his wife. "When the hell did you hear this?"

"He told me."

"What?"

"Yes, he told me that night—not long after he apologized. You had left to go to Exley House and I ran into Visel at McNair's." McNair's was a notorious gambling den so vile even the Runners avoided it. Byer, of course, adored the place.

Gabriel shook his head in disgust. "He told you because he wanted me to know."

"Precisely. Which is exactly why I *didn't* run and tell you."

"If Visel is so damned happy at trapping me into marriage, then why is he lurking about my bloody house and what the devil is he plotting with Rowland?"

The waiter dropped off the fresh drinks, and Byer handed one to Gabriel before picking up the other. "That, my friend, is something I do not know," Byer admitted, and then grinned at Gabriel like a mischievous boy. "But I'm bloody curious to find out—aren't you?"

Chapter 18

Gabriel finished tying his cravat and stepped back to examine the results. His clothing looked well enough, but there were dark circles beneath his eyes and the grooves that ran between his nose and mouth seemed twice as deep as they'd been at the beginning of the Season.

He slipped into the coat Drake held out for him, exhausted. He'd been burning the candle at both ends since the night he'd caught Rowland in the garden, but so far he had learned less than nothing. In fact, it seemed as if Visel had disappeared. Gabriel couldn't have said why, but an absent Visel made him almost more nervous than a lurking Visel.

As for Rowland? Byer had sent his valet—a sly, clever man who'd spent a stretch in the Steel—to the tea shop where Drusilla's group met. Gabriel had protested, feeling as if it were spying.

"It *is* spying, Gabe—on Rowland. And that brings to mind something else. I think you should hire somebody to keep an eye on your wife anytime she leaves the house." Gabriel had bristled, but Byer had rolled his eyes. "It's not *that*, you daft bugger. It's in case Rowland or Visel try anything."

"Like what?"

"Who knows, but it is better to be safe than sorry—is it not?"

So Gabriel had engaged a Runner, yet another of Byer's acquaintances. The man was slight, not at all what he'd expected of the famous Bow Street Runners.

"Don't worry," Byer had assured him. "Tompkins might be small, but he's as tough and wily as a terrier."

Drake held out Gabriel's ring, the only piece of jewelry he wore. The ring was gold and encircled in fine Berber script. The center bore a ruby with a falcon in intaglio—the symbol of his Berber tribe. It had belonged to the sultan—the only thing he had from his father.

Drake cleared his throat, and Gabriel looked up from his woolgathering to find him holding his cane and hat.

Gabriel took both. "Ah, thank you."

He left his chambers, heading toward the stairs, but stopped outside his wife's room: it was quiet within, so he resumed walking. It was past noon; no doubt she had already gone out. He had slept late as he'd returned home close to five in the morning.

He was more on edge than ever and had no idea what the devil was going on—especially when it came to Visel's mysterious absence. But he and Byer had done everything they could, short of invading the duke's house and demanding he produce his heir.

Gabriel smiled to himself at the foolish thought as he made his way down the stairs.

When he reached the foyer, it was to find Drusilla, her maid, and one of the footmen just preparing to leave.

"Ah, good afternoon, Drusilla." Acting on impulse, he kissed her cheek, causing her fair skin to blush. "Where are you bound?"

She paused in the act of pulling on her gloves. "To Hatchards and then to the dressmaker's."

"Perhaps I might steal a ride with you?"

She blinked up at him, her flush deepening. "Of course. I've ordered the barouche."

He offered his arm once her second glove was on. "I wasn't aware we had a barouche," he said, leading her down the front steps to a rather magnificent equipage.

Her hand tightened on his arm. "I hope you don't mind that I had it brought over, but it was my father's and I just thought—"

"Lord, what an ogre you must think me. Of course I don't mind using your father's barouche." He motioned away the waiting footman and helped her into the carriage. Fletcher hovered a few steps away, uncertain. Gabriel smiled down at her. "You too, Fletcher." He held out a hand, and the rather homely, narrow-faced woman blushed just as fierily as her mistress at the small courtesy. "You sit beside Mrs. Marlington, Fletcher. I'll take back-facing."

"Where to, sir?" a footman Gabriel did not recognize asked before he shut the door.

"I'll disembark with the ladies; I need no special stop."

"So," he said, after he'd settled himself in the seat. "How is your aunt feeling?" he asked his wife.

"She is doing much better this past week."

"And did you convince her to pay us a visit before she leaves town?"

"Yes, she will stay with us for three nights before she departs for Bath."

"Excellent. I look forward to having her in our household." He could see his words pleased her. "Buying anything special today?"

"A few books I've ordered have come in and I'm going to try on some gowns Fletcher believes might suit."

Gabriel's eyebrows leaped. "New gowns?" he said with a

playful smile. "Perhaps I should join you—I can act as your cicisbeo."

The maid choked back a laugh and even his stern wife smiled. "I'm sure you have better things to occupy your time."

Gabriel realized, suddenly, that he would actually like to spend some time with her doing something domestic. Although they'd been together often in the week and a half since establishing their tenuous truce, they were rarely alone.

Besides, he was not to see Samir today or tomorrow as Giselle and Maria had taken him out of the city to visit one of their many friends from France. The friend in question had a little boy who was Samir's age. They'd invited Gabriel, but he knew they would rather reminisce and gossip without a man in attendance.

"I'm at liberty today and would join you." He hesitated at her wide-eyed reaction. "That is, if you do not mind?"

"Oh," she said faintly, glancing down at her hands, which were gripping her reticule in a death hold. "That would be very . . . nice."

Drusilla sneaked a look over the top of the book she was considering purchasing. Gabriel sat in one of the chairs reading, his hat balanced elegantly on one knee, his cane propped against the chair. Why had he decided to join her? He'd been treating her like a stranger—a polite stranger—ever since the night she'd told him the truth about Rowland.

Every night she'd wondered if he'd come to her, and every night she'd been hurt and disappointed. Why? Why was he avoiding her? Was this the way it would be from now on? Had he gone back to his mistresses? She'd heard him return near dawn several mornings and had been seized with a mad, furious desire to burst into his rooms and demand where he'd been.

But then she'd wondered if she really wanted to know. Or was her imagination even worse? A man and two women . . . The thought was enough to drive her mad with jealousy. And something else: a tingling sensation between her thighs, a heaviness in her hips, a low, insistent pulsing inside her. In that place he had woken and now ignored.

She had gone so far as to leap out of bed and storm toward his door a few times, but then she'd stopped, her body throbbing. No. She could not demean herself so—she refused to beg.

And now here he was: Drusilla allowed her eyes to wander from his highly polished Hessians over his pantaloons and come to a rest on his magnificent torso. Why was he accompanying her on her daily errands as if it were the most natural thing in the world? Just what did he want from her?

He looked up and caught her staring. His gorgeous face creased into a smile, and he closed his book and stood. Drusilla took control of her rampaging thoughts and assumed a cool expression.

He held up *Waverley.* "Have you read this?"

"I do not read much fiction."

"Ah, only improving tracts?"

She shut her book and showed him the spine, a biography of Leonardo. "No, not *only* improving tracts."

He grinned. "I stand corrected." He reached out, and she handed him her book. "Here, let me buy this for you, to make up for my ignorant comment."

"Oh, you needn't."

"Oh, I *need,*" he teased.

He paid not only for that book, but for the two she'd ordered. They went out to the waiting barouche, and he handed the parcel to her footman.

"How far is your dressmaker? It is a lovely day—perhaps we might walk?"

A thrill of pleasure rippled through her. "You were not jesting then?" she blurted. "You really wish to come to my dressmaker with me?"

"I never jest about ladies' garments." He glanced down. "Do you have proper shoes for walking?"

"I am wearing my half boots." Drusilla couldn't help wondering what he thought she'd be wearing. And then she recalled the type of woman he normally consorted with.

He turned to John Coachman. "I shall see Mrs. Marlington gets back safely. Fletcher, you may go with him." He turned to Drusilla. "That is, if you do not need her?"

Drusilla's face heated at her maid's curious look. "No. I shan't need you, Fletcher."

The streets were busy and they passed more than a few people one or both of them knew.

"What are you collecting from the dressmaker's?" he asked her.

"Two new gowns."

"You have a riding habit, I trust?"

"Yes."

"Good. It is my hope we will get the chance to ride together when we are in the country."

She glanced up at him, ridiculously pleased by his words.

"You would like that?" he asked, cutting her a quick look before leading her around a steaming pile of animal manure.

"I've always wanted to ride more, but the only times I seemed to get around to it were those visits to Exham every summer."

"Those visits will not cease. We are not even a day's ride from Exham."

"I am glad."

"Are you? You and Eva have patched up your disagreement?"

Had they? "Things are slowly going back to the way they were before." She chewed her lip before adding. "I'm afraid she feels betrayed by me."

"She will get over it in time."

Drusilla wasn't quite so certain. "I also think she has developed other interests. At least she seems somewhat distracted."

"Oh? You mean new friends?"

Drusilla thought about Eva's confession that she'd been spying on Visel. She could not betray her friend yet again. So she said, "I don't know." It was a truthful, if evasive, answer.

"Eva has her quirks, but I'm sure she'll come around eventually. You are her best friend, after all."

Drusilla wasn't sure it was only the issue of the duel that was bothering Eva.

"Are you still riding with her in the morning?"

"I haven't gone the past few days but I know she goes with Byer." He glanced down at her, his lips twitching. "I have always wondered if she might be a little sweet on him."

"Byer?"

"I can tell by your tone you do not agree?"

"Indeed, no. She teases him, but I believe she views him as yet another brother."

"Hmm. Has she any particular partiality for any of the young gentlemen?"

"Not that I've seen." In fact, her friend seemed to have closed off the possibility of love and marriage in her mind. Although they never spoke of it, she knew the strain of madness in her mother's family was an issue that weighed heavily on Eva's mind. Her elder sister, Catherine, had married, but to a young baron who'd been injured in the war and could not have children, which was exactly what Eva's shy, quiet sister had wanted: no chance to pass along the potential taint of insanity.

Drusilla understood all too well that any man wanting

children, or with the responsibility of providing an heir, would probably not wish to take a woman with such questionable family history.

"Ah, here we are—Maison d'Hortense," he said, opening the heavy wood–and–beveled glass door to the Frenchwoman's elegant little shop.

Any opportunity for private conversation was over.

It was a few days after their shopping trip—and the first night since their marriage—that they had no plans for the evening; at least not beyond dinner.

They ate at Exley House, along with three other couples and an assortment of unmarried young men and women—no doubt invited for Eva and Byer. Drusilla found she enjoyed going out in public, now that she could put behind her the days of awkward introductions to young men who clearly had no interest in meeting her. Behind her also were the days of worrying about chaperones. So, when dinner had finished, she and Gabriel were free to wander the extensive Exley House gardens by themselves.

Although there had been no resumption of flirtation like that the night of the Renwick ball, they'd conversed on a wide range of topics without devolving into an argument as they used to do.

Drusilla had wanted to tell Gabriel that she'd severed ties with Theo. She'd been eager to terminate her relationship with the young man, so she had contacted the members of her small group and called a special meeting. His behavior that day had been a sore disappointment. In spite of his letter, he'd continued to behave just like a rejected lover. It had made her and the other members of her small group intensely uncomfortable. She had regretted that she'd misjudged him and was glad that was their last meeting.

She'd been on the verge of telling Gabriel about Theo during their walk in the garden, but she hadn't wanted to drag such a negative subject into what was a lovely evening.

They stayed at Exley House for another hour, and then Gabriel, to her surprise, begged his mother's pardon and asked to leave early.

Lady Exley had looked at her son with a concerned notch between her eyes. "You are tired, Jibril—the skin beneath your eyes is bruised." She glanced at Drusilla. "Take my son home and pamper him, my dear. Every man is a big baby who loves pampering."

Gabriel rolled his eyes and fired off something in Arabic. Lady Exley laughed and waved goodbye.

After they were settled into the carriage, he turned to her. "I told my mother her tongue was so loose it would fly away if it wasn't attached."

Drusilla gave a scandalized laugh. "What a dreadful thing to say to your mother."

He grunted. "It is the *only* thing to say to a mother like mine." He turned to her, his gorgeous features shadowed but still distinct thanks to the small lantern in the carriage. "I am an ignorant oaf and have never asked about your mother. She died when you were young?"

"Very young—she died in childbed."

His warm hand covered hers. "Ah, my poor Drusilla," he murmured, gently caressing her.

Drusilla was not expecting what happened next: her eyes watered, her throat tightened, and a tear slid down her cheek.

"What is this?" he asked, his voice wondering. "I have made you cry?"

"I don't know *why* I'm blubbering," she said, her voice approaching a wail.

He slid an arm around her and held her tightly. "There's nothing wrong with crying, Drusilla. All of this has been a strain on you—on both of us."

His kindness was the last straw. "I don't wish to live at odds with you, Gabriel—I *hate* it when we quarrel."

His expression was arrested and her face heated under his tiercel-like gaze. "I don't wish to live at odds with you, either."

A sob of relief tore out of her before she could clamp her jaws shut.

He leaned down and kissed away her tears. "Shhhh, *ya amar*," he whispered.

She sniffed in a most mortifying fashion. "What does that mean?"

He kissed her cheek, using the tip of his tongue on the path of her tears. "My moon."

That just made her cry harder. "I'm so sorry. I don't know what has gotten into me."

He kissed her temple. "I know what *will* be getting into you."

Drusilla gasped. Surely he could not mean . . .

He chuckled. "There, see? You are no longer weeping."

"That was so—so—*wicked*." There had to be a better word, but she could not think of it.

"Mm-hmm." He kissed the tip of her nose. "You have a nice nose—small and with a sweet little tip that turns up."

"Ugh, I hate my nose. But yours . . ."

"What? You like this beak?"

"Yes." The single word somehow managed to waver and the naked desire in her voice made his nostrils flare.

"Well, there is no accounting for taste." The carriage rolled to a gentle stop and his lips curved into a smile just before his mouth covered hers. Although she was ready and eager for his touch, he kissed her with a passionate thoroughness that left her head spinning.

When he pulled away, they were both breathing heavily. "Thank God. We are home . . . at last."

* * *

Gabriel was so hard he was tempted to barrel into her chambers and lift her skirts. But, wisely, he gained control of himself before reaching the third floor.

He turned to her on the landing outside her room. "I will come to you in—"

"Ten minutes."

He'd been about to say a half hour, but grinned at her answer and kissed her—hard. "Ten minutes," he said, watching her disappear into her chambers before going to his own room.

Gabriel felt like a bull going into rut and it was a struggle to sit still and allow Drake to shave him when all he really wanted to do was burst naked into his wife's room and mount her.

Luckily he restrained that barbaric instinct and allowed Drake to handle the razor since he could not trust his own hand. In his heightened condition he could very well cut off the nose his new wife appeared to like so much.

He recalled the husky desire in her voice, and his cock throbbed, the cool slide of the silk brocade torture against his hot, sensitive skin. Was there any aphrodisiac as potent as the stare of an eager lover? If there was, Gabriel could not think of it. Especially not a lover who managed to appear so cool and unmoved, but was really boiling beneath her icy façade.

Gabriel had no idea at what point he'd started wanting her so much; it had sneaked up on him like one of the desert storms, the sudden attacks his people called khamsins, for which there was no English translation.

He studied his puzzled expression as Drake shaved him. Perhaps it was these days of self-imposed abstinence that had heightened his desire. He had gone much longer without a lover before, of course; one did not have time to engage in bed sport in the middle of a desert war. But never had he been in such prolonged contact with a woman he desired without taking her. Something about delaying his pleasure while they became easier with each other had increased his ardor tenfold.

It also helped that she'd gazed at him with desire, rather than judgment or recrimination.

She'd looked very well tonight. The gown she'd worn, a primrose silk with a tight, low-cut bodice, flattered her far more than her normal run of gowns, white muslins that were primly cut and better suited to a schoolroom miss. She was the sort of woman who should wear colors and should not be shy of accentuating her voluptuous curves. Gabriel thought of what he'd bought—unbeknownst to her—at the dressmaker's today, smiling in anticipation of seeing it on her body.

"Sir?"

"Hmm?" He looked up to see Drake had finished. "Ah." He took the hot linen cloth from his valet and pressed it against his freshly shaved skin.

"Thank you, Drake." He handed back the towel, and his eyes flickered toward the door for the millionth time. "That will be all for tonight. I shan't need you again."

Drake dropped a quick bow. "Very good, sir."

Gabriel's eyes narrowed; was that a smile on his valet's face? He'd never seen the dour, highly efficient man smile before. He shrugged. Who cared if he was smiling?

He pushed out of his chair and made for the door, knocking once before entering.

Chapter 19

Drusilla was in front of her window, her back to him. He grinned like a fool: she was wearing the negligee he had purchased for her.

"Drusilla?"

She jumped a little and then turned.

Gabriel sucked in breath and said a silent prayer as his eyes ate her body.

She ran her hands awkwardly down her sides and plucked at the diaphanous skirts with her fingers. "Thank you for this; it is—it is . . . lovely."

His eyes had become stuck at the level of her chest. She had the kind of nipples he loved—big, dark rose peaks that thrust up when erect and aroused. Like right now.

He looked from the flushed skin over her sternum, up her throat, to her slightly parted lips.

How had he ever thought she was not attractive? True, she wasn't pretty, but she was sensuality personified.

"You look delicious." That was the only word for it. He wanted to eat her.

She turned her face away, her expression one of mortification.

Gabriel laughed and caught her chin, forcing her eyes to his. "My wife is shy. Delectable, and shy."

"You speak of me as if I am food."

He grinned the moment what she'd said dawned on her face, which she promptly hid between her hands.

"You are so—" She appeared to run out of words. His articulate, clever wife was out of words. His smile grew even bigger.

"This gown is perfect for your body," he said, taking her wrists and gently pulling them away from her face, exposing the bodice of the lacy nightgown to his hungry gaze. The rosy pink lace had been cunningly designed so that it swirled around her breasts, exposing only a glimpse here and there. But her nipples . . . Those refused to be concealed.

Gabriel leaned forward and took one in his mouth and sucked it. Hard.

"Gabriel." Her voice was scratchy, raw, needy. She arched into him, pushing into his mouth. "Please."

It was the most erotic word he had ever heard.

He took her waist and held her motionless while he switched to her other breast, teasing it until she vibrated beneath his touch.

"Pull up your gown," he said as he released her nipple. She hesitated. "Do it. Now."

Her hands scrambled over her hips and he felt the silk fabric bunching between them. He walked her backward toward the bed, not stopping until her thighs hit the mattress. When the nightgown reached the apex of her thighs, he slid a hand between their bodies, and between her legs.

A vulgar word slipped out of him before he could stop it, and she shuddered, her thighs tightening on his hand.

"You are so wet for me, Drusilla." He thumbed her peak while pushing a finger inside her. He stroked and she tightened, her sheath unspeakably soft and hot. "You like it when I talk to you—tell you what I feel, what I like, what I'm doing."

It wasn't a question, but she nodded.

Gabriel nipped the pebbled tip of her breast as he worked her with his hand. "I'm going to take you in my mouth and make you orgasm."

Panic flashed across her face as he slid to his knees.

"Wh-what?

"Hold your gown up higher." He didn't stop stroking and probing. "Better yet, remove it."

She was looking down at him, her lips parted, bright red stains of passion across each cheek.

"Take it off, Drusilla." He punctuated his demand with a quick, deep thrust that made her body shake. "Do it now."

Her hands fumbled to unfasten the bodice, which had a row of diabolical, tiny buttons that he'd thought about today when he'd purchased it for her. He'd imagined removing it slowly, teasingly. But now . . . his eyes dropped to her sex, mere inches from his mouth, from his tongue—now it was *her* teasing him with her wet, tight arousal. And all for him.

The material fluttered, and he looked up in time to see her yank it over her head, the sound of a seam tearing rending the silence.

"Oh no!" Her brow was wrinkled with concern when her head emerged from the yards of blush-colored silk. "I've torn it."

"I'll buy you another," he growled. "Now sit."

She flopped onto the bed as if her legs had stopped functioning.

Gabriel parted her lips with his thumbs and groaned when he saw her tiny pink pearl. He had wanted to work her slowly to a punishing climax, but he needed to taste her first.

She pushed up onto her elbows. "What are you doing?"

"I want to taste you."

"Wh-why?"

"Did you like the way I just made you feel with my hand?"

Her skin darkened and she swallowed, her breath quickening, making her breasts rise and fall faster. She nodded.

"This will feel even better," he promised, his thumbs exposing her to his view. "My God, you are so beautiful." He draped one of her thighs over his shoulder, nudging her other leg. "Open for me."

She obeyed, and he took her into his mouth.

She gave a guttural cry and fell back against the pillow. Gabriel laved her extrasensitive flesh with care, lightly flicking only her exposed pearl.

In a matter of seconds she was thrusting against his mouth, her movements desperate and demanding: she wanted more. He gently entered her with one finger while his mouth worshipped and his tongue stroked.

Her brain was stuffed with one thought: he'd purchased a negligee for her. She had come home from the evening to find a large box on her bed, a huge bloodred ribbon around it, and a brief note:

Ya amar, I saw this and thought of you today. Put it on for me and I will take it off for you. G.

Drusilla had never seen his handwriting before. The letters were shaped with a foreign flare and the powerful strokes were like his distinctive personality.

It was the first garment she had ever worn that she'd not chosen. And, oh, what a garment it was . . .

Even with him kneeling between her widespread thighs, she could think only of that. He'd chosen something especially for her—for her *body*. And now he was—

She threw back her head and released a sound that should

have made her disappear with shame. But any embarrassment she felt was swamped by the wave of pleasure that rolled up her thighs, womb, and exploded in every part of her body.

When she thought she couldn't take the intense, concentrated pleasure any longer, he released her, and his mouth settled on the tender skin of her inner thigh as she orgasmed: as she *came*.

"Drusilla," he said into sensitive skin before sucking her hard enough to mark her.

Somewhere during her pleasure a second finger had joined the first inside her, although both were motionless now. "I can *feel* your climax as you contract around me," he said, his breath hot on her sex. "I can't wait to feel you around my cock."

Another wave of lust slammed into her at his raw words and a shocked thought flitted through the background of her mind: what kind of woman found such talk arousing? Shouldn't she be slapping his face instead of quivering beneath his touch?

He stood up before her, the sight of him driving all other thoughts from her head. He picked her up without any effort and moved her farther up the bed, until she was lying in the middle. Drusilla was *not* a small woman, but the way he handled her left her feeling delicate and desired.

His red, slick lips curled. "Put your feet flat on the bed."

It took a moment before his words sank in. She realized, when she tried to obey, that it was impossible to place her feet on the bed without bending her knees.

"Good," he said when she did so, his hand going to his sash. One tug and the garment fell open, exposing a broad swath of hard body. She let her eyes drop to that most masculine part of him. It was long, thick, and erect. And the ruddy tip, she noticed, glistened with moisture.

Without realizing it, she ran her tongue over her lower lip.

His body shook and he groaned. "If you do that, I'll make

a fool of myself before I even enter you." He smiled at whatever he saw on her face and shrugged, the red silk sliding from the sculpted, taut curves of his shoulders, his biceps bulging as he plucked the robe off and tossed it across the room. His hand went to his erection—to his *cock*; Drusilla throbbed just thinking the word—and he stroked.

His eyes glittered beneath heavy lids. "You like it when I do this?" He demonstrated by stroking himself from root to tip, the gesture sending saliva flooding her mouth, making it impossible to talk. He jerked his chin at her bent but tightly clenched knees. "Open them." His hand had stilled and the message was clear: closed legs, no stroking.

She parted her knees a little and he gave a half-hearted stroke.

Drusilla took a deep breath and slowly spread wider.

His chest began to move faster, as did his tightly clenched fist. Power mingled with mortification—and an addictive, impossible-to-resist urge to watch him surrender to passion. She kept opening until she lay before him, as spread open as a butterfly, her knees almost touching the bed. His hand had stopped, frozen, his lips parted, his expression taut and wanting as his eyes flickered up to hers and then quickly back down.

"My God." He shook his head, as if in disbelief. "You are so beautiful." He released himself and dropped to his hands between her thighs. "I need just one more taste." His mouth covered her exposed sex, and this time instead of taking her aching peak into his mouth, he thrust his tongue inside her. She cried out and pushed toward him, her hands in his hair, pulling him tight against her body as he used his tongue, fingers, and even teeth to drive her yet again into delicious madness.

His hands on her thighs held her open, and when her crisis came, all she could do was thrust her hips into his face, her back arching and straining until she thought it would snap.

She was lost in a blur when she felt the hot, slick head of him at her opening. He entered her in one smooth thrust and then lowered himself over her, their eyes mere inches apart, his mouth open as he breathed in sharp puffs, his hips still, his body buried deeply inside hers.

"I can feel your climax—the last of it." His nostrils flared with pride, his hips pressing her down on the bed. "Now I'm going to fuck you."

Her body clenched tight at the sound of the wicked word—which she had only ever heard once, when she'd inadvertently overheard a stable hand and maid at her father's house.

"Ah, God, that was exquisite—I want you to do that again. Tighten around me—squeeze me."

She wanted it, too. But . . . "I—I don't know how."

He leaned low and whispered against her temple. "I'm going to *fuck* you, Drusilla."

This time they both groaned when she tightened around him.

Gabriel laughed. "That is your secret weapon." His expression turned from amused to hard and severe in an instant. "Now let me show you mine."

Chapter 20

It was still dark when Gabriel woke up. His arms were full of his wife's lush body and her head rested on his biceps, their chests against each other, his body still inside hers and beginning to harden again.

"Gabriel?"

He pulled back a little, but not enough so that he left her. Streetlamps or moonlight filtered through the gap in the drapes and cut a stark line across her features. He carefully pushed a lock of hair off her cheek and tucked it behind her ear. "There, that is better. Now I can see you."

Her face took on an expression he'd once thought of as haughty, but now realized was merely shyness. His cock, already stirring, hardened the rest of the way. Her eyes widened.

Gabriel pulsed his hips. "You keep me aroused, Drusilla." She tightened her inner muscles and he sucked in a breath. "You are a very fast learner." He leaned down to nuzzle and bite her exposed throat. "Do you want me? Tell me. I want to hear you say the words; I want to hear you say my name."

"Please, Gabriel," she said without hesitation. "I like it." She held his gaze captive. "I love it."

They made slow, languorous love on their sides, staring into each other's eyes and making the joining last and last, as if they both knew what had to come afterward.

He held her tight, buried deep inside her after he'd spent. Her body seemed to change its structure as she came back from her small death. And his soft, pliable lover slowly stiffened into a woman with something on her mind.

Gabriel pulled himself from her with reluctance and rolled onto his back. They lay in the near-darkness, their hot, sweaty bodies cooling in the night air.

"You wish to say something, Drusilla?"

He felt her nod.

His lips twitched. "But you don't wish to start a disagreement."

A soft sigh and then, "Yes."

He turned onto his side and propped his head on his hand. "We need to learn how to get along with each other—and not only in bed."

Her lips curved into a slight smile. "I want to talk about your son, Samir."

He felt his own smile stiffen. "Yes?"

"You said he was with a nurse—surely that is not the only person he lives with?"

Gabriel worked his jaw back and forth as he considered her question.

"He is living with some friends."

He felt her shift and turn beside him. "Friends?"

Gabriel passed his hand over his face; he'd known this day would come, but had hoped it would not come so soon. They'd only begun to get over their last misunderstanding. But he supposed now was as good a time as any.

"Yes: friends."

Tension inserted itself between them, much like a third person in their bed.

"Is it—well, is he living with your mistress, um, mistresses?"

"Who the devil told you about *that*?"

Her eyes were wide, and he realized he'd raised his voice.

"I apologize, Drusilla, I should not have spoken to you that way." He closed his eyes and rolled onto his back. Why was he even surprised that she knew? His life appeared to be an open book; the entire world knew of his amorous relations.

"Yes. He has been living with Maria and Giselle. They are both French speakers and adore children so they were glad to take him in while I considered what I should do."

Silence met his declaration.

Gabriel inhaled deeply and slowly let his breath out before sliding both hands beneath his head and forcing himself to relax.

"Will you tell me about him?"

He knew it was a reasonable request. Still . . .

He sighed. "It is a confused and rather sordid story. I'm not sure how much you care to know."

"I'm your wife and he is your son. I would like to know what there is to know."

He chewed his lower lip; he was asking her to bring a child into their home. Did she not deserve a little of his background?

"His mother and I were promised to each other from a very early age and—"

"You mean, you were *married*?"

"No, we were not. The ceremony was to be at the beginning of our cool season. Every year my father's subjects would make the journey to Oran to pay homage. That year there was to be an added celebration: my marriage."

"Marriage? But you couldn't have been more than—"

"I was sixteen."

She lay on her side, her head propped on her hand. "So young," she said wonderingly.

"It is not much different from here. Some girls come out at seventeen—almost all by eighteen. And here you might only talk to a prospective mate a half-dozen times before you are betrothed. Fatima and I had known each other all our lives."

She remained quiet and Gabriel wished he knew what she was thinking.

Even in the low light Drusilla could see his expression was pensive. Asking about his past had probably not been wise. After all, it would make no difference to her feelings about Samir. She would take the boy—was in fact eager to meet Gabriel's son—and did not need to know of his past to accept him.

Likely anything he told her would only make her yearning for him more painful. Already she wasn't sure if she felt better or worse knowing the boy was the child of a woman who was to have been his wife, rather than one of his mistresses.

And speaking of his mistresses . . .

She swallowed her curiosity along with her jealousy and waited for him to finish. She'd started the boulder rolling and there was no stopping it now.

Drusilla let him think rather than pushing for confidences, taking advantage of the opportunity to study his body.

He'd thrust both hands behind his head, his action unconsciously displaying acres of velvety skin and chiseled muscle. Unfortunately, the blanket covered most of his abdomen and hid that intriguing V of muscle that separated torso from hips. She wished she could light a candle and then spend some time inspecting his body at her leisure, uncovering him, touching him—maybe even *licking* him. Would he let her do such a thing—the way he had done to her? Was that what one of his mistresses would do for him—*to* him? The thought was like a sharp stab to her chest. She could not bear thinking about another woman having him in a way she could not. She would ask him—tell him that she wanted to—

"There is—was—a tradition in my father's family."

His voice pulled her from her lustful fantasies and Drusilla was glad he was not looking at her. Instead, he was staring up at the canopy.

"When a boy turns fifteen, he is taken from his family and sent off to . . . well, to prove himself, I suppose." He turned to her. "By the time I was fifteen, there were only three of us—three sons—left. My older brother, Assad, and my much younger brother, Malik." His mouth creased into a frown. "Malik was a sweet boy—very loving and innocent. But he was simple. He would never offer a challenge for my father's kingdom." His frown turned thunderous. "Which should have stopped Assad from—" He broke off and heaved a sigh. "Never mind about that. When I was fifteen, I went to another of my father's palaces, a smaller holding. Assad had been there for several years already, but my father brought him home."

"Did you like your older brother?" she asked when he lapsed into thoughtful silence.

"I loved and worshipped him from the moment I could crawl after him. But then—" He scrubbed a hand through his hair. "Lord, Drusilla, this is a tangled web and—"

She laid a hand on his chest. "You don't need to tell me anything you do not wish to. We don't need to speak of this at all. I will accept and grow to love Samir no matter what I know."

He grabbed her hand in a crushing grip and kissed her knuckles, his lips hot and almost feverish. "You could not have spoken kinder words, Drusilla. It's been a heavy weight on my mind. Even before our marriage, I worried about his future and what I should do. I've long considered how I would tell my mother."

"Your mother doesn't know?" she blurted before she could stop herself.

He gave her a wry smile. "I know, foolish, eh? But now that you know, it will be less . . . difficult to tell her. Besides, it was not until recently that I decided that England would not be such a terrible place for him—but I have gone ahead of my story." He replaced her hand on his chest and absently rubbed it over his skin, brushing it back and forth over his small hard nipples. She was on the brink of losing control of herself and crawling on top of him, but he resumed his tale.

"Fatima's father was in charge of the palace where I was sent. I'd not seen her much in the prior four years. At one time she'd run freely with the children of my father's palace. But all that changed when we turned eleven or twelve. Her family moved away, and I only saw her a few times every year.

"But after I went to her family's home, we became closer. It was not easy to get time away from the eyes of her many chaperones, but we were driven by desire to find ways, and the understanding that we would marry caused us to become . . . careless." He turned toward her. "We made love. More than once."

The words were the sharp talons of a raptor. He'd said that he'd made love to Fatima, but was that what had just happened between them? He had certainly never mentioned the word *love*. Had he merely *fucked* Drusilla? Thinking the word sent both despair and desire spiraling through her body. Would he ever come to love her or to make love with her?

"I had only been there about half a year when I received word my father was dead and my brother had seized control of the palace."

"If he was your elder brother, why was he not your father's heir?"

Gabriel rubbed his thumb over the thin skin on the back of her hand, which he now held over the rippled musculature of his abdomen, moving in ever-widening circles. The gesture seemed absentminded on his part, but she had begun to melt, to become liquid between her thighs. Her body's response should have been embarrassing, but she could not bring herself to regret the sensations—no matter how much pain it would probably bring her.

"Assad's mother had poisoned the sultan's oldest two sons. She'd been careless and over a dozen people died."

His words made her forget all about the pulsing sensation in her sex.

"My God. What happened?"

"To Isabella?"

"Was that Assad's mother?"

"Mm-hmm. She was an Italian lady of good birth. She'd given the sultan six children—two of them boys. For years she reigned supreme—until my mother had me."

"What happened to her—Isabella?"

"The sultan found out she was behind the poisoning and beheaded her." Drusilla gasped, and he frowned. "I think it was too good for her. The poison she used was not a kind one and her victims suffered. Isabella had not been a well-liked woman. Assad's mother was vicious to all the children except her own. None of the other wives would leave their children alone with her—especially not their sons." He shrugged. "The sultan decided her son would not profit by her crimes, so I was raised up and Assad humiliated. It was the end of my relationship with the brother I loved so much."

Drusilla could imagine.

"To make a long story much shorter, it turned out Fatima's father was in league with Assad, and I barely escaped the palace with my hide. If her father had known what I was doing with his daughter—" He shook his head. "Let us just say I doubt he would have had the nerve to offer a soiled dove to Assad. As for Fatima? Well, she had no say in her future; she would marry whoever her father ordered her to marry."

"Oh, Gabriel," she said.

He turned and smiled at her, running the knuckles of one hand down her jaw. "Oh, Drusilla," he teased.

"You are making light of it, but you must have been heartbroken."

"I was. And it was fuel on the fire of my anger against my brother. Ever since he'd been disgraced, my mother had warned me to take steps against Assad, but I could never bring myself to do such a thing. Even though he'd certainly eliminated any of our siblings he believed might cause him trouble—some of our more assertive sisters in addition to our unfortunate brother Malik."

She stared, the horror of what he was saying sinking in. "Steps? You mean your mother wanted you to—"

"Do not judge her, Drusilla. It was a different world where we lived."

"I would not presume to judge. It's just that—"

"She is so small and seems so loving and affectionate?"

"Well, yes."

"She can afford to be soft now. But all the years I was growing up, she was alone and foreign and had given the sultan a son. Such a coup made for uncertain relations in the harem. My mother had always to be vigilant."

What a horrible, horrible life. Something suddenly occurred to her. "Your son—you said Fatima married your brother?"

"Yes, they were married immediately after Assad secured my father's palace in Oran and drove me and my small band of men into hiding." He frowned. "I'm ashamed to say that did not take him very long."

"So Fatima married him quickly after you left?"

He nodded. "I can see you understand."

"You don't—"

"I do not know which of us is Samir's father."

She raised her hand to her mouth. "Do you think your brother ever suspected?"

"No. Fatima would have suffered a dreadful punishment if he'd known. She must have taken steps on their wedding night to fool him. And if the child happened to come early? Well, that could always be explained away."

Drusilla had no idea what to say.

"Samir's mother was killed when Oran was bombarded. Perhaps you heard something of it?"

She frowned in thought. "Yes. Yes, of course. It happened some months after the navy attacked Algiers, did it not?"

"Three months later."

"And the casualties were considerably less?"

He hesitated and then said, "Yes, they were. Unfortunately, Assad, Samir's mother, and another of their children were among those killed."

"Oh, Gabriel."

"Samir was the only one of the royal sons who survived, and he had no family nearby. So I brought him back with the intention of finding his grandparents or any of his aunts or uncles on his mother's side who might take him."

Drusilla gaped. "But . . . wait—you were *there*?"

He paused, took a deep breath, and sighed heavily. "I was there—right before the siege and right after."

"But—but—wasn't that dangerous?" She shook her head,

as if trying to shake away cobwebs. "Didn't the navy go with the intention of taking the city—as they had done in Algiers? Why would you be there? How did that happen?"

His expression was beyond bleak. "I was there because I am the one who told the navy how to seize my brother. I also told them where to fire the bombs if they could not capture him."

Chapter 21

Gabriel had known that this day would eventually come. He could not keep his past a secret from Drusilla forever—not when they were both trying to make a life together. But this was his greatest shame and he was about to lay himself bare before her. He could not avoid his past forever—nor did he wish to.

Yet still he hesitated, considering what he was about to disclose. The regret, sadness, and loss that rose inside him every time he thought about his brother's death did not fade, no matter how often he told himself he'd sacrificed Assad to save hundreds, if not thousands, of others.

But regrets were pointless and they certainly had no place in this new life he'd chosen.

"I'm sorry, Gabriel. I shouldn't pry. You needn't tell me any—"

He gave her a swift kiss on the lips, stopping her words. "Yes, Drusilla, I do need to tell you this. You are my wife."

She swallowed audibly, but nodded.

"During my last term at Oxford I was summoned to London. Lord Admiral Singleton wished to speak to me about my knowledge of Oran—specifically about my father's palace."

Gabriel had been speechless and furious at the man's audacity—at what he expected from Gabriel—until he'd explained the alternative.

He glanced at Drusilla, who was watching him with an expression of concern. He smiled and took her hand. "I won't go into the two weeks that followed. Suffice it to say he explained what the Royal Navy was planning, how many casualties there'd been in Algiers, and how I could make a difference in Oran." He stroked the soft skin on the back of her hand with his thumb, recalling Singleton's final argument—the one that had made his decision for him.

"You have family in that palace, Marlington," the dignified older man had all but shouted at him. They'd been in his offices at Whitehall. Though Singleton hadn't sent armed men to bring Gabriel to London, he'd certainly made no secret of his willingness to do so. As a result, Gabriel had gone when summoned.

"I cannot betray them by sharing the details of their home—of their defenses and their city. Would *you* give such details to men who wished to bombard *your* family home, Admiral?"

"It is because we do not wish to bomb Oran that we are asking for your help." He'd leaned across the massive expanse of his desk, his pale blue eyes hard. "You know what happened in Algiers—it was a bloody slaughter. You can stop the same thing from happening in Oran. Do you know how many casualties there—"

"Yes," Gabriel said through clenched jaws. "Thousands."

"We don't even *know* the full extent of the losses suffered by the Regency of Algiers. And those losses were *senseless*—the dey accepted our terms. He could have spared his people the—"

Gabriel raised a hand. "Enough, Admiral. Enough." His sense of dread had almost made him ill, but he'd looked the older man in the eyes. "Tell me what it is you would have me do."

"Gabriel?"

He blinked at the sound of his name and looked at Drusilla. "I apologize," he said to his wide-eyed wife. "I'm afraid I was—"

She lifted their joined hands to her mouth and kissed his knuckles. "You don't need to apologize. I can't even imagine how terrible that was for you." She shook her head. "But whatever you told them, it must have helped? There was very little said in the newspapers about the whole affair. But I recall there wasn't much loss of life—nothing like Algiers."

"That is true. Thousands died in Algiers. In Oran, twenty-three people died that day: twenty of my brother's people, and three Englishmen." He looked at her. "Three of those twenty were my brother, Fatima, and their daughter. Most of the others who were killed during the fighting were their personal guards. I led them into the palace, Drusilla. Me—I'm the one who led them to kill my brother and the others."

Two tears slid down her cheeks. "That must have been dreadful—I cannot imagine how terrible. But you saved so many, Gabriel. You saved Samir."

That was the one thing that gave him comfort. Not only had he stopped a bombardment that would have killed far more than twenty-three people, he'd been on hand when they'd discovered Samir crouched in a cupboard, terrified and alone.

"Because all the family had fled for their lives, I took Samir. I sent men searching for any remaining relatives. Thus far I've received word that a few of his aunts are alive." He turned to Drusilla and kissed each cheek, his lips lightly brushing the damp trail of tears. "I've been lying to myself. None of his mother's family will take him—it would not be safe for him *or* them. Part of me has always known I cannot send him back to our people. As Assad's son, he would always be in danger. And if the truth were ever known—that he might be *my* son—that would be a death sentence for him." He kissed the tip of her nose and gave her a sad smile. "Don't cry, Drusilla."

She gave a loud sniff and wiped the back of her hand across her cheek. "But it is a dreadful situation. I know the problems you face here—the prejudice, ignorance, intolerance. Just look at Visel and what he—"

"Shhh." This time he kissed her lips. When he pulled away, he shook his head. "We will make sure Samir has all the love and family that was taken from him."

He paused, waiting until she nodded before continuing. "When I returned home, I found a letter waiting for me. I don't know how she managed it, but Fatima must have sent it before matters became so bad. In the letter she told me her parents knew about Samir's questionable parentage."

"My God! How?"

"From her. Fatima sent them a letter when it was clear Assad would lose control of Oran. And in it she confessed the truth."

"But why—after so much time?"

"I daresay she believed it would make Samir safer if he was not believed to be Assad's. The political situation had become dangerous for my brother over the past few years and she must have known he could not hold onto power for long." He shrugged. "It is my belief she hoped her parents would send the boy to me if anything ever happened. I daresay they would have if I'd not been there to take Samir."

"But he is their *grandson*. No matter who his father is, Fatima is still his mother—still their daughter. Wouldn't they have wanted him?"

"Samir is now a political liability. If he is Assad's, then he will always be viewed as a threat by the new sultan. If he is mine, then he is a bastard and his mother has brought shame on her family." He stared grimly. "I'm sure you can see how difficult this is. If I give him the protection of my name, I am dooming him to bastardy. If I don't? If I tell him that he is Assad's son am I dooming him to war—making him believe it is his duty fight for control of the sultanate—as both Assad and I did?" He shrugged. "If I tell him he is *my* son, then he will live knowing his father is a man who abandoned his own people to become English and helped in the attack on his very home—might have been responsible for the death of Assad and Fatima. Also, if I keep him with me, I will deprive him of his heritage." He grimaced. "And nobody knows better than I just how unwelcome a man of mixed race often feels in this country. Even if he wishes to return to Oran one day, being raised in England will ensure he is a stranger in his homeland." Gabriel shook his head at the tangle of problems. "No matter what I tell him or what I do, I will hurt him. You tell me, Drusilla—what should I do?"

Gabriel could see by her expression she understood the magnitude of his quandary. He also knew she would have no simple answer—because there wasn't one.

Gabriel stayed in her bed all night, making love to her again just before dawn.

Afterward, he pushed up onto his elbow and looked down at her. "I want you to meet Samir today. Perhaps we can then make plans to bring him home."

Drusilla was glad her face was still flushed from their vigorous lovemaking so he could not see how foolishly pleased she felt at his words.

"I would like that."

He tucked a lock of hair behind her ear and she hated to think what a crow's nest her hair must resemble.

"Thank you for that, Drusilla." He cocked his head. "But I need to ask more of you."

She stared into his serious green eyes, her heart pounding. What now? What . . . *now*?

"Samir came to Maria and Giselle not long after his mother died, and he has developed an attachment to them."

Drusilla clenched her jaws.

"I will bring him to live with us, but it would be cruel to deprive him of their company—or they of his—when he has lost most of his family so recently."

She could only stare. Good Lord, what was he saying? Did he expect to bring these women to *live* with them? Was he going to—

His beautiful lips pulled into a rueful smile, and he leaned close to kiss the tip of her nose.

"I can see by your expression that you are imagining the worst. I know this cannot be easy—nor is it the accepted or normal way of doing things. But this situation is *not* normal. There is bound to be discomfort and unhappiness, but I would prefer Samir not suffer any more than we can help." He cupped her jaw, his warm hand holding her lightly. "Giselle and Maria are not my mistresses anymore, Drusilla, but they *are* friends to me. You are my *only* lover and have been since our betrothal."

Joy, jealousy, anger, fear, and a dozen other emotions swirled within her at his words. Logically she knew these women had been a part of his life long before she was. But logic played little part in the feelings she had for him.

But he had called her his lover.

He cocked his head. "You need never see them, but I do not wish to end his contact with them. It is best he stay with them for the last few weeks we are in London. And I will see to it that—"

She forced herself to smile. "I'm not so fragile as that, Gabriel." Her lips trembled a little. "We can take matters as they come—can we not? The most important thing is to make Samir feel loved after what he has endured."

"Thank you, Drusilla. I know most wives would not be so understanding."

Most wives? She wanted to yell—she doubted *any* wife would understand. Drusilla burned to tell him that she was boiling with jealousy about his bloody mistresses. Instead she told herself to remember that he was no longer a lover to either of these women—that everything between him and the two Frenchwomen had happened before they'd become betrothed.

She met his concerned gaze and told herself that she could do this; she could master her jealousy for Gabriel and for Samir. She nodded.

"Thank you."

The words were simple but Drusilla heard the sincerity beneath them.

"Now," he said, his manner brisk. "I am to meet Byer and Eva this morning."

Drusilla was relieved to change the subject, not sure she could take too many more revelations without giving in to her baser emotions. "I shall see you at breakfast?" she asked for lack of anything better to say.

"Do you wish to join us?"

"I have no horse."

"My stepfather keeps mounts for all three of my sisters and my mother. Melissa is close to your height. I will send word to have her mare made ready. Can you be dressed in an hour?"

Drusilla was riding between her gloriously beautiful husband and the outrageously garbed Viscount Byer.

"You have a good seat, Mrs. Marlington," Byer told her.

"And you, sir, are an excellent liar."

He grinned, his handsome face lighting up. "Not good enough, it would seem. Are you looking forward to going to the country at the end of the Season?"

"Yes, I am." Relieved, was more like it. "And what will you be doing this summer, my lord?"

"I will be staying at my family seat for the first time in many years." His normally lazy expression was replaced by pensiveness. She knew he'd lost his brothers in rather horrifying succession. She also knew he was in dire straits financially. Even so, she'd never seen him pursue any heiresses, not even the delectable Miss Kittridge. Although it was difficult to see past his foppish clothing and jocular façade, she suspected he was more than half in love with Eva, who, of course, did not view him—or anyone else—in a romantic light. Poor Lord Byer.

"Hard to imagine you a farmer, Tommy," Eva said. She'd smiled at Drusilla this morning, seeming almost happy to see her. Drusilla had been ridiculously relieved. She had so very few close companions, and Eva was her dearest friend in the world.

Lord Byer gave Eva a mock haughty look. "What? Can't imagine me as king of my demesne?"

"No, more like court jester."

The conversation devolved into teasing and taunting until they were almost back to the park gates. Eva rode up between Drusilla and Byer.

"Excuse me," Byer said as Eva's horse shoved his aside. "Am I in your way?"

"Yes. Go away. I wish to talk to my sister."

"Come on, Tommy," Gabriel said, laughing. "You know better than to get in Evil's way."

"I'm sorry," Eva said, once the men were far enough ahead so that they couldn't hear.

Drusilla didn't need an explanation. "Me too."

"Friends again?" Eva asked, her eyebrows raised high.

"I never *wasn't* your friend, Eva."

"Good. I hated not talking to you—especially since I will be leaving London before the end of the Season."

"You will? Where are you going?"

"Mel keeps begging me to come to stay with her at Lily Repton's." She gave a sudden grin. "She says they've got a lovely goer that Lily's brother is training."

By Mel, Eva meant Melissa, the youngest—and most reserved—of her two sisters. Lady Melissa was only seventeen and not yet out. Drusilla knew the girl was not looking forward to her Season. Although nobody had ever said the words out loud, it was obvious Melissa was not Lord Exley's blood relative. She was taller than Drusilla, with fair, sandy hair and broad sunny features that were nothing like either the marquess or her two sisters. The only characteristic she'd inherited from a mother who was reputed to be the beauty of her age were her unusual blue-violet eyes. Well, and possibly a strain of madness.

"Ahh, now I know the *real* reason you are deserting London: for a horse."

"Guilty as charged." Eva hesitated, her smile draining away. "But I also miss Mel. She is not happy about the approach of her eighteenth birthday. I hope to reassure her—to tell her that a Season is not nearly as dreadful as we'd both feared."

Drusilla's eyebrows rose. "Really? I never believed I would hear such words from you."

"Well, it is boring and tedious and annoying, but not dreadful." She cut Drusilla a look that was almost shy. "Especially not if you've a friend to endure it with you."

They rode in silence, Drusilla far too emotional to speak for some moments. When she'd gathered the reins of her feelings, she turned to Eva. "I'll miss you greatly. When are you leaving?"

"Not too early—perhaps a week before Mama and Papa."

"But surely you are staying for the Richland ball? I know how much you love masquerades." Indeed, Eva's childish enjoyment of costumes had always made Drusilla fear she might run off and join a troupe of actors.

"I shall hate to miss it, but I keep putting Mel off. Besides, I want to be out of the house before the packing madness starts."

"Well, I wish you were not leaving, but I certainly understand." Drusilla wasn't lying. She'd been hoping to persuade Eva to come and stay with her and Gabriel. And Samir. But she didn't know when Gabriel would tell his family about the boy.

"Don't look so sad, Dru—I'm not leaving yet. Tell me, what is your costume this year?"

"Nell Gwynn."

Eva laughed. "You're so lazy—you're always Nell."

"I know. But the costume is so easy. And I can always eat the oranges if nobody asks me to dance."

"You'll have at least one partner." Her eyes slid to Gabriel, who was laughing at something Byer had just said. Drusilla's cheeks heated as she recalled last night.

"I'm so glad you two seem happy."

"We do?"

Eva shook her head. "Lord! Love really *is* blind. If you two were any more lovey-dovey this morning . . . Well, suffice it to say, it will soon be plain to the entire *ton* this marriage of convenience has turned into a love match." She reached across and squeezed Drusilla's hands. "I am so glad for you."

It always had been love on Drusilla's side. Was Eva saying she believed Gabriel might feel the same way?

She smiled at her friend. "Thank you, Eva. So am I."

"There he is." Gabriel took her hand and led her toward The Serpentine, to where a little dark-haired boy in short pants was throwing crumbs to ducks and laughing as they squabbled. Beside him stood a woman dressed in a domestic's clothing. The nurse saw them first and leaned down to the little boy.

He dropped his bag of crumbs and ran at full speed toward them. Gabriel released her hand to bend down and pick up Samir, swinging him around in circles while he shrieked.

Other nurses and children looked on. At this time of day—long before the fashionable hour—they were the only people in the park.

"Jibril! Jibril!" he shouted when he'd stopped spinning enough to speak. "There is a duck who keeps climbing on top of another duck and being mean to him." The boy spoke rapid, fluent French, and it was all Drusilla could do to keep up with him. She'd learned it in school but had never spoken the language with a native speaker.

Gabriel looked over the boy's head at Drusilla, his eyebrows raised, his expression one of barely suppressed glee. "A mean duck beating up on other ducks, eh," he said in the same language. "Well, let's make sure he stops his wickedness, or there will be no bread." He planted a smacking kiss on the boy's cheek and lowered him to the ground. "Now, you little savage, turn and give this lady your best leg."

The boy turned to Drusilla, suddenly shy, stepping closer to Gabriel and blinking up at her with huge hazel eyes. He had the same warm skin tone as Gabriel and she detected some reddish glints in his hair although it was considerably darker. They bore a certain resemblance to each other, although she did not believe they were enough alike to make their relationship a certainty.

He dropped a courtly bow. "It is a pleasure to meet you, mademoiselle."

"It is a pleasure, Samir. I am Drusilla," she replied in less than fluid French.

Gabriel laid a hand on Samir's shoulder. "This is my lady, Samir—my wife."

The boy's brow wrinkled. "Like Gigi and Maria?"

Gabriel laughed, his face flushing. *I'm sorry,* he mouthed at Drusilla. She arched one brow, trying to suppress the stew of jealousy. After all, that was in his past and she was in his future. Or so she would have to keep telling herself whenever jealousy threatened to get the better of her common sense.

Gabriel dropped onto his haunches, at eye level with the little boy. "Gigi and Maria are my friends, Samir. Drusilla is special—she is my one and only wife."

She felt a thrill at his words, even though they were just meant to reassure a child.

Samir cocked his head, and she realized he would have lived the bulk of his life in the harem, among many wives. "Your favored wife, Jibril?"

Gabriel tweaked his ear and made him giggle. "My only wife, you little monkey. But she is a good one." He winked up at her and swung Samir onto his shoulders as he stood, causing the little boy to shriek with laughter.

"Oh no," Gabriel said, pointing toward the pond. "There is your duck, Sami—he is on top of that other one." He grinned down at Drusilla and took her hand, giving it a hard, quick squeeze. "Let's go see—what could that wicked duck be up to now?"

The next day Gabriel asked his wife if she had any objection to canceling their plans for the evening.

"You mean you don't wish to go to the Carews' ball?" she asked, looking up from the desk in the library, where she was engaged in writing a letter.

Once again, they'd spent the afternoon with Samir. Today, they'd taken him to a rather spectacular toy shop on Oxford Street. It seemed Drusilla was very well known there as she often bought toys in such quantity as to make her their most welcome customer.

They'd purchased a fine box filled with soldiers for Samir as well as several books that had been written expressly for children.

Afterward they'd brought Samir to Upper Brooks Street and introduced him to the senior members of their staff, all of whom would be accompanying them to Sizemore after the Season was over.

Gabriel suspected his servants already knew more than they let on, but it made him feel as if he'd taken a step in the right direction by bringing the two parts of his life together. As for his mother? Well, he had determined to wait to tell her anything until they left London in a few weeks. He assured himself that he was not afraid of her reaction—and he mostly believed that was the truth—but he did not wish to add yet more tension to what had already been a difficult Season.

After he'd taken Samir home, he'd returned to find Drusilla in the library and had settled down to do some much neglected paperwork. They'd spent the past few hours in companionable silence.

As the dinner hour approached, Gabriel realized he wanted more of her company—that he did not wish to share her tonight.

"Gabriel?"

He saw she was waiting for his answer, her graceful eyebrows arched and her full lips slightly parted in a way that sent a buzz of arousal through his body. She was, he thought with a shock, a remarkably sensual creature in addition to being clever and caring. He loved their time in bed, but he wanted more than that—no matter how wonderful their sexual relations might be.

"I would rather spend the evening at home. With you," he added, diverted by the way she turned away, giving him her shoulder. A few weeks ago, he would have viewed such an action as rejection. But Gabriel was beginning to understand she was at her most prickly when she was most emotional.

"I shall write to express our regrets," she said to the far wall.

Gabriel smiled, as eager for the evening as Samir had been for their visit to Gunter's this afternoon. He strode toward her and took her upper arm, turning her.

She was a fiery red, her expression flustered. He lowered his mouth to hers, claiming her with all the hunger he felt. Her body shifted and molded itself against his, her arms circling his neck while she opened to him, sucking his tongue in a way that made his entire body hum with want. His wife was a very fast learner in many areas.

Gabriel was breathless when he pulled away. "I shall notify Parker that we will dine in our room tonight." He took in her full, parted lips and slightly flaring nostrils and gave a growl of frustration. "I think we will have dinner early this evening. Very early."

Chapter 22

Everything changed after that night.

Oh, they still needed to attend the interminable parties, routs, and balls that filled the Season every evening, but they spent part of every day together—days that sped by in a blur of happiness.

As Gabriel had suggested, Samir remained with his former mistresses until they departed for Sizemore.

Though Drusilla agreed that two moves in a brief time would be hard on him, she could not be comfortable with Gabriel's frequent visits to their house to either bring Samir out for the day or read him a story before bed. It wasn't that she didn't trust him; it was just that she felt . . . excluded.

To his credit, Gabriel tried to include her in his time with Samir. She saw the little boy every day, and, after a few weeks, she felt as though she'd known and loved him for years. She didn't know if he was Gabriel's son, nor did she believe the blood relationship mattered to her husband.

For a child who'd just lost both his parents, he was remarkably happy, but Gabriel told her Samir was plagued by nightmares, so Drusilla knew he was not as serene as he appeared on the surface. It would take years to help him overcome his grief.

The best way to do that was to give him security and love. She was eager to begin their life as a family and could hardly wait for the day they could leave London for the country.

But, in the interim, there was the remainder of the Season to be gotten through.

In the evenings they went to balls, routs, soirees, and every other type of foolishness. She soon discovered that a Season with the man she loved was far more exciting and interesting than a Season as a wallflower. Drusilla was stunned by what a difference happiness made to activities she had always considered vapid.

Eva often accompanied them, and Drusilla was relieved to resume their friendship. She did not believe Eva felt excluded by the growing closeness between herself and Gabriel, although it seemed to her there was a new distance between herself and Eva. It was probably natural that their relationship had changed; they were now separated by a vast gulf of experience.

But it wasn't only the fact she was now married; sometimes she felt as if Eva might be hiding something from her—or, at the very least, was distracted by somebody or something.

It was selfish of her, but Drusilla could not apply herself to discover whatever might be bothering Eva. Her daily life was simply too magical. Indeed, she could scarcely believe this was *her* life, that she had somehow managed to end up with the man she'd wanted and dreamed of all along. And that he seemed happy to be spending his days and, *oh*, his nights, with her.

He came to Drusilla every evening, often remaining until morning.

It was on one of those nights, not long before the last ball of the Season, when Gabriel said to her.

"Perhaps you might pay a visit to *my* chambers one of these nights," he said in a teasing tone. They'd made love earlier and then dozed for a while, neither of them falling asleep. Drusilla loved these times—usually after a vigorous session in bed—when they talked, the subjects ranging from serious and emotional to playful and light.

A single candle burned low in its socket, allowing her to see the outlines of his face. His full lips were curved into a smile, his expression almost . . . loving.

"Why should I go to your room, Mr. Marlington? What would I find there?"

"You might find me."

"Ah, I see. Would I like what I found?"

"I would make sure you did." He traced a line down her jaw and across to her lips, outlining them with his finger.

She caught his digit between her teeth and held it there, lightly touching the sensitive pad with the tip of her tongue.

He groaned. "Again? You will break your poor husband, Mrs. Marlington." He took her hand and pressed it against his tumescent organ, giving a soft grunt of pleasure as her fingers closed around him and her hand began to move on its own. He pushed the covers down, exposing his male beauty to her greedy eyes. The sight of her hand wrapped around him, his muscles taut and flexing, made her own body tighten.

"Mmm, that feels so good." His hips pulsed against her hand. "Harder—grip me tighter."

"It doesn't hurt?" she asked, daunted by the thought of squeezing him any harder than she was.

"It hurts in a good way." He spread his thighs, and his hand went between them. She stared in fascination as he tugged at the skin of his testicles. They locked eyes, and he thrust into her hand with increasing savagery.

"Drusilla," he said, his tone urgent.

It was almost impossible to tear her gaze away from the hard, ruddy length of him and the increasing slickness in her hand.

"Yes?"

"I want you to suck me."

Her hand stuttered and she gasped.

He chuckled and settled his hand over hers, resuming the stroking motion. "Should I apologize? I daresay that is not something one says to a well-bred lady."

Drusilla's mind rebelled against his words even as they sent spirals of heat to her sex. What he meant was that it was the type of thing he could ask of a mistress.

How could the thought of him asking another woman to do *that* to him be both arousing and infuriating? But there was no denying it was. One of those beautiful actresses she'd seen—had *they*—

His hips stilled and a notch formed between his eyes. "I *am* sorry—that was—"

"Is it something a man would say to his m-mistress?"

He hesitated, his lips slightly parted, his chest seeming to freeze in midbreath. And then he nodded, his eyes heavy, his hips resuming their thrusting, the head of his penis slick, hard, insistent. "Be my mistress, Drusilla."

She shuddered at his words—at the way he devoured her with his eyes.

Drusilla opened her mouth and was surprised that she could force words out of it. "Will you tell me how to do it?"

He spread his thighs wider in answer and released her hand. "Come. Kneel between my legs."

She scrambled up onto her knees.

"Come closer and lean back; sit on your heels so I can reach you."

She complied, and he stroked her jaw with a light touch, his middle finger drifting over her lips, back and forth, back and forth. "Take my finger into your mouth."

She parted her lips, and he pushed inside. Her eyes widened when she realized the musky scent on his hand was hers—from the pleasure he'd given her during their earlier lovemaking.

He gave her a wicked grin. "You taste good, do you not?"

Her face flushed and, luckily, he didn't seem to expect an answer.

"Cradle my finger with your tongue. Yes, that's good," he praised, wincing slightly. "Be careful with your teeth, both top and bottom." He began to move his finger in and out, slowly. "Caress me with your lips and tongue, yes, suck me." His expression was sensual and eager. "Your mouth is so unspeakably soft and hot. I cannot wait to fill it."

Blood pounded in her ears at his words, his blissful expression, and his gently pulsing hips. He'd taken himself in hand again. The sight was so erotic it sent excruciating pleasure rippling through her body, the sensations pooling and swirling in her lower belly—in her sex. Was it possible to climax just from watching him and sucking his finger?

"I think you're ready," he murmured, his eyes lazy slits. "I know I am."

She released his finger with a soft *pop*.

"Find a position that is comfortable."

She lowered herself, her knees between his thighs, pushing his legs wider as she brought her face closer and closer, until she was mere inches away from his erect organ: it looked far too big to fit in her mouth without chafing him.

"Take me in your hand."

She did.

"Explore and get the sense of me."

Her mouth immediately went to the slick head. She tongued the small slit, and he groaned, his buttocks tightening and his hips pressing up—just as hers had.

She smiled, thrilled by his reaction, and ran her tongue around the underside of his flared head, fascinated by the growing moisture, which tasted mildly salty.

He tilted his chin down to look at her. "You are teasing me."

She tongued the slit, and he jolted.

"I have created a monster." His head dropped to the bed.

Drusilla laughed, heady with her newfound power.

Gabriel hadn't been this hard in his life. His wife was inexperienced, but she made up for that with eager curiosity. He had to keep reminding himself this was the starchy, stern Miss Clare kneeling between his thighs. That it was her sharp, acerbic tongue and clever mouth that was laving and sucking. One of her hands stroked him with increasing skill while the other explored his pelvis, stomach, and, *oh!*, his nipple.

She chuckled against his stiff, slick flesh, her laughter echoing up his erection straight to his heart. He wanted to savagely thrust into her, to feel her throat tighten against the exquisitely sensitive skin, to fill her and to claim her in this manner, as well as every other.

Instead he lightly caressed a naked shoulder, her throat, her jaw, his fingers drifting to where she held him in her mouth. The feel of her lips stretching tight to accommodate his girth drove him beyond endurance.

"Come up here," he growled, hooking his hands beneath her shoulders and pulling her off his far-too-excited cock. "Up on your knees, straddle my hips," he said when she looked adorably confused.

"Was it not good?" she asked, wiping a wet sheen from her pouty lower lip with the tips of her fingers.

"It was very good, but I want you this way."

Her eyebrows crept up her forehead and she looked down, realizing, apparently, that she was naked. She covered her breasts with her hands and then gasped as her fingers grazed her erect nipples, surprise and arousal on her face. So, his little sensualist had never fondled her pretty breasts. He would enjoy watching her discover them.

He took his cock and nudged it between her thighs. Once he was positioned, he grabbed her by the hips and pulled her down while thrusting up. Hard.

Her eyelids fluttered and her head dropped back. Gabriel took her hips in a punishing grip and drove them both to ecstasy.

"Gabriel?"

"Hmmm?" He lay beside her with his eyes closed, holding one of her hands on his bare chest and absently moving it in circles.

"When will you tell your mother about Samir?"

He groaned.

They'd discussed the matter earlier in the evening, but he'd not given any indication of when he would go.

"I will go to her in the morning."

That was exactly what she'd wanted to hear. "Good. I want to go with you today."

His eyes opened, and he turned. "I thought you said you didn't wish to be there for that conversation?"

"I don't."

"So where do you wish to go with me?"

"I want to go with you today when you fetch Samir."

"Oh, Drusilla, that—"

"These women—*Giselle and Maria*." She had to force herself to say their names. "They are part of his life and he speaks of them with great affection. I can hardly pretend they do not exist."

"No."

"Why?"

"Because it is—" He muttered something she could not hear. "Because it is not done; that is why."

"A lot of what we are doing is not done. Besides, I have never given any credit to not doing things simply because they haven't been done in the past." The bed shook, and she realized he was laughing silently. "What? Why are you laughing?"

"I'm laughing at the sheer understatedness of your words."

"I don't believe understatedness is a word."

He laughed outright this time and kissed her shoulder.

"I am serious—I will not be distracted on this subject."

He leaned onto his side and kept kissing, over her arm, and down, twitching off the sheet that covered her, his lips settling over one hard nipple.

She groaned. "Gabriel . . ."

"Mmm?" His mouth was full of her breast.

"I will not be distracted," she said, far less emphatically.

And then he raised himself up over her and demonstrated—once again—his exceptional skills when it came to distraction.

Chapter 23

The last ball of the Season—and it hadn't come soon enough in Gabriel's opinion. He felt an almost childish excitement when he thought about taking Drusilla and Samir to the country.

"Your costume will be delivered today at noon, sir."

Gabriel glanced up from the mirror at the sound of his valet's voice, surprised to see that his hands had managed to tie his cravat into a respectable knot without any direction from his brain.

"Costume?" he said as Drake handed him a stickpin in the shape of a plain gold bar.

"Er, yes, sir. The Duchess of Richland's ball tonight is a masquerade."

"Damn! I'd forgotten all about that." He ran a hand through the hair Drake had just carefully coiffed, the action causing his valet to wince.

"I thought you might have, sir, so I took the liberty of ordering three costumes for you to choose from."

"Ah, excellent."

"It is my understanding Mrs. Marlington will be going as Nell Gwynn, sir."

Gabriel laughed. Could there be a better costume for her than the allegedly sharp-tongued and quick-witted mistress of Charles II?

"You know far more than I do, Drake," he said. "Just select one of the costumes and have it ready for me."

His dour valet gifted Gabriel with one of his rare smiles. "Very well, sir. It will take an extra half hour to dress you."

"That sounds ominous." Drake held out his coat, and Gabriel struggled into the navy superfine.

The other man just smiled as Gabriel buttoned up his coat and checked his reflection one last time.

Drake handed him his hat and cane, and he descended to the foyer. It was a remarkably clear, sunny day: perfect for walking.

Also perfect for delaying the inevitable, his conscience mocked.

Gabriel ignored the voice; he would not engage in any further internal arguments with himself. He had made up his mind: today was the day he would tell his mother and stepfather about Samir.

He would do so alone, even though he had invited Drusilla to join him last night.

"I don't know, Gabriel." She'd been lying atop him at the time, their bodies joined from shoulders to toes. "I believe this should be a private conversation between you and Lady Exley."

"You do not need to come with me." Gabriel ran his fingers through her heavy dark hair, which was so shiny and fragrant and soft he could not keep his hands out of it.

"Does it disappoint you that I don't think I should be there?"

"No, you must do what you feel best. Although I daresay you will get a visit from my mother soon afterward. She will want to speak to you—to see if you are truly as sanguine about the decision as I say you are." He ran both his hands up her arms and then down her sides, letting them rest on her waist. "*Are* you as sanguine as you say?" He stretched up and kissed her chin before lying back down.

Her eyes were grave. "Never more so—I look forward to moving to the country more than you can imagine."

So here he was, strolling toward a confrontation he could not look forward to, even though he very much looked forward to the aftermath. His mother would be disappointed in him for behaving recklessly, of course, but she would welcome Samir with all the affection she showed to everyone who belonged to her. And she would immediately set about spoiling her grandchild with a vengeance. Certainly, Samir was a little boy who needed a great deal of spoiling after all he'd been through.

Whether Samir was Assad's or his own, he was still Gabriel's flesh and blood, not to mention a delightful child.

When Sami was of age, Gabriel would tell him everything, and he could seek out his mother's family and make what connections he desired. Gabriel would see to it that he was raised with knowledge of and respect for his Berber connections.

He nodded at a passing acquaintance, his heart lighter than it had been for months—perhaps even years; most certainly since the British navy had approached him.

Life, he decided, giving his cane an extra flourish as he crossed the street, was turning out to be very good, indeed.

Drusilla was ready to leave the moment she heard Gabriel depart. She knew Lady Exley would be thrilled by the discovery of a grandson. She might not, however, be so thrilled with her son for hiding the truth for so long.

But when the marchioness met Samir, she would forgive Gabriel everything.

Drusilla pulled on her gloves as she considered Samir. Gabriel might not be sure whether the boy's mother had spoken the truth, but Drusilla now was. Samir not only resembled his father, but he was also as sunny, sweet, and loving as Gabriel. Whatever other traumas had marred his early life—the bombing of his home and the tragic loss of his mother and the man he believed to be his father—Samir had been raised with a great deal of love.

In truth, she did not think it mattered to Gabriel if the boy was his or his brother's. She could see he'd loved his brother greatly. Perhaps raising his son was something he could do to ease his conscience about leaving his people and what he'd done for the navy.

Drusilla checked her appearance in the mirror. Her walking costume was one of the new garments she'd purchased at the encouragement of her husband. She'd discovered that it was far more enjoyable to go shopping with one's husband than with one's maid. Gabriel not only seemed to like helping her choose her clothing, but he had exquisite taste. The walking dress was a deep teal blue-green that made her eyes an almost silvery gray. The fabric so rich and vibrant it practically glowed.

And the hat she wore was a tiny fluff of a thing she never would have purchased for herself. It was not to cover or protect, but to display. The peacock feather that jutted out over one eye made her look sophisticated beyond anything she'd ever worn.

Fletcher appeared in the doorway. "You rang, madam?"

"Yes, we are going for a walk." Drusilla would tell her maid the true destination once they were away from the house.

What she was doing was . . . well, there was no word for it other than outrageous.

Would Gabriel be angry? She thought back to his irritation about her questions regarding the duel with Visel and grimaced. Surely there was no subject more private than a man's mistresses?

She should turn around and go back immediately.

Instead, she turned to Fletcher when they were two streets over and stopped. "Will you hail a hackney cab for us?" She felt foolish asking, but she'd never done such a thing. Did one merely stick out one's arm and wave?

"You want a hackney?" Fletcher said.

"Yes, Fletcher. That is correct. I wish to go somewhere."

"We are not far from the house—shouldn't we just—"

"A hackney, Fletcher."

Her maid's forehead wrinkled with concern, but she nodded before glancing up the street to where several carriages were approaching. She raised her hand and just as quickly dropped it. An oncoming carriage pulled up a short distance ahead of them.

So that was how it was done. Not so difficult.

The driver, a remarkably handsome young man, grinned down at her, his eyes bouncing from Fletcher to Drusilla. "Where can I take you two lovelies?"

Drusilla's jaw dropped at his familiar greeting. Before she could speak, Fletcher edged her much smaller body in front of Drusilla.

"You mind your manners or I'll climb up there and box your ears."

The driver laughed and touched his cap. "Aye, missus. Where may I take you ladies?" he repeated, mockingly stern.

"Number twelve Alder Street," Drusilla said.

Fletcher opened the door and lowered the steps, pulling them up once they were both inside.

"Miss Drusilla—"

"I am going to visit the two women who have been taking care of Mr. Marlington's son."

Her maid's face reddened. "But—"

"You won't dissuade me, Fletcher. But I can understand if you do not wish to visit with me. I can have the driver set you down at the next corner. Do you have money enough to take yourself home?"

Fletcher's expression settled into martyrish lines. "I shan't let you go alone, Miss Dru."

Relief flooded her at her maid's words, and she sat back against the worn squabs of the carriage, watching the busy afternoon streets flicker past. Discovering where the well-known actresses lived had not been as difficult as she'd feared. But making the decision to visit them had been exceedingly difficult.

She and Gabriel had taken Samir out dozens of times in the preceding weeks, and one of the things she noticed with every visit was how much Samir spoke about his "aunts" Gigi and Maria. He'd only been with the two women for a few months but he'd grown very close to them. He seemed to be a boy with a great capacity for love and had taken Drusilla into his heart without hesitation. She was grateful for that because he very well could have felt threatened to share his precious Jibril with anyone else. Instead he even seemed to look forward to seeing her now.

But that didn't make this decision to disobey Gabriel and pry into his life any easier.

The carriage rolled along far faster than she would have liked, and it seemed only minutes had passed when they came to a stop.

Fletcher laid a hand on her arm. "Are you sure about this, Miss Dru?"

Was she? If she didn't meet these women now, she would always wonder.

She gave her maid a reassuring smile—which was as much for herself as it was for the other woman.

"Yes, Fletcher, I am very certain."

Chapter 24

The door to Drusilla's dressing room opened, and a king walked in.

Drusilla laughed.

Gabriel put one hand on his hip and wagged a regal, be-ringed finger at her. "You risk our displeasure with such disrespectful laughter in our presence."

Even Fletcher, who'd been kneeling to stich up a small tear in the hem of her simple dress, laughed.

Drusilla curtsied low. "Your majesty."

"That is better." He smirked. "You may rise."

She cocked an eyebrow at him. "You look regal but . . . warm?"

He lifted the long brown curls of his wig. "I was going to be Cromwell, but the breastplate was even hotter. Besides, the last masquerade I went to was swarming with Cavaliers. It's worth a man's head to show up as the Protector." He came closer and took her hands, holding out her arms to inspect her.

"And you, my dear"—his eyelids lowered—"are a woman fit to be my queen."

She gave him a saucy look and spoke a slightly altered version of the infamous line: "You are mistaken, sir, I am satisfied with the role of Protestant *whore*."

He threw back his head and laughed. "Your ready wit pleases us greatly," he said, giving her a look that would have done the lascivious Charles II proud.

Drusilla picked up her basket of oranges, hung it on her arm, and cut him an arch stare. "Your pleasure awaits, Highness."

They gazed out the windows of the carriage, both of them shaking their heads.

"I've never seen anything like such a crush of carriages," Gabriel said.

"Nor I."

The coaches crammed the streets in all directions leading to Richland House, packed so tightly a person could have walked across the roofs with ease.

"You did not come last year?" he asked.

"I was not invited last year." Her lips—which he had a difficult time not kissing—twisted into a wry smile. "I doubt I would have been invited this year, either—but for you."

He grinned at her. "Your king is good for something, then?"

"One hopes one will find many uses for him," she said primly.

Gabriel laughed. He delighted in her acerbic wit almost as much as he did her willing body and insatiable appetite for him.

"You didn't say how your visit with Lady Exley went today?"

Gabriel stopped laughing immediately.

"Ah," she said, her expression filled with sympathy. "She was angry."

It was not a question. And, yes, his mother had been angry.

She had railed at him at length—and at high enough volume to catch the attention of the marquess, who'd been several rooms away. Luckily she'd done most of her yelling in a language other than English. Indeed, Arabic had not been enough to express her thoughts—she'd switched to Berber and French, as well.

He turned to his wife, who was still waiting for his reply. "She was, er, rather disappointed in me for acting irresponsibly six years ago, but mostly for not telling her sooner." He didn't tell her what his mother had said when she'd learned where Samir was staying. When she'd demanded he bring the boy to her house, Gabriel had put his foot down. The marquess, who'd stayed to keep his wife calm and stop her from working herself into a state, had—for once—come down on Gabriel's side.

"She wanted me to bring Samir to live with her, but eventually came to accept that would not happen."

Drusilla nodded, her smile wry. "I imagine she possesses quite a temper."

Gabriel snorted. "You have no idea."

Drusilla glanced out the window, and Gabriel realized the carriage hadn't moved for several minutes.

"We have not moved even a foot. Shall we walk?" She looked at him and then raised her hand to her mouth to hide her grin. "Or perhaps not. It will be easy for me—but you?"

Gabriel wore a huge wig and more clothing than he'd ever donned at one time. The heavy velvet and ermine-trimmed cloak was stifling.

"Perhaps if I remove my—"

"Oh no." She shook her head. "You mustn't remove even a stitch—not until everyone has seen you."

"But, darling, they won't know me because I will be wearing this." He lifted the mask Drake had given him.

"They will know you," she assured him.

"What does that mean, Miss Clare? Are you referring to my nose?"

She giggled. His serious wife giggled.

Gabriel heaved an exaggerated sigh. "Very well, we shall suffer in all our court finery. Come. It will be better to walk than swelter in here."

The streets were full of costume-clad guests with the same idea.

"There seem to be an unprecedented number of Cleopatras," he murmured in her ear as they approached the head of the receiving line.

She shivered.

"What, are you cold?"

"No, only thinking of all those asps."

He chuckled as they reached the head of the stairs.

"My goodness," she said, her eyes wide as they handed their cloaks over to the footman and looked at the scene below.

There were Greeks, Romans, figures from all eras of English royalty, explorers, and other, less recognizable characters milling around the packed ballroom dance floor.

"You were right about the Cavaliers," she said, adjusting the basket on her arm before pointing to a clutch of Royalists in a far corner.

"Good God," Gabriel muttered. "It is sweltering in here. Why are all the windows closed?"

"I understand it is not unusual for the Regent to attend. He is great friends with the duke."

Gabriel doubted the rotund monarch would be up for such an arduous trek as they had just taken.

A tall, uncharacteristically blond Cromwell approached them and pointed at Gabriel. "Seize him! And bring him to the tower," he ordered nobody in particular.

Gabriel cut him a haughty look. "I'm the other Charles—

or can't you tell? Besides, it would appear your men have deserted you."

Byer glanced over his shoulders and frowned. "What the devil happened to them?"

"How did you know it was me? Oh, never mind—it was Drake, wasn't it?"

"I will not reveal my sources." He cut a glance at Drusilla and bowed low. "And how arrogant we are to assume it was Your Highness I knew. It was your lovely companion I recognized."

"Kind sir." Drusilla dropped a curtsy and then handed him an orange. "And who are you? The Protector of lobsters?"

Gabriel laughed.

"Sharp-tongued Nell." Byer ran a finger around the ruff at his neck, his exposed skin indeed an alarming shade of red.

"Hot?" Gabriel asked with a snicker. "I almost took that costume, but I am wiser than you."

"I can't imagine yours is much better," Byer said, eyeing the heavy cloak.

"It isn't." Gabriel cut his wife a pitiful look.

She heaved a mock sigh. "Very well, you may take it off, Your Highness."

Gabriel opened the heavy gold clasp that held the garment on and swept it off with a flourish. He gestured to a passing footman. "Put this in the cloakroom, please."

The man sagged when Gabriel laid the burden in his arms.

The ballroom became even stuffier as more guests made their way from their carriages.

The doors remained closed in anticipation of a royal visit and the massive room was stultifying, a heavy fog of perfume and sweat hovering above the crush of bodies.

The dance floor was cramped and Gabriel was grateful his costume did not allow for much dancing as he could barely see past his wig. Drusilla, on the other hand, had danced with a very stiff Byer and a half-dozen others by the time supper rolled around. He looked over the dancers on the floor, searching for her plain bonnet, which was conspicuous among all the sparkling finery. He'd last seen her dancing with a man dressed as what he supposed was a corsair. But they were nowhere to be seen, now.

Drusilla leaned heavily on the tall corsair's arm as she limped beside him. "Are you sure you are quite all right?" he asked, "Or shall I carry you."

She cringed at the thought of making such a spectacle—even though she was in costume. "No, I do not require carrying. Perhaps you might help me to a seat on the terrace and then fetch my husband."

"Ah, of course. And who might he be in this wild menagerie?"

"His Royal Highness Charles II."

Her companion chuckled as he opened one of the closed French doors and guided her through before closing it behind her. "Better than Charles I."

Drusilla smiled at the small jest. She had no idea who the corsair was, although there was something about his voice that teased at her memory. He had coal black hair that made his light blue eyes striking behind the full black velvet mask he wore.

He began to lead her down the steps and into the garden. Drusilla hesitated.

"It will be more private," he assured her. "There is a seat just there—beside the fountain."

Drusilla saw he was right and allowed him to help her to the stone bench. The garden had been lighted with colored lanterns, but the two nearest the fountain had gone out. There were other couples in the gloom, but nobody close by. A slight flutter of worry settled in her stomach before she recalled that she was a married lady: her reputation was no longer more delicate than an orchid. Still . . .

He crouched down in front of her, his colorful robes billowing as he dropped to his haunches. "Would you like me to look at your foot? After all, I am the oaf who may have broken your toes."

Drusilla wiggled her toes, which indeed did feel crushed. But she hardly wanted some strange man looking at her foot. "That won't be necessary. I would much rather you find my husband, if you do not mind."

He hesitated, and then stood. "Stay right here—don't walk on your foot or you might make it worse."

Drusilla wanted to roll her eyes, but instead she forced out a smile. "Yes, of course."

She looked down at her foot when he turned and left, grateful for the second time tonight that she'd worn sturdy shoes for her costume. If she'd been wearing dancing slippers when the clumsy corsair trod on her foot, it might indeed be broken.

She leaned down and untied the laces, reflecting on the odd evening. She'd danced almost every dance—a first in her life. The corsair had come upon her when she'd been looking for Gabriel. She was tired—they'd had a very energetic evening the night before—and she'd wanted nothing more than to go home early and curl up together in one of their beds.

Her face heated at her thoughts, even though she was alone. "Silly," she muttered beneath her breath, toeing off her sturdy shoe, wincing when she tried wriggling her toes. The mysterious corsair had caught her before she could reach Gabriel and had begged for the next set so insistently it would have been uncomfortable to say no.

The first dance had been a waltz, which she had danced only a few times before—all this past week and just the one time with her husband. A dance that had seemed romantic and delightful with Gabriel had felt uncomfortable with a costumed stranger. She had not liked feeling another man's hands on her. Nor had she liked his probing questions after she'd told him she was married. He had proceeded to winkle increasingly private details from her, his manner gentle but persistent.

"Even though your face is concealed from me, you seem to be a very happy lady," he said at one point.

What did a person say to *that*?

"Yes, I would call myself happy."

"Ah, you must be in love."

She'd drawn the line at sharing something she'd not even told her husband yet. Her silence must have told him that he'd stepped over the line.

"I apologize, that was ill done of me. But I can't help noticing you are glowing."

She knew he was correct: she *was* glowing. Eva had noticed it, Fletcher had noticed it, and Lady Exley—in her direct manner—had commented on her appearance a few nights ago at dinner. She was in love with a man who seemed at least to be very fond of her, if not actually in love himself.

"Thank you," she'd said, her voice cooler than usual to hide the joy she felt that even a stranger would notice her happiness. "I am very fortunate."

"Indeed," he had murmured quietly, and that had been the last they'd spoken until he'd trod on her foot.

As she massaged her toes she realized the corsair had been gone long enough to have found Gabriel, even in *this* crowded ballroom. She released her foot and sighed. Well, she would just have to put her shoe back on and go find him herself.

She should have guessed a pirate could not be trusted.

Gabriel removed his wig the moment he shut the door to the carriage.

"Feel better?" Drusilla asked as he lowered the window and let the breeze ruffle his damp hair.

"Much. Although I'll need to bathe as soon as I get home." He was distinctly ripe smelling. "Are you sure you don't want me to sit in the other seat?"

"I am sure," she said in the cool, prim manner he now knew hid great depth of feeling.

"How are your toes?"

"Sore, but uninjured."

He took her hand in his beringed fist, wondering—not for the first time—how Byer could stand to wear so much jewelry. He lifted her hand to his mouth and kissed her knuckles. "I will inspect them myself when I come to you tonight. Closely."

She flashed him a shy smile.

"If I had met the blackguard who injured you, I would have had him dragged to the Tower."

"That seems a severe punishment for mere toe treading."

"He also abandoned you in your time of need."

She chuckled. "To be honest, I was rather glad. There was something about him . . ."

"Oh?"

"Yes, he was asking odd questions."

"What kind of questions?"

"About our marriage, me, you, us." She shrugged. "Personal questions."

"I don't like the sound of that—you have no idea who he was?"

"None."

"Hmm."

She squeezed his hand. "It was nothing. I'm just glad to be going home—glad this is the last big event of the Season." She leaned against his shoulder. "Glad we will be going to Sizemore with Samir soon."

Gabriel released her hand and slipped his arm around her. "He is a good little boy."

"He is. I think he will make an excellent elder brother."

Gabriel had to play her words over in his head before he gasped and grabbed her by the shoulders. "What?"

She looked up at him, the streetlights giving him brief glimpses of her smiling face. She nodded. "I believe it is true. It has been almost six weeks since we married and I should have started my courses by now."

He pulled her into a crushing embrace, until he realized she was making slight choking sounds, and he released her, kissing her hard.

"You are happy?" she asked in a breathless voice.

He laughed. "I am happy." She stiffened in his arms. "What is it?" he asked.

"I just realized that our child shall be only a bit younger than his or her aunts or uncles."

Gabriel blinked. "Why, so they will." He thought of something else, too. "And what of you, Drusilla? Are you happy with this? I know a marriage, husband, and children were not what you had planned for yourself." She said something into his shoulder. "What was that, darling? I couldn't hear you."

"I said I never dreamed I could have such a thing with you."

"Oh, why is that?"

She chewed her lower lip, her expression anguished.

"What is it, Dru?" he asked, the diminutive form of her name slipping easily from his tongue. "Why do you look so sad?"

"I'm just so happy." The words were hard to understand they were so soft.

He chuckled. "And that is a reason to look sad?"

"I am afraid my happiness will not last."

Gabriel made a *tsk*ing sound and drew her close. "My little porcupine," he said into her plain straw bonnet. "We should both rejoice in our good fortune in finding each other. I will not lie to you, Drusilla; I did not enter this marriage with a great deal of optimism. But as you gave me glimpses beyond your mask, I realized what a treasure I had inadvertently—and undeservedly—been given." She pulled away and looked up at him, her cheeks damp.

"Don't cry, my lovely Drusilla." He leaned in and kissed away her tears. "Have you not realized that I've come to love you?" He stared at her stunned expression and shook his head. "And here I thought you were so clever."

Her jaw dropped. "Y-you love *me*?"

He laughed softly at her marveling tone. "I love you. I should have told you when I first deciphered my emotions, but you are so—self-contained, so stern, so remote. I couldn't imagine you would appreciate my messy feelings."

"When? When did you know?"

"I believe I began to love you when you were so generous and accepting of Samir. But every day I have found more and more about you to admire, respect, and—yes—to love very much. You're kind, intelligent, generous—"

"Oh stop," she said, burying her face in his chest. "You're making me blush terribly."

He laughed softly.

"Are you certain I'll be enough, Gabriel? After all, you were raised to believe—"

He gave her a gentle squeeze. "You forget, my love, that my *mother* also had a hand in my raising. All my life she has taught me that love is real. Even before she found it herself, she always believed in it. It's true I would have lived as my father lived had I stayed." He stroked her soft cheek. "But I chose to come to England and live a different life. I love you, Drusilla—and I want you. Only you—there will be no other woman in my life."

She shook against him, as if the violence of her emotions was too much.

"Shhh," he murmured into her hair.

She said something against his chest.

"What was that, sweetheart?"

"I've loved you since that first summer we met."

All the air left his lungs, and he turned to face her, taking her chin between his fingers and forcing her to look at him. *"What?"*

"Yes, I did. But I knew even then, before I saw how many women pursued you—hurled themselves at you—that you would never want a woman like me. So I—I—"

"So you abused me at every opportunity."

She choked out a watery sound that was half cry, half laugh. "Oh, Gabriel! I was so afraid you could never care for me, that you would take lovers and that I would die inside."

"You goose," he said, brushing back a spiraling strand of hair. "Besides, I can see you killing me before I see you dying."

She sniffed loudly. "I might have."

Gabriel pulled her soft, feminine, and already beloved body against him. "Your strength of purpose is one of the things I love and admire most about you."

"Oh? What other things do you love and admire?"

He grinned into the darkness. "Well . . . I like the way you win some of our arguments—"

"Some!"

"All right, *most* of our arguments. I like your beautiful, wild hair and the feel of it across my body. When I'm naked," he added in a rough whisper. "And I like the way you look when I am thrusting inside you and—"

"Gabriel!"

"Am I making you blush?" he asked as she pulled away and straightened her bonnet.

"I'm as red as a beet."

"I love beets."

They were enjoying a deep, languorous kiss when she broke away, her expression suddenly pensive.

"What is it?" he asked.

She bit her lower lip, her forehead furrowed with worry.

"Drusilla—"

"I went to see Giselle and Maria today."

Drusilla had expected him to yell. Or to look angry. She had *not* expected him to laugh.

She frowned, inexplicably peeved by his response. "What is so funny?"

He shook his head, still chuckling. "I'm laughing because I'm imagining their surprise."

Drusilla grunted. It was true, the two women had been flabbergasted to find her in their small but charming sitting room.

"I'm sorry for going behind your back on this matter, but I felt a persisting aura of mystery between us would only give my rather fertile imagination more, er, fertilizer."

"I daresay they both admired you very much."

Drusilla could not answer to that, but she *had* felt an unexpected twinge of admiration for them—of course that was nothing to the jealousy she felt. She didn't know what she had expected to find, but it hadn't been two well-spoken and attractive women in a house that had been decorated with exquisite taste. And it had almost ripped her apart to imagine Gabriel making love with them in that house.

Gabriel took her hand, no longer laughing. "I should have taken steps to introduce you to them myself—but I was far too cowardly. I've noticed before that women are frequently braver than men."

She gave him a slight smile, unable to scrub her imagination of disturbing pictures of him with his ex-lovers: touching them, being touched.

It would take time, but she would conquer her emotions.

Gabriel lifted her hand to his mouth and kissed it. "I am pleased you made their acquaintance, Drusilla. You are correct in saying it will make future relations much easier."

The carriage rolled to a halt just then and Drusilla was spared from responding—which was an enormous relief. While she had wanted to establish contact for Samir's sake, that didn't mean it was an enjoyable activity. The fact that the women were so elegant and well spoken might have actually made matters more difficult.

A footman opened the carriage door, but Gabriel handed Drusilla down. It wasn't until he was halfway up the steps that he realized the door was open.

Parker stood in the opening, his face tight and tense.

"What is it?" Gabriel demanded, his voice harsher than he had intended.

Before he could speak, Byer came up behind Parker. "I've just come from Giselle and Maria's; Samir has been kidnapped."

Chapter 25

Drusilla had always believed she'd seen her husband at his most angry when he'd attacked Visel. But this . . . he sat across from her, engaging in low-voiced conversation with Byer, and his eyes—his lively green eyes—seemed to have become stone.

Gabriel had only stopped long enough to strip off his cumbersome costume before accompanying Byer to Alder Street.

He hadn't been gone long and Byer did not return with him.

Drusilla had changed into a comfortable gown and paced until his return. She led him to the library. "Sit, have some tea."

He did not demur, his expression almost crazed.

"What happened, Gabriel?"

"Giselle and Maria's maid discovered Sami's nurse, Mrs. Banks, in her room with a large lump swelling on her head."

"Is the lady hurt?"

"Not seriously, thank God. She was already awake when I got there, but she remembered nothing as both she and the boy had been asleep when it happened. The open window in the schoolroom makes it clear how the person—whoever it was—entered the house.

"It is a steep climb with very little to hold on to," Gabriel said, his expression taut with worry. "I hope to God Samir took no harm or—"

The door opened to the library, and Parker stood in the doorway, a full tray in his hands. He glanced nervously from Gabriel's angry face to Drusilla.

"Right here will be fine," she said, smiling at the obviously upset servant and gesturing to the table in front of the fire. It had seemed chilly tonight, although she knew it was most likely an emotional chill they were all feeling.

"Thank you, Parker."

She began to prepare the tea, unable to wrap her mind around what had happened. She shook her head and turned to Gabriel. "Who would kidnap the boy? Could it be somebody from his mother's family, Gabriel? Perhaps they want him back? Or maybe—"

"Byer and I believe we know who is behind this."

He told her how he'd seen Rowland meeting with Visel at least twice.

"Why didn't you tell me, Gabriel?"

"Because I had no idea what they were doing. I assumed that if Visel was involved, it would be something to do with me." He shrugged. "As for Rowland? I thought perhaps he would be helping with whatever Visel had planned."

"Yes, his cousin. Although he always indicated he was not close to him—that he despised his wealthier relatives as lazy, useless spendthrifts."

Gabriel set down his cup, his jaw tight. "Did Rowland ever tell you about his gambling?"

"No—he said he hated gambling, that it was the downfall of his father."

"The second part of what you say is true. But as to the first—well, Rowland owes money to several people. A great deal of money."

Her cup and saucer clattered, and tea sloshed over the side. Gabriel reached across and took it from her, setting it down on the tray before continuing.

"He lost his lodgings and sold most of his possessions about ten days ago. He's been living with his cousin since then. It seems they had a falling out over something and Visel turfed him out. I lost track of him after that."

"Wait—you mean you've been following him?"

"Yes, since the night he met you in the garden. Byer and I split the task and his valet also helped." He grimaced. "I'm ashamed to say we lost track of Rowland on my watch. He went into a—" He stopped, his cheeks darkening. "Well, he went into a brothel."

"You followed him into a brothel?" It was all she could do to force the words out.

"It is because I *didn't* follow him inside that he was able to disappear." He gave her a wry look. "You see how well you've trained your husband without even realizing it?"

It was Drusilla's turn to blush.

"I waited for hours. And when Byer came, *he* waited for hours." He coughed. "Although he waited *inside*. Which is how he found out that Rowland had left hours earlier—that he'd gone with another man to a card game in an adjacent building. The men had left through the servants' entrance for convenience." He shook his head. "And that was the last we saw of him."

"Why do you think he would have taken Sami? What could he—"

A sharp rap on the door interrupted her. Parker rushed inside the room, his cheeks flushed. "This just came for you, sir."

Gabriel took the folded rectangle. "Who delivered it?"

"A boy from The Greenman," he said, naming a posting inn on the north end of the city. "But he said he was paid in advance to deliver it—double his usual amount. He said the man who paid him was slight with curly dark brown hair."

Drusilla and Gabriel stared at each other: Rowland fit that description.

"You may go, Parker." Gabriel waited until the door closed before breaking the seal.

Drusilla felt sick. "My God, it *is* Rowland."

He read it out loud:

"Marlington:

"By now you will know the boy is gone. He is unharmed and will remain so as long as you do exactly what I say. I want 10,000£ and I will give you until tomorrow night to gather it. You will receive a message tomorrow at nine o'clock telling you where to take the money and how to go about it. If you do not follow the directions to the letter—if you think to send a Runner, for example—you will never see the boy again. I know Drusilla has the money, so I will not tolerate any delaying tactics. Also, don't try any tricks. I will not hesitate to carry out my threat. I shall accept the money from nobody other than Drusilla—alone."

Gabriel handed her the note. "Of course he did not sign it—do you recognize the handwriting?"

Drusilla glanced at the letter and then handed it back. "It is his writing."

Gabriel strode to his desk, tossed down the letter, and then pulled a sheet of paper from a drawer and sat.

"What are you doing?"

"Writing to my mother."

Drusilla went to stand over the desk. "Does she know Rowland has been stalking us?"

"No, but she will be able to get the money quickly. I'm afraid I simply do not have such an amount lying around. It would take me days to assemble it."

His words were like a slap. She leaned forward and splayed her hand in the middle of the piece of paper, forcing him to look at her.

He was already shaking his head. "No. I will not take your money. Nor will you deliver it to that worm." He frowned, his expression fierce enough to make her shiver. "The nerve of—"

"It is *our* money, Gabriel. And Samir is *our* son. How can you think I would ever want anything else?"

His face flushed darkly. "While I appreciate your sentiment, he is either my estranged brother's son or my bastard child by a former lover, Drusilla. How can I expect you to pay?"

"First," she said, yanking the paper from his hands and crumpling it in a ball, "I never want to hear that word spoken out loud again. Second, we are *family*. Do you think I would give tens of thousands of pounds to help strangers yet begrudge money to save our son—no matter *who* his mother was?"

She could tell he was angry—at her, at himself, at Rowland? Probably all three.

He closed his eyes and slumped back in his chair, dropping his head into his hand. "I should have known he was up to something like this—he and Visel were—" He stopped, shook his head, and snapped his fingers. "Visel!" He was halfway to the door before she realized what he was doing.

"Gabriel—wait. You're going to see him *now*? It is four o'clock in the morning."

He yanked open the door and said over his shoulder. "Don't you know, Drusilla? Nighttime is the best time to hunt rats."

* * *

Drusilla had hoped Gabriel would be home when her man of business came to see her at eight o'clock sharp, but—as it turned out—she was very glad he wasn't.

"Hello, Mr. Jenkins, thank you for coming so quickly." Of her three trustees, she had always liked Mr. Jenkins the best. He wasn't warm or affectionate, but he was always forthright and treated her as a thinking being. She'd decided to keep him as her personal man of business after she had married. Her plans for expanding her charitable endeavors were not yet fully developed, but when they were, she would need help implementing them.

"Would you like tea?" she asked once he'd settled in the chair across from her. She had decided to meet him in the library, by far the most comfortable room in the house.

"No, thank you, Mrs. Marlington. I had some before I left." He opened the large black leather satchel he'd brought with him. "If you hadn't summoned me today, I was going to ask for a meeting with you."

Oh dear. This did not sound good. "And why is that, Mr. Jenkins?"

His mouth settled into a grim frown. "I'm afraid I received some rather disturbing news late yesterday."

She could have told him it was going around. "Nothing wrong with Mrs. Jenkins, I hope?"

"No, no, nothing of that sort." He cleared his throat and then opened one of the ledgers he'd brought. He was acting almost . . . nervous. "I received word from my man up in Leeds. He went to look at the house you purchased for the women's home."

Drusilla had a bad feeling developing in her already churning stomach. "What did he find?"

"There was no such house. The address doesn't exist."

She could not speak.

"After he found that, he hastened to Manchester, and then he went to Birmingham."

"He found the same thing." Her voice was the husk of a whisper.

"Yes. In all three situations false papers had been prepared—right down to the architectural plans. It appears Mr. Rowland employed a competent forger." He closed the folder. "I hope you won't take it amiss, but I had a Runner look into Mr. Rowland even before I sent my man up North."

"He is in debt—gambling debts."

Jenkins raised his eyebrows.

"I found out last night," she explained. "In fact, Rowland and his activities are the reason I asked you here today."

Jenkins looked perplexed. Drusilla stood and went to the bellpull.

"You might not need tea, Mr. Jenkins, but I certainly do."

The valet's face had turned an alarming shade of red.

Byer's hand landed on Gabriel's shoulder. "Perhaps you might loosen up on him a bit, Gabe. I believe he's trying to tell you something."

Gabriel grudgingly loosened his grip.

"I don't kn-know," the man wheezed.

"That was not what I wanted to hear," Gabriel said, flexing his fingers.

"Wait—wait! Give me a moment. I'll tell you what I know." He repeatedly cleared his throat. "May I have a drink, please?"

Gabriel's hands began to tighten, but Byer said, "Come on, Gabe. Let's all have a drink."

Gabriel dragged the servant to the only armchair in the room and shoved the man into it, glaring down at him while Byer went to fetch the drinks.

Gabriel had met Byer's Runner—Tompkins—outside Visel's

apartments. He could see by the man's surprised expression that Byer had not sent word to him yet about Samir's abduction. When Gabriel told him, the short, slight man let out an unspeakably vulgar curse.

"Beggin' your pardon, sir, but I'm a right fool for not suggesting we watch the boy's house."

"Well, so was I," Gabriel had admitted. "Is there anyone inside?" He gestured to the lodgings with his chin.

"Nobody came or went from Visel's apartments last night except his valet, who left at around seven, came back at ten, and then left again early this morning."

"Is there a way to get inside?"

The Runner had grinned.

Byer had joined them not much later and waited with Gabriel while Tompkins went off to see what he could find from his sources.

They'd grabbed the valet the second he'd entered Visel's lodgings. And then Gabriel had begun to question him.

Gabriel turned to where Byer was pouring out what appeared to be brandy.

"Care for a glass?" the viscount asked, cocking a brow.

"No." Gabriel didn't care for hard spirits even at the best of times. Right now was not the best of times.

Byer brought the valet a glass and then propped his hip on the desk and took a sip.

The man gulped half the glass, dragged the back of his hand across his lips, and then threw back the other half.

"That's enough," Gabriel growled, taking the glass from his hand before the valet could convince Byer to give him more. That's all he needed, for the man to become even more insensible.

Byer grinned down at their captive. "I won't be able to hold Mr. Marlington back much longer, old chap. Why don't you tell us *everything* before my savage friend here tears it out of you piece by piece? Let's start with your name," the viscount suggested.

"Symond, sir."

"Talk," Gabriel ordered.

"I haven't seen Lord Visel since last night—before he went to the masquerade party and he—"

Gabriel lunged at Symond, who pressed himself back into his chair.

"*What?* Good God—what did I say?" he squeaked as Gabriel grabbed the lapels of his coat and loomed over him.

"Visel was at the Duchess of Richland's masquerade party?"

Symond nodded vigorously. "He was going to the party but he said he would come back afterward—only briefly—and that I should have everything packed." He cut Gabriel a sly look. "He said he would have a ladybird waiting in his carriage and that he wanted to set out immediately after he loaded his bags."

Gabriel had noticed the luggage and trunks in the small entry hall.

"I packed first thing—I didn't want to anger him. His lordship is a man with a short fuse." He tapped his temple. "It's my opinion he's not quite right in the head." He gave Gabriel a suggestive look.

"Keep your medical opinions to yourself. What else happened last night?"

"He was in a right ugly mood. He'd ordered his costume in advance, but they delivered the wrong one—a Roman outfit. Anyhow, he went storming off to the tailor's shop where I'd found the costume." Symond shook his head. "Madness. What difference could it make?"

"Let me guess—he went as a corsair."

The valet looked arrested. "Why, yes, that's right, sir. Did you see him? Not that his own mother would have recognized him. He even dyed his hair. Looked just like those corsair villains you see in the broadsheets." He stopped abruptly, his eyes suddenly widening as he realized what he'd just said and to whom he'd said it.

But Gabriel was no longer listening to the man's babbling. He released the valet's coat and thrust him away, commencing to pace.

All he could think was that something had happened last night to have foiled Visel's plan with Drusilla. Why else would he have injured her and taken her out to the garden? Perhaps he had planned to spirit her away? But for what? What could he possibly have planned?

Byer's voice interrupted Gabriel's frantic imaginings.

"Why was he leaving so late and in such a furtive manner?"

"I don't know. I assumed he and his lady friend didn't want to be seen hanging about together."

Symond's slimy expression made Gabriel's hands twitch to strangle him. "Where was he going?"

"I don't know."

"What do you mean you don't know?" He reached for Symond's coat again, but the man held up his hands.

"I don't—it's the truth. He only hired me a few months ago—at the start of the Season."

That stopped Gabriel. "He didn't have his own man?"

"No, he said he'd been killed—a while ago in the Peninsula—and that he'd not gotten around to replacing him." His expression turned sullen. "He told me only last week he would not be keeping me on."

Gabriel could understand that; Symond was not only slovenly, but he also had an unsavory air about him and it had taken very little effort to get him to turn on his master.

"What about Rowland—his cousin?"

"That one." Symond scowled with disgust. "The master let him stay here for almost a week. What a pig."

"Did the two spend a lot of time together?"

"Not much. They came back from some club together a few times, but I heard them arguing." His eyes shifted between Byer and Gabriel. "It was loud; it woke me up," he explained, although neither of them had said anything. Gabriel knew a man like Symond probably spent a good deal of his time hovering around keyholes.

"Could you hear what they were saying?"

"They were arguing about a woman and some boy."

"What?" Gabriel took a step closer. "Tell me every single detail. Every. Single. One."

Symond gulped, his shifty eyes filled with fear. "There wasn't much. Rowland wanted to take some boy; he never did say who. He said taking a child was easier than taking a full-grown woman. Lord Visel said he would not countenance such a thing—that they should stick with the original plan. But they started to really row when his lordship said he would thrash Rowland if he learned he'd done anything with the boy and that he'd turn him over to the constable."

Gabriel and Byer exchanged looks.

"And when was that?" Gabriel asked the valet.

Symond shrugged. "Less than a week ago. Not long afterward Lord Visel found out Rowland had stolen and sold some of Lord Visel's odds and sods, like a family ring—something that had belonged to his lordship's father." He grimaced. "I thought I'd seen him get mad before, but that was nothing compared to this. He was in a proper taking over that ring."

"Did he report Rowland's thieving?"

"That's the funny thing," Symond said, scratching his head. "He didn't. He smacked him around a bit—until Rowland told him where he'd pawned it—and then told him he'd find somebody else to help carry out his plan if Rowland did anything else stupid." His mouth twisted into a derisive sneer. "Rowland actually cried and begged his forgiveness."

"Where did he sell the ring?"

"At a pawnshop down by the East Docks—Hurley's, I think the name was."

Gabriel turned to Byer and could see his friend was thinking the same thing he was: a rat always returned to its lair.

"You mentioned a plan," Gabriel said. "What plan?"

"Whatever it was, they were doing it after the masquerade ball. Rowland met him here, and they left the house together."

"Was Rowland in costume?"

"No, sir. Just his regular cheaply made togs."

"They must have meant to do something at the ball but it fell through," Byer said.

"So they left Drusilla and came for Samir."

Byer pushed off the desk and stood over Symond. "Is there anything else?"

"I've told you all I know, sir."

"Everything?"

"Yes, sir. Everything."

Byer turned to Gabriel. "You ready?"

He nodded, and they headed for the door.

"Sirs!"

They both turned to find the valet standing in the middle of the room, his hands out.

"What?" Gabriel asked, impatient to be moving on.

Symond gestured around the room. "What should I do?"

"About what?"

"About Lord Visel. He should have been home already—I think something might have happened to him. Surely I should do something? Tell someone?"

"You could go tell the local constable," Gabriel tossed over his shoulder. "But given what Lord Visel was up to, I doubt he would thank you for that."

It was almost eight o'clock in the evening and Drusilla was half-mad with worry as she paced her study. She'd been waiting for *hours* for Gabriel to return or at least for a message from him. It was getting to the time when somebody should take the money and go meet Theo. What *could* he be doing? Why hadn't he at least sent a message? Something must be terribly wrong—she felt it in her bones.

There was a soft tap on the door, and Parker entered. He looked as raw and tense as she felt.

"A message for Mr. Marlington, ma'am. But I thought you should have it."

Drusilla recognized the handwriting immediately: it was from Eva.

"The messenger is from the Swan with Two Necks, madam. He said he was paid double and that it was urgent."

"Is he waiting for an answer?"

"He said the young man instructed him not to wait for an answer."

Young man? *What* young man. Oh Lord. What had Eva done now?

Drusilla realized her butler was still waiting. "Thank you, Parker," she said, staring down at the message as the door shut. Drusilla chewed her lower lip. There was no name on the delivery, only the address—did that mean it was for either her or Gabriel? She thought about how oddly Eva had behaved the last time she'd seen her—and now this about a young man. She was up to something; Drusilla knew the signs. Who knew when Gabriel would get back? She tore open the seal.

Gabe:

She paused at the name—it was to him, not them . . . But then her eye caught her name on the next line.

You're going to wonder how I know this, but I can't tell you. I hope it didn't happen, but if Drusilla is gone, she will be down by the East Docks in an empty corder's warehouse between an inn called the Jolly Taxpayer and a pawn broker called Hurley's. If she is not gone, watch her closely because a man named Rowland has decided to take her for ransom. This might never happen as I know at least half of his plan was foiled.

Don't believe everything you hear about me, my favorite brother. I am fine and will be happy. Take care of my best friend and yourself.

Love,

Eva

Drusilla considered the last few sentences, which were even odder than Eva usually was. What did she mean, not to believe everything she heard?

She bit her lip so hard it stung. She simply did not have time to worry about Eva, too. At least not right now. Already it was eight o'clock and she had heard *nothing* from Gabriel. Should she go?

If she left now, she could make it in time to meet Rowland's instructions.

She knew that Gabriel was furious—that he didn't wish to spend her money nor want her to be the one to deliver it. But time had almost run out.

Drusilla groaned—she just wanted it over—all of this was her fault. Rowland wouldn't have even known of Samir if not for her.

She would never have guessed he would do such a thing. But she probably should have. She recalled his angry accusations the last time she'd seen him—that she'd led him down a false path: all those private talks, sharing their hopes and dreams. Drusilla still didn't believe his accusations—that she'd led him along—but she did realize it hadn't been wise to spend so much time with him. And now he'd done this. If Gabriel got his hands on Rowland, he would kill him.

She pulled the bell. "Summon a hackney, Parker. I shall be ready to leave in ten minutes."

"You promise me you will wait until I return, Gabriel?" Byer asked for the second time. "I know you're eager to retrieve your son, but we have no evidence he's there. If we spook the kidnappers now, we might—"

"I'm not a fool, Tommy. I'll wait here and keep a lookout. You go notify the constables and have them ready and waiting—at a *distance*—when the time comes."

"Of course."

"And—" Here Gabriel heaved a heavy sigh. "Pick up the money from Drusilla and bring it in time for the meeting. Let her know—" He broke off. Let her know what?

Byer laid a hand on his shoulder. "Don't worry, I'll tell her we have things well in hand. Now, I know you can watch out for yourself, but this is one of the most dangerous spots in the city. I'd advise you not to leave the taproom until I return."

"You watch yourself, also, Tommy." They'd hired a hack but had dismissed it hours ago. Finding transportation in this area was not without dangers; finding *reliable* transportation was all but impossible.

"I will, Gabe. See you in a few hours."

That was over four hours ago, and it was now eight o'clock.

They'd left Visel's lodgings and spent the day searching the area around the pawn shop. Nobody had heard of Rowland or Visel—and they'd distributed enough bribe money to loosen tongues.

They'd decided, just after five, to follow Rowland's plans with a few important exceptions.

So Gabriel sat, waiting. He'd ordered a pint of home brew and a meal. He'd stopped drinking the second pint when he noticed the fly smashed on the bottom of the glass—the *inside.* He'd not touched the meal.

The waitress, whom he tipped far too well, drifted by his table. "You ain't touched yer food, sir." She exposed a gap-toothed smile. "Not 'ungry? Or maybe not for food." She put a foot up on the chair opposite him, her dirty green skirt slipping enough to show her battered half boots and a scabby shin. "Maybe it's somefing else you want?"

Gabriel forced himself to smile. "The necessary—where is it?"

That made her hoot. *"The necessary,"* she repeated in a dialect he supposed was meant to be his own. "That be the back wall—out in the alley." She flounced away, pausing at another table, where two sailors looked more interested in her wares.

Outside a dense fog had drifted up from the river and it was drizzling. He walked around the corner, not wishing to do his business out in front of the building. The alley was narrow and dark, and the stench . . . Lord, it was enough to make a man's eyes water. It was littered with rubbish, and rats as big as cats were scurrying between the refuse piles, making no effort to hide from humans. He'd never spent any time down at the London docks even though many young men liked to frequent the area to drink too much and enjoy rough sport. He'd done enough of that kind of thing back in Oran, where the wharf had been a favorite spot for getting into trouble.

He was about to face the wall when something flickered at the end of the alley. It was the bar wench.

"Oi there, pretty. Ye left this on the chair." She held something up but it was too dark to see.

"What is it?" he demanded, walking toward her. He got close enough to see, and she dropped her hand into her skirt. "What—"

He was alerted by a slight scraping noise behind him, but then his head exploded.

Chapter 26

Gabriel woke up tied to a chair with a pounding skull that felt as if it had been cracked like an egg. He was in a small, dimly lighted room, the only illumination coming from the gap beneath the door. As his vision sharpened, he saw piles of something—rope—covering most of the floor. It must be the rope-making business on the other side of the pawnbrokers. So, somebody from the inn must have alerted Rowland, who—

The light beneath the door flickered, and it swung open. Gabriel squinted against the lamplight, which was not bright but still made his head throb. The man in the doorway was not Rowland.

He grinned, an expression that did not communicate humor, but rather sadistic enjoyment. " 'Ello, me lordship!"

"I told you, he isn't a lord. He's a bastard." Rowland hove into view and frowned at Gabriel, his face twitching with worry, anger, hate, and a half-dozen other emotions. "And you shouldn't have let him see your face. It will not be safe for you now. He may be a bastard, but his mother is a marchioness and his grandfather is a duke."

"Safe? For me, or for 'im?" The big man gave an unpleasant laugh. "I don't care if he's the bloody King 'imself." he said, the light behind him casting his face into darkness. "I ain't goin' anywhere. I'm keepin' my 'alf of the money and livin' like a lord. Right 'ere."

"Half?" The word was a hoarse squawk. "But we agreed on—"

The second man spun around, and his arm shot out grabbing Rowland by the neck. "It 'curs to me I don't need you any longer, neither. You wrote the letter and sennit, the mort should be 'ere any minnit."

Gabriel could hear choking sounds as the big man reached down, snatched up a piece of twine, and began to truss Rowland's hands together as efficiently as a butcher trussed a hen. There wasn't a chair to tie him to, so when he'd finished tying his hands, he pushed the younger man onto a pile of coiled rope and grabbed his ankle. When Rowland kicked him, he swung his arm and Gabriel heard a muffled cry. Rowland's legs were not moving as the man tied them tightly together.

"There," he said, brushing his big paws against each other, as if to get rid of dirt. "Now the dosh is *all* mine." He turned, and the light slanted across his face, his expression sending ice down Gabriel's spine. "You'll both wait in here till Big Paul comes back and I can fix things right and proper. Don't think o' yellin'. Nobody 'oo cares can hear ye, and I'll do you like I did 'im." He jerked his head in Rowland's direction and reached for the door.

"Where is my son?"

"The nipper? Oh, 'e's with my Dolly. She's right fond o' 'im already. 'Er own boy died lass winter and she's too old to 'ave anovver. She'll take good care of 'im." He winked. "Don't you worry none." He slammed the door and Gabriel waited for his steps to recede.

"Rowland!" he whispered.

The man didn't move. Gabriel's feet were bound to the legs of the chair, but if he jerked his body, he found he could inch forward—which sent fierce pain hammering in his skull, but brought him close enough to Rowland that he could nudge him with his boot.

"Rowland! Wake up, you wretched piece of refuse." He was just about to tip his chair over and land on top of the man when Rowland moaned. "Wake up, before your partner in crime returns and kills us both."

"Marlington? Wh-why am I here?"

Gabriel ignored his question. "Get up and untie my hands."

"I can't move. My head—"

"Your big friend will be returning soon, and you will no longer have a headache *or* a head to worry about. The man is going to kill us after he gets the money." An image of Drusilla showing up—disobeying him, of course—with a sack of money invaded his mind. He gritted his teeth against the horrifying thought. Surely Byer was only late? Surely he'd told her everything was fine. Surely she would not—he bit down on the paralyzing fear this line of thinking created and focused on what he *could* control.

"Get up, Rowland. Your crony is bringing a man named Big Paul. How many of these devils are working with you on this?"

"It—it was only supposed to be one—Jed—but he brought his friend into it and then he took the boy, keeping him with some woman—"

"Do you know where Samir is?"

"No. I never actually saw him—they had a sneak thief steal him."

Gabriel briefly closed his eyes before continuing. "Get over here and untie my hands."

"But how?"

"Dammit, roll, crawl, fly for all I care. Just do it—don't you want to live?"

Rowland moved a little and groaned. Gabriel was ready to

howl with frustrated rage, but then the man pushed again and slid off the coils, landing with a soft thump on the floor.

"Oh God," he wailed.

"Keep your voice down, fool, and hurry."

Gabriel stared at the narrow slit of light beneath the door, living a hundred years in the next few minutes while Rowland inched his way over like a worm. Their captor had tied Rowland's hands in front of his body so he was able to roll onto his knees and reach the knots that held Gabriel's hands tight.

His mind went to what he would do once he was free. He had no pistol, no sword, but if he could get his hand on even a stick or perhaps a—

The bonds that had been cutting off the blood to his hands loosened. He flexed his hands and felt a thousand sharp needles stabbing into his fingers.

Ignoring the pain, he worked at the ropes around each boot, each second lasting a year. By the time he freed the second knot, his hands had regained most of their mobility. He stood and stretched, working circulation into his feet and hands.

"What is outside this door?"

"It's the warehouse where they store the rope-making supplies. Er, would you untie me?"

"I didn't hear him locking anything," Gabriel said, ignoring the question. "Is there a lock on this door?"

"No, he's an arrogant bastard. He told me he could handle a toff with one hand tied behind his back."

Gabriel's lips curved into a smile. He hoped to use that arrogance to his benefit. "What about the warehouse—which side are the doors on?"

"You'll see them straight ahead. A big rolling door with a smaller one cut in it. It's the only way in. They won't be waiting in the warehouse; they're in the pawnbroker's next door—they keep an eye on the street from there. They saw you come with Byer earlier and watched him leave. They knocked him on the head before he could find a hackney."

Sudden and severe sickness almost crippled him. Good God—Byer. "Is he dead?" He had to force the words through clenched teeth.

"No, Paul said he looked like he might be worth something, so I think they have plans to ransom him."

Thank God!

Gabriel put his friend from his mind and concentrated on the here and now. He was good with his fists—he'd trained at Jackson's and with his stepfather—but he could hardly take on two men at once.

"Can you untie me now?"

Gabriel pressed his face against the rough wood and squinted through the crack. He couldn't see much—although he did see something that might be a door straight ahead. He needed to get out of here before they came back. He reached for the latch.

"You can't leave me here." Rowland's voice reminded Gabriel of a pig's squeal.

"I'll knock you on the head if you don't shut your mouth," Gabriel whispered furiously.

"I swear, Marlington. I swear on my life that I'll help."

Gabriel snorted and pushed down the latch. "That's not worth much right now, is it?"

"I brought a pistol."

His hand froze, and he half turned. "Where is it?"

"Not until you untie me. I swear on my honor as a gentleman."

A pistol would make all the difference. If he could get his hands on it, that was.

"Tell me where it is, and I'll let you out."

"But—"

"That is all I will offer. Take it or stay here."

There was a long pause and then: "There is a barrel near the entrance; it has bits of rope ends that are frayed or worn. The pistol is tucked in with the rope."

Gabriel wanted to leave the scoundrel here, but he'd given his word. He huffed out a breath, grabbed the much smaller man under his arms, and lifted him onto the chair, untying his hands. It was less of an ordeal than his had been; Gabriel got the distinct impression the thug had considered Rowland even less of a threat than Gabriel.

He turned to the door and let Rowland untie his own feet. He checked to see if anyone had entered, but it looked the same. The door gave a shrill squeak he didn't recall from before, and he grimaced, expecting to hear the sound of footsteps. But nobody came. They'd left a lantern hanging on a hook near the door. A big barrel stood not too far away. Gabriel ran to the barrel and began pushing through the rope.

"I lied."

When he turned, Rowland was holding the pistol in his hand. He hadn't wasted time to free his ankles and they were still tied, meaning he had to hop. His mouth was set in an ugly line.

Gabriel laughed—a sound with no humor in it.

"What?" Rowland asked when he saw Gabriel's expression. "Did you expect the honor of a gentleman?" He snorted, gesturing with the pistol to the door of the smaller room. "Honor and other lofty ideas tend to fall by the wayside when one is facing debtor's prison and public humiliation."

"You'd do better to worry about saving your life just now."

"Shut up. If not for you, I'd be married to that bossy harpy and have no worries except how many mistresses to keep—just like yourself. Now, put your hands where I can see them, and get back into this room and onto your chair." His voice had gotten louder and his hand shook with anger.

Gabriel raised his hands and walked slowly toward Rowland. "He's going to kill you."

"No, he isn't. Because when he opens the door I'm going to—" He glanced over Gabriel's shoulder at something. It was only a second's distraction, but it was all Gabriel needed. He threw himself into Rowland's midriff and knocked him to the ground. Unfortunately, the pistol also hit the ground, skittering across the rough plank flooring.

"What do we 'ave 'ere? You ladies 'avin' a dance?"

Gabriel rolled onto his side and up onto his feet, immediately dropping into a crouch.

It was Jed, and he was alone. Gabriel lunged for him. For such a big man, he stepped out of the way nimbly, and Gabriel skidded past him.

He heard laughter as he turned around. Jed was grinning, rolling up his sleeves. "A milling-cove, are ye? It's some o' the home brew you want, aye?"

Gabriel dropped into a boxer's stance and raised his fists, sweeping the room with his eyes, looking for the gun. Rowland was rolling and moaning on the floor, his knees tucked up to his chest.

The gun had slid all the way to the far wall.

Gabriel began sidling toward it, but then Jed launched his body directly at him and he had no time for anything else.

Drusilla wished she'd listened to Parker.

"Please let me come with you, madam. Or perhaps one of the footmen. Mr. Marlington will skin me alive when he learns I let you go alone."

"No, he won't." That was a lie; Gabriel would be furious. But, hopefully, it would all be over by then and she could take the brunt of his anger, rather than their servants. She'd been tempted to tell Parker about the pistol she had in the big leather satchel with the money, but she knew how men were.

He would not feel assured at the knowledge she had a gun; he would be even more nervous.

"I can't, Parker. The note said nobody but me or the consequences would be dire. I cannot take chances. If Mr. Marlington happens to return in the next fifty minutes, please wait until after nine and then you can tell him where I went." She personally doubted the butler would be able to make him wait even ten seconds—she'd seen Gabriel in a rage—but it was the best she could do.

She opened the satchel and looked inside, as if the money and gun might have gone somewhere. No, both were still there. Ten thousand pounds—a fortune for most people. But for a gambler? She doubted Theo would make it last very long. But that would not be her problem.

The carriage came to an abrupt halt, and she had to cling to the strap above the door to keep from falling off her seat. The panel slid open, and the hack driver looked at her. "Are ye sure this is the place ye wanted, missus?" he asked, concern clouding his voice.

Drusilla looked out the window onto a dark, narrow street that had at least a thousand places to hide. She swallowed hard. "Yes, this is the place. I want you to wait for me."

He hesitated but then said, "I'll wait for ten minutes, no more. Those 'oo run these streets are like to 'ave the wheels offa my carriage afore I even know it."

Drusilla opened the door and stepped out before answering. She held up a gold coin, and his eyes widened. "You will wait until I return and I will give you this."

He nodded, his expression grudging. "Aye. If you still *'ave* it in ten minutes."

There was no window on the squat two-story building, which displayed an ancient-looking and crooked sign saying LIONEL SNIVELY & SONS, PURVEYOR OF SPECIALTY GOODES. She knocked on the door and waited. A full minute passed, and she knocked again. Still nothing. She looked at the building next door—it appeared to be a ropemaker's. There was light coming from the gap around a small door cut in a larger door.

There was also an inn, but the raucous voices spilling from the cracked and hazy window made her shudder; the Jolly Taxpayer public house would be her last choice.

The driver had taken a flask from somewhere and was busy with it, paying Drusilla no attention. She took the pistol out of the bag, slung the satchel over her shoulder, put her hand on the handle, and opened the door.

They were surprisingly well matched when it came to skill. Unfortunately, Jed outweighed Gabriel by a good three stone. Every hit the other man landed was like two of Gabriel's.

They were breathing hard and the big man's face was sheened in sweat.

"Where's Big Paul?" Gabriel taunted, wanting to know when some other man—a man *this* one called "big"—might be arriving.

Jed gave a wheezy laugh. "Never you mind about Paul. You'd best be minding yersel'." Like a bolt of lightning his fist shot out. Gabriel dodged, but it clipped him on the shoulder. It was like being struck with a mallet.

"Quick, ain'tcha?"

"Not fast enough."

That made Jed laugh. "I tell you what. If you—"

The door opened, and both he and Jed turned to stare. It was his wife, and she was holding a pistol.

She saw him, and her taut features brightened. "Gabriel!" The pistol wavered in her hand. "Oh, thank God, Gabriel!"

"Have a care," he said as Jed began inching toward her. "Hold the gun steady on him, Dru. I'll get some rope." No problem there, at least.

"Ye wouldn't really shoot me, would you, lass?" Jed took a step toward her and Gabriel opened his mouth—but his wife was already ahead of him and took a step closer to Jed, raising the gun higher, her expression grim and her hands steady.

"You are a big target, sir. Even I cannot miss you."

Jed raised his hands and took a step back.

Gabriel grinned and snatched the end from a huge spool of rope, yanking to get enough free to reach Jed. "Good girl, Dru."

"Yes, good girl, Drusilla."

Gabriel whipped around just as Rowland stood up from where he must have been hiding beneath the piles of spooled rope. He had the bloody gun in his hand, and it was pointed at Gabriel.

"Theo, where is Samir?" Drusilla began to move the pistol.

"No, keep that on Jed, my dear. Do it," Rowland snapped when she hesitated.

"Keep it on Jed, darling," Gabriel urged, giving her a reassuring smile.

Rowland nodded when she obeyed. "Good, now you," he said to Gabriel, "go tie that big ape's hands."

"What?" Jed wailed. "I'm yer partner in this—ye need—"

"Shut. Up." Rowland's voice shook with barely suppressed rage and his hand trembled. "What are you waiting for?" he demanded, glaring at Gabriel.

"Drop your hands," Gabriel told the towering man.

"You would have taken all the money, stuffed me in a sack full of rocks, and thrown me in the river," Rowland continued, his voice shrill.

Jed prudently kept his mouth shut.

"Where is Samir, Theo? I know you don't want to harm a child. Tell us—"

"He's safe. He's not here. I'm not a monster, Drusilla. I wouldn't hurt him."

Drusilla's expression shrieked disgust and disbelief, but she made no comment.

"Make sure to tie him nice and tight," Rowland said to Gabriel.

At least they agreed on one thing. Gabriel finished tying a double knot on Jed's giant wrists and turned to Rowland. "I need a knife to cut the rope."

Rowland gave a high-pitched, whinnying laugh. "Not likely. Get on your knees, Jed."

The big man looked from Rowland to Gabriel, his expression suddenly pleading.

Gabriel snorted. "You'll get no help from me, mate."

"On your knees or I'll shoot."

While Jed awkwardly dropped to his knees, Rowland began to inch sideways toward Dru, keeping the gun trained on Gabriel.

"Good," Rowland said once Jed was down. "Now lower the gun and slide it across the floor, Drusilla." She cut a look at Gabriel, and Rowland saw it. "I won't hurt either of you. That was never in my plans. I just want the money—it's in that bag?"

She nodded.

"Go ahead, Dru; do as he says," Gabriel urged.

She lowered the gun to her waist, but before she could lay it on the floor, the satchel slipped from her shoulder and knocked the gun from her hand. The explosion was deafening in the enclosed space, and it reverberated endlessly.

As if in slow motion, Gabriel saw Drusilla raise her hand to her mouth, her eyes fastened on Rowland, whose arm wavered.

"I'm . . ." Rowland looked down at his stomach, clutching at himself with one hand. "Shot." The pistol in his hand wavered and then hit the ground. Gabriel winced, waiting for a second shot—but the gun just clunked harmlessly on the wooden slats. Rowland swayed, both his hands on his midriff, which had darkened with a growing blossom of red.

Drusilla ran to Gabriel. "Have I killed him?"

Gabriel quickly picked up Rowland's unfired pistol and turned to Jed. The big man was already on his feet and halfway out the door, rope trailing behind him.

"Gabriel?"

He put one arm around Drusilla, and they went to where Rowland lay; the man was gutshot. He wouldn't last long, and his end would be agonizing.

The sound of rope unspooling caught his attention. He tucked the gun in the waistband of his pants and grabbed the rope. Jed almost jerked him off his feet, but Gabriel managed to loop the rope around a big metal cleat bolted to the floor—no doubt something used in the making of rope. The thick cord snapped taut, and he heard a yowl of pain beyond the door.

Drusilla dropped to her knees beside Rowland's prostrate form and stared up at Gabriel. "There must be something we can do?"

He glanced from his wife's distraught face to the man on the floor.

"Please, Marlington," Rowland gasped, cradling his middle with a shaking arm. "Don't let me die this way."

"Where is my son?"

"I don't know—I swear, Jed took him. Please—" tears streamed down his agonized face.

"I think he's telling the truth," Drusilla said.

So did Gabriel.

"We'll get you to a physician, Theo," Drusilla said in a shaky voice. "He can take out the bullet."

Gabriel strode toward the door. He needed to keep hold of Jed or he'd never find Samir. Rowland could bloody well wait.

A crowd of customers from the inn had gathered, and somebody was already helping Jed untie the rope. The serving wench saw him first.

"There 'e is!"

The mob turned as if it were one creature, all eyes on him.

"'E's a no good dirty tea leaf 'oo was trying to steal from my shop," Jed said, throwing Gabriel an evil grin.

Gabriel lifted the pistol. "Stay where you are."

The mob hesitated.

"'E can't shoot all of us," one of the men yelled.

"No," Gabriel said, aiming his pistol at the man—obviously the leader. "But I can kill you."

Jed flung away the rope. "Gimme back what's mine, and I'll tell 'em to let you go."

"Where. Is. My. Son."

"I'll tell you after I get what you've taken."

"Come and get it."

Jed slid a look at his mob, whose spirits were rapidly cooling. "Let's get him, lads."

"Let's not," a bored voice said. Byer stepped out from behind the pawnbroker's shop, his normally impeccable attire dirty, his coiffeur mussed.

"How the devil did you get free?" Jed growled.

"That hardly matters. What matters are these gentlemen."

Men began filing out from behind the building: constables and Runners.

The crowd broke apart and scattered like cockroaches exposed to lamplight. When Jed looked ready to join them, a half-dozen men raised pistols.

"Not you, I think," Byer said as five men came forward and grabbed the huge man.

Gabriel lowered his arm and strode toward Jed, prepared to rip him limb from limb. "Where is my son? Tell me now or so help me God I'll—"

"We've already found the boy, Gabe." Byer limped up to him, his buckskin breeches torn and bloody on one thigh. "He's safe with the Parkers, who are spoiling him rotten by the way."

"Thank God! How did you find him?"

"From this fine fellow." The Runners dragged a tiny man out from the shadows.

Jed gave a sound of amazement. "Bloody 'ell, 'ow the devil did they get you, Paul?"

Gabriel stared: *This* was Big Paul? The man was not even as high as Byer's shoulder.

Big Paul shrugged miserably at Jed's question.

"I'm afraid Mr. Tompkins has far better connections than you, old chap," Byer said, nodding to the men holding Paul. "You can take them both away now."

Gabriel turned and ran toward the open door to the rope warehouse. Inside, Drusilla's head was bowed and her shoulders were shaking.

He crouched down beside her, and she turned an anguished, tearstained face toward him. "I killed him, Gabriel."

He wrapped an arm around her. "It was an accident, Drusilla."

"I know, but . . ." Her voice broke, and she sobbed.

Gabriel knew what she meant: taking a life was never pleasant, no matter how it happened.

He lifted her to her feet. "Come on, darling. Let's get away from all this."

"But—what about Samir?"

"He's at home. Byer's man already found him."

"Thank God!" She swayed, and Gabriel held her tightly against him and started to lead her away. But she stopped, turning back toward Rowland's unmoving body.

"What will happen to him?"

Gabriel looked at Byer.

"The constables will report him dead due to an accident."

He was beside the door, his face a grim mask. "I hate to say it, but it is better this way, Mrs. Marlington. His life would have been over and he would have shamed his family. This way—" He shook his head and opened the door wider. "Well, don't worry, we shall take care of it."

"Come, darling. Let's get you home." Gabriel led her toward the waiting carriage.

"Gabriel, you forgot this." He turned to find Byer holding out the satchel.

"Thanks, Tommy."

Beside him Drusilla shook her head. "Money," she said, the word dripping with disgust.

Yes, money—Gabriel agreed silently, and the things people would do for it.

Epilogue

Two mornings later they were lazing beneath the blankets, even though they would be leaving for the country today and should have been up and about an hour ago.

They lay side by side on Gabriel's bed, slick with sweat.

"There," Gabriel said, turning only his head to kiss her shoulder. "I think I can face hours closeted inside a carriage now."

Drusilla chuckled weakly. "That's not very flattering to me as your travel companion."

"I did not mean you, my dear." He gave an exaggerated shudder. "You've never taken a two-day carriage ride with a child before, Dru. Trust me," he went on before she could reply, "I've done it several times with my young brother and sisters, and it is not an activity for the faint of heart."

"It can't be *that* bad, Gabriel."

Gabriel thought about his mother's three youngest children—the twins and the heir, all of whom were under the age of five. It wasn't enjoyable for anyone to be closeted in a coach for hours—but it was especially difficult for little bundles of energy.

"Besides, half the coach is full of toys and books. It will be a delightful journey," his blissfully ignorant wife said.

It was Gabriel's turn to laugh. "That just goes to show you how—" A sharp rap on the door interrupted him. "Who the devil could that be?"

Drusilla shrugged. "I don't know. But it is *your* room, so *you* should have to get up." She stretched and then pulled the covers up to her chin.

"You lazy thing," he chided, kissing her hard on the lips before swinging his feet to the floor and pulling on his robe. "I told Drake last night that we would leave when we chose to leave and not to disturb us at the crack of dawn," he said, somewhat unfairly, since bright sunlight was piercing the gap in the drapes.

Parker stood outside in the hall, his expression pained. "I beg your pardon, sir, but this just came for you."

Gabriel glanced at the note—it was his mother's handwriting.

"There is a messenger waiting below, sir."

"Give me a few moments, Parker."

His butler nodded, and Gabriel closed the door before cracking the wafer.

"What is it, Gabriel?" Drusilla called from the bedchamber.

"A message from my mother." He unfolded the note: it was brief. He read it once, and then read it again. And then he read it a third time when the words continued to make no sense.

"Good God!" He yanked open the door to find Parker hovering in the hall. "Tell the messenger I shall head over to Exley House directly."

Gabriel shut the door and strode through the bedroom to his dressing room. He snatched up the buckskins he'd been planning to wear today and turned.

Drusilla was kneeling up on the bed and holding on to one of the posts. "What is it? You look as if you've seen a ghost."

"It is Eva."

"Oh no, what? Is she—"

He cursed in every language he knew, allowing himself full rein.

"Gabriel!" she said, her eyes round with shock. "Tell me what has happened?"

"My sister is headed for Scotland with Earl Visel."

Drusilla's hand flew to her mouth. "Oh no. *That* is why he didn't return the night of the ball—he wasn't going to take me—he was planning to abduct her all along." She frowned. "But Eva wasn't *at* the ball—she was with Melissa in the country. I don't understand."

Gabriel laughed. "No, that was where Eva was *supposed* to be. Now she is with *Visel*."

She flung aside her sheet and hopped down off the bed, momentarily distracting him with her fetching body. She planted her fists on both hips and glared. "He is a brute *and* a liar. You must go after him, Gabriel—but if they've been gone—"

"If Eva's groom is to be believed, they left the night of the Richland ball." Gabriel laughed, and the sound was more than a little hysterical. "This is—well, this is absolutely bloody unbelievable! Even for Eva this is beyond everything."

"It's hardly fair to blame Eva for her own abduction, Gabriel. It is Visel who should be caught and strung up and—"

"It was Eva."

She cocked her head, her brow wrinkled with confusion. "What?"

"It was Eva, Drusilla. Visel didn't abduct Eva; Eva abducted *him*."

Please read on for a preview of OUTRAGEOUS,
the next novel in Minerva Spencer's Rebels of the *Ton*.

Chapter 1

London
1816

Godric Fleming, Earl Visel, vowed to kill his cousin Rowland when he got his hands on him.

He strode down the alley, feeling like a fool as his ridiculous cape billowed out behind him as if he were some Barbary corsair. Which was, of course, exactly how he was dressed—or at least the English public's perception of a corsair.

When he reached the alley entrance he gaped. "Good God."

The street in front of the Duke of Richland's house was crammed with dozens, maybe even hundreds, of carriages. No wonder Rowland hadn't been waiting for Godric near the duke's garden gate as they'd planned. Godric considered the mob of unmoving carriages, his mind as chaotic as the scene before him. Perhaps this mess was a sign he should call off his asinine plan. Perhaps there was still time to—

"Lord Visel?"

Godric spun around to find a huge boy dressed like a stable lad.

"Who the devil are you?"

"Mr. Rowland sent me to tell you the carriage is waitin' at the back entrance, my lord." The young giant hesitated. "Mr.

Rowland said he needed to talk to you before taking the woman."

Godric clenched his jaws so tightly his head throbbed. It was a struggle to contain his fury; trust that idiot Rowland to bring in even *more* conspirators. It was bad enough the two of them were planning to kidnap the woman—now this *boy* was part of the plan? Who else had the fool told? The bloody *Times*?

"No." He shook his head. No, he would not do it. He *could* not do it.

"My lord?" the boy asked, his expression one of nervous confusion.

"Come along," Godric said, ignoring his question and marching toward the other end of the alley.

The oddest sensation filled him as he walked: as if he were emerging from a dense fog, his head clearing with each step and his vision shifting slowly into focus the closer he got to the street ahead.

Good God! What the devil have I been thinking?

His gait stuttered and the air whooshed out of his lungs as the enormity of what he'd been about to do hit him: he'd actually planned to abduct this woman and he was on the brink of carrying out his plan.

He *must be* barking, bloody mad.

The sudden, blinding clarity left him dizzy. Why the *hell* had it taken him so long to realize he was behaving like a lunatic?

Instead of wondering why it took you so long you should be grateful you came to your senses before *you did something irreversibly stupid and cruel,* his conscience—which had been muffled of late—said.

Godric thought about the woman he'd just left—a woman whose life he'd schemed and planned to wreck—and his stomach churned. Drusilla Marlington had done nothing to him—

they hardly even knew each other—and yet he'd humiliated her and forced her into a marriage with a man who'd been courting another woman.

And when her unwanted marriage had—against all odds—showed signs of becoming a love match? Well, then Godric had decided to use her *again* to get to the man she'd married: Gabriel Marlington.

To be perfectly honest, her husband had done nothing to him, either. Yet all Godric had done since returning home to Britain was harass the man.

I've been telling you this for months, the dry voice in his head observed, louder and stronger.

"Blast and damn," he cursed under his breath. Sod it all to hell; this was bloody lunacy. He would get in the carriage, go home, and try to forget these past few months of insanity.

He would have a devil of a time with his cousin Rowland—a man so desperate for funds he'd ransom his own grandmother—but Godric did not doubt he could handle the little worm.

The hired carriage waited at the end of the alley. Godric yanked open the door and peered into the dark interior

"We're going," he said to the figure sitting on the back-facing bench. "I won't—"

Something hard slammed into the back of his head. His vision exploded with red-hot pain, and he staggered forward. "Wha—"

"Push him in, James!"

Big hands grabbed his shoulders and shoved. Godric went headfirst into the carriage, turning his head just in time to avoid landing on his face and breaking his nose. Even so, the pain from the impact was so intense it was nauseating and his stomach cramped, preparing to void itself. He gritted his teeth to keep back the flood of bile while huge hands grasped his ankles and folded his legs up against his chest.

A face lowered over Godric's: huge blue-violet eyes creased in a frown; red lips, parted; a lock of silky black hair . . .

He blinked, "Y-you—"

"Hallo, Lord Visel."

Whoever was holding his ankles gave him a shove, and his head struck the opposite door. The last thing he heard was "He's out cold, James, but you'd best tie his hands."